Neck bones] his face eclipsing were dull purple, glazed over with a foggy film, and deep-set wrinkles radiated from the corners of his eyes like arrows drawing attention to them.

A shudder caused the keys to slip from my hand and clank on the ground. My face burned with shame that the poor man's appearance had startled me. My rudeness would have disappointed Mom.

"I'm sorry, but really—" I snagged my keys.

His hand slithered out of the brick-colored sleeve as his arm rose, trembling as he strained to hold the weight of his own limb. Gloved in loose, veiny skin, his skeleton hand had yellowed fingernails so overgrown they grew in on themselves like curly birthday ribbons. As his fingers unfurled, he revealed a ring nestled in his palm.

It was large. Too large. The ring resembled the toy jewelry Jason's sister played with or something from a Halloween costume. Grimy gold with a single dull purplish jewel that matched his eyes.

His hand trembled under the heaviness of the ring. "Take it."

Shifting my backpack to my other shoulder, I took it. "What is this?"

The corners of his thin lips curled into a grin as a gust of warm, dry wind cut through the chilly October night and swirled around me.

From Brick & Darkness

by

J. L. Sullivan

This is a work of fiction. Names, characters, places, and incidents are either the product of the author's imagination or are used fictitiously, and any resemblance to actual persons living or dead, business establishments, events, or locales, is entirely coincidental.

From Brick & Darkness

COPYRIGHT © 2022 by J. L. Sullivan

All rights reserved. No part of this book may be used or reproduced in any manner whatsoever without written permission of the author or The Wild Rose Press, Inc. except in the case of brief quotations embodied in critical articles or reviews.
Contact Information: info@thewildrosepress.com

Cover Art by *The Wild Rose Press, Inc.*

The Wild Rose Press, Inc.
PO Box 708
Adams Basin, NY 14410-0708
Visit us at www.thewildrosepress.com

Publishing History
First Edition, 2022
Trade Paperback ISBN 978-1-5092-4008-1
Digital ISBN 978-1-5092-4009-8

Published in the United States of America

Dedication

To Kara, Sloane, and Paige for always indulging my fantastical storytelling.

Acknowledgments

Thanks to The Wild Rose Press team for believing in my story and giving it a home. In particular, thanks to my incredible editor, Melanie Billings, who guided me through the process and gave my novel a much-needed polish.

Special thanks to Holly Ingraham for her insightful suggestions that shaped my manuscript into the book I always wanted it to be.

Being a writer means talking with people who love to read and write—powerful tools in early drafts. Thanks to Michael Penrod, Robin McMinn, Jenni Chafin, and many others for having those conversations with me and providing unfiltered feedback on very rough drafts.

Of course, a huge thank you to my friends and family who always supported me, including my parents. If they hadn't bought me a word processor in the sixth grade, I would have never started cranking out my first weekly science fiction serial for classmates.

I owe so much to the St. Louis Writer's Guild for introducing me to the industry and community of publishing, and to Emily Lammers, Kate Manfull, and Jennifer Mossman for making my online presence look so legit.

Last but certainly not least, thanks to my beautiful and patient wife for listening to all the ideas I blurt out late at night.

Chapter 1

My phone glowed in the dark. Forty-five minutes past curfew. Our neighborhood wasn't exactly the safest in the city, so Mom didn't like it when I walked home by myself after nine p.m. Especially when she worked late. But I was so close to passing level forty in *Archer Annihilation*, I couldn't have torn myself away any earlier without being a horrible friend to Jason.

Besides, I deserved the time to zone out after another mandatory hour with the school counselor, even though I hadn't had one of my "episodes"—as Mom called them—in over a year.

Still a block away from my building, I stopped abruptly.

What the hell?

I squinted to see through the fog crawling near the ground. A man, probably homeless, sat on my apartment's concrete stoop like he'd set up camp right in front of the entrance.

That's bold.

In some buildings, the doorman would have removed him, but we didn't have a doorman. Instead, we had an entrance with a lock that didn't work half of the time.

I started forward with cautious steps, straining to make out the details of my building's still-shadowy visitor.

Maybe he wasn't homeless. I had always fantasized something big would happen to me, like in a comic book. Something life-changing like developing a superpower, inheriting an island nation, or finding out I came from another planet. But I never envisioned my Something Big might arrive by way of a creepy homeless-looking dude.

Closer to my building, his image sharpened as the streetlights radiated off his silhouette like a faded halo. Wispy tufts of white hair sprouted out of his head and glowed under the smog-filtered light. His clothes were pretty clean for being homeless but sloppy like he'd recently lost weight. And I couldn't put my finger on something odd about the color of his coat.

As I stepped up to the entrance, it hit me. The reddish-brown of the coat matched the brick of my building—exactly. Frayed threads of the cloth even gave it a textured appearance as if the man materialized out of the brick itself.

He stared straight ahead, studying the closed thrift store across the street. I did a double take, but Sally's Second Hand remained dark and empty.

His concentrated focus made him oblivious to my approach, which thankfully allowed me to avoid eye contact. I slipped by him and up the cement stairs.

Of course, the lock on my building's front door chose that moment to work, denying me a quick escape. As I fumbled with my key to unlock it, the man's voice rasped, "Can you help me?"

Ugh.

I ignored him. He just wanted money. So much for my Something Big.

"Please?" His pained voice groaned.

Against my better judgment, I glanced over my shoulder.

Neck bones popped as his head rotated toward me, his face eclipsing the rays of the streetlight. His irises were dull purple, glazed over with a foggy film, and deep-set wrinkles radiated from the corners of his eyes like arrows drawing attention to them.

A shudder caused the keys to slip from my hand and clank on the ground. My face burned with shame that the poor man's appearance had startled me. My rudeness would have disappointed Mom.

"I'm sorry, but really—" I snagged my keys.

His hand slithered out of the brick-colored sleeve as his arm rose, trembling as he strained to hold the weight of his own limb. Gloved in loose, veiny skin, his skeleton hand had yellowed fingernails so overgrown they grew in on themselves like curly birthday ribbons. As his fingers unfurled, he revealed a ring nestled in his palm.

It was large. Too large. The ring resembled the toy jewelry Jason's sister played with or something from a Halloween costume. Grimy gold with a single dull purplish jewel that matched his eyes.

His hand trembled under the heaviness of the ring. "Take it."

Shifting my backpack to my other shoulder, I took it. "What is this?"

The corners of his thin lips curled into a grin as a gust of warm, dry wind cut through the chilly October night and swirled around me. Leaves and litter scooted along the street and in the gutters.

I just accepted a gift from some creeper outside of my building. Something every little kid knew better than to do. Who knows where that ring came from? But before I could return it, his hand smoothly retracted into his sleeve and his arm lowered.

"Greg Allen." The ambient rumble of cars on surrounding streets muffled his voice. "The ring is for him."

The blood drained from my head, like during one of my episodes, and the ring grew as heavy as it had appeared in the old man's palm. "Greg Allen?"

He nodded, neck bones creaking and popping.

"That's my dad."

"Ahhhhh." He exhaled. "Superb. Then you will give it to him? It is a gift. He showed me kindness years ago. My time in this world is expiring."

If Greg actually knew this guy, the ring made a bizarre thank you gift.

"Why are you looking for Greg here?"

He closed his eyes as he spoke. "I searched for Allens in this neighborhood and located this building. You happened to be the first person to answer my plea."

I swallowed, vowing no more conversations with homeless guys. Served me right. Though the odds of him asking *me* about Greg were one in a million. Or at least one in however many people lived in my building.

"I'm sorry, but he's not here. Greg's never lived here."

"But you said—"

"Yeah, he's my dad, but he doesn't live here. Do I need to explain every detail?" My voice got louder. I didn't owe this weirdo an explanation.

"Ahhhhhh." He exhaled again, deflating. "Then it is yours. Time will not afford me the luxury to continue my search."

A woman in a long black coat glanced from the old man to me as she hurried down the sidewalk but quickly averted her eyes when I noticed. Probably thankful she'd avoided the old man herself. But if he had roped her in, she wouldn't have known Greg Allen. What would he have done then?

"I don't think I want it." I extended my hand—and the ring—back to him, holding it between my thumb and forefinger. While I'd always wanted to learn more about Greg, for some reason, the ring didn't seem like the way to do it. Something about the old man felt off.

"Please." His sad gaze bored into me. "You can sell it. It is valuable."

A vivid image of moving out of our apartment and into a nicer one flashed through my mind. An apartment with a pool and home theater. One with a doorman who kept away homeless dudes. In a neighborhood where Mom didn't worry about me walking home alone.

I pulled the phone out of my pocket—9:55. No time to keep arguing with him. I needed to get inside before she got home.

"Um, okay. Thank you. I have to go."

He nodded. "Your father was a kind and noble man." He closed his purple eyes in reverence as if conjuring up fond memories of Greg.

When his eyes didn't open again, it left me, like an idiot, staring at an old man who may have fallen asleep sitting up.

"Thanks for this, I guess." Dropping the ring into my pocket, I hurried to unlock the door to my building and shouldered it open. I didn't look back at the old man, not wanting to risk him talking to me again.

Past the elevator, I skipped every other step in the stairwell, including the broken one. The black scuff marks on the light gray walls zipped by until I reached the third floor.

The old man had to be at least forty years older than Greg, but he said they were friends. Close enough that he came back—while dying—to thank Greg for being "noble." To give him a gaudy piece of costume jewelry as a gift he claimed was valuable.

Inside our apartment, my backpack smacked on the hardwood floor after I flung it into my room, and I headed to the living room, turning on the lights as I went. I pressed my forehead against the chilled glass and scanned the stoop below, then the street. No old man.

As I dug into my pocket to reexamine Greg's thank you gift, Mom rounded the corner of our street. She walked home alone after nine p.m. all the time, but whenever I pointed that out, she said coming home from work didn't count.

The living room looked like I'd just walked in the door. Snatching the remote, I flipped on the TV, got a glass of water in the kitchen, and skidded down the hallway to my room.

Lights on, water glass on my nightstand, I kicked off my shoes and plopped onto my bed. I snagged a comic book from the floor and rolled onto my back as Mom's keys jingled outside of our door.

"Bax?" Mom called. Her keys rattled on the table as the door clicked shut behind her.

"Hey." I said the word soft and slow, pretending to be absorbed in my reading. "In my room."

Her footfalls reached my door before she did. She

leaned against the white doorframe to slip off her shoes, one at a time. "Super crazy at Zia's Candles tonight."

I smiled, envisioning mad rushes of people fighting with each other, desperate to grab up spiced and floral scented candles at nine p.m. on a Wednesday night.

Mom pulled her chestnut hair—the same color as mine—back into a ponytail. She kept it long, just past her shoulders. "Jason's fun?"

Jason's? Boring. The excitement happened after I came home.

"Fine." The open comic book rested on my chest. "Mrs. Franklin said to tell you 'hi.' They want us to come over for dinner soon. Oh, and we finally finished *Archer Annihilation*."

"That's great, hon." She attempted enthusiasm but sounded tired thanks to back-to-back shifts and two jobs. Besides, she didn't appreciate the hard work required to master a game like *Archer Annihilation*.

The ring in my pocket poked my thigh as if nudging me. I should tell her about it. More importantly, I should tell her about our visitor. But anything regarding Greg always sunk her mood. Who wanted a reminder of the man who left her to raise a two-year-old alone? After working a double shift, she didn't need to be upset.

And if I told her about the ring, she'd demand to see it. She might make me toss it out. I couldn't do that—not yet.

At six or seven, I found an old comic book in a box of Christmas decorations called *The Haunting of the Ravine*, *Shade Slayer, #276*. When I asked her about it, she told me Greg collected comic books and must've forgotten it when they separated. I kept it but could see by the look on her face that keeping something of his hurt her.

And I'd innocently stumbled into the comic book. A man with overgrown nails and purple eyes, who stalked our building waiting for Greg, hadn't given it to me. The ring was way different. No way she'd give this memento the same leniency as *Shade Slayer*.

But finding out if Greg had any older friends might help me figure out his connection to the strange man. If a connection even existed at all, which I still couldn't get my head around.

"Did Greg have any close friends?" As soon as the words left my mouth, I cringed.

Her body tensed, and her face muscles strained.

After a pause, she shook her head. "A few. A couple of electrician buddies. Why?"

Not helpful. I blew off my question for her benefit. "Just curious."

"So anyway," she changed the subject, "I took a shift tomorrow night after committing to Friday night. That means every night this week. We could use the money." Her face fell with guilt over working too much. I wished she'd stop torturing herself. She did the best she could.

"It's fine, Mom. Really. I'll hang with Jason or something."

Her smile dripped with an apology, though she didn't say anything.

"Seriously. No big deal. Besides, it's hard to keep up my drug habit with you around so much, you know?"

She didn't laugh.

"For real, it's all good."

Mom sighed. "How about a movie night on Saturday? Order pizza?"

"You know it's my turn to pick the movie, right?" I smirked.

Her head fell back, and she talked to the ceiling. "Right. Well, then I'll prepare for a violent movie with too much cursing."

"Hey now." I wagged my finger. "I sat through that horrible romantic comedy where the dude never wore a shirt."

She couldn't stifle her grin. "It's hot in Florida."

"At least there weren't any love scenes."

"Agreed! Well, as tired as I am, I'm gonna have a glass of wine, then go to bed. My shift at the hotel isn't until ten a.m. tomorrow. I'm sleeping in!" She shook her fist in the air triumphantly.

I smiled. "Sounds good."

"Night, hon." She eased my door shut. "Love you."

"Night, Mom. Love you."

After a minute, voices from the TV floated into my room as she turned up the volume and changed the channel.

Exhausted from the long day and weird night, I undressed and pulled the chain on my lamp, then crawled under the covers.

In the dark, the man with the long nails and purple eyes materialized in my mind. Definitely not an electrician buddy of Greg's, and too old to be his father. Grandfather? No, he said "old friend."

Reaching over the side of my bed, I dug around for the ring in my wadded-up jeans. It clinked as I placed it on my nightstand to stare at it. A thank you gift for Greg that's now mine. It'd be the second thing of his that I owned. The old man said the ring held some value, but I'd bet I could sell the comic book for more.

The jewel began emitting a subtle purple glow. A strange sound rose behind me—a growl, low and deep, like a gigantic dog threatening an enemy.

Guttural and buried underneath the throaty rumble came my name.

Baaaaaaaaax.

I rolled over in bed, jerking the covers with me. I searched the empty, dark room but found nothing out of the ordinary.

What did I expect to see?

The sound stopped as suddenly as it started. Only the distant television disrupted the silence. The purple jewel went dark again.

It must've been my imagination.

"You're a freak," I muttered to myself as I pulled the covers up. I closed my eyes but couldn't fall asleep right away, thinking about the old man.

Chapter 2

The bell jingled against the glass as I pushed open the door of Warren's Cosmos. I stopped by the comic book store every couple of weeks on my way to school, and at some point during my visit, I always asked the same question. The owner always answered the same way, but after the old man's visit, a small voice in the back of my mind whispered, *Maybe this time the answer will be different.*

Warren balanced his massive frame on the wobbly iron stool behind the counter. The mustiness seemed to emanate from him and crawl through the aisles of paper, saturating every inch of his cosmos. So early in the day, we were the only two people in the store, which I preferred.

"Mornin', Bax." A smile stretched across Warren's leathery skin, his yellow teeth peeking out from between cracked lips. A modest, three-inch *Shade Slayer* scythe symbol adorned his navy-blue T-shirt on the right part of his chest. I couldn't imagine Warren without a superhero image somewhere on his person.

"Morning." I flipped through some random comic books on my way to the counter, careful to return them to their exact place to avoid Warren's scolding eyebrow raise.

I had no idea how he kept his store organized. Comic book covers plastered every inch of the walls, comic books and graphic novels crowded the shelves, and boxes littered the floor with no signage anywhere. But somehow, Warren never struggled to locate a specific back issue when asked.

He shook his head. "Haven't gotten in anything new. Not since your last visit. Well, a couple of contemporary ones. I know you don't care for those." Years of smoking had sandpapered his voice.

Perusing through the aisle, I grabbed a *Confederation of Assassins* comic and slapped it down in front of Warren. "So…"

He grinned, waiting for me to ask the question I asked every visit, even though he knew it by heart. As he waited, he picked up the comic and punched the UPC from the back cover into the ancient cash register. With each jab of his thick fingers, the machine rang and clanged. Old machines needed to make lots of noise to add numbers.

"Anyone, by any chance, come in asking about *Shade Slayer, #276*?"

"The one called *The Haunting of the Ravine?*" He didn't take his attention from the register.

I smiled. He knew the name. "It is, in fact."

Warren paused, and for a moment, he sucked me in. My anticipation swelled. Maybe his answer would be different today than every other day since I started visiting Warren's Cosmos. Maybe the old man with purple eyes had heard Greg returned.

Warren shook his head. "No, sir. I truly wish someone had come in about that issue so I could tell you."

I exhaled. Over the years, when my internet and social media searches for *Greg Allen* hit dead ends, I would reread Greg's forgotten comic book, thinking it'd provide some kind of insight into him. Like a mysterious note he'd left behind for me to find. However, it only revealed that I spent too much time searching for nonexistent clues, trying to connect nonexistent dots. Turned out, *The Haunting of the Ravine* was just a *Shade Slayer* story, and not a great one.

But that didn't stop me from spending most of my allowance in Warren's Cosmos, starting my own comic collection, and creating something Greg and I had in common. Like sitting through tennis matches with Jason and his dad, the game bored the hell out of me, but I sat through it to bond with them.

"One day," Warren caught his breath, "I'll give you a different answer. I'm certain."

"Maybe. Maybe not." I shrugged casually.

Thirteen years after Greg left, I pretended my question had just become a fun tradition with Warren, but deep down, I still held on to the sliver of hope that Greg would return to the comic book store closest to the place he'd left his lost issue in search of it. Stupid. Kinda like thinking the old man's visit might have been some kind of omen.

As I paid Warren, heat began to spread across the side of my thigh like someone drizzled coffee into my pocket. Like the ring had started melting into a hot liquid, singeing my leg as it crawled toward my knee.

I jumped back from the counter, expecting to see my jeans on fire.

"You okay?" Warren heaved himself up from his stool.

"I-I don't know—"

I slapped the side of my leg rapidly with both hands, but the burning dribbled down my leg. Then, just before I dropped my pants in Warren's Cosmos, it stopped.

Gone as quickly as it started.

My fingers traced the ring over the outside of my pocket, not wanting to take it out in front of Warren. The undamaged fabric of my jeans still radiated the chill of the outside air. Not even warm.

"Probably a bug."

Warren settled back on his stool. "Well, it happens. They all come inside for the winter."

I reapproached the counter, my face warm with embarrassment. I must've imagined it.

Warren handed me my change with his right hand, his pointer and middle fingers severed at the knuckles. After I took the money, Warren tapped what remained of his fingers on the counter, reminding me.

I shook off the weird incident. Warren waited. "Warren?"

"Yup?" His tiny eyes sparkled.

"What happened to your fingers?" This question began our second tradition.

Warren leaned back, careful not to topple the stool. He held his hand up, giving me an unfettered view of his missing digits. "Well, Bax, you ever hear of noodlin'?"

I shook my head.

"As a kid, we did it nearly every Saturday morning. We'd head down to the creek and wade in until about waist deep. Much shallower or deeper, and it doesn't work. Anyways, we'd search the shores for underwater holes. Catfish burrows. When you spotted one, you'd ease your hand into the hole. If you found a catfish, he'd bite 'cha. Latch onto your hand." He used his other hand to demonstrate on his severed fingers.

"They ain't strong enough to do any damage, so once they latched on, why, you'd yank 'em out and grab 'em with your other hand. There you got dinner."

My body cringed even though I smiled. "You couldn't pay me a million dollars to shove my hand into an underwater hole. So a catfish ate your fingers?"

"Like I said, they ain't strong enough. However, the turtles hiding in the catfish holes are. On one particular noodlin' expedition, I found myself a snapping turtle squattin' in a catfish hole." He snapped his free hand over where his other hand's fingers should have been again. This time, he moved with lightning speed.

Snap!

I jumped.

"Wow." Warren's stories about his missing fingers grew more detailed every time. "Classic."

A proud gleam shone in Warren's eye. He probably never went noodling. I didn't know if people even did that. I could look it up but wouldn't. With Warren's stories, truthfulness ruined them.

"You get on your way now, Bax. Don't want to be late for school." He sounded like Mom.

"Thanks. See ya."

I had no idea how Warren really lost his fingers. He created a different story every visit. Once, he lost them rescuing his platoon buddy in Vietnam from an exploding grenade. Another time, he lost them in a knife accident during sous chef training in Spain.

Shoving the comic book into my backpack, then

slinging my backpack over my shoulder, I headed to school.

****

Mr. Buchannan scribbled on the whiteboard, his blue marker squeaking with each hurried stroke. He wrote "Super Blue Blood Moon" and spun around to face us. "Besides a horrible naming convention, any guess what this is?"

Ashley Bryant's hand launched upward like a rocket.

"Ms. Bryant?"

"A super blue blood moon is happening next Friday." Ashley beamed. "I read about it online."

Ashley never stopped quoting random facts she read about. She lived across the hall from me, so if I left for school too early, she'd catch me and explain—in excruciating detail—whatever she had learned about the night before. Every subject excited her. Two weeks ago, she spent the entire walk to school explaining the political history of some country named Chad. Ashley would have made a popular study partner if she weren't so annoying.

"Well, before you share what you've read online, Ashley, let's dissect the phrase and figure it out based on what we've learned about lunar anomalies in class." Mr. Buchannan leaned back against the front of his metal desk, arms crossed over his wrinkled dress shirt. The stark whiteness of the shirt called all kinds of attention to the small coffee stain dotting his stomach. "Can someone refresh us on what a super moon is?"

Several hands raised, more participation than in any other tenth-grade class on the planet. Unlike required classes, students had to earn an A in freshman biology to take astronomy. That meant the astronomy students wanted to be there because they actually liked the subject. I liked it fine, but the main reason I worked my ass off in biology sat one row over and three seats ahead—Scarlet Lane.

"Bill?" Mr. Buchannan pointed the dry erase marker at the student.

"A super moon is when the moon's orbit brings it closest to Earth, which makes it appear really big."

"Correct. Super moons can be thirty percent brighter and can appear fourteen percent larger." Mr. Buchanan strolled around his desk, back to the dry erase board. "How often do those occur?"

Papers shuffled as students scanned their notes.

Three times per year. That's the answer. Mrs. Bronson kept encouraging me to speak up more in class. She said it'd help with my anxiety, which in turn would help with my episodes. She challenged me to raise my hand in class at least twice a day.

Here goes.

I raised my hand.

Not waiting for Mr. Buchannan to call on him, Bill blurted out, "Two to three times per year."

Too slow. I needed to stop thinking about it so much.

"Correct again. Can someone remind us what a blue moon is?"

Ashley's hand shot up first, but Mr. Buchannan avoided looking in her direction. "Ron?"

Ron flinched when Mr. Buchannan called on him. He scratched the back of his head. "Um, it's when two full moons happen in one calendar month?"

"You sound unsure," Mr. Buchannan said as the

class chuckled. "But your guess is right. Every two and a half years or so, two full moons appear in one calendar month. Which is relatively rare."

"Hence the expression, 'Once in a blue moon.' " Ashley couldn't contain herself.

Mr. Buchannan nodded. "True, Ashley. Scarlet, why don't you refresh us on the last part of our mystery phrase and explain what a blood moon is? The final piece of our puzzle."

Scarlet shifted in her seat, brushing her hair over her shoulder. "The moon passes into the Earth's shadow when the sun, Earth, and Moon are in a perfect line. Basically, no sunlight hits the moon, only refracted light from Earth's atmosphere, making it appear red. It happens, like, two to four times per year."

Scarlet—smart, beautiful, and a huge heart. The whole package.

We'd met in the hallway of our building right after Mom and I moved in, and she offered to walk with me to the first day of fifth grade at my new school. Scarlet noticed my nervousness and reassured me the entire way. When we arrived at school, just before we separated, she told me not to worry. That it'd be the same classes, just different kids. Then she gave me a peck on the cheek and skipped off, her wavy red hair bouncing off her shoulders.

We'd walked to school every day together for most of the fifth grade. Then, when Scarlet's parents split, she moved apartments, and we didn't talk much.

Ashley's family moved into Scarlet's old place. Not the upgrade in neighbors I'd hoped for.

"Correct, Scarlet. Anything else notable about a blood moon? Can anyone recall our discussion on blood moons?" Mr. Buchannan knew someone would remember it. Someone always did. Teachers dreamed about classes like this one. Mr. Buchannan also taught senior physics, where I doubted the students learned with a fraction of the enthusiasm.

Scarlet raised her hand again. From behind her, I pictured her long eyelashes flickering at Mr. Buchannan as she answered.

"Continue, Scarlet."

"Because the refracted light makes the moon appear red—like blood—many superstitions evolved from it."

"And murders!" Bill blurted out, apparently unable to understand the concept of raising his hand before speaking.

"Scary, right?" Mr. Buchannan made a silly ghost sound. "Throughout recorded history, the blood moon has been blamed for all kinds of unexplained events. Christians thought it to be a sign of the Rapture. Mayans believed a blood moon turned jaguars murderous. Most ancient cultures believed a blood moon opened a gateway between the physical and metaphysical worlds, allowing demons to pass back and forth."

Mr. Buchannan stroked his thin beard. "But sadly, as Ms. Lane informed us, it's only the Earth's atmosphere reflecting on the moon's surface. Now, many urban legends attribute aberrant behavior to the blood moon's influence on the human psyche. While there's no proven connection, Bill is right, crime rates do actually increase during a blood moon."

Seeing an opening, I didn't hesitate. I didn't think about it. I raised my hand.

"Yes, Bax?"

As my hand came down, it grazed the thick brown curls on my head. I needed a haircut. The longer my hair grew, the more curls popped out. "Um, so if it's all superstition, why do crime rates go up during blood moons?"

Mr. Buchannan smiled. "Excellent question. What you're referring to is a self-fulfilling prophecy. People believe there's a connection and use it to justify bad behavior. That, Mr. Allen, is the difference between correlation and causation. I may get hungry at noon every day, but the clock striking twelve doesn't *make* me hungry."

Ashley's hand shot up again, desperate for some attention from Mr. Buchannan. It *had* been almost a minute without her commenting on something, after all.

"Yes?"

"What's a super blue blood moon? All of the above?"

Mr. Buchannan glanced at the clock. "Yes. Next week, we will see a super blue blood moon. Which means," he began bulleting under the phrase he'd written on the board, "Super = moon will be close to the earth. Blue = second full moon of the month. Blood = lunar eclipse." He whirled on his heels, his face aglow with nerd enthusiasm. "All three of these during one night. Next Friday, people. Take some pics, and you'll receive five extra credit points."

He glanced at the clock again. "And the last time these events lined up in North America?" He beat his desk like a drum, building suspense. "One hundred fifty years ago!"

The bell rang. "Read chapter six!" Mr. Buchannan

called over the commotion of the exiting students. Everyone liked astronomy, but it was still a class. "Mark your calendars for next Friday! Five points!"

By the time I dove into the chaotic river of bodies flowing in both directions of the hallway, Scarlet had already locked hands with Nick Ruiz, and they strolled toward the cafeteria. King and queen of the school. She giggled at something lame he said, and he flashed his toothy smile back.

Barf.

Her IQ probably doubled his.

"Oh, Scarlet, I love you! Please come back!" a voice sang from behind me.

I lifted my middle finger over my shoulder, flipping Jason off. No one had a worse singing voice. Well, maybe me.

His palm rammed my back, shoving me forward.

"Hey." I spun around.

"You have some drool coming out of your mouth." He wiped my dry chin clean with his thumb.

I swiped his hand away. "Shut up."

"You know I think she's hot for a white chick, but dude, you got nothin' on Nick Ruiz. Unless you suddenly become a football god, grow a few inches, and pop some serious biceps."

Jason and I became friends on the first day of fifth grade. He knew everything about me, from my natural talent at video games to my embarrassing passing out episodes, both of which he'd witnessed firsthand. In the case of my episodes, we stayed friends despite it.

The current of kids dragged us toward the cafeteria for lunch, closer to the source of the bleach-and-fried-chicken air. Metal lockers slammed shut on both sides of us, and random shouts flew over us. A brief shoving match broke out down the hallway to my right. Truman High was one of those public schools with super-rich kids and really poor kids from all backgrounds, which sometimes caused stupid nonsense fights.

Jason elbowed me. "How'd it go last night? You beat your mom home, or did she bust you for curfew?"

I choked on a sudden inhale. I hadn't seen Jason since yesterday. Since my visit from the old man. I could tell him the creepy details, and he wouldn't send me straight to Mrs. Bronson for a counseling session.

"Man, who cares about curfew? Get this…" I filled him in on the old man's visit.

He didn't comment or react when I finished. He usually didn't, though. Jason liked to process things before giving an opinion. After a moment of my story settling in, he tugged on the front of his black T-shirt and said, "You're making that up."

"I'm so not."

"Then show me the thank you gift."

We detoured away from the flow of students and into an alcove in front of the boy's restroom.

"Check it out." I displayed the ring in the palm of my hand.

A glimmer of disappointment, magnified behind his thick glasses, flickered across his eyes. "It looks like something Michelle plays with. From your story, I imagined, like, a one-hundred-carat diamond."

"Me too. I'm not even sure the jewel is real. What kind of precious stone is an ugly purple?" I turned the ring over on my palm.

"And the guy with the crazy nails told you it held some kind of value?"

I nodded. "Yeah, but he didn't exactly look like a professional appraiser. He also said he's friends with Greg, but he'd be at least forty years older than him—at a minimum."

"What are you gonna do?"

"Dunno. Maybe go by a pawn shop or—" Someone cruising past bumped my elbow, shoving my arm forward. The ring rolled across my palm, but I clenched it in my fist, saving it from dropping into the stampede of tennis shoes.

"Too close. Come in here." Grabbing Jason's sleeve, I yanked him into the restroom.

I checked under the wobbly metal stall walls. No feet. Good, we were alone. I didn't need anyone hearing about old men coming to visit me late at night.

"I mean, I want to keep it because it's Greg's, but if it's worth something, how incredible would that be? What if I'm sitting on a winning lottery ticket?"

"Well, I wouldn't buy your yacht quite yet." He snickered. "As dirty as it is, I can't imagine you'd get more than a buck for it."

"It just needs a shine." I rubbed my thumb over the ring to wipe off the grime. After a few passes over the jewel with the pad of my thumb, a frigid shudder slammed down on the top of my head like someone dumped ice water on me from two stories above.

The tingling trickled its way down my face, fell over my shoulders, and dripped down my torso, not stopping until it frostbit my toes. My knees buckled, and I wobbled but managed to stay standing.

"What the hell? What's happening to you?" Jason grabbed my elbows, ready to hold me up. "Are you having one of your…your things?"

The dizziness waned as my senses settled back into place. "No, and stop calling it a *thing*."

A distinct odor seeped into the bathroom, overpowering the urine-saturated air. We pinched our noses. "What's that smell?" I searched the bathroom for the source of the rankness. "Did someone not flush?"

"Shit doesn't stink like that."

I fanned the air in front of my face. "It's like burnt hair."

"Yeah. Maybe—" Jason's eyes, already large under his glasses, grew more enormous as something caught his attention over my shoulder. He stumbled a few steps backward into a stall door. "What. The. Hell."

He pointed behind me, his finger trembling. For a moment, I couldn't turn around. No, I didn't want to. Jason's expression paralyzed my lungs, and I couldn't take a breath, confident a zombie loomed behind me, ready to eat us both alive.

Following the direction of his finger, I pivoted, bracing for the smelly thing that caused Jason's mouth to hang open.

While not a zombie, I couldn't identify what we were staring at. Under the sink, with one hand on the water pipe to steady itself, a creature leaned against the mildew-covered tile.

I stumbled backward, like Jason, stepping on his sneakers. He must not have felt it because he didn't budge.

The creature stood a little over a foot tall, with long arms like a monkey, floppy ears like a beagle, and dull purple eyes that matched the jewel on the ring and the old man's eyes. White mangy fur covered it, and pink ape-like feet capped its squatty legs.

It looked from Jason to me and back, as apprehensive of us as we were of it. It blinked and rubbed its oversized, glassy eyes like a toddler waking up. Nothing about it appeared dangerous, but I'd never seen anything like it.

"HOW CAN IT SERVE?" Its shrill voice ricocheted off the tiled walls, blasting my ears.

The sharpness of its voice startled me into tripping over Jason again, who remained frozen behind me, except this time, he shoved me off his feet.

"Its eyes—" Jason muttered.

"Like it's connected to the ring."

"HOW CAN IT SERVE?" it repeated. "YOU SUMMONED IT."

I took a cautious step forward, needing to examine it closer. Needing to make sure the creature existed. "By rubbing the ring? Is that how I summoned you?"

If Jason hadn't been with me, I'd have sworn a mental breakdown created the creature's image in my mind.

"You're like a genie?" Jason's voice quivered.

It wrinkled its nose. The word *genie* offended it. "IT IS JANN. A JANNI."

"A janni?" I fought the urge to touch it. I didn't want to scare it off. "Like a genie?"

The creature shrugged. "JANN ARE A TYPE OF DJINN, OR AS YOU SAY, GENIE."

"So djinn is the same as genie," Jason's words trickled out of his mouth, "and jann are a kind of djinn."

Normally, I'd have teased Jason for repeating what we just heard, but not this time.

The edges of the ring dug into my hand, but I kept

my grip, afraid to break the potential connection between the ring and the creature. "Do we call you jann or janni?"

With an exasperated tone, the thing spoke as if teaching a child the same lesson for the hundredth time. "ONE JANNI, SEVERAL JANN."

My heart thundered in my chest, beating in my eardrums. Who cared about grammar and naming lessons? We'd discovered a full-on genie! The old man gave me a winning lottery ticket after all—a short, hairy lottery ticket.

"Do I get, like, wishes or something? For summoning you?"

Janni cocked his head. "IT WILL SERVE. YOU CAN CALL THEM WISHES IF YOU PREFER."

"Do I only get three?"

It squinted its purple eyes at me, like I'd just asked the strangest question, then shook its head, ears swinging like long hair. "IT SERVES AT YOUR PLEASURE. FOR AS LONG AS YOU POSSESS THE RING."

The ring grew hot in my clenched fist. Given Janni's reassurance, I relaxed my grip. The purple stone emanated a bright glow between my fingers.

Now what?

"Dude." Jason poked me in the back. "Touch it. I need confirmation it's real."

"You think we're imagining the exact same thing?"

"I'm not sure what the hell is going on."

Janni waddled toward me and held out his long arm, inviting me to touch him. I extended one finger. As a kid, a zookeeper offered me the opportunity to touch a snake, so I carefully stroked a tentative finger on the scaly skin, ready to jerk back at the slightest hint of danger. Similarly, I skimmed my pointer finger across the dirty, matted fur of Janni's arm.

"Well?"

"It feels like…um…fur." I took my hand back. "Like a stray dog or something."

The creature put his fists on his hips. "DOG?"

The door yawned open, and chatter from the crowded hallway swelled in the bathroom.

Janni jumped a foot off the floor, purple eyes wide with fright.

"Crap!" I barely finished the word before Janni jumped again. This time, leaping into my chest. My arms closed around him like someone had passed me a ball. A very stinky ball. His entire body vibrated.

Jason spun and turned on the water to wash his hands. "In a stall! Quick!"

I dove, with Janni in my arms, into the nearest stall and slammed the flimsy door shut, throwing the latch. Hopefully, before our visitors spotted Janni.

"IT WANTS TO LEAVE."

"Shh! Be quiet." I couldn't see anyone through the gap between the door and the stall.

Boys' voices filled the bathroom, loud and obnoxious. Janni trembled in my arms, making him hard to contain. "Stop moving!"

"IT DOES NOT LIKE NOISE! OR TOO MANY PEOPLE!" For a little guy, his voice sliced with ease through the hallway chaos, water running, and bathroom visitors shouting.

"What's that smell?" one of the voices asked. As the bathroom door eased shut, the hallway noise gradually quieted.

"Nasty."

Jason gave an awkward chuckle. "I don't recommend the nachos for lunch."

"Damn, bro!"

Janni squirmed. "IT DOES NOT LIKE—"

I pressed my hand over the janni's mouth.

"What was that?"

"You mean the weird voice?"

I couldn't let them find Janni. Who knew what they'd do to him?

I made an obnoxious grunting sound, pretending to push out the most giant shit of my life.

"You alive in there?" one of the boys hollered. "Don't pop your poop shoot out!"

They cracked up, at least four separate laughs. I responded with another loud, intentional grunt. "Like he said, stay away from the nachos."

Janni bit the inside of my hand. "Ow!"

Someone—likely Jason—turned on the hand dryer, providing cover. Good thinking.

"CAN IT LEAVE?" Janni failed to keep his shrill voice quiet.

I whispered into his floppy ear. "If you leave, will you come back?"

"RUB THE RING, AND IT IS AT YOUR SERVICE. PLEASE LET IT LEAVE!"

"Who the hell is in the shitter? That voice is insane." A guy's shadow fell over the crack between the stall door and stall wall, about to peek in. We were trapped.

I couldn't risk anyone seeing him. "Fine, leave."

Janni vanished. No cloud of smoke or magician-like explosion. He just stopped existing. And in his wake, he left a fresh injection of burnt hair odor.

An eye peered in through the crack.

"What's up, pervert?" I kicked the metal stall door, which rattled against the latch.

The eye disappeared, hopefully before he realized I sat on the toilet, supposedly taking a dump, with my pants still on.

"Definitely staying away from the nachos!" one of the guys said. Hands slapped, then a urinal flushed. "Let's go."

Jason forced a very awkward chuckle, pressing the button on the air dryer again. No one questioned how Jason's hands could be so wet.

The bathroom door opened, then swung shut again.

"They're gone, Bax. You can come out."

I flipped the latch and shoved the stall door open. It swung, bumping the next stall.

Jason's mouth still agape, he stared at me. "Um…"

"Yeah, um."

"Where'd he go?"

"Vanished. He said I could call him back by rubbing the ring again." The air dryer cycled off, and silence settled back into the bathroom. My mind spun with excitement, my thoughts tripping over each other. I'd found a genie, djinn, or whatever.

"This is jacked up." Jason, always the practical one. "I mean, what do we do with it?"

"You mean, what do we do with an albino rat-dog-monkey thing asking to serve me? Yeah. Jacked up is one way to describe it."

The bell rang, rattling the bathroom speaker.

"I'm not sure I can concentrate on anything else today. I mean, we found a genie." I worried the smile on my face might become permanent. "What are you doing tonight? Mom's working."

Jason shook his head. "I think I just remembered our overdue project. I may need to spend the night at your house to get a jump on it."

Nodding, I ran my fingers through my hair and flashed Jason a nervous smile, about to laugh like a crazy person. The surge of emotion pumping through my entire being came from a tornado of excitement, fear, and nervousness at what we'd stumbled into.

"See you at four?" I asked Jason.

"I can't get there fast enough."

Chapter 3

When the final bell rang, I practically fell out of my desk as I scrambled out of World History. I barreled down the hall, knocking people aside and ignoring their angry shouts. They'd be in a hurry, too, if a djinn waited for them at home.

Could I wish for a palace in the middle of downtown and it'd appear on Market Street? Or with a snap of my fingers, maybe Scarlet would stand devotedly at my side with Nick Ruiz as our house servant. Maybe I could wish Greg's return to Warren's Cosmos where he'd hug me, then reunite with Mom, all in time for Thanksgiving.

After hitting the street, the cool air beat me in the face as my feet pounded the concrete, racing home like a true Olympian. Jason would need some time to tell his parents we had a project due before he came over. I'd start seeing what I could find online until he arrived.

As much as more waiting killed me, I wanted Jason with me when I summoned Janni. He'd be a reliable witness for whatever happened. Besides, I needed his help. Jason knew way more than me about pretty much everything.

School always came easy to him. If I had half of his brain, I'd coast through high school, but Jason studied his ass off. Mom insisted I get a summer job, while Jason's parents told him studying *was* his job.

And he took his job very seriously, with extra classes every summer.

His dad taught African American Studies at Washington University, and since he taught there, Jason had guaranteed admission. But his dad insisted Jason earn his place like everyone else. He had this whole speech about how "Black people had a history of disadvantage in this country, so Jason's fortunate family would not take advantage of systemic benefits allocated for the disadvantaged." I could recite the speech by heart.

At home, I flung my backpack into my room and headed to the kitchen to check the fridge—sparse pickings. On second thought, who could eat? I found a Janni.

I grabbed a glass of iced tea, set it on the end table, then plopped onto the couch and powered up my laptop.

I typed *Janni* into my browser.

The browser asked, *Did you mean, jann?*

Janni had told us, "One janni, several jann."

I clicked.

My screen filled up with links to sites related to genies, djinn, jann, and several other related words that sounded alike. I clicked *genie*, starting with the only word I'd heard before today.

More links populated my screen. One for an American feral child (whatever that meant), one for a Canadian tennis player (had Jason heard of him?), one for a wrestler, several companies named Genie, and then pages of links about "spiritual creatures from an astral plane."

Bingo.

The first site defined *djinn*—which appeared to be

the proper term for a genie—as the catch-all name for a spiritual being. Then there were specific kinds of djinn, jann being one. Hundreds of ancient stories portrayed djinn differently through tales mainly from Asia and the Middle East. Some djinn did good things, some did bad, and some stories described djinn who tried to do the right thing but accidentally wreaked havoc.

A fist banged on our front door, yanking me out of Internet World.

"Come in!" Mom hated when I blindly let people in since I didn't know who waited on the other side of the door. Good thing Jason wasn't a serial killer.

"Man, I ran all the way here." He panted, trying to catch his breath as he dumped his jacket and backpack on the floor.

"How'd it go with your parents?"

"They weren't crazy about a sleepover on a Thursday night. I'm gonna have to come up with a fake project." He shook his head. "You got it? I haven't thought about much else all day."

"Yeah, and me neither."

I tossed my laptop to the couch and pulled it out of my pocket. We stared at the cheap-looking ring in my palm for a few seconds. The wide gold band and its oversized purple jewel displayed in all its gaudy glory. It did seem like a fancier piece of jewelry since we'd discovered what it could do.

"Do it here, I guess?" With Janni's small size, my living room would have plenty of space.

"Do we need to decide, like, what to do with Janni first?" Jason never acted without a plan. Exactly why I waited for him before using the ring.

"I have lots of questions to ask him. Figured we

start there." I pushed up the sleeves of my sweatshirt, anxious to start.

Jason nodded. "And you can always command him to leave, right?"

"Yeah. That's all I did earlier today. He said he'd come back whenever I wanted."

"You keep saying *him*. I have, too. Is it a *he*?" Jason always had a plan and always wanted to be polite.

"It's weird calling Janni *it*, isn't it? Although that's what he calls himself."

"Yeah." Jason scratched his head. "I'm guessing if he wanted to be called *it*, he'd tell us."

"True." Okay, enough talk. "You ready?"

Jason puffed out his chest and exhaled a lungful. "As I'll ever be."

"Here goes."

I rubbed the jewel between my thumb and forefinger, applying some pressure, unsure how much to apply. Before I could worry about it, a familiar sensation trickled from the top of my scalp down my body, like millions of icy pellets under my clothes, scampering down my skin. I shuddered, shaking my shoulders.

"What does it feel like?" Jason whispered with funereal reverence.

"It's strange," was the best answer I could come up with before the smell wafted through my living room. Freshman year, in biology, I reached over a Bunsen burner, and the flame singed the hairs on my arm. The same stench saturated the air now, but way more intense like someone had burned the hair off their entire body.

Jason searched for Janni. "The smell reminds me of

the time Michelle used Mom's hair straightener and burned her hair."

"I thought the same thing." I dropped the ring back into my pocket—I couldn't risk setting it down somewhere and losing it—and searched my living room with Jason.

"HOW CAN IT SERVE?" Its voice didn't sound any softer than it did in the bathroom at school. I jumped, even though we'd been expecting him.

I whirled around. Janni balanced on the back of our tan couch. His pink monkey feet clutched the fabric so he wouldn't fall backward.

"Um, hello?" How did I properly greet a djinn?

Janni nodded. An animal-like creature responding like a human would take some getting used to.

"HOW CAN IT SERVE?" he repeated, tapping his foot with impatience, even though he'd just arrived.

Jason nudged me. "You have lots of questions. Go for it."

I started with the basics. "I read jann are a type of djinn. We keep calling you Janni. Do you have an actual name?"

He shrugged his furry shoulders. "IT DOES NOT HAVE A NAME. JANNI IS FINE."

"Are there others like you?" Jason asked.

Janni reached up under his armpit, and in true monkey form, scratched. "THERE ARE OTHER JANN. IT THINKS. IT HAS NEVER MET ONE."

"Wow. You're isolated from others like you?" Janni cocked his head, not understanding. I moved on. "Where are you from?"

"THE RING."

"Yeah, but I mean, like, where did the ring come

from?"

Janni shrugged his tiny shoulders again, bristling his matted white hair. "IT HAS ALWAYS EXISTED."

Jason anxiously cut right to it. "Do you grant wishes?"

"IT IS HERE TO SERVE."

Jason whispered into my ear, "Ask him to do something. This is it. Test him out."

This *was* it. What every person dreamed of—a genie to make impossibilities a possibility. A genie who could end world wars or poverty. A genie who could grant all kids an education. But my ask would be way more spectacular than those things.

I cleared my throat. "Can you give me the ability to turn invisible?"

Janni's small face contorted into a wrinkled scowl. "IT CANNOT DO THAT."

I rephrased my question. "Can you make me invisible? For a day or something?"

He shook his head, ears swinging side to side.

The idea of limited powers landed on me like a punch in the gut, but I tried to hide my disappointment.

"I'd have done the same thing." Jason rested his hand on my shoulder. "Can I ask him something?"

"Have at it."

"Can I have perfect eyesight? Nothing crazy. Just so I don't need glasses?"

The sincerity of Jason's wish caused a twinge of guilt to knot in my stomach. He wanted to modestly correct his vision, while I wanted a super power.

"IT ONLY SERVES ONE MASTER."

Jason and I exchanged glances.

I squared my shoulders. "Give Jason twenty-twenty

vision."

"IT CANNOT DO THAT."

"Well, why didn't you say that when he asked?"

Janni shrugged.

"Then what can you do?" Irritation leaked into my tone.

"IT IS HERE TO SERVE."

"Yeah, heard you." I asked the first thing that popped into my head, "Can you find out the answers to our astronomy quiz?"

Janni vanished.

"Where'd he go?" Jason pushed his glasses higher up the bridge of his nose. "I guess he can't, like, change people."

"I guess not. How long will it take him?" I squeezed a blue throw pillow. I'd envisioned my afternoon with a djinn going way differently. So much for flying on magic carpets through the clouds.

Jason nodded to the pillow in my hands. "If you're not careful, you're gonna have to use a wish to replace that pillow when you rip it apart."

I threw it back on the couch. "Should I summon him again? What if we're only allowed three asks per visit? Did I just waste one?"

As I reached into my pocket to grab the ring, Janni reappeared, perched on the couch again. At the end of his long, monkey-like arm, he clutched some papers stapled together. He handed them over.

I flipped through them, bouncing over the pages, recognizing the familiar words about lunar anomalies. "It's our quiz for next week. With Mr. Buchannan's answers."

Jason grabbed the quiz and leafed through it. "Did

you steal this from Mr. Buchannan's desk?"

"HE ASKED." Janni pointed at me.

My neck grew warm under Janni's accusation. "Let me get this straight. You can't do, like, crazy stuff, but you can find things?"

"IT IS HERE TO SERVE."

"Yeah, I know." All the buildup in my mind all day long, and we ended up with a dog that could play fetch. Great.

"I kinda think you should return this." Jason handed me the quiz.

"Yeah." Pulling down a solid A minus in astronomy, I agreed. Would I have given my history test back so willingly? I think so. Maybe.

Janni sighed, exasperated, took the paper, and vanished.

"He can't seem to do stuff real genies can." Jason shook his head. "I get why you're frustrated."

I chuckled. "Real genies?"

"You know what I mean."

"Then what do we do with him?" I ran a hand through my hair, my fantasies dissolving as quickly as they'd bombarded me earlier. Hours before, I couldn't sort through the possibilities fast enough. Now, I drew a blank on how to use Janni's abilities. If you could even consider them abilities.

Janni reappeared. This time, he announced his presence behind us. "IT IS HERE TO SERVE." He stood in front of the door leading to the fire escape. "ANYTHING ELSE?"

We both spun around.

Fine. If he could fetch things like a dog, I'd see how far Janni could go. "Bring me one hundred dollars."

Janni vanished.

Jason raised an eyebrow. "What are you trying?"

"Not sure. Aren't you curious? Can he get into any place? I mean, if he can't make a palace appear downtown, then maybe he can help me buy one somewhere."

"A palace?"

"Never mind."

"Yeah, but if he stole the test from Mr. Buchannan, then he'll probably go steal money from some unsuspecting old lady." Jason sat on the couch. "Besides, we need to calm down on sending him back and forth. The stench gets worse every time he appears and disappears."

"I'm sorry you can't handle the bad odor." My words slipped out sharper than I intended.

After a few seconds of weirdness, I said, "Sorry. We have the only genie—or djinn—in the world, and I can't think of an exciting way to use him. It's irritating."

"Yeah, I get that, but you should relax. We just found him earlier today. I'm sure he can do stuff we just haven't discovered yet."

Who wanted to wait to stumble upon cool djinn stuff? I plopped down on the couch across from Jason and hiked my feet onto the coffee table, a personal habit Mom detested, but I couldn't seem to break. It wasn't – like the coffee table cost a million dollars, and it was older than me.

I sighed. "You're right."

"I always am."

Janni reappeared, holding a newly printed, crisp

hundred-dollar bill.

Jason grunted at me but pointed at Janni.

I sat up. "Where did that come from, Janni?" I dreaded what his answer would be.

"MIDWEST BANK AND TRUST."

"Jesus! You robbed a bank?" Jason leaped to his feet. "That's worse than robbing an old lady."

"NO OLD LADY THERE. BANK CLOSED."

"Ugh! Go put that back, too." I stood. "Then, how about something to drink. Can you do simple tasks?"

Janni vanished again. The smell of burnt hair thickened the air. I opened the door to the fire escape to clear out our apartment. The fire escape overlooked the alley, though, which included the building's dumpsters. Not sure if our air quality improved much.

"Not exactly like the genies in the movies." Jason's disappointment matched mine. I shouldn't have lashed out at him.

"Yeah. We found a thief who looks like the offspring of a monkey and a dog."

"A stinky thief."

We both laughed, lightening the mood.

Janni reappeared. This time, he held two margaritas, half the size of him, one in each hand. He struggled to keep his balance.

"Margaritas?" Jason and I asked at the same time.

"When I asked you for something to drink, I meant something from our fridge, Janni. Let me guess, you got those from—"

"DOS CANTINAS."

The Mexican restaurant on the corner was our go-to for most celebrations. The neon sign in their window flashed *Best Margs in the City* twenty-four seven.

I grabbed one of the massive glasses out of Janni's hand and took a drink, then wiped the salt from the corners of my mouth. Jason gaped, holding his breath like I'd started a game of Russian roulette. "What? It's not like he can return them. I want to see if they're the best in the city."

"Do you have many to compare it to?"

I rolled my eyes. "Look, something about this night should be fun."

Jason paused for a second, then, with a shrug, grabbed the other margarita from Janni and took a swig. His face twisted. "Too salty."

"Janni, can you go chill out for a bit? I need some air. Don't leave yet." I stepped out onto the wrought iron fire escape. At the end of the alley, peeking over apartments across the street, the downtown skyscrapers towered in the distance. Their windows lit up even with most of the offices closed for the day.

Mom called the fire escape our grand vista, even though we only lived on the third floor of a ten-story building. One of her desperate selling points when I told her I didn't want to move apartments. But, like all kids not wanting to move, almost five years later, I barely remembered our old place.

A car's tires squealed, followed by a honk. A man yelled, "You son of a bitch!" at someone near the alley's entrance, his voice bouncing between the brick walls and up to our fire escape. I imagined these weren't noises typically heard on a grand vista.

"Janni is still kinda cool, right?" Jason took in the view of the dumpsters below. His shirt flapped in the breeze. "It's like having a pet you don't need to walk and feed."

I shrugged. "I guess. I was just hoping…you know."

Janni waddled outside through the open door and climbed up the railing, balancing on the rail. Like a scolded puppy, his long ears hung low, and his large purple eyes blinked. Cute in an ugly sort of way.

"Seriously? I hurt your feelings?"

"IT IS HERE TO SERVE." Janni's voice sounded quieter in the depth of the city night.

I couldn't blame him. He could only do what he could do. Maybe he had some kind of spiritual insight, or all-knowingness, if that's a thing. It couldn't hurt to try. "Any chance you know Greg Allen?"

He shook his head. Strike three.

Jason perked up. "What about a creepy old dude with long-ass nails?"

Janni squeezed his eyes shut, and his ears slunk back against his head. He grabbed his elbows and started trembling. The October night wasn't that cold.

My heart skipped a beat. Jason's a genius. Janni might be able to explain the old man's connection to Greg.

"Who is he? The old man." I set down the margarita and squatted in front of Janni, keeping his attention on me.

Janni shot glances over my shoulders, worried someone would hear us. "IT DOES NOT LIKE TO TALK ABOUT HIM."

"Why?" I pulled myself closer to the rail. Janni's trembling almost vibrated him right off the fire escape. I prepared to catch him if he fell.

"PLEASE DO NOT MAKE IT TALK ABOUT HIM."

"Is he a bad guy?"

Janni's eyes widened as they flickered over my shoulder. He leaped off the rail and dove behind Jason's leg. His small monkey hands clutched Jason's jeans around his shin.

"IT WANTS TO LEAVE!" He pressed his face against Jason's pant leg and pointed behind me.

I envisioned the old man on the fire escape next to ours, reaching out with his long fingers, his purple eyes glowing in the moonlight.

Instead, Ashley Bryant, my neighbor and pariah of the tenth grade, peered over the rail of her fire escape. One of her short stubby fingers pointed at Jason's leg. "What the freakin' hell is that thing?"

Chapter 4

"What's what thing?" I couldn't smooth out the guilt from unsteadying my voice. Of all the people in the world, it had to be Ashley Bryant who saw Janni.

She folded her arms across her chest, and when I didn't elaborate, wagged her finger at Jason's leg. "That thing!"

The breeze blew Ashley's tangled brown hair across her face, but she didn't bother brushing it away. Her oversized red T-shirt rippled around her. "Is it a pet monkey?"

I debated going with Ashley's idea. He did kind of resemble a monkey. Before I responded, though, Janni answered, "IT IS JANNI!"

Apparently, calling him a monkey offended him.

Jason slapped his palm against his forehead.

Ashley squealed, piercing the night, almost sounding like Janni. "It talks? Holy freakin' crap! I'm coming over."

"Wait! You can't." I lurched toward the rail of the fire escape with my hands out, thinking I could grab her and stop her.

"I can't what?" She awaited my answer.

"Y-you can't come over."

"Why?"

I hadn't thought it through. I scrambled. "Because Mom's not home. I can't have friends over when she's not home."

Ashley pressed her fists on her hips and grunted. "First of all, I've lived next to you for years and never heard that rule. Second, is Jason an illusion or something?"

Next to me, Jason made his *that's your excuse?* face. Thinking fast on my feet had never been one of my talents.

"Besides," she wagged her stupid finger at us again, "if you don't let me come over, I'll tell my parents. Don't make me play that card. I'm too old."

"Fine." I sighed. She left us no option. "Door's open."

Ashley disappeared into her apartment so quickly that if she'd been a cartoon, she'd have left a puff of smoke in her wake.

"What now, Bax?"

"I don't know. We try to get Ashley in and out of here as quick as we can. What else can we do?"

"SHOULD IT LEAVE?"

I scooted Janni inside. Jason followed. "You're the reason she's coming over here, so you aren't leaving. Why couldn't you just pretend to be a monkey?"

"IT IS JANNI."

"Argh. Don't go anywhere. If you leave, she'll *never* leave."

Janni climbed onto the couch, sitting on a cushion. His stubby legs stretched straight out in front of him, the pink pads of his feet facing us like a dirty stuffed animal.

"What do we tell her?" Jason bit on his thumbnail.

"I'm open to ideas, but she saw him. If we don't tell her the truth, I'm not sure what kind of believable

45

lie I could come up with. I mean, how do we explain *him*?" I pointed at Janni.

"True. We all just witnessed your ability to lie under pressure. You can't have friends over when your mom's not here? Really? With me standing right behind you?" Jason spun a throw pillow at me.

I batted it away. "I didn't hear you coming up with anything better."

The doorknob slammed against the wall as Ashley barreled in. Grace wasn't her thing. "Where is it?"

The noise caused Janni to spring to his feet and thrust his head behind the cushion.

"Seriously, Ashley, you have to calm down. He scares easily." I sat on the couch next to him, resting a hand on his back. "Look at him. He's shaking."

She stared at Janni's back end sticking out from behind the pillow. "Sorry." She dropped her voice to a whisper. "What is it?"

Jason shrugged, trying to sound casual. "A genie."

"Sorry, what? A genie?" It seemed physically impossible for Ashley to keep her voice down.

"You can't tell anyone." Why did I let Ashley in? What a mistake. Even with the best of intentions, could she be discrete?

Janni squirmed his head out from behind the cushion but stayed tight against the back of the couch. His purple eyes stayed suspiciously on Ashley.

"Whoa." She took a step back.

"We're not kidding." Jason repeated my warning, "You can't tell anyone."

"Duh." Ashley waved her hand. "I'm not a freakin' moron. I've seen enough alien movies to know you can't talk about the alien, or scientists will come, take him, and do tests and stuff on him."

Janni's ear fell back against his head. "TESTS?"

"He can understand you, you know." I rubbed the top of Janni's head, unsure if it helped calm him, but he didn't pull away. "And he's not an alien. Stop getting him worked up."

"Whatever."

In addition to always sharing random facts she learned, Ashley had what Mom referred to as a "big" personality. While a nice enough person, most could only handle small doses of her. No one called me Mr. Popular, but at least I had a friend, and people didn't avoid eye contact when I entered the room. Ashley, on the other hand, turned people off in seconds. In a way, I admired that she didn't seem to notice or care. For a tenth grader, I'd never met anyone more confident and comfortable with themselves, for better or worse.

"What's the story? Spill it. How'd you find him?"

I glanced at Jason to see if he agreed. He gave me a nod and shrug. Not necessarily an unwavering endorsement.

She was in it with us, so no backing out now.

I explained everything, starting with the old man's visit and even showed her the ring, which continued to emit a dull purple light with Janni around.

For the first time since I'd known her, Ashley had nothing to say for a full minute after I finished. No random facts could compete with my story. And by the time I finished, Janni had calmed down enough to lounge on the couch, his attention bouncing between us as we talked.

When she did respond, Ashley simply muttered, "No freakin' way."

For whatever reason, she didn't question the two massive margaritas on our table. So after spilling everything to her, I took a gulp of the warm margarita and set it back on the coffee table with a clink like we were exchanging small talk at a work cocktail party. "He seems to be able to teleport and fetch stuff but no other real genie things."

"REAL?" Janni scoffed.

Ashley put her fists on her hips, ready to command an army. "You boys are just not creative enough to challenge him. I mean, he's so little and can teleport. That alone is enough to do cool things."

Of course, Ashley went into I-know-more-than-you mode. After dumping the two margaritas in the sink, I threw the plastic glasses in the trash, shoving them down deep. Didn't need Mom finding them.

I called back to Ashley from the kitchen, "So what amazing ideas do you have, then?"

"Freakin' dumbasses." Name-calling was one of Ashley's awesome personality characteristics. Or *freakin'* awesome personality characteristics, as she'd say.

She leaped to her feet, raised a hand, and pointed at Janni. "I command you to go see what my parents are doing!"

Janni dove under the cushion again.

I hurried back to the living room. She'd give him a heart attack. "Stop yelling at him. You're scaring him. Jesus, Ashley."

"Sorry." She lowered her hand.

"Besides," Jason wiped the water rings the margaritas left on our coffee table with his sleeve, "he only listens to Bax."

She turned to me. "Send him to see what my parents are saying. You could use him to spy on people, I bet."

I bristled at the way she said "use him" but liked the idea. "I'll *ask* him. Janni, can you listen in on what Ashley's parents are talking about across the hall? Don't let them see you."

In a blink, he vanished.

"Whoa." Ashley fanned the air in front of her face. "Is the stink always around?"

"Whenever he comes and goes." Jason scratched his chin. "Must be a result of how he shifts time and matter in order to teleport."

Ashley and I looked at Jason like he started speaking Martian. I chuckled. "What's that, dude?"

"What's what?" He raised both hands defensively. "You don't know!"

Ashley brushed it off with a shake of her head. "So, how do you think the creepy old man knew Greg?"

"I'm not sure." I fell back onto the couch. "And it worries me how the mention of the old man spooked Janni."

"If that guy scares Janni, maybe we should be scared, too," Jason mumbled. He bit at one of his fingernails.

No way I'd bail on Janni yet. "What are you getting at?"

"What if we're messing with something we shouldn't? This whole magic thing is kinda...unknown."

"I hear you. But what do we do? Everything happened so fast. Janni seems harmless."

"Yeah." Jason agreed but didn't sound convinced.

The old man, the ring, Janni, the voice in my bedroom that first night. They all had to connect.

Jason, lost in his thoughts, jumped two feet out of his seat when Janni suddenly reappeared on my coffee table, engulfed in a fresh wave of burnt hair. "I wish you could warn us when you were about to pop in and out." Jason shook his head. "Like a buzz or something."

"Well?" I ignored Jason, anxious to see if we discovered a new ability. "What did Mr. and Mrs. Bryant say? Did you listen in?"

"YES." Then, Janni started speaking, but instead of his shrieking voice, he sounded like a recording of Mr. and Mrs. Bryant.

Mr. Bryant: When did you tell Ashley to come home?

Mrs. Bryant: Nine. She said Jason Franklin is there, too.

Mr. Bryant: As she gets older, I'm not sure I like her hanging out with two boys.

Ashley shifted in her seat.

Mrs. Bryant: Hon, you won't meet two nicer boys than Bax and Jason.

Mr. Bryant: I agree, but hormones kick in, and kids find themselves in all kinds of trouble. I see it happen every day.

Mrs. Bryant: Well, I've always said she and Baxter would make a cute couple. I'm glad they're finally hanging out. Maybe they'll be future prom king and queen of Truman—

"Enough!" Ashley screeched, leaping up from the couch. For a minute, she looked poised to slap Janni, desperate to trigger his off button. "We get the idea! Jesus, Mom!"

Janni stumbled as he backed away from her and fell off the coffee table, tumbling to the area rug with a thud.

I grabbed his ice-cold hand and helped him back up. "Come on, Ashley!"

She fidgeted with her fingernails as pink blotches erupted all over her neck. "Moms can be so embarrassing." We stood in awkward silence for two excruciatingly long seconds.

Who knew what our moms said about Jason and me when we weren't around? Maybe Ashley had a crush on me, maybe not. For everyone's sake, I pretended we hadn't heard the last part of Janni's recording. "So, um, yeah. He sounded just like your parents."

"He did." Jason jumped in, giving Ashley time to recover. "Should we ask him any other questions?"

"Janni, do you, like, eat or anything?" Ashley reengaged.

"Excellent question!" Jason used way too much enthusiasm, but we all appreciated it.

Janni shook his head. "NO. BUT IT IS GETTING TIRED. JUMPING IS TIRING."

"Is that what you call teleportation?" Jason asked. "Jumping?"

Janni lay down on the couch and curled up like a puppy as if we'd all vanished. "JUMPING IS HOW IT TRAVELS. AND IT CAN ONLY SLEEP IN THE RING."

"Time to let him go, I guess." I patted the ring in my pocket. At least we found another ability. Still nothing like I expected, but something.

"He's so cute. Can we watch him sleep for a

while?" Ashley bit her bottom lip.

I rolled my eyes. "You can leave, Janni. Thanks."

Janni closed his eyes, and as he did, jumped back into the ring.

"Well, I should head home." Ashley walked backward to the door. "Have to be home by nine." She chuckled awkwardly. "But you all heard that I guess."

"Later." I smiled and gave her a casual wave.

"I can't wait to see what I can find out about djinn." Ashley's constant scouring of the internet for random and unusual facts might come in handy. While her personality made her a social outcast, her grades rivaled Jason's. She'd be our perfect researcher.

"Sounds good."

The door barely clicked shut behind her when Jason's white teeth lit up his face. "You guys would make the cutest kids."

"Shut up."

"Seriously adorable. With your wit and Ashley's personality—"

"Shut up!"

Laughter drowned his words. "I mean, the kids would be *freakin'* cute!"

I dove, tackling him to the couch. "You're jealous." I pinned him to the cushion.

While cracking himself up, he coughed, "Okay, okay! I'll stop."

I climbed off him, laughing myself. "Play some *Archer Annihilation*? We could start over and see how easy it is now."

"Have I ever said no to *Archer Annihilation*?"

I plugged in the game console, my reward for spending two summers as a camp counselor. The kids were kindergarten age, so no diapers, just hanging out by a pool and bandaging scraped knees. Way better than doing dishes at the hotel where Mom worked, which was her threat if I didn't find anything else.

Tossing Jason a controller, I plopped back onto the couch. "I need a break from magical things."

****

In the expansive ballroom, the long dining room table resembled doll furniture. A fireplace covering half of the wall emitted a flickering glow that cast long shadows across the floor. A meticulously groomed dog lounged in the corner, ears perked, waiting for my command. The food towered on the table: pizza, pasta, chips, and cakes. We'd never make a dent.

The food didn't matter. The people did. Jason, laughing, his family on each side of him. His parents chatted and joked with each other in the regal setting, and his sister played with her dessert. Jason's family, for once, seemed elated to be part of my life instead of the other way around.

Next to me, Scarlet wore a form-fitting emerald dress that matched her eyes. Her auburn hair piled on her head in one of those styles meant to look casual but instead looked royal. She resembled a princess who'd stepped right out of a fantasy book. Her eyes sparkled in a way I'd never experienced, with a sheen of adoration she normally reserved for Nick.

She smiled, her lips shimmering in the firelight. "I'm glad you did this. I'm so happy."

I turned away as my face burned. How do I react? No girl ever looked at me like that.

At the other end of the table sat Mom and Greg. Her hand rested on his, and they talked casually like they'd never been apart. Tall and handsome, his dark hair needed a trim, like mine. He laughed heartily at whatever Mom whispered, and instead of worn and exhausted, her face glowed.

As the warmth of the scene wrapped around me, a shudder crawled from my chest and over my shoulders. Happiness and contentedness almost overwhelmed me. They swelled anxiously inside me like a kid waiting for his parents to allow him out of his room on Christmas morning.

I had so many questions for Greg. Where had he been? Why did he leave? Did he miss *Shade Slayer, #276*? I tried to stand, but Scarlet reached over, her hand on mine, in a motion that mirrored what my mom did to my dad, keeping me seated.

"Hey, Bax!" Jason beamed from across the table.

I acknowledged him with a nod.

"Janni will always be my favorite, but this new djinn is the best thing that ever happened." He raised his glass, and everyone followed. "To the new djinn."

Glasses clinked.

"New djinn?"

Besides Janni?

Jason's face glowed. "Yeah, man. The new djinn."

The life I'd envisioned when we'd first found Janni—a living fantasy—had become a reality. No rules of what could or couldn't happen. Maybe a new djinn would be my Something Big.

Scarlet's breath tickled my ear. "Get up."

"Huh?"

Mom stood and slammed her hands on each side of her plate, vibrating the entire room. "Get up, hon!"

Her smile morphed into a worried grimace. "Get

up!"

I jerked back and forth in my seat, nearly falling out of it. An invisible, giant hand had wrapped itself around my torso and shook me like a rag doll.

****

My eyes couldn't open under the blinding light at first. As they adjusted, the outlines of Mom and Jason began to hover over me.

Mom shook my shoulders. "Bax! Wake up!"

"I'm up. I'm up." My dry voice rasped as if I'd gone years without water.

The sheet, soaked in sweat, fell to my waist as I crawled to a sitting position. My Truman High T-shirt clung to my skin, instantly turning to ice in my bedroom air.

Jason stood behind Mom, both in rumpled sleep clothes and with concerned scowls.

"You were shouting and thrashing around like a guy possessed." Jason scratched his stomach. "Like you were having night terrors."

"Really?"

"Some dream." Mom's gaze bounced over me, checking to make sure I hadn't hurt myself in my sleep. "You woke us both up. You kept yelling, but we couldn't understand you."

I rubbed my eyes. "Sorry."

"No need to apologize. You all right?" Mom's eyebrows came together over her puffy eyes.

I nodded. "I guess too much stuff happening lately."

"You think?" Jason glanced at Mom and said nothing else.

"How about some milk or something? A glass of

J. L. Sullivan

water? I'll get you some water."

Before I could say, "I can get it, Mom. I'm not five," she left.

"Some nightmare," Jason said.

"Not a nightmare." The dream returned in flashes: the mansion, the food, the family, Greg, the *new djinn*.

"What do you mean?" Jason dropped his voice so Mom wouldn't hear.

"I mean, you woke me from the happiest dream ever. You were there, Scarlet, Mom, Greg. All because of some new djinn. Not Janni. A djinn who made everything perfect. Perfect."

Jason scratched his head. "It was a dream, man."

I leaned back against the headboard, the wood cold against my sweaty hair. I closed my eyes, trying to conjure up the feelings of contentedness and happiness from the dream. "I know it was just a dream, but isn't it odd the dream filled me with happiness, even though you guys said I—"

"Bax?" Jason pointed to the drawer of my nightstand.

A bright purple light—more brilliant than we'd ever seen—lit up the inside of my nightstand. As I slid open the drawer, purple beams from the ring streaked across my room.

"Woah," Jason mumbled, his eyes hidden behind the purple reflecting off his glasses.

"Yeah, woah." The purple beams shone on the ceiling like spotlights, blanketing my room in a violet hue. I gasped, then reminded myself to breathe. "You know what this means, don't you?"

Jason wrinkled his eyebrows like he had earlier when Janni freaked out about the mention of the old

56

man. "That we may have started something we don't understand?"

I ignored his skepticism. "It means my dream isn't made-up. It means there's at least some reality to it, some connection between my dream and the ring. What if it's true? What if the ring's trying to tell me there's another djinn?" I grabbed Jason's T-shirt sleeve, shaking it with excitement.

"All right, Bax—" Mom said, coming down the hallway.

I slammed the drawer shut, extinguishing the purple supernova before she noticed. To be safe, I grabbed a shirt from the floor beside my bed and tossed it over the nightstand.

"Here." She came in and handed me a glass of water.

"Thanks." I took a drink and glanced at the drawer, which appeared dark under the T-shirt.

"All right, Jason, back to the couch. You guys have school in a few hours." Mom tousled my hair, then discretely wiped it on her pajama top. It must've been sweaty. Finally, she left, giving Jason a pat on the shoulder with her dry hand.

Before turning to leave, Jason whispered, "What have we started?"

I shrugged, not having a better response. I couldn't disagree with Jason's concern, but we also didn't know everything. If another djinn existed who could make my dream a reality, I wanted it.

Chapter 5

The sun shone through my living room window, casting a bright square on the floor that had already begun its morning crawl across our apartment. The ceiling thudded with irregular intervals. Had to be young kids since the stomping only happened first thing in the morning.

"You really think the ring caused your dream? I mean, it's on your mind, so I'm not shocked you dreamt about djinn. But you think the ring literally sent you a message?" Jason shoved a spoonful of cereal into his mouth.

"You saw it glowing. That means the dream wasn't my imagination. And the weirdest part of the whole thing was how happy the dream made me feel. Happy isn't the right word. More like euphoric. So how in the world could I feel euphoric while you and Mom watched me have some kind of night terror?" I swirled the last swallow of juice in the bottom of my glass.

"If, and I say *if*, the ring spoke to you through the dream, where would we even begin searching for another djinn? If the old man hadn't given you Janni's ring, we'd have never known he existed. Do we hunt down the old man and say, 'Pardon me, Creepy Old Guy, any other djinn on you, by chance?'"

We both laughed. "Yeah. 'Excuse me, Creepy Old Guy, the first djinn did some cool things, but can we upgrade?'"

Jason scrolled on his phone while he finished his breakfast. "There's a ton of different types of djinn. Jann seem to be pretty low on the ladder as far as power goes, from what I'm reading."

"Given what Janni demonstrated last night, I can't say I'd disagree." I sighed but still held out hope Janni had untapped power we just needed to discover. He couldn't be some furry consolation prize. I refused to accept that.

I dropped my bowl into the sink. "Crap."

"What?"

"I told Mom I'd do the dishes before we left."

Jason didn't raise his head from looking at his phone but eyed me over the top of his glasses. A smile spread across his face.

"What's so funny?"

His smile widened. "Or you could have your genie do the dishes?"

My smile matched his. "You think?"

He shrugged and stood up from the table. "What could happen? If anything, he'll just say, 'IT CANNOT DO THAT.'" Jason's horrible impersonation of Janni rivaled his horrible impersonation of Principal Clark, which always cracked him up.

"Let's give it a try."

I fished the ring out of my pocket and rubbed the purple jewel. After a few seconds, my skin tingled like I'd stepped out into freezing rain naked. The cold droplets raced down my arms and legs. I shuddered.

"HOW CAN IT SERVE?" Janni appeared on the kitchen counter, leaning against the toaster with one hand on the top of it. The smell of burnt hair wafted through the kitchen.

"Janni." I hesitated.

Jason nodded, *go-ahead*.

"Can you do the dishes?" I pointed to the sink.

He cocked his head. "DO?"

"Like, wash them and put them away." I turned on the warm water and handed him the soap scrubber to get him started. "And hurry. We need to get to school."

Janni examined the scrubber in his hand, then squeezed. Soapy water dripped off his elbow fur, so he shook his arm. With a furrowed brow, he studied the sink, plotting his chore. Then he jumped, vanishing.

He reappeared, holding a plate under the water, rubbing it with the soapy scrubber. The water raced from the faucet, across the plate, and then pooled on the counter briefly before creating a waterfall to the floor.

"IT WILL HURRY." He glanced down.

"Keep the water in the sink, Janni." I grabbed a towel and tossed it on the puddle, an ominous sign of things to come.

Janni rinsed the plate, coated in slippery bubbles. His tiny pink hands lost their grip, and the plate launched. It banged on the edge of the sink, then crashed to the floor, splitting in two.

"UH, OH."

"Maybe this wasn't a good idea," Jason mumbled as he picked up the broken plate.

"Yeah, Janni, maybe—"

Janni jumped.

"Where'd he go?" Jason tossed the plate into the trash.

Janni reappeared with a bowl in hand, holding it under the running water. This time, the water ran into one side of the bowl, then shot up the other side like a ramp, splashing him in the face. Janni dropped the bowl into the sink and rubbed his eyes.

"Just stop, Janni."

He didn't hear me—too busy shaking his entire body at once like a dog in the rain. His ears flopped back and forth.

He jumped again.

"Get him to stop," Jason hollered.

"I'm trying."

A crash sounded from inside the cabinet above the sink.

"What's he doing?" I opened the cabinet door. A stack of plastic bowls tumbled out, crashing on my head. Startled, I stumbled backward.

"IT IS TRYING TO—" Janni started as he lost his footing in the water puddle he'd made underneath himself in the cabinet. Arms flailing, he instinctively reached for something. Unfortunately, he latched onto an unstable tower of cups.

Both Janni and the stack of cups—luckily plastic—rained down from the cabinet. Some plummeted to the floor, some rolled into the sink. Janni landed on the counter.

In a dash to save the falling dishes, Jason slid in the water on the floor and flew forward. He caught himself on the counter just before whacking his chin on its edge.

Determined to carry out my command, Janni picked up another plate, already struggling to maintain a grip on it.

"Stop!" I yelled. "Put everything down. Just stop!"
Knock, knock, knock.

"Who's that?" Jason pulled himself to stand and threw another towel on the floor. Water droplets speckled his glasses.

I looked at the front door as if I could see through it.

Knock, knock, knock.

"Everything okay in there?" a voice called from the hallway outside our door. With all of the banging dishes and water running, I didn't recognize it.

"It's eight in the morning." I shut off the water, fearful Mom forgot her keys. It wouldn't have been the first time. "Janni, go away!"

He jumped.

Knock, knock, knock, knock.

"Hold on! Mom, is that you?"

"No, it's me!" Ashley replied.

I stopped and took a deep breath.

"Thank God," Jason mumbled. "I'll let her in."

I started gathering the dishes from the floor, drying them off, and putting them away. Fortunately, Janni only broke one plate. Mom wouldn't notice.

"What the freakin' hell is going on in here?" Ashley barreled inside, pushing past Jason. "I could hear all the banging and yelling in the hallway! You two having a wrestling match?"

Jason wiped the water off his glasses with the hem of his T-shirt. "We asked Janni to do the dishes."

"I take it that didn't work out so well?" Ashley chuckled.

I started mopping the water up. "Not so much. Ashley, would you mind getting our backpacks from my room? We need to get going, or we'll be late for school."

"Sure."

As soon as she was out of earshot, I whispered to Jason, "Let's not tell her about the dream. Not until we know more."

Ashley overreacted to things, and I didn't need her reacting at all until Jason and I figured out how we wanted to play the whole dream thing.

"Up to you. She's your girlfriend."

I punched him in the arm.

****

We weaved between the people on the sidewalk headed to work or school. Some just sat on their stoops having coffee. Primarily residential, mornings tended to be the only time of day my neighborhood bustled with pedestrians.

"What did you find?" I flung my backpack over my shoulder. "Yesterday, I looked up djinn, and there're a butt load of sites. Like, a ton."

"True." Ashley's hair bounced off her shoulders as we walked. "But there are also some facts on almost every site. I figured those must be closest to the truth."

As I suspected, the girl who loved sharing random information would end up being very helpful.

We separated to let a guy on a bike speed between us, then regrouped. Had we not separated, he would have run me over.

"What are those facts?" Jason asked.

Ashley brushed her hair behind her ear, a smile exploding across her face as she reveled in being an authority. "Well, it sounds like genies, or as they're formally called, djinn, have existed forever. Some sites say they're mentioned in Sumerian writings back in two thousand four hundred BC."

"Sumerians?" I should have paid more attention in history class.

"Sumerians are considered the oldest civilization in history." Jason told me things I should know in a way that didn't make me feel stupid, which happened a lot. If someone ranked our team of three on intelligence, Jason would be a solid number one, Ashley, number two, and I'd place firmly at number one hundred. I'd never figure all of this out without them.

Ashley continued. "Most sites said God created djinn before he made humans. The story goes that after he created all these different types of djinn, they angered God by causing so much mischief in the world. As punishment, he imprisoned them in…guess what?"

"Bottles?" I may not know about Sumerians, but I'd seen genie movies.

"Bingo. It could be any inanimate object, though. So then, after he sorted the whole djinn thing out, he tried his hand at creation again, but this time, he created beings without magic. He called them humans."

I kicked an empty liquor bottle into the gutter. "So are djinn good or evil?"

"Both. Like all beings, there're good ones, bad ones, and some kind of in between." The words fell out of her mouth in rapid succession.

"Do they all look like monkey-dogs?" Jason asked without the slightest trace of humor.

"Actually, most shape-shift. In their natural state, some are covered in fur, some have hooves, some don't have any heads, and some are nothing *but* floating heads." Ashley's hands flailed as she spoke. "There are all kinds."

"And the whole 'big blue guy singing songs'?" I

had to ask. We were all thinking it.

"Movie studio propaganda. Interestingly, the original djinn lore evolved and embedded itself into different cultures in different ways. For example, a type of djinn called *shaitan* later became known as Satan in Christianity. Another type, called *ghuls*, are what we now refer to as ghouls or poltergeists. Each kind of djinn varies in power and what they can do. There are nasnas, marids, ifrits, jann…the list is endless."

We were almost at school. Time to reign Ashley in. "Interesting trivia, but what did you learn about Janni?"

"Right. From what I read, jann are the weakest of the djinn. Unfortunately for us, they're scraping the bottom of the djinn ladder."

Same thing Jason read during breakfast.

He elbowed me. "So maybe Janni is at the bottom of the hierarchy, but think about the problems we'd have with a more powerful djinn. Right, Bax? Ashley said one became Satan."

Clearly, Jason had decided not to pursue the djinn in my dream, but I wouldn't give up that easily—not yet. "There are also more powerful *good* djinn. Right, Ashley?"

She squinted at us. "Riiiiiiight. Why did Jason elbow you? Am I missing something?"

"No," Jason and I said in unison.

"I don't believe either of you. Anyway, do you have the you-know-what?"

"In my pocket."

"When do we play with Janni again?" She giggled. "I have tons of questions after everything I read."

I shook my head. "Play with him?"

"Damn, Ashley," Jason said, "he's not a doll or

something."

"That's not what I meant. And I resent the fact that a toy I want to play with has to be a *doll* because I'm a girl. Why couldn't you say he's not a soccer ball? Or football? Couldn't I play with those?"

"You've never kicked a soccer ball in your entire life."

"Whatever, Jason. What if I said you thought of him like a *basketball* just because you're Black? Believe me, I've seen you play basketball, and you couldn't draw one on paper—"

"Enough." I eased them apart. "We're here."

The line of empty school buses idled at the curb while kids swarmed around the outside of Truman High School like bees around a flower garden. Some moseyed into the tan brick building. Some stalled on the lawn—dead from endless trampling—as they waited until the absolute final second to go to homeroom. I knew myself well enough to know I'd end up being tardy if I stayed outside talking any longer.

I held a fist to Jason. "See you at assembly?"

"Yep." We bumped.

Ashley gave me a pat on the shoulder. "Yep. See you guys there."

Before I could say, "We didn't ask," she spun on her heel and trotted inside.

****

All four grades of Truman High congregated for our monthly assembly. The giant scoreboard hung at one end of the gymnasium while the navy banner adorned with a yellow Truman Lancer hung at the other, both over metal doors propped open with folding chairs.

Chatter filled the space in between as students strategically chose their seats on the bleachers, myself included. Assemblies created the perfect time to *accidentally* sit next to someone you wouldn't dare approach during the openness of lunch period. They provided an excuse to be forced to squeeze in during the forty-minute all-school meeting.

After locating my target, I took a seat on the cold metal, pretending not to notice who I sat next to. Then, after an adequate pause, I casually scanned the crowd before my gaze landed on my neighbor. I put on my best surprised voice. "Oh, hey."

"Hey, Bax." Scarlet brushed her perfect red hair over her shoulder. The silver flecks in her fuzzy sweater sparkled. "You ready for our English exam?"

"As ready as I'll ever be. You?"

She nodded. "I think so. Nick's tutoring me."

Fighting back an eye roll took every ounce of strength I could muster. "Nick's a literature buff?" Picturing Nick in a tweed jacket, smoking a pipe, and discussing Moby Dick brought a smile to my face.

She giggled, probably realizing how ridiculous it sounded, too. "No, but he took the class last year."

"Ah. The benefits of dating a junior, I guess." I snickered like I had a long list of juniors in my dating history.

She scanned the bleachers, noting where everyone chose to sit. "You going to the game next week?"

Did Nick have to be the subject of *everything*?

"I think so," I answered after a pause, pretending to mentally organize my many engagements next Friday. "Should be an exciting game."

Please don't ask me who the opposing team is.

"Nick is nervous. Scott Armington is supposed to be there."

Hoping he wasn't someone I should know, I took the risk. "Scott Armington?"

She giggled again, but not in a ridiculing way. I loved her giggle. She turned to face me, her green eyes somehow sparkling like her sweater in the sterile gym lighting. "He's a scout. A football scout for Missouri State. Nick has a strong chance of getting a full ride to college, even though he's just a junior. Isn't that amazing?"

It physically pained me not to roll my eyes. Of course, they'd give him a full ride. Nothing less than perfect ever happened to Nick Ruiz. "Yeah. Pretty amazing."

"Oh my gosh. I have to go, Bax." She leaped to her feet as if the bleachers had disappeared beneath her.

I stood with her. "Everything all right?"

She rested her hand on my arm for a moment, raising goosebumps in its wake. "Yeah. Casey's had a tough day. She and Preston might break up. I should be a good friend and sit next to her."

Might break up? Was she proactively consoling *before* the breakup? Casey and Preston spent their entire relationship in a constant state of breaking up and getting back together. Was she trying to get away from me? Upgrading her bleacher neighbors?

"Yeah, of course. You're such a good friend. I hope they work it out."

She gave me a sad, patronizing smile. "I'll tell her you wish her the best."

She began crawling over people to reach her potentially sad friend. Down several rows, Casey did appear sullen—for a hot girl with a perfect life. At least Scarlet hadn't made up Casey's impending breakup to get away from me. I needed to chill.

I plopped back to the bench, noticing Jason next to me.

"Oh, hey. When did you get here?"

He smacked his forehead with his palm. "Like ten minutes ago, but you didn't notice. Too busy making googly eyes at Scarlet. I didn't want to interrupt."

"Whatever. We're friends."

"You walked to school together for, like, half a year. In fifth grade. You use the term *friends* pretty loosely."

"Whatever. She's always nice to me." Nicer than her snobby friends like Casey, who probably didn't even know my last name.

Hooting and applause rose from the bleachers as Nick Ruiz strutted to the middle of the gray gym floor. Nick embodied the perfect cliché. Tall and buff, golden blond hair, and a dimpled smile, all packaged around a star athlete. No wonder Scarlet practically fainted when he entered her general area. Hell, I'd date him.

Principal Clark strolled to Nick's side as the cheering faded, appearing short, fat, and generally troll-like in comparison. "Everyone, take your seats." His voice crackled in the cheap gymnasium speakers.

After everyone quieted down, Mr. Clark began. "Good morning!"

"Good morning," the bleachers responded in messy unison.

"Couple of housekeeping things." He straightened his suit coat. Mr. Clark always wore a suit. None of the other faculty did. He never explained it, but whether field day or graduation, the man would be in some shade of gray suit, a white shirt, and a tie matching his mood. During December, when the holiday spirit possessed him, he'd go crazy and break out the candy cane tie.

"First, the Student Council is hosting a tailgate party before next Friday's home game. They'll be selling hot dogs for two dollars and hot chocolate for one dollar. All proceeds will go to the prom fund, so cash only."

The student body gave an obligatory round of applause.

"Next, before Nurse Masson's health tips, I believe you all know Nick Ruiz?"

Cheers erupted as Nick's fists launched into the air, accepting the praise of his legion of followers. I clapped as Jason leaned over. "It's your boy."

I snarled.

Nick gave everyone a cut-it-out gesture like it overwhelmed his modest sensibilities. As the crowd noise lowered, Mr. Clark handed him the microphone. With more confidence than any high school junior in history, Nick took a few steps forward to make sure all eyes focused on him.

"Fellow students of Truman High," he began. "I hope you're planning on attending next week's game against the lame, talentless Lafayette Bruins!"

Hooting and cheers exploded from the audience again.

The assembly would drag out all day at this rate.

"That's what I like to hear. As a thank you for your support, we have special prizes for a few lucky attendees."

Malcolm Reardon, the Lancers starting running back and boy-built-like-a-mountain, jogged up to meet Nick. His broad shoulders stretched his yellow-sleeved letterman jacket to the point of ripping apart. He held a fishbowl stocked with folded papers.

Nick pointed to Malcolm. "In this fishbowl are the names of every freshman at Truman."

Malcolm whispered to Nick, and Nick closed his eyes, shaking his head with overly dramatic disappointment.

"Sorry, everyone, it sounds like we're starting with sophomores. We'll do freshman next. Not sure why Malcolm would start in the middle, but he seems challenged by arranging things in order."

Everyone laughed, including Malcolm, who bowed to the crowd.

"I will select a name out of this fishbowl. If that person can answer a Lancer football question, they will receive front row seats, free popcorn and soda, and a Lancer T-shirt for themselves and a friend at our homecoming game next week!"

Everyone cheered as if Nick just announced a million-dollar giveaway.

"And don't worry. We'll draw one winner from each grade."

Mr. Clark leaned forward and mumbled to Nick, who had to lean down to hear him.

"I'm hurrying." Nick answered Mr. Clark without lowering his mic, causing muffled chuckles to spread through the audience.

Nick dug into Malcolm's bowl. He removed a piece of paper, read it, then announced the sophomore winner. "Baxter Allen!"

My stomach lurched. Nick's voice reading my name rang in my head like a bullhorn.

Are you kidding me?

The students clapped.

I wished I could jump like Janni. Vanish and leave a burnt hair odor in my seat. Maybe I could summon him as a distraction? That would take the focus off me, for sure.

Don't be stupid, Bax.

"Stand up." Jason nudged me.

I should have skipped the stupid assembly. I didn't know jack about Lancer football and had zero interest in attending the homecoming game. Why did football players always think everyone loved football as much as they did?

The audience searched for me. Maybe if I didn't move, they wouldn't see me and would draw another name.

"You gotta stand, man. It'll be fine," Jason muttered.

My lips didn't part. "You know any Lancer Football trivia?"

"No, but you can't just sit there."

Focusing my strength, I rose. My weak knees wobbled under my weight. The blood in my head plunged to my feet. I blinked a few times, willing myself not to throw up. I stretched a smile across my face.

An episode started forming deep inside of me. It stirred in my core. It'd been a year since the last one—a year. And it picked now for its mighty return. Just perfect.

I tried to shove it away. Force it down.

Too late. My heart rate picked up its already quickened rhythm.

Relax. Focus on breathing.

I needed to sit down and put my head between my legs. The doctor told me that could prevent it. But how could I sit down with everyone watching me?

"Get ready, Bax. This is an easy one." Nick's voice boomed in the mic. The red and white lights in the scoreboard, set to zero, suddenly became blinding. "Name the quarterback who scored the most touchdowns in one season in Lancer history."

You've got to be fucking kidding me.

I could name one quarterback in the entire history of Lancer sports. Nick Ruiz.

"We'll take first or last name."

My field of vision shrunk. My legs tingled.

I could make up a name. Maybe it's easy because the answer was Nick. That's dumb. He's only a junior, and it's the middle of the season. I should say Nick Ruiz. At least I'd get a rise out of the crowd.

My knees vibrated. Could anyone notice?

Jason tapped my leg with the back of his hand, almost toppling me over. "Someone said the answer is Ray Folds."

"Anyone help out Bax?" Nick chided me over the mic, taunting me.

The name Ray Folds echoed all around me, spoken by every single person in the bleachers. In front of me, *Ray Folds Memorial Gymnasium* stretched in huge black letters above the opposite side of the bleachers. The answer literally stared me in the face.

I had to spit out two stupid words, but my throat had sealed shut. I'd gotten too worked up. I hadn't sat down. My heart pumped blood out, but my blood vessels constricted, cutting off the blood to my brain. That's how an episode happened.

My body reacted to anxiety on its own, and I couldn't stop it. It no longer operated under my control.

Orange spots exploded across my limited field of vision. My voice abandoned me, too embarrassed to be associated with the rest of me.

I'd transformed into a stone statue before the entire school, unable to repeat what people around me kept chanting.

Ray Folds.

Ray Folds.

Ray Folds.

I hated Ray Folds. Despised him.

Then finally, the orange spots became a solid orange curtain over my vision. My legs melted. The blood cut off from my brain.

I passed out.

Chapter 6

My eyes opened, and I rolled my head to orient myself. The backside of Nurse Masson jiggled in front of me as she furiously scribbled something on the counter. The nurse's office came into focus: cabinets— some refrigerated and some locked—a desk, two beds, and two emergency medical kits, all within stark white walls.

She must've heard the paper-covered bed crackle underneath me because she spun around. Despite Nurse Masson's constant preaching of being active and making healthy choices, she didn't look like she practiced much of what she preached. She lumbered over to my bed.

"Hellooooo, Mr. Allen." She massaged a blob of hand sanitizer between her hands. As she approached the bed, a few drops splattered onto the floor.

I rubbed my dry eyes. "How long's it been?"

"Not long at all. We pack you kids into those bleachers, so your classmates caught your fall. Whether they intended to or not." She winked, proud of her insulting joke. I didn't hold it against her.

My brain rebooted to life, sprouting details of my episode in my mind through a series of rapid flashes. I squeezed my eyes shut to stop the images, trying to erase them from my memory. Goddamn Ray Folds.

My episodes began in fifth grade. Right after we

moved and I changed schools. They only happened maybe once a year or so. Dr. Barkley called it *vasovagal syncope*, a panic attack where the person actually passed out, not just where they felt like they might. The heart rate sped up while the brain's blood vessels constricted, causing the person to lose consciousness.

Dr. Barkley couldn't find a physical cause for it. He said that improved the odds that the episodes would stop on their own. However, not finding a physical cause meant it didn't have a cure.

So essentially, each episode could be my last, or it could be a regular occurrence for the rest of my life. Awesome diagnosis.

This episode, however, had the distinction of being the first where I passed out on top of my classmates, in front of the entire school, as everyone watched. Every sophomore's dream come true.

Nurse Masson saw it on my face. "No one really noticed."

She picked up her phone. "Mrs. Bronson? He's awake." She hung up. "It was a nonevent. You know how kids are. They've all moved on to the next exciting thing by now, I'm sure."

"A nonevent?" My voice cracked from dryness. "I fainted like a lady in one of those old movies who can't handle the sight of blood."

She clicked her tongue. "You're being dramatic. You could have hurt yourself, and you didn't. That's what's important. Besides, you don't need to worry about the homecoming tickets. Nick said they were yours." She handed me an envelope. "Such a considerate young man."

I ground my teeth, pressing the back of my head deep into the paper-covered pillow. Of course he became the hero by giving the prize to the poor, pathetic sophomore. You couldn't force me to go to that stupid game at gunpoint. Frustration and embarrassment pooled in my eyes in the form of tears. I swiped them away with my sleeve.

Great, now I'm crying.

Totally like a lady in one of those old movies. Enough humiliation. I couldn't handle any more. I couldn't. I willed my eyes to dry up.

Nurse Masson didn't notice or at least showed mercy on me by ignoring it. "Mrs. Bronson's on her way to check in, then you'll be free to go."

Everyone watched me pass out because I couldn't answer a question about a football player when the answer stared at me in six-foot-tall letters. I had escaped public ridicule after my episode last year, but I'd never survive this. I'd never be able to show my face again at Truman High.

The door opened, and Mrs. Bronson entered the Nurse's office, her white blouse and modest dress pants the outfit of someone way older than her, even though she looked around Mom's age. The glasses she never wore poked out of her shirt pocket.

Nurse Masson nodded. "I'll give you two some privacy." She left, closing the door behind her.

I couldn't deal with Mrs. Bronson. Not now.

"Do we have to do this?" I closed my eyes. "We met Wednesday, and I don't have anything else to say. I'm not really in the mood to talk about it."

She ignored my request. "Are you feeling better?"

She balanced on Nurse Masson's stool. She never

wore makeup, but her excessive hair spray made her red hair glisten like a waterslide in the afternoon sun.

"Yeah. I'm fine. Couldn't be better." My focus stayed on the ceiling and away from her.

"What happened?" She eased into her counselor-calm tone.

"I didn't know the answer to a question about football. I felt it coming on but couldn't stop it."

"Did you try the breathing exercises? Or putting your head between your knees?"

"Yeah, sitting down and putting my head between my legs with everyone watching would have been way less embarrassing."

Silence.

Even though I couldn't see her, I knew she wore The Look. She wore it every time I shut down in a session. Her trademark we'll-wait-in-silence-until-you-start-talking-again look.

I took the bait. "I don't know what happened. The pressure, I guess."

"Everything good at home?"

Ugh.

The Home Question. Thanks, Mrs. Morris.

We moved apartments right before I started fifth grade because they raised the rent. Mom blamed gentrification at first. Then, blamed herself for not making enough money to avoid uprooting me right before middle school. Regardless of the reason, Mrs. Morris, my new middle school's counselor, told my mom the change in homes and schools all at once may have triggered the VS. A perfect storm to give Mom enough guilt for five lifetimes.

Mom shared this revelation with Mrs. Bronson,

forever heightening her sensitivity to my stressors at home and school.

"Everything is fine. I just can't handle speaking in public. Too much pressure. This was, like, the *ultimate* speaking in public."

"You may need to go back to the doctor, Bax. He can prescribe some beta-blockers. I'm gonna write your mom a note."

Not happening. Mom couldn't afford a psychiatrist. If Mrs. Bronson sent her that note, Mom would pick up even more shifts and never sleep in order to make enough money to send me to some doctor who'd just end up diagnosing me as a big baby.

No way I'd give her the note.

The bell rang.

A commotion of kids stampeded down the hallway outside the nurse's office door as they scrambled to get to their classroom. My imagination raced with the potential gossip flying around. How many people already started theories on my "condition?" What did Scarlet think? Were they teasing Jason just because we were friends?

The whispered discussions on the other side of Nurse Masson's door sent my heart rate soaring.

"Can I go home? It's Friday. Can I skip the final period?"

Mrs. Bronson stared. "Hiding from this isn't the—"

"Argh, please. I can't do this today. I'm not asking to transfer schools, just miss one class. Please." Tears started to blur my vision, and I didn't hide them, hoping they'd strengthen my plea.

Mrs. Bronson picked the notepad out of her shirt pocket, behind her glasses, and scribbled a release. She handed it to me. "Let's not wait two more weeks to talk. Let's schedule some time together next week."

"Fine." Shoving the pass into my pocket, I swung my legs over the edge of the bed. Classes still had fifty minutes left. I could escape before running into anyone.

"Bax, everyone has things they're dealing with. You're not alone." Mrs. Bronson's profound words of wisdom. She meant well. I appreciated that.

My legs wobbled, but nothing that wouldn't work its way out in a minute or two.

I gave her a smile, opened the door, and threw a quick glance up and down the empty hallway like a fugitive. Locked metal lockers lined the hallway walls, and a few random balls of wadded-up paper rolled on the floor like tumbleweed.

After a deep inhale, I sprinted out of school, successfully avoiding all contact with anyone.

****

Lying on my back with my phone at arms' length in front of my face, I read the latest text from Jason. The latest in a series of texts since the assembly. All different versions of *You okay?*

I couldn't alienate my best friend. I started typing.

—*I'm fine.*—

—*You totally faked it to get out early on a Friday.*—

—*Yeah, you caught me.*—

—*Playing with your new pet???*—

I smiled. Maybe Janni could help with dishes again.

—*No.*—

—*I'll call later.*—

—*K*—

I dropped the phone on my nightstand, staring at a long crack in the ceiling, wishing it would open up, swallow me, then spit me out in some other high school. Luckily, the football game in Granite City tonight meant no big group gathering at school, but my classmates would have all weekend to gossip about my episode. Plenty of time to invent nicknames for me, crazy reasons why I passed out, or maybe even create a contagious disease I'd contracted. The gossip ship plowed ahead at warp speed, or at least at the speed of text messaging, and I couldn't do anything about it.

Jason's text resonated. *Playing with your new pet???*

I sprang up.

Dishes weren't his thing, but maybe Janni could somehow stop the gossip, or he could find out what people were saying, so I could prepare. If I knew what they'd be whispering on Monday, I'd be able to develop a response—a defense.

Digging into my pocket, I pulled out the ring. It rested on my palm, the jewel catching the late afternoon sun and throwing a purple spot on my gray wall. I'd never summoned Janni alone, but Jason wouldn't approve of what I intended to ask my djinn to do.

My thumb traced the smooth surface of the jewel, igniting the violet glow. The invisible, tingling pellets rained over my skin. I stood next to my bed on wobbly legs, balancing myself with one hand still on my mattress. Within seconds, the scent of burnt hair crept through my bedroom.

"Janni?"

The djinn emerged from under my bed, poking his head out from beneath my hanging comforter. "HOW

CAN IT SERVE?"

Janni heaved himself up by grabbing hold of the blankets, hand over hand—like a monkey—until he reached my mattress. He plopped down, making himself comfortable against my pillow.

The bedsprings squeaked as I sat across from him. "Can you go listen in on Scarlet? Find out if she's talking about me. Like you did with Ashley's parents."

I couldn't bring myself to use the word *spy*, even though the word applied perfectly. *Listen in* somehow eased my guilt, sounding less criminal, less horrible.

"WILL DO."

Janni stood up, but just before he jumped, I grabbed his arm. "No, wait!"

He retook a seat, sighing as he folded his arms across his chest. "WAITING."

I couldn't spy on Scarlet or anyone. The simple fact that I only considered the idea because Jason wasn't around to disapprove should have told me something.

"Don't do it." Cross-legged on my bed, I buried my forehead in my hands.

There had to be a way to utilize Janni's abilities without blatantly spying. Besides, if Janni reported back that Scarlet called me a loser, it'd just make me feel worse. It wouldn't help anything.

"I don't want to know what she's saying."

Janni stood up. "RIGHT BACK."

He jumped.

"No!" I shouted at the empty space. "I told you not to go! I said I *don't* want to know!"

I threw my head back and closed my eyes. So much for obeying my command. Why would nothing go my way? When he returned, I'd cover his mouth before he could say anything. Then, we'd have a long talk about the definition of *serving*.

Janni reappeared on my bed.

I sprang forward. "Don't say a—" I stopped midsentence. My hands, about to cover his mouth, dropped to my lap. I sat back on the bed.

Janni cradled a battered brown teddy bear, almost as big as him. Stains spotted its tan fur, worn thin, especially on its belly, and scuff marks dulled its marble eyes. On its side, stuffing poked through a small split in the seam.

Mr. Cuddles.

I'd spent most of my toddler years with Mr. Cuddles. Mom said Santa gave him to me on my second Christmas—our first without Greg. Of course, I don't remember unwrapping him, but I had vague memories of dragging him around and not being able to sleep if Mom didn't tuck him in beside me.

Janni offered me the bear.

I took him tentatively, unsure why Janni brought him or where he even found him. As I stroked the matted fur of Mr. Cuddles' belly—feeling like that's what I used to do—warm nostalgia washed over me.

"Where did you get him?"

"FROM A BOX UNDER THE BED OF YOUR MOM."

"Why did you give him to me?" I couldn't take my eyes off Mr. Cuddles.

"YOU HELD HIM IN A PICTURE." Janni nodded to our hallway.

I knew the picture. I sat at the same table in our kitchen now, though it didn't have as many dings in it.

Mr. Cuddles rested on the table at my side, his arm up against the icing-covered side of the cake, decorated in script that read, "Happy 3rd Birthday, Baxter!" My face glowed, and my eyes sparkled from the three burning birthday candles in front of me. Air filled my puffed-out cheeks to capacity, ready to unleash a windstorm down on my cake.

"YOU LOOKED HAPPY IN THE PICTURE. TODAY, YOU SEEM SAD. IT THOUGHT BEAR MIGHT MAKE YOU HAPPY AGAIN." Janni cocked his head to the side. "WHY IS IT MAKING YOU CRY?"

I wiped my eyes with the back of my hand. "It's just been one of those days."

Mom said whenever she'd shove Mr. Cuddles into my arms, I'd instantly feel better. Easy as that. Quick snuggle, and all would be right in the world. Things were simpler then. I didn't need to worry about VS embarrassing me in the middle of a school assembly. I didn't need to worry about anything.

But Mr. Cuddles didn't fix problems. He just helped me forget them. As a toddler, that was enough. But I had an actual situation to deal with and no solutions ready to go.

If Janni could do more than just jumping into a room and listening to what people said or fetching long-lost stuffed bears, he'd be able to help. I needed him to do something to fix my situation. Like erase the memory of the Truman High School student body, or stop my episodes entirely.

I needed a djinn with stronger magic.

My dream. The message from the ring.

I tossed Mr. Cuddles to the bed and scooted closer

to Janni. "Are there others like you? Or djinn with different powers?"

Janni's ears fell back, and his gaze dropped to his hands, folded in his lap as if he knew my next question. "YES. ALL DJINN ARE UNIQUE."

I lowered my voice. "Was that old man a djinn? The one who gave me the ring?"

"NOT REALLY." Janni wrung his hands together, holding something back.

"Where can I find another djinn? Do I need to ask the old man?"

Janni didn't answer.

"Look, I need a djinn who can fix my...situation. Unless you have a solution?"

This time, he answered with a scowl.

"You're great and all, but I need some other, um, tricks. Better magic. No offense."

Janni began picking at a loose thread in my comforter like he couldn't look at me. "THERE ARE HUNDREDS OF OTHERS. ALL AROUND. BUT A VERY POWERFUL ONE IS NEAR."

A breath caught in my throat. "How powerful?" The dream replayed in my mind, my fantasies one step closer to becoming reality.

"YOU DO NOT WANT TO SUMMON HIM." Janni shook his head.

"Why?"

"HE IS VERY POWERFUL."

"That's what I need. I need to fix some things."

Janni continued to shake his head in despair. "FOLLOWING YOUR DREAMS IS A BAD IDEA. THEY ARE ONLY DREAMS."

I raised my hand. "Hold on. How did you know

about my dream? I never told you about it."

"IT ALWAYS STARTS WITH A DREAM."

Janni still refused to make eye contact with me.

"Will he be obligated to do what I want? This other djinn?"

"OH YES. HE IS BOUND TO DO WHAT YOU WANT." Janni's response sounded almost mechanical. He'd had this conversation before. But so far, he gave me no reason to avoid the new djinn.

"What's the downside? I'm only hearing the upside. How do I call him?"

Janni didn't move.

"I'm commanding you." I paused, my own tone surprising me. "Unless there's something I'm missing? Tell me the downside."

Janni's face hung. "HE IS BOUND TO DO WHAT YOU WANT."

A shiver scampered from my head and down my back, my Something Big coming within reach. "So where is this other djinn?"

Janni's tiny chest expanded, then contracted. "NOT FAR."

"And you can show me?"

His subtle nod hardly qualified as movement.

"Tonight?"

Janni nodded again, still avoiding eye contact, probably jealous I'd ditch him for another djinn. Life in that ring had to be boring. He probably liked being out of it.

"Look, I just need a djinn who can help me out with something. I'll still summon you. I promise."

Janni scoffed.

"Why don't you put Mr. Cuddles back where you

found him, then you can leave. I'll call you later."

Janni and the bear vanished before I finished my sentence.

Jason worried about summoning another djinn after my dream, but now I knew more. According to Janni, this new djinn would be "bound to do what I want." I could summon this djinn to fix my school situation, correct Jason's eyesight, build us that house from my dream, and so much more.

Grabbing my phone, I texted Jason.

—*Coming over later? Big news.*—

—*Be there around six. You gonna tell me?*—

—*Be here at six.*—

Chapter 7

"Hello, Jason." Mom held the door open. "Oh, hi, Ashley."

I flew from the couch as if Mom's words vaporized it from underneath me. "Ashley's here?" It'd be hard enough convincing Jason to go after this new djinn. I didn't need to talk Ashley into it, too.

"Baxter! Don't be rude. You're welcome here anytime, Ashley."

"Thanks, Ms. Allen," Ashley said with syrupy sweetness. As soon as Mom turned around, Ashley flipped me off.

I signaled them to follow me into my room. Mom came home an hour ago, and so far, no mention of the assembly or my early release from school. Maybe I'd gotten lucky, and Mrs. Bronson forgot to tell her—one of the benefits of an overworked counselor.

In my room, Ashley made herself right at home, plopping onto my bed. Jason took the chair at my desk.

"Really?" I nodded at Ashley. I didn't want to deal with her on top of everything else.

"She saw me in the hallway and invited herself over." Jason shrugged. "What was I supposed to do?"

"You guys aren't cutting me out of the djinn thing. Besides," her tone softened, "I wanted to make sure you were okay."

My cheeks warmed as Ashley sincerely waited for

a response. She might have been the most annoying person at Truman, but I needed to be nicer. Enough people at school already treated her like she carried a contagious disease.

"Thanks for asking. I'm good." I responded with as few words as possible, not wanting to rehash the entire event.

"That's not important." I clapped my hands together, clearing the air of that topic. "I have news. Big news."

"Your text said that. Out with it." Jason rocked back on two legs of my desk chair.

"Janni told me about another djinn. One with better magic."

"Like in your dream?" Jason's tone dropped. "Or nightmare, depending on how you look at it."

I hid the irritation from my face. I'd expected that reaction and needed it. A devil's advocate would keep me grounded. "Yeah. Like my dream."

"Doesn't it bother you? We're not even sure if it *was* a dream or nightmare."

"What dream?" Ashley scrutinized Jason and me. "What aren't you guys telling me?"

I waved my hand dismissively as if she asked about an insignificant detail. "I had a dream that a new djinn completely changed my life. Janni told me where to find him."

"Another djinn? Holy freakin' crap. Janni told you where to find him?"

"That's what he just said." Jason started pacing in very small circles. The twin bed, desk, dresser, and pile of dirty clothes covered most of the available floor space in my bedroom for anything bigger. "I still think

Janni can do more. We just haven't discovered it."

"But," Ashley shrugged her shoulders, "jann are the weakest kind of djinn. So there's a good chance we've seen his maximum potential."

Maybe involving Ashley would be helpful after all.

Jason turned on her. "You were the one who read there are bad djinn. We don't need an evil super djinn destroying the world because Bax wants to live in a castle."

Ashley lit up. "You lived in a castle in your dream? Like as a king or something? Cool."

I ignored her, needing to focus my effort on Jason. "But there are good djinn, too, like Janni. That's the point. We won't know until we summon it."

Jason shook his head. "I think it's a bad idea, man."

"How do we control it?" Ashley asked. "We don't want to accidentally start an apocalypse or something."

"Janni said the other djinn would be obligated to do what I want. We've all seen genie movies, right? They do what their master says. So I don't think we'll be unleashing a monster into the world. Unless, of course, we tell it to destroy the Earth."

Jason remained silent, creases cutting across his forehead. I trusted Jason's judgment and wanted him on board. I wouldn't go down this path without him.

"Look, Jason." I laid it out. "I want this. I need this. But I want you guys with me. Even Ashley, if you can believe it."

She stuck her tongue out at me.

"If you really truly think this is a mistake, we won't do it, but don't you want to find out if this is our winning lottery ticket? Think about what we imagined

Janni could do. I don't want Mom working two jobs anymore. What if Ashley got a full ride to Harvard? What if you had perfect eyesight? What if my episodes stopped, and I didn't have to worry about passing out at school assemblies?"

The mention of the assembly quieted the room.

"Our lives aren't so bad," Ashley said. "You freakin' passed out. Whoopee."

"*You* think it's a bad idea now?" I threw my hands in the air. I'd planned on her helping me convince Jason, not work against me.

"*But,*" she yelled over me, "Let me finish, Baxter. Knowing we have an opportunity to discover a djinn with stronger magic…that's huge. What if it could significantly change our lives? Or other people's lives? Like end cancer? Or save the environment? I mean, years from now, how do we tell our kids we passed on making life better for billions of people because we were scared?"

Focused so much on what a djinn could do for me and my friends, I hadn't considered it that way. What if we *could* make the world better?

We both turned to Jason, awaiting his answer. He'd begun fiddling with a dusty Little League soccer trophy from my shelf. One of those trophies every kid got for just being on the team. I'd forgotten I still had it there.

"Aren't you the least bit curious?" I piled on.

After the silence hung for a few more seconds, Jason returned the trophy to my shelf. "Where did Janni say we'd find this other djinn?"

Yes!

A smile exploded on my face, and my stomach did a double flip with a twist from a high dive.

"As long as we take it one step at a time," Jason added.

"Of course." We were actually doing this. We were about to summon another djinn. "All right. Janni said the other djinn was nearby. I'm assuming in another ring. Let's ask him."

Ashley spread the blinds, looking down to the street. "We can't do it in here. Your mom will smell him. By the way, we should think of a cover story if she ever does catch a whiff of him. Eventually, someone's bound to ask why your room reeks."

Jason shook his head. "Too many people outside, though."

"The roof! No one goes up there this time of year."

"Good call." Jason opened my bedroom door, and the three of us acted about as casual as amateur bank robbers on their first heist.

Mom didn't seem to notice. "We're heading out for burgers!" I called to her on our way out.

The old elevator crawled up seven stories to the tenth floor, occasionally making a loud clanking sound that echoed in the shaft. Living on the third floor, I rarely took the elevator. Feeling it lurch and rumble, I'd likely continue sticking to the stairs.

My stomach continued doing flips. I took a deep breath, minimizing any sound or movement so Jason and Ashley wouldn't hear. Nervous excitement made it hard to stay focused, and I had to look calm and confident in our decision. Jason didn't need a reason to change his mind.

Like he said, we'd take it one step at a time.

The elevator door slid open with a ding, and we jogged down the hallway. We charged through the red door labeled *Roof* and up the last flight of concrete stairs, finally outside.

The October air bit at my skin, so I zipped up my jacket. Even with the high, clear plastic walls around the roof's perimeter, the autumn air whipped across the rooftop in sporadic gusts. Since most of the other buildings around us were the same height, the roof felt like the top of the world.

The roof used to be one of my favorite places to read or do my homework, but the timing had to be just right. If not, the summer sun would turn the roof into a frying pan, or the winter winds would transform it into a tundra.

"No one will smell Janni up here, that's for sure." Ashley squinted as her curly hair smacked her in the face.

"Ready?" I held the ring out on my palm for them to examine. "Here goes."

I rubbed the purple jewel, anticipating the familiar tingle seconds before it arrived, working its way from the top of my scalp down to my toes. Even in the chilly breeze, I couldn't resist a shudder as the frigid sensation made my shoulders twitch.

Janni's distinct odor cut through the air briefly before the wind whisked it away.

"Do you see him?" I searched the empty rooftop.

"There?" Ashley pointed. A small shape came around one of the massive silver air-conditioning units. "I hope that isn't a rat. I hate rats."

As the form hit the light, it took on a familiar waddle. "HOW CAN IT SERVE?" The wind softened Janni's voice.

"Hey, Janni." I knelt in front of him. The sun-heated asphalt of the roof warmed my knee through my jeans. "I want you to show us where to find the djinn you told me about."

Janni's ears fell flat against his head. His glassy gaze went from me to Jason to Ashley and back again. "HE IS VERY STRONG."

I cringed.

Don't freak Jason out.

"Why are you so scared?" Jason nudged his glasses up higher on the bridge of his nose. "Or let me ask it this way, should we be scared?"

A fair question. Take it one step at a time, and don't jump in blind. Exactly why I wanted Jason along. I didn't want to accidentally unleash Armageddon.

"HE IS VERY POWERFUL."

"But he only does what I want, right? That's what you told me."

"YES. ONLY WHAT YOU WANT."

"Why are you scared, then?" Jason folded his arms across his chest.

"He's scared of everything," I answered for him. "Janni isn't exactly Rash Grey."

"Who's Rash Grey?" Ashley asked. "I'm confused."

"From *Archer Annihilation.*"

Ashley shook it off. "Let me try." She knelt in front of Janni, like I did. "Is this other djinn evil?"

Excellent question.

Janni paused for a moment. Not a question he should have to think about. "IT DOES WHAT ITS MASTER WANTS. IF MASTER IS EVIL, SO IS DJINN."

Problem solved. Unless I wanted to destroy the

world, the new djinn would be safe.

Ashley snickered. "I'm ninety-five percent sure you aren't evil."

The setting sun reflected off Jason's glasses, hiding his eyes. "This other djinn will *only* do what we say?" he asked.

"ONLY WHAT MASTER WANTS."

Jason nodded.

I sucked in the cold air, held it, then exhaled. "Where can we find him?"

Janni spun on his heel and walked to the edge of the roof. He pointed through the plastic barrier to the street below. "THERE."

"On the street? The alley?" Jason asked.

Janni nodded.

I knelt in front of him again. "Can you meet us there?"

Janni jumped.

"Let's go."

We stampeded down the stairs, skipping the slow crawl of the elevator: tenth floor, ninth floor, eighth floor. By the sixth, we were all panting, but no one stopped to rest. Finally, outside, we rounded the corner and ducked into the alley.

Ashley wrinkled her nose. "If I wasn't so out of breath, I'd be holding it right now. The stink is worse than Janni."

The dumpsters overflowed with white and black trash bags, many laying on the ground around them. The streetlights had just kicked on, but they did little to light the depth of the alley. The small metal light fixture on the brick wall above the dumpster had no bulb in it.

"Do you see him?" I searched the shadows.

A form quivered in the dark up ahead, among the mound of garbage bags in front of the dumpster. "THIS WAY." Janni's voice ricocheted off the brick walls.

Our heads all snapped to the alley entrance at the same time—all clear.

"COME." Janni shuffled deeper into the alley on his stubby legs. He didn't have a tail, so his body resembled a gorilla more than a monkey. We followed him into the intensifying stench, leaving the glow of the street behind, walking deeper into the darkening alley.

About midway, Janni pointed to the ground.

"A trash bag?" Ashley kicked at it.

"No." I shoved the bag out of the way, exposing an old wooden door leading into the cellar of my building. "In there?"

Janni nodded.

"We've had a freakin' djinn living in our building's basement this entire time?"

"What's down there?" Jason asked.

"Not sure," I said. "Other than a djinn."

Jason tapped the padlock with the toe of his shoe. "Locked."

"Before we go any farther," Ashley fingered the lock, "I'd like to point out that we're breaking and entering. Doesn't matter if we live here. Don't forget, my dad's a cop. Crimes are discouraged in my family."

"Like they're encouraged in our families?" Jason's voice cracked.

We didn't need to break it open. "Hey, Janni, Mr. Reynolds lives in 1-A. Can you get the keys from him?"

Janni jumped. The smell of garbage quickly absorbed the burnt hair cloud he left.

"Nice thinking." Jason concentrated on the door as if his glasses gave him X-ray vision. "Seriously, what do you think is down there?" The deep crease returned to Jason's forehead.

Neither Ashley nor I answered Jason's question. We didn't know, but we wanted to see it through. I couldn't spend my life wondering *What if?*

Janni appeared in front of us, along with the sound of jingling metal. He handed me a key ring with at least fifty keys. Turns out, some landlord stereotypes were true.

"How do we figure out which one?" Ashley flicked a random key on the ring.

"Do you know?" I crossed my fingers. It'd take forever to try each key.

Janni sighed, taking the key ring back. He seemed to have only two emotions—fear and annoyance.

Janni flipped through keys, separating one from the others. He handed the ring back.

"How do you know this is the one?" I didn't doubt him, but maybe we'd discovered another ability.

"IT SAYS CELLAR ON IT."

I flipped the key over to find a worn piece of freezer tape with the word *cellar* written in black magic marker on it.

I grinned at Jason and Ashley.

Done waiting and debating, I squatted down and stuck the key into the rusted padlock. It didn't slide in, so I jiggled it as I pushed. No one had used the key or the lock in a while. Once the key seated, I turned it.

Click.

The padlock sprang open.

I removed the lock and threw open the door. It hit

the brick of the building with a bang, making us jump and check the alley entrance. No one there. We could have been murdering someone, and no one would have noticed. I kept that to myself.

We peered into the hole. A set of rotting stairs descended into blackness.

"If either of you says, 'Ladies first,' I swear I'll freakin' punch you."

"It's your djinn, Bax." Jason put his hand on my back but didn't shove. "You do the honors."

"It's just a basement, guys." The dark opening seemed bottomless. "Flashlight, anyone?"

Jason and Ashley shook their heads.

"We're the worst burglars ever," Jason said.

"We're not burglars." I tapped my phone's flashlight on.

Jason stared at the keys. "Do you think Mr. Reynolds will—"

"You're in or you're out, Franklin. Make the decision." Ashley cut him off.

Grumbling under his breath, Jason dropped his gaze to his shoes.

"Look, guys," I said to them both, "we've never done anything like this before, right? So they're not gonna throw us in jail or anything."

I aimed my phone's beam of light into the cellar. "Let's go."

Moisture and age darkened the color of the stairs. They bent softly under my weight, and there couldn't have been more than nine or ten steps to the floor of the shallow cellar. The dark played tricks on my vision, and once my sneaker touched concrete, it felt like only a foot or two of space separated my head from the cobweb-infested rafters.

"You sure the djinn's down here?" I whispered.

I shone the light on the floor near Janni. He nodded.

Spinning the light beam in as many directions as I could, I mentally assembled the layout of our surroundings in the darkness.

The mildew-scented blackness stretched on infinitely in all directions. Rotting shelves filled with splintered crates transformed the dark cellar into a foreboding labyrinth. The random movement of rats scurrying away sent shivers up the back of my neck.

Once Jason and Ashley joined me at the base of the stairs, Ashley's fingers wrapped around the hem of my shirt.

"Whoa," Jason mumbled. "I wonder if Mr. Reynolds ever checked this place out?"

"It's just a storage cellar." I forced a chuckle that sounded a bit too much like a crazy person as I swatted a cobweb off my face.

Janni trotted on ahead of us, undeterred by the dankness. For a creature so skittish about almost everything, he'd found his bravery in the cellar's creepiness. Maybe the musty darkness reminded him of life in the ring.

"THIS WAY."

We followed Janni between narrow aisles walled by rotting wood shelves. Occasionally, since I led, I cleared cobwebs blocking our path. Ashley's grip on my shirt grew tighter the farther into the cellar we ventured until finally, the neckline dug into my throat. I pulled my shirt forward a little for some breathing room.

Behind her, Jason whispered, "I'm trying to remember our path so we can find our way back out of here."

"Great thinking," I whispered back. That's all we needed. We'd find a new djinn, then spend the rest of our lives trying to get him out of my building's cellar.

Ashley shrieked.

Janni jumped into my chest, my arms instinctively wrapping around him. With my sudden stop, Jason rammed into the back of Ashley, who bumped into me, and we all stumbled forward.

"What the hell?" I whispered over my shoulder.

"I think I saw a rat." Ashley clawed at my shirt.

"Jesus, girl. They're all over down here. Have you not seen one until now?"

"Not the best way to calm her down, Jason."

"I told you on the roof, I hate rats. They freak the crap out of me."

Janni wiggled out of my arms, landing on the floor. He scowled at Ashley. "GIRL SCARES JANNI."

Ashley's fingers maintained their grip on the back of my shirt as we plowed forward again, deeper into the cellar, which seemed to stretch on for miles.

Up ahead, my light reflected off a cracked concrete wall. Janni stopped and turned, pointing to an unremarkable corner. "THERE."

A pile of cement chunks and broken bricks had fallen from the disintegrating wall to the cement floor. Imagining a diamond and glass jewelry case containing the djinn's ring might be a little extreme. Still, I'd expected more than a pile of rubble.

"Dead end?" I scanned the wall for a seam to indicate a secret entrance.

Janni tugged on the leg of my jeans and pointed to the mound of brick pieces. "THERE."

"Huh?" I squatted in front of the pile, sweeping the cement rubble and bricks around with my hand. The dust cloud I unleashed worked its way into my lungs. I coughed.

As I caught my breath, I noticed a gap in the wall where the cement foundation met the brick of the building. The hole could have been the result of erosion and time, or something else. It looked like an open mouth that had spit out the aged brick and cement. Like something birthed itself through to the cellar from the earth on the other side, resulting in the mound of rock I searched.

"Anything?" Jason peered over my shoulder, scanning in front of me with his phone's flashlight.

"Shine the light over here." I dropped my phone back into my pocket.

I dug through another pile nearby, my mind conjuring images of spiders and rats lurking under the disturbed rocks, waiting to bite my finger off. Now that'd be a good story for Warren.

A streak of dark brown wood revealed itself beneath some gray chunks.

I cleared away the remaining debris. An old wooden box lay nestled in the pile of rubble.

"Is that it, Janni? Is the ring in the box?" I tossed the rest of the concrete rocks quickly off its lid, anxious to unbury my discovery.

"THAT IS THE DJINN YOU SEEK."

With a final tug, I yanked the box free and fell onto my backside, the wooden box landing in my lap. Jason and Ashley hovered behind me, Jason shined the light on our find.

Like the ring, the wooden box was extraordinarily unremarkable, its rotten wood split and splintered in places. It resembled an old storage crate, like on the shelves around us, but shrunken down to the size of a jewelry box. The only distinguishing mark was a familiar purple jewel seated on the lid.

"It's got the same jewel as your ring." The light beam quivered in the dust settling around me.

"Open it." Ashley's statement sounded more like a question.

For some reason, I almost said no. Something nagged at me, something in my gut. But when Jason added, "Yeah, do it," I couldn't turn back.

With my thumbs, I eased the lid open, ready for something to spring out like a jack-in-the-box. The box creaked on its hinges. Jason shined the light inside.

Empty.

"It's just a wooden box." Where was the ring? "Janni?"

"RUB THE JEWEL ON THE LID TO SUMMON IFRIT."

Duh.

I closed the lid and rubbed the jewel with my pointer and middle fingers.

"Wait, did Janni say *Ifrit?*" Ashley grabbed my shoulder. "Stop, Bax! Stop!"

Too late. Warmth spread through my hands as the jewel injected invisible fire into my fingertips. The swelling heat raced through my veins, up my arms, and met in the core of my chest where my heart pumped it back out again. Every hair on my body tingled. The hairs on my arms stood at attention.

Jason pointed to my head, his mouth agape. "What's happening to you? Your hair is standing up."

Ashley bit her nail. "We shouldn't have done this."

My heart pounded and sweat seeped through every pore. Even though Jason and Ashley didn't appear to be the slightest bit warm, the cellar became a sauna. Then an intense stabbing shot the back of my eyes from somewhere deep in my brain.

"Ow!" I pressed my palms to my eyes.

The pain subsided as quickly as it came, and my temperature lowered, returning to normal.

Jason scanned the basement, searching the dark for the new djinn. "Did it work?"

For a moment, I hoped it hadn't.

Then the smell rolled into the confined space of the basement. More intense than Janni's, with a sinister depth to it. Like what I imagined burning flesh smelled like. My stomach turned.

"Ick." As the odor wafted through the stale air, Ashely pinched her nose. "I think we should go, guys."

Wood ground on cement, the sound screeching in the cellar as old shelves scooted breezily across the floor like they were made of paper.

Ashley screamed. Not like when the rat startled her. She screamed as if she were witnessing a murder.

I leaped to my feet. The box crashed to the floor.

I spun.

In the corner, the djinn's head smashed against the ceiling, unable to rise to its full height. Below the waist, it had the body of a goat, with massive cleft hooves and a long pointed tail. Above the waist, the djinn resembled a man with bulging shoulders and a barrel chest covered in dense black hair. The head of what looked like a ram topped its thick neck, and curved horns twisted in on themselves while wisps of smoke curled from its wet snout. It watched us with dull purple eyes, like Janni's, and as it opened its mouth to speak, fire glowed in the back of its throat.

"It is here to serve," it said. Instead of the shriek of Janni's voice, this djinn spoke with a deep, guttural growl like a dog. I recognized the voice. I'd heard it calling my name in my room the night the old man gave me the ring.

Ashley, Jason, and I huddled back against a wall. "You guys see that, right?" My voice jumped an octave.

Janni clung to my leg, shaking. Between us and the new djinn, the box lay open, its jeweled lid glowing triumphantly.

"You're…you're a djinn?" I swallowed. We'd made a mistake. We'd brought something horrible into the world. *I'd* brought something horrible into the world.

"I am Ifrit," the djinn growled.

"I thought that's what Janni said when you were rubbing the jewel." Ashley's warm breath and fast words battered my ear. "We shouldn't have done this."

"Why?" My gaze remained fixed on the djinn.

"Remember how I said there are good ones and bad ones?"

"Yeah."

"Ifrits are the second kind."

"Janni said he had to do what Bax wanted," Jason whispered.

"I'm just telling you what I read—"

"You have released me." Ifrit took a step toward us on one of his massive goat-like legs. His pointed tail whipped around, snapping a chunk of rotted wood off the shelf behind him.

We screamed.

"We have to get around him to get out." Jason's words flew out rapidly. "We're trapped."

Ifrit leaned down, thrusting his head forward. His nostrils quivered, sniffing us like a dog. The ends of his goat-like mouth curled into what resembled a smile.

"I shall make all your wants a reality, Baxter Allen." His long tongue traced his sharp teeth, and a small line of drool dripped to the floor where it sizzled on the cold cement.

"Why don't I believe you?" I should have trusted Jason's instincts from the start.

His growl morphed into a sinister chuckle.

Janni trembled so much he vibrated my entire pant leg.

"Tell him to freakin' go away." Ashley's fists pressed into my back as she clutched my shirt. "See if he obeys."

I pointed a trembling finger at the box between us. "Get back in the box!"

Ifrit's head retracted. He tried to stand, but the low ceiling forced him to stay hunched over.

"Get back in the box! You have to do what I say!"

Ifrit snarled once, his violet gaze piercing mine defiantly.

But then he vanished.

I bolted forward, shaking off Ashley, Jason, and Janni. Grabbing the box, I slammed the lid shut, wanting to lock him away.

The thick silence in the cellar made my ears ring while disrupted dust—previously still for decades—

began to resettle around us.

I spun on Janni. "What the hell?"

"IFRIT IS THE POWERFUL DJINN YOU WANTED."

We waited for him to continue, but he offered no further explanation. What else could he say? He did exactly what I told him to do.

"We unleashed an Ifrit." Ashley's voice wavered.

I wiped the dust, caked with sweat, from my brow. "He's gone."

Janni's volume became as quiet as I'd ever heard him. "GONE FOR NOW."

Chapter 8

The sun peeked over the tops of the trees, and leaves crunched under my tennis shoes as I trudged through the park. Yoga classes, runners, and dog walkers crowded the tiny green space. Jason and I claimed the park years ago since it fell about halfway between our places and used to be mostly empty. Lately though, more people started crowding our private meeting area.

Jason had texted first thing, wanting to meet. Like me, he'd barely slept. Ifrit's odor lingered in my nose all night. The heat from its breath still burned my face. How did I stupidly think summoning another djinn would be my ticket to a better life? Nothing came that easy.

Before I left home, I checked on the box in my closet. The jewel remained dark, but Janni's ominous warning, *Gone for now,* echoed in my head

The rusted swing set came into view—the one we usually met at—but Jason wasn't swinging alone.

Seriously?

Ashley had become attached. I took a cleansing inhale of the morning air. After last night, could I blame her? She was probably freaked out like us. Besides, I'd promised myself I'd be nicer to her.

"Hey." Without tree cover, the bright sun warmed us on an otherwise chilly day. I tossed my jacket to the grass.

"You answer Jason's text but not mine? I've been freakin' texting since everything went down. I thought the ifrit came back and ate you or something."

"I texted you back saying everything's fine." I hopped up on the third swing but let it hang, swaying with the breeze.

Ashley rolled her eyes. "A reply of the single word *fine* does not reassure someone. We," she dropped her voice, "brought a monster into the world, for cryin' out loud."

"Good morning, Jason." I looked over her head to get her to move on.

Jason chuckled, pumping his legs forward and back on the swing like a kindergartener. "She texted me every time you didn't respond. After we decided to meet, I invited her so she'd calm the hell down."

"Are you guys totally calm after what we saw? By the way, I can hear you describing my pity invite."

Jason laughed. "Do you care if it was a pity invite?"

"Not really."

I kicked back, letting the swing glide. "I hardly found anything about ifrits on the web."

"You're not kidding." Jason dragged his feet, stopping his swing. "There are endless websites, books, and movies about djinn in general, but specific information on ifrits is sparse."

Ashley skidded her swing to a stop as well. "I wish we knew an old man in an antique or used bookstore we could visit. Those old guys always have answers to supernatural crap like this. At least in movies, they do. No matter how small the town, there's always one."

I smiled. "True."

"Since we don't have that," Ashely continued, "why don't we try to track down the old man with the long nails?"

"Absolutely not." I shook my head. "We're not digging around into the Djinn-verse anymore. Researching online is one thing, but hunting down the old man is another. We need to quit while we're ahead."

"But what if the old man knows something?" Ashley grabbed the chain of my swing, stopping me.

"Knows something about what? Ifrit is safely back in his box—problem solved. I shouldn't have been so greedy to begin with. You even said it—'My life ain't so bad.'"

Ashley had no response. Jason kept quiet, too.

After a few moments of listening to the birds singing in the trees behind us, she started again. "Aren't you curious what the connection is between the old man and Greg? How did your deadbeat dad become friends with some old dude with purple eyes? Purple eyes like a djinn, in case you haven't connected those pieces of the puzzle yet."

"He's not a deadbeat. God, Ashley! They parted ways amicably, then Mom lost track of him."

"Because he skipped out. He's not sending child support, or she wouldn't have lost track of him. That's the definition of—"

"Okay, okay!"

Maybe Greg fit the definition of a deadbeat. Maybe not. We'd never met, and Mom refused to talk about him. I owed him the benefit of the doubt before labeling him a loser.

Across the park, a group took over the basketball court, dribbling and passing a ball back and forth. Nick Ruiz and his football friends. Exactly who I wanted to bump into on a Saturday. I'd hoped for a weekend off before having to deal with the humiliation at school.

Jason followed my line of sight. "You wanna head out?"

"No. It's fine," I said, even though I watched for any indication they noticed me, ready to jump off the swing and get the hell out of the park.

Oblivious to our new conversation, Ashley kept at it. "How would we even start to locate the old man? That's the first question. Could we summon Janni and ask him?"

"Seriously?" I threw my head back. "Let it go. No more Djinn-verse. I don't think we should be summoning anything."

"Summoning Janni never resulted in bad stuff."

"Yeah, but what if we summon him, and it also calls Ifrit? Maybe we opened their connection. You're the one who reminded us that the one truth all websites agree on is that ifrits are dangerous. Right?"

"True." She sighed. "That about sums up the info out there."

"I can't say I'm curious enough about the connection between the old man and Greg to summon the Big Bad," Jason said. "I'd be fine never seeing him again."

Three girls approached the three-on-three basketball game across the field. Scarlet, Casey, and a third girl I didn't recognize giggled and waved at the guys. Nick passed the ball to Malcolm, jogged over to Scarlet, wrapped his arms around her waist, and kissed her like they'd just reunited after years apart.

Gross.

He returned to his game while Casey laid out a blanket on the grass. The other girl unloaded a small cooler. As they set up, Scarlet caught a glimpse of us.

She waved.

Crap.

I waved back, flattered she waved, but also worried it would draw the others' attention. No one else on her side of the park noticed.

The basketball game finally caught Ashley's attention. "Oh, your girlfriend's here."

"Cut it out."

As Casey and the other girl made themselves comfortable watching the guys play, Scarlet said something, then trotted toward us.

"She's actually leaving Nick to come and say hi." Jason grunted. "I had her all wrong."

"Come on, be cool, guys." Jason and Ashley needed to keep their snarky, under-their-breath comments to themselves around Scarlet. I had enough to deal with. I didn't need a new enemy.

Malcolm pointed at Scarlet from the court, smacking Nick in the chest with the back of his hand. The game stopped momentarily, and Nick raised his hand to block the sun, trying to identify who his girlfriend ran off to meet.

He must've recognized us because he said something to Malcolm and everyone on the court. The two girls courtside looked in our direction. Malcolm started laughing and said something to the rest of the team, who cracked up.

A taste of what's in store for me come Monday. I

couldn't wait.

"Hey, Bax." The wind whipped Scarlet's red hair in front of her face as she tucked it behind her ear. The late morning sun behind her created a halo outlining her entire body.

I squinted. "Hey."

"Hi, guys."

Ashley and Jason waved politely.

"How are you feeling? After the, um, assembly?" Scarlet dropped her tone like Jason and Ashley had missed the spectacle. She sounded sincere, not mocking, but I had no interest in being a broken person she pitied.

"I'm fine."

I should have been appreciative she cared about me enough to ask, but having a girl like Scarlet call attention to my most embarrassing moment made my skin crawl.

We needed another topic, fast. "Who's winning?" I nodded back to the basketball court.

"Huh?"

"The game."

"Oh." She giggled. "I have no clue. We just got here."

Awkward silence.

I asked Jason and Ashley to be cool, not mute. Their quiet just added to the weirdness of our exchange. Ashley never shut up until I actually needed her to talk.

"Did you see a doctor or something?"

Oh my God. Let it go.

"Yeah. Stress-related. That's all."

She brushed her hair behind her ear again. "You should journal. I do every night. It helps, like, ground me."

My face grew warm.

Oh my God. Oh my God. Oh my God. Stop talking about it.

"Yeah. I'll try that."

More awkward silence, broken only by the birds chirping. Why wouldn't my friends say something? Anything.

I picked a new topic. "So, you guys going out tonight?"

After I asked it, panic swept over me. Would Scarlet think I just asked her out or invited myself along? What an idiotic thing to say. How could she answer my question without inviting me?

"Yeah. Movies, I think." She paused, then added, "You guys are welcome to come."

"Great. Thanks." I didn't ask what theater, time, or movie, and she didn't offer.

"Well, I'm glad you're feeling better. I should head back."

"Okay. Thanks for stopping by."

Thanks for stopping by?

What was wrong with me?

She jogged back to the basketball court, hair bouncing behind her, probably preparing to tell her friends about her conversation with Bax the Weirdo.

When she couldn't hear, Jason chuckled. "Thanks for stopping by?"

Here it came, the snark they'd been holding back. "Well, you guys sure didn't help. I didn't tell you not to say *anything*. I would have appreciated a little chatter."

"Did you just get us all invited on a date with Scarlet and Nick?" Ashley giggled.

"At least she checked on me and didn't make fun of me behind my back like her friends probably are." I kicked the dirt mound under my swing.

"Yeah, she's a total saint," Ashley said.

I shook my head. "I had my first episode in fifth grade. I'd just started a brand new school. No one knew what to make of it…or me. Everyone just stared at me like I carried something contagious, but not her. She asked if I was okay when no one else did."

Jason cleared his throat—loudly.

"One of two people to ask. Sorry."

"Oh." Ashley lifted her feet and let her swing sway in the wind. "I was in English class with you when it happened. I remember it. The teacher asked you to stand up and introduce yourself to the class."

I hadn't intended an awkward stroll down memory lane. A stroll that made my feeling of impending dread about Monday a hundred times worse.

"I should have asked if you were okay." An apologetic tone resonated under Ashley's words. "You were the new kid who didn't know anyone."

I squirmed. "It's fine. Can we drop it?"

Ashley kicked back on her swing. "Who'd have guessed Scarlet Lane cared more about people than me?"

"Oh my God. Drop it."

"Looks like they're all caring people." Jason watched the court where, with Scarlet's return, Nick and his cronies pointed in our direction, cackling and slapping each other on the back.

"What do you think they're saying?" Jason asked.

"I'm sure I'll find out on Monday."

****

I lay on top of my covers in the dark. My headphones blared my favorite band as loud as I could take it, but my mind still spun. When Scarlet returned to the basketball court, did she defend me or make fun of me along with Nick's crew? Her concern seemed sincere, but I didn't truly know where I stood with her. I wanted her to like me, not be a loser she felt sorry for. That would've been the worst. I'd rather not even be on her mind at all, good or bad.

I reached over and opened my nightstand drawer, taking out the ring. I rolled the tarnished gold band between my fingers, careful to avoid touching the dark jewel.

I'd stopped myself before, but I could find out what Scarlet thought about me. No more guessing. No more wondering. I'd know if our casual interactions gave her ammunition to embarrass me or if some genuineness existed.

She wrote in a journal every night about Nick. Maybe she wrote about me.

I clicked on my lamp, lighting up my room, and yanked off my headphones.

Staring at the purple jewel for only a second, I rubbed it.

The jewel glowed, sending the tingles from the top of my head down to my toes. I shuddered. The feeling never dulled.

When the goosebumps faded, I sniffed the air but smelled nothing unusual.

What if Ifrit scared Janni off? What if we were only allowed one djinn?

Before the panic grew too large, I inhaled again. Found it—burnt hair.

Relieved, I exhaled and shoved a couple of T-shirts, already on the floor, against the gap at the bottom of my door. I didn't need to risk waking Mom up.

Janni crawled up the comforter at the foot of my bed.

"HOW CAN IT SERVE?"

"Shhh." I pressed a finger over my lips. "Mom'll hear you."

Janni cocked his head. He started to speak, but before he did, I cut him off. "I need you to go to Scarlet Lane's house. Bring me her journal." As the words left my mouth, my stomach quivered with guilt.

Unlike the last time I'd almost sent Janni to spy on Scarlet, he jumped before I could change my mind. After my episode at the assembly, I'd done the right thing and told Janni to do nothing. And reading the journal seemed like a way bigger intrusion of privacy than listening in on Scarlet at one moment in time.

I'd only read a little. Just today's entry. Maybe yesterday's. To see if she mentioned my episode. The words she used to describe it would totally tell me what she thought about me. That'd be enough to determine if she pitied me or considered me a friend. That's it—a day or two of entries.

Janni returned, holding a brown leather book in his pink hands. On the cover, gold script letters read, *Secrets.*

Secrets.

"HERE IS—"

"Shhh. I got it. Thanks." I took the journal.

What if I read that she hated me? I couldn't act differently around her. What if she's secretly in love with me? I couldn't do anything different then, either. I'd look crazy if I just asked her out from out of nowhere. Besides, she already had a boyfriend.

I tossed the journal to my bed, disgusted with myself. The blood rushed to my head, embarrassed, even though I was alone in my room. I couldn't violate Scarlet's privacy.

"Return this, Janni." The words felt dirty in my mouth.

"YOU HAVE NOT—"

"I said put it back! Then you can go back to wherever you…wherever you go."

With a shrug of his shoulders, Janni took the journal in his hands and jumped.

I collapsed onto my bed, staring at the ceiling again. The strong desire to pat myself on the back for not reading Scarlet's journal meant nothing compared to the guilt of stealing it. Plus, I'd lectured Ashley at the park about the riskiness of summoning Janni again and possibly awakening Ifrit. My own rules didn't apply to me.

Such a hypocrite.

Tossing the ring into my nightstand drawer, I slammed it shut. Whatever Scarlet felt, I'd find out when she wanted me to.

Chapter 9

Monday morning arrived.

I woke up to Jason's three-word text exploding in my mind like a grenade.

—*Ready for school?*—

The question sent tremors through my gut. I couldn't avoid reality. Based on my preview Saturday at the park, today would be as bad as I imagined—or worse.

I'd barely slept and skipped breakfast, certain I'd have puked it back up, and kept telling myself the unknown made it worse than it would probably end up being.

Yeah, right.

It wasn't like I'd topple from Mr. Popular to Social Pariah. Still, at least before last Friday, I maintained a safe, invisible existence. No one paid me any attention, positive or negative. I liked it that way—no pressure to perform, with no stigma to exist.

Since speaking in front of people triggered my VS, I'd spent middle school honing the skill of high-pressure situation avoidance. Gradually, I became the kid in the back of the room that people forgot about, which suited me fine.

And it worked. After no episodes for all of the eighth grade, I'd convinced myself the VS finally ran its course. As a bonus, three middle schools fed Truman

High, so only one-third of the school would even know about my episodes going into freshman year. I pretty much had a clean slate to start high school—every invisible kid's dream.

Then the first week happened.

The teacher asked each student to stand and introduce themselves, just like when I started fifth grade. And just like in fifth grade, my VS came roaring back. Right in freshman homeroom on day one.

Fortunately, the first week of high school gave me a once-in-a-lifetime advantage—cliques and social groups were still forming. So people reacted sympathetically to my episode, quick to forget. No one raced to judgment. Who knew, at that point, if I'd end up the football powerhouse instead of Nick? You had to hedge your bet on who you alienated.

But an assembly during sophomore year was not the first week of high school. The kid in the back of the classroom could quickly become the joke of Truman High. Especially if he panicked over a trivia question when the answer literally loomed over his head in massive block letters.

"Hey, Bax!" Ashley panted, running to catch up with me, her ponytail swinging behind her.

I pulled my jacket closed, though the sun warmed my shoulders. I shook my head to reset. "Hey."

"How are you feeling about today?"

I threw my backpack to the other shoulder, on the side Ashley walked. "How do you think?"

A garbage truck backed up, beeping its obnoxious warning to pedestrians. Ashley waited for the beeping to stop. "Right. Sorry. Any discoveries in the Djinn-verse?"

"Why would you ask me that?" I came to a dead stop and glared at her. She stopped, too.

How did she know I'd summoned Janni to steal Scarlet's journal? Impossible. Her eyebrows raised in sincere confusion. I needed to calm down. Maybe I shouldn't walk with her right now. Maybe I shouldn't walk with anyone right now.

"Sorry. I'm just tense."

"I understand." We continued in silence for a few blocks. The droning sounds of cars, public buses braking, and people talking on their phones calmed me.

"I wish I could give you some sage advice." An Ashley with no opinion made me even more anxious.

"I just need to get to school and have it all out in the open. See how bad it'll be." The morning sun shone unusually bright in the clear sky. I focused on that. Maybe Scarlet told them to back off. Maybe they listened.

Yeah right, again.

As we rounded the corner to Truman High, a silent alarm sounded that everyone on the front lawn heard but me. All heads turned. Some gossiped and pointed. Some hid giggles under their hands. Some shook their head pitifully. The second episode in my high school career elicited the whole gamut of emotions.

Noticing, Ashley whispered, "Don't worry about that. Trust me, they can say all they want, and it won't change your life one bit. You have a freakin' djinn. They can't top that shit."

As much as I appreciated Ashley's effort, it didn't help.

I navigated through the kids, keeping my head down and pretending this Monday was no different from any other. Pretending the whispers weren't floating around me. Pretending I hadn't given the school the most memorable assembly in modern history.

I arrived at my locker unscathed—at least physically. Ashley must've gone to her locker. I hadn't said goodbye, not sure when she detoured.

As I entered my lock's combination, Jason came up behind me.

"Hey, man, how's it going?" I appreciated his attempt at a casual tone, even though it sounded forced. He felt the gawking, too.

"Hey." I matched his casualness, needing something to talk about other than the obvious. "How about last Friday night, huh?"

"Bet you'd like to unleash that thing right here." Jason chuckled.

For a minute, the idea landed on me with a bit too much consideration. Truman needed a new distraction. One that stood eight feet tall with a nasty growl.

Jason leaned against the locker next to mine, seeing me smile. "They'd shit their pants."

"Like you did?"

He shoved me. "You should've seen *your* face."

I laughed, and my insides untwisted some.

I got this.

"Uh oh." Jason spun around to face a random locker as if it was his.

"Looky here, gents. It's our delicate flower." Malcolm Reardon's voice sliced through the chaos of the hallway like he shouted on a megaphone. Students nearby stopped talking to each other, ready for a show.

Here it came.

The hammer of embarrassment whacked me over the head. My face burned.

I turned around, my eye line hitting Malcolm in the chest. The kid towered over everyone at Truman, including the teachers. I wanted to look him in the eye, but the act of looking up at him would make me feel like a scolded child.

I stepped back, then met him in the eye.

"Are you gonna faint if I make fun of you, Flower?"

His crew went hysterical. Among them, Nick Ruiz, his flawless white teeth gleaming.

Malcolm started fanning himself with a folded piece of paper and spoke in a southern accent. "I do declare! This is too much for little ol' me. I don't think I can take it." He rolled his eyes into his head and fell back into the arms of Brad Crafton, who bounced him back up.

Gerald, the team's fullback, chimed in. "Um, do you know what school you go to, Flower? Let me help you. It's the name all over the building in *huge block letters*!"

Nick grinned, flipping his blond hair off his forehead. "Guys, leave Flower alone. We don't want him passing out under pressure."

They all hooted, slapping each other on the back like they'd won a stupid football championship before drifting down the hallway in a tight pack—a pack of hyenas.

They cut through the small crowd whose chatter to each other started up again as the show ended. Everyone moseyed off to homeroom.

All in all, it could have gone worse.

I turned to my locker and opened it up again. I already held the books I needed, but wanted to hide my face and regroup.

Flower?

Next to me, Jason muttered, "It'll all blow over, man."

"I don't think so. My free pass expired after the last time." I slammed my locker shut. "*Flower* better get to class."

****

The morning incident with Nick and his minions set the tone for the rest of the day. Probably the rest of my life. For example, a chalk daisy appeared on my locker by lunch period.

And in history—my only class with Nick—a strategically placed dandelion waited on my desk. I spotted Nick snickering with Malcolm in the back of the room as they gave each other congratulatory punches.

As everyone took their seats, I swept the weed off my desk, knocking it to the ground. I needed class to start.

Mr. Prescot, of course, chose that moment to glance in my direction. His bushy eyebrows crinkled together, and his gaze stalled on me before dropping to the dandelion on the floor.

"Mr. Allen, trash goes in the trashcan, please." He turned back to the whiteboard.

I stayed in my seat. No way I'd touch that thing like Malcolm wanted. I wouldn't go near flowers ever again.

Prescot stopped writing on the board to talk to Becky, who handed him a note. He thanked her, then caught a glimpse of me, still in my seat. He wouldn't let it go. With his free hand, he pointed to the wastebasket. "Trash can is up here, Mr. Allen."

Malcolm squealed behind me, unable to contain his jubilation. Mr. Prescot somehow didn't notice.

As if I hadn't been through enough, now I had to pick up that fucking dandelion and walk it up the aisle, delivering it to the yellow plastic trashcan like a nightmarish parade of shame.

Everyone had settled into their desks watching me while Mr. Prescot scribbled on the whiteboard, oblivious to the swelling chatter in the room. Unaware of the class giddiness over a kid nicknamed Flower taking a literal flower to the trashcan.

My face burned from my forehead down to my shoulders, almost catching fire. I clutched that stupid yellow weed in a fist, its wetness leaking into my palm. My other hand clutched into a matching fist to hide the shaking. But, unfortunately, holding the flower so intentionally, so angrily, focused more of the spectators' attention on my hands.

The aisle stretched out for miles in front of me. The wastebasket on the distant horizon of a vast ocean of humiliation. Every one of my footfalls slammed on the floor. The soft rubber of my sneakers on the tile defied physics and banged with each step.

The whispers bombarded me.

"Oh my God, it's not funny, but it kinda is."

"It's like he's bringing one of his own to its grave."

"Do you think he'll pass out right now? This must be stressful."

Mr. Prescot turned to face the room, dropping one of the dry erase markers on his desk. "All right, class…Mr. Allen, let's move it along. That thing must weigh a ton, as slow as you're moving."

The class exploded with laughter, Prescot's horrible joke giving everyone permission to openly laugh at me.

Mr. Prescot smiled, assuming he won his students over with his insightful wit.

I threw the flower at the wastebasket. But, of course, it floated down, then sideways, easing itself onto the floor next to the trashcan.

Oh my God! You stupid yellow piece of shit!

Mr. Prescot wasn't watching, so I pretended not to notice I missed the target and slinked back to my desk, keeping my head down. After landing safely back in my chair, I sighed, praying Nick or one of his douchebag lackeys didn't point out to Prescot that the dandelion didn't make it into the trashcan.

Mr. Prescot began describing the politics behind some war long, long ago. I couldn't focus on anything but the flower procession that replayed on an endless loop in my mind. I wiped the dandelion juice on my palm across my pant leg.

The longest day in history would never end.

About halfway through class, a knock rattled the door.

Visibly annoyed, Mr. Prescot called, "Yes?"

Ms. Hamilton, the school receptionist, hurried in, her modest gray skirt swaying with her stride, her blond hair in a tight bun. She passed a pink note to Mr. Prescot, then folded her hands in front of her as she smiled at the class.

Prescot unfolded the paper and read it.

A proud grin spread across his face. "Mr. Ruiz, you

have a visitor."

Nick looked up from his desk, having not listened to anything in class until Mr. Prescot uttered his name. "Huh?"

"Scott Armington is here to see you."

"No shit?" Malcolm blurted out.

"Mr. Reardon!" Mr. Prescot scolded Malcolm, but the smile didn't leave his face.

"Man, you're getting a personal visit from a football scout? That's huge." Malcolm punched Nick in the shoulder.

Murmurs of awe exploded across the classroom. Nick Ruiz officially began his journey into local history books. Whether he ended up with a free ride to Missouri State or not, a football scout came to recruit him in person. Right before our eyes, Nick Ruiz had become a celebrity.

He rose from his desk and strutted to the front of the room, basking in his classmates' amazement. He dragged a hand through his perfect hair, winked at Malcolm, then blessed us all with a thumbs up.

I stared at his thumb, wanting to rip it off his hand. How would his football career go then?

Ms. Hamilton escorted Nick out of history class with a congratulatory pat on the back.

Before returning to his lesson, Mr. Prescot beamed. "Well, let's wish Nick the best of luck when we next see him."

And once again, for the second school day in a row, my humiliation grew while Nick remained a hero.

Just awesome. Or, as Ashley would say, just *freakin'* awesome.

Chapter 10

Nick fumbled with his tie in the front seat of his parents' luxury sedan. His pressed shirt and stiff collar suffocated him, but his mom assured him the outfit gave him a sharp, focused college student look. His dad thought it odd Mr. Armington had scheduled the interview without parents, but Mr. Armington told Nick he liked to get to know his potential players without their families. The family meeting would be the next step.

A flicker of something unfamiliar raced through Nick—nervousness. He ran his hands across the leather steering wheel and repeated to himself in the quiet of the car, "I'll nail this. I'll nail this. If I don't, tons of other schools will be fighting for me."

He locked the car door with a chirp of the key and headed inside. He couldn't be late. He wanted to make a positive first impression.

People packed Randy's Bar and Grill. The loud classic rock belting out of the speakers probably belonged to one of those bands Dad listened to. They all sounded the same.

Mr. Armington waited at a four-top wearing the sport coat and pants he'd been wearing earlier during his visit to Truman. He sipped on some tea with a lemon wedge way too big for the glass as he scrolled through his cell phone.

"Mr. Armington?" Nick kept his voice solid and confident as he approached the table.

He'd nail this.

"Please, call me Scott." The man rose to shake Nick's hand. Nick shook it firmly, with a single pump, like Dad coached him.

"Have a seat." Scott gestured to the chair across from his.

Nick straightened his shirt as he sat. His mother's voice rang in his ear: *Don't fidget!*

"Thanks for joining me on such short notice." Scott dropped his phone into his pocket. "I had a last-minute engagement in town, so figured I'd try to squeeze in some preliminary visits. Then, if we decide to continue talking, I'll come back and sit down with you and your parents. Sound like a plan?"

"Absolutely."

"Why don't you tell me about yourself."

"Well, St. Louis is home. I go to Truman. I have a three-point-three GPA, not great, I know, but—"

"I'm sorry to interrupt. Did you want something to drink? Eat? I should order before we start."

What was proper etiquette? Should he order something or politely pass? Just a drink. "Um, a soda? Cola?"

"You bet. Be right back." Scott scooted his chair back and headed to the bar to place their order.

Nick fingered the napkin. He'd never been to Randy's Bar and Grill before. Malcolm said he brought Sheila here once. He also said their burgers were off the charts. Nick's stomach grumbled at the thought of a burger, but his nerves told him to wait. He didn't need ketchup dribbling down his chin during the interview.

A waitress with huge breasts pressed against the inside of her tight blouse set down two beers and two glasses of water, then turned to leave.

"Miss?" Nick raised two fingers, trying to politely get her attention.

She turned around, irritated a kid called her back to the table.

"I don't think these are ours." Nick pointed to the beers.

The waitress rolled her eyes and dug around for her order pad in her apron. She flipped through it. "Table seventeen. Two waters. Two beers."

Are you kidding?

This type of thing sure as hell never happened when the guys hung out. Just his luck, a waitress mistakenly serves him on the one occasion he couldn't drink.

Maybe Scott had orchestrated a test. He hated tests.

Before Nick could say anything else, the waitress left him with the beers.

He stared at the frosty glasses, practically salivating. It would sure help douse his nerves. But that'd be bad if Scott returned to Nick chugging a beer. It had to be a test. A test to determine if he'd party his way through college or focus on his classes and football.

Scott returned before he made a bad decision and slid the soda over to Nick.

"What's this?" Scott nodded at the beers and waters on the table.

"The waitress brought them over. I told her they weren't ours, but she seemed annoyed and ignored me. I didn't order them, I swear." Nick quickly corrected the defensiveness in his voice.

Keep calm, dude.

Scott laughed. "Too funny. It's fine, Nick. Honestly, I've been interviewing all day. You're my last one, so I hope you don't mind." He dragged the glass toward him, leaving a trail of condensation on the table, and took a swig. "Otherwise, it'd go to waste, right?"

As Scott arranged his water, iced tea, and beer in front of him, he must've noticed Nick eycing the beer. "Part of this process is about making adult decisions. So drink it if you want. I'm not your mom. We're two adults discussing your options."

This had to be a test. Scott ordered the beers, and Nick successfully passed by trying to give them back. Now, the second part of the test started—an open invitation to drink.

Scott smiled, exposing long yellow teeth. "Seriously, Nick. Do it or don't. It won't affect our interview or my assessment, but please stop staring at it. Now, moving on." He took a notepad from the briefcase next to his chair. "Tell me about you. What are your strengths as a quarterback? What sets you apart from other players?"

Not a test—so, bottoms up. Nick took a drink. The carbonation tingled his throat and relaxed his mind. He dabbed his upper lip with a napkin to wipe away any remaining foam.

Scott didn't react in the least. He watched Nick, but in anticipation of his answer to the question.

What a score. If this is what college would be like, he was all in.

Nick mentally smacked himself to focus and stop

thinking about the stupid beer.

He recited his rehearsed speech about his playing ability, including his opportunities to improve, as his dad advised. And he drank. Scott did, too. Like two grown men hanging out.

Scott gave Nick several reassuring smiles as he spoke, and by the time Nick finished his beer, his confidence soared. He'd hit all of Scott's questions out of the ballpark.

Nailed it.

"Tell me why you think you're the guy for Missouri State."

"Well, academically, your business program is world-class—" Scott's phone rang.

Scott glanced at the screen and scowled. "I'm sorry, but you'll have to excuse me. I need to take this." He scooted back from the table as he answered and hurried outside to talk.

Nick leaned back in the wooden chair, satisfied with his performance so far. He'd come across as confident but not cocky. Humble in all the right places while not stammering during a single answer.

The annoyed waitress with the massive breasts returned. She set down two shots.

Seriously?

"Vodka." She spun on her heel, back to the bar.

Nick didn't say anything this time.

He stared at the two shot glasses, then glanced around the bar and grill. No one he recognized. Scott paced in small circles out the window, his free hand flailing as he yelled at someone on his cell.

Nick downed the first shot. The vodka seared his throat. He checked on Scott's pacing, then did the second shot of liquid courage. The interview would only improve from here.

The next time they went out after a game, the guys were totally coming here. They'd sit in the annoyed waitress' section for sure. She was the best server in the history of waitressing.

But today, he should stash the evidence. The beer was one thing. Scott wouldn't be able to overlook two vodka shots.

Nick strolled to the bar, set the shot glasses down, then returned to his table, muttering a "thank you" to whoever paid for the mistaken orders.

Malcolm always said you couldn't smell vodka on someone's breath, and Malcolm would know. He regularly stole shit from his parents' bar, but Nick couldn't risk it. He took out the pack of mints from his mom and chewed on three.

They'd just dissolved when Scott returned.

"I am very sorry." Scott grabbed his briefcase from next to his chair. "I have to run. We got through a lot, though. The next step is scheduling some time with your parents. Before you ask, yes, you are proceeding to the next step." He flashed his long yellow teeth again.

Nick pushed back from the table, rose, and extended his hand, hoping to contain his beaming. "I've got time if you want to talk more later this evening?"

He sounded too desperate. He needed to act like he had other scout meetings lined up.

"I appreciate it, but that won't be necessary. You did a great job tonight. Really. Pleasure meeting you."

The two shook hands.

"Nice meeting you, too." He nailed it.

Scott threw some cash down. "I'll be in touch."

Nick stood idly by the table as Scott walked out of the restaurant. After he'd gone, Nick searched for Big Tits. Not seeing her, he left before anyone could ask what happened to the vodka shots and beer they'd ordered.

Safely in the parking lot, Nick dialed Scarlet as he flicked the hair back from his forehead.

"Hey! It's over. I nailed it, babe."

Scarlet squealed. "Of course you did! I'm so proud of you. What happens next?"

"He'll call. He said I made it to step two."

"I'm so proud. I already said that. But it's true. I am."

"Thanks, babe. I'll text you later."

"Buh-bye."

Nick dropped the phone back into his pocket.

He took out his keys and stood still for a moment. He lifted his left leg enough to force himself to balance on his right, but not high enough to attract attention if anyone glanced in his direction. He balanced for several seconds.

Yep, sober—okay to drive. It took more than two shots and a beer to do him in. Hell, two weeks ago, some guys from the team and him polished off half a bottle of whiskey. Couldn't have driven home that night, for sure.

He started up his dad's car and drove out onto the road. He checked his speed, not wanting to risk a run-in with the highway patrol. The streetlights and lane stripes were sharp and unwavering. Yep, sober.

On the highway, Nick did sixty-two mph in a fifty-five mph speed zone. He reviewed the interview in his mind. Missouri State would be begging him to attend. He wouldn't have done anything differently.

Bright headlights bounced off Nick's rearview mirror and blinded him. Some asshole rode his bumper, less than a car length behind. Nick had set the cruise control to sixty-two, with empty lanes on both sides. Why didn't the guy just pass?

The car honked.

Nick gave the finger to the rearview mirror. "Just pass!"

The car jumped lanes and accelerated, zipping up alongside Nick's side of the vehicle.

"What the hell?" Nick glanced over to give the asshole a dirty look.

Scott Armington drove the car in the next lane.

At first, Nick's face grew hot. He'd flipped off a football scout. What was he thinking? He'd just blown the perfect interview.

He looked over at Scott again, and a chill crawled down the back of his neck. Scott still stared at him, but not a quick glance, like people do when they're driving. Scott full-on stared, his head turned, looking completely over his right shoulder with a long, creepy smile. Yellow teeth in all their glory. Somehow, he kept his car on the road while intently focused on Nick.

What kind of game was he playing? Another test?

Nick stole another glance left. Scott's eyes widened as if he'd taped his eyelids open, and his broad, toothy smile sent a fresh wave of shivers over Nick. Somehow, Scott's entire body had rotated, and he sat sideways in the car, facing Nick straight on.

Nick flinched, tapping the brake, letting Scott's car roll ahead.

As soon as his car cleared, though, Scott jumped lanes, moving in front of Nick. Nick slammed on the brakes to create some space between them. Scott then rolled to the other lane, on Nick's passenger side, and slowed to meet him again. Both cars cruised at fifty mph.

Nick didn't look. Out of the corner of his eye, the passenger window of Nick's car lined up with the driver's-side window of Scott's. He resisted the urge to turn his head. Ignore him. Was this a test to determine if he could stay focused? Was Scott drunk? Maybe he'd been drinking before Nick arrived.

Scott honked. A couple short honks, then one long, relentless one that dragged out for at least five seconds.

HOOOOOOOOOOOOONK.

Nick wanted to exit the highway. To pull over and see if Scott had something to say. Now that Scott's car rode on his passenger side, he'd have to speed up or slow down to get around him and off the highway.

This was too dangerous to be a test. Scott must've had a nervous breakdown or something.

Nick turned to mouth, "What?" to Scott, but as his focus landed on the driver, Nick's muscles melted temporarily, and he swerved in his lane. Scott no longer sat in the driver's seat. Instead, a tall, handsome kid with perfect hair met his gaze.

It was him.

A mirror image of Nick drove Scott's car.

Nick rubbed his eyes. The only difference between himself and the Nick in Scott's car was the impostor's glowing purple eyes.

"What the fuck—"

Nick rear-ended a van in front of him.

The impact sent his parents' sedan into a tailspin, like on a sheet of ice.

Nick steered in the counter direction to steady his car, but he couldn't regain control. He skidded across one lane as another vehicle rammed him on the driver's side. Both cars now spun, taking with them a third and fourth into what became a fiery explosion of metal and flesh.

Nick raised his hands to protect himself as the sides of the car collapsed inward, the dashboard crushing his lap. Glass shattered and sprayed him.

He yelled but only heard the shrill grinding of metal. Then, in a split second, he heard nothing at all.

****

I shot up in bed, my heart high in my throat. Something squeezed my chest, causing me to struggle to pull air into my lungs. I grabbed my sheet, wet with sweat, as my brain began to comprehend that I hadn't died in a four-car pileup. The sun shone brightly through my closed blinds, but I flipped on my lamp, needing as much light as possible.

My chest loosened, and I took several deep breaths. On the nightstand, my phone vibrated frantically. As I watched it light up with a missed text, something caught my eye.

From the crack between my closet door and its frame, a purple glow radiated into my bedroom. I shuffled toward it, dread clawing up from deep in my gut. I paused like a child afraid of the imaginary monster in his closet. Though my monster wasn't imaginary.

As if my closet door handle were red hot, I yanked it open with my fingertips.

On a pile of sweaters, the jewel on the old box emitted a familiar and chilling violet.

"What the hell is going on?" My wet T-shirt became icy against my skin.

"You up, hon?" Mom called from the kitchen. "Time to rise and shine!"

I jumped, almost pissing my pants at Mom's shout. With a few hurried strides, I dove onto my bed and grabbed my vibrating phone. Jason.

—*Nick died in a car accident last night.*—

The phone slipped from my hand, crashing on the floor with a bang.

Chapter 11

"I guess you heard?" Ashley jogged up alongside me. "I mean, it's not like we're friends with him or anything, but to think someone at our school…died."

"Yeah. Jason texted me this morning." I couldn't shake the feeling of cars crushing me on all sides, the impact sucking the wind out of my lungs, and Armington's blank, purple-eyed stare.

Why would Ifrit go after Nick? I never ordered him to, and Ifrit only did what I commanded. That's how djinn worked. That's what Janni told us.

No way my dream was a freak coincidence. I woke up to a glowing jewel on Ifrit's box. That meant something we'd awoken in the djinn-verse had a connection to Nick's death.

Ashley and I stood at a crosswalk, waiting for traffic to stop. "My dad's at school right now," she whispered like the pedestrians around us were trying to listen in. "He's working the case."

Just perfect. The cop living across the hall from me is investigating the murder I caused.

Ashley missed the flicker of panic on my face. "It's so freakin' weird. I mean, why would a talent scout invite Nick to some bar and get him drunk? That's what I read, anyway. Nick had alcohol in his system. Totally unethical. Dad said that guy will go away for a long time if that's what happened. And why would Nick drive home drunk? I'm sure Scarlet would have picked him up or something."

I bit my tongue, fighting the urge to defend Nick. Resisting the urge to tell Ashley that Scott Armington wasn't an actual talent scout and that Nick didn't drive drunk. Sure, he drank a beer and two shots, but he didn't seem hammered. Then, of course, she'd ask how I knew. I'd have to explain, and I wasn't sure what I'd be explaining.

Nope, not yet. Not until I got Jason's opinion. Ashley would have an immediate reaction, and I needed Jason's help to think through the best way to handle everything.

When we arrived at school a full fifteen minutes before the morning bell, not many students milled about on the front lawn like usual. The buses sat empty. The few small groups outside talked in hushed church voices.

Same inside where a dense sullenness hung like a fog. People whispered to each other, shook their heads, and reminisced about Nick. A few girls cried. Even the teachers seemed somber.

No one called me Flower. No one even noticed me walking the halls. My invisibility made a welcome return. Maybe the students of Truman High realized life was short, we're all in this together, and all that other stuff. Maybe Nick's death had shown them all life— and all kids—were the same. Maybe they imagined if something happened to me suddenly, there'd be no way to make it right.

Or maybe their attention simply shifted to the next bigger headline.

The guilt nagged at me for thinking it, but I

appreciated the distraction from my notoriety. If I could lay low, the whole episode at last week's assembly might disappear from memory.

God, what an asshole.

Jason caught up with Ashley and me—finally. "Hey, guys. This is crazy. I heard we have an assembly this afternoon. Probably a lecture on drunk driving."

With Ashley glued to my side, I'd have to tell Jason about the dream later.

"My mom knows Mrs. Ruiz from her Endangered Wolf Group," Jason whispered as if describing a secret relationship. "She sent her an email with condolences but didn't get a response yet."

We passed Ms. Hamilton. Her face, streaked with tears, plunged in and out of her hands. Her hair, typically in a small, tight bun, hung loose and messy. She had introduced Scott Armington to Nick when he visited our school yesterday.

Two plainclothes police officers, including Ashley's dad, interviewed her. Mr. Bryant wrote notes in a small notepad as his partner rubbed Ms. Hamilton's shoulder.

Next to us, two girls whispered.

"Ms. Hamilton hasn't stopped crying since she found out."

"Well, it's not her fault that sleazy scout got Nick drunk. How could she have known?"

"I heard they sent the cops to arrest him. He deserves the chair for what he did." She glanced over, catching me listening.

"Sorry."

She curled her lip. "Whatever."

At least she didn't call me Flower.

At my locker, I stacked up my books, stalling, waiting for Ashley to leave so I could talk to Jason before first period. I didn't need to wait long.

"Later. See you guys this afternoon."

Jason sensed something because Ashley had barely left earshot when he asked, "You okay? You're acting strange. I mean, besides the obvious. But you weren't his biggest fan or anything."

"I didn't want him dead!" I didn't know what Jason was getting at. No, I knew what he meant.

Jason held up his hands in surrender. Usually, we'd be shouting over the noise in the hallway, but not today. Instead, Jason checked to see if my outburst caught anyone's attention. "Calm down. I didn't say that."

I slammed my locker door shut but kept my voice quiet. I fought to form the words and force them out of my mouth. "I think Ifrit or Janni had something to do with Nick's…you know."

"Wait, what?" Jason slid closer, his eyebrows high on his forehead, way over the top of his glasses. "Why do you think that?"

I bit on my thumbnail, suddenly hesitant to tell him. What if Jason blamed me? What if Jason thought I committed murder, even if by accident?

No, we were best friends. He wouldn't think that. Besides, I had to tell him. "I saw everything happen in a dream last night. Nick's dinner with the scout. Even his driving and the accident."

Jason's shoulders dropped with relief. "Well, you were thinking about him. The odds of dreaming about his death are odd and all, but that doesn't mean anything. He tormented you yesterday. You saw that scout get him out of class. It's a coincidence."

I closed the space between us, practically touching noses. "Coincidence I dreamed he died in a car accident after leaving the same restaurant they actually met at? Oh, and there's the fact that when I woke up, the jewel on Ifrit's box lit up like a purple bomb exploded in my closet. And the vividness of the dream...I experienced what Nick did. I felt what he felt. All the way up until he..."

Jason rubbed his eyes. "Wait. You mean like that dream—or nightmare—about the perfect life when the ring glowed?"

"Yes! Similar, but more intense." Saying it out loud to another person lifted a massive block of guilt from resting on my shoulders. I did this. My stupid desire for a djinn with better magic did this. I killed a guy.

I slammed the back of my head against the locker.

"Let's not talk crazy." Jason kept his voice just above a whisper. "I mean, you didn't, like, wish him dead or anything." He paused. "Did you?"

"Of course not! Look, he wasn't my favorite person. Especially after the bullshit yesterday, but dead? No. I haven't seen Ifrit since last Friday night in the cellar with you guys."

I squirmed, hoping he didn't ask if I'd seen Janni since then. I couldn't handle admitting I almost used him to spy on Scarlet. Besides, those two things were unrelated. Janni had nothing to do with Nick. Ifrit's box glowed, while the ring stayed dark.

The bell rang.

"Let's continue this tonight." Jason closed his locker door. "We'll figure it out. We'll ask Ashley to help. If her dad has info on Nick's accident, we may be able to eliminate our *thing's* involvement."

I sighed. Jason always came through with a plan. "Can we trust Ashley?"

"She's been involved from the start. Seems pointless to cut her out now."

"Yeah." Ashley said she was all in when we unleashed Ifrit. That meant the good and the bad. "I'd want to know if I were her."

"Try to relax." Jason patted my shoulder. "We didn't do anything intentionally. At this point, we're not even sure of the connection between Nick and Ifrit."

I shifted my books under my arm and gave Jason a fist bump. Time for English, though I wouldn't be able to concentrate on anything, let alone *The Grapes of Wrath*. Then again, being far away from here, traveling through the dust bowl during the depression seemed like a welcome vacation.

As I rounded the corner, the halls cleared, and one person remained in the empty hallway in front of me. Scarlet faced her open locker, shoulders vibrating. Her posse of orbiting girlfriends were gone. I'd never seen her more alone.

Jason liked to point out we weren't friends anymore, but at one time, we talked like friends. Acquaintances, at an absolute minimum. I couldn't ignore her. Not now.

I stopped behind her, unsure of the right way to approach her. Because my entire family consisted of Mom, me, and her sister in Chicago, who Mom talked to maybe three times a year, I never experienced a grandmother's or grandfather's death. I had never consoled a person after losing a loved one. I'd attended one funeral in my fifteen years for Mom's work friend, who I'd met once.

I fidgeted awkwardly, trying to figure out the proper protocol for consoling someone. "I'm sorry, Scarlet."

She turned. Her cheeks were wet, her emerald eyes bloodshot and puffy. My insides melted to mush. She clutched a used tissue in her hand so tightly her knuckles glowed white.

Maybe we weren't friends anymore, maybe we never were, but the sight of someone in so much pain made my throat close and a rock form in my gut.

Before I could say anything else, she threw her arms around my neck. She sobbed into my shoulder, making noises I didn't know a person could make. Her entire body convulsed against me. Not knowing what to do with my hands, I rested them on the small of her back.

"It's okay."

The wetness on my shirt spread where her face pressed into it, and I hated that the scent of strawberries in her hair distracted me.

After a few minutes, she eased back from me. "I'm sorry." She wiped her face with her sweater sleeve, stretched out from a morning of constantly wiping.

"Don't apologize."

"I can't believe it." Her sobs tapered off.

"I know."

"He called me. After the interview. Said he did amazing. He didn't even sound buzzed." She wiped her cheeks again.

My stomach flip-flopped. Of course, he called her. I saw it in the dream. I wanted to ask if he said anything about making it to step two, but she didn't need that question now.

"I need to go." She gave me a crooked smile. "Sorry about your shirt." She swiped at the wet patch on the front of my shoulder, creating a wake of goosebumps.

"It'll dry."

I couldn't have had a stupider response.

****

School dragged by in painful slow motion. Minimal chatter filled the halls between classes, and students participated even less than normal in class. The teachers didn't care. They lumbered through their day just as distant. Robots had populated Truman High performing automated activities.

A lengthy address from Principal Clark over the intercom system replaced the rumored assembly. He didn't mention the drunk driving but instead commented on Nick's generous spirit, phenomenal sense of team, and untapped potential the world would never experience. He closed by encouraging all students to contact Mrs. Bronson to talk or pick up one of the pamphlets outside her office with an eight hundred number for a free counseling session.

When the final bell rang, I texted Jason and Ashley to meet at my place. Of course, with a police officer dad, Ashley may feel obligated to turn us in. Still, a djinn couldn't exactly be a murder weapon. At least, not in the traditional sense.

If only we understood more about ifrits, or djinn, to figure out what we were up against. Ashley joked at the park that we needed an old guy in a bookstore, an expert in the supernatural. Every town in every movie had one. Where was ours?

I stopped, causing a woman on the sidewalk to stumble into the back of me. She cursed under her breath and continued around me.

We did have one—our version of an old guy in a bookstore.

Time for a quick detour to Warren's Cosmos.

I opened the glass door under the green and white striped awning. The silver bell dinged, and the familiar mustiness wafted out into the sunny afternoon.

Inside, Warren sat where he always sat, perched on his stool, a metal *Captain Shield* symbol pinned to his shirt. I could have counted on one hand how many times I'd seen him somewhere else in the store. Even if I'd asked him where to find a specific issue, he'd just point to the section from behind the counter.

"Hey, Warren. Anyone come in looking for *Shade Slayer, #276*?" I had to get our tradition out of the way if I wanted his help.

He smiled. "Afternoon, Bax. And nope. Not today."

Warren noticed I skipped past the shelves of comics, headed directly for the counter. "A man on a mission, eh? What can I do for you?"

"Do you have any comic books on djinn?"

I crossed my fingers in my pocket.

Come on, Warren. Don't let me down.

One of Warren's caterpillar eyebrows lifted. "Genies?"

I nodded. "Villain or hero djinn. I'll take either."

Warren leaned back on the tiny stool. It creaked under him as he scratched his belly. "Well, there's *Greta Genie*. Kind of a silly comic, though." He snorted. "She got her powers from making people

146

laugh."

I grunted. "No. I'm looking for, like, *realistic* djinn."

Warren folded his arms. "Realistic? That section over there is all real-life comics. World War II stories and such, but I can't recall any comics based on *real-life* djinn." Warren sized me up, anticipating a punchline to a joke.

My shoulders slumped—a dead end. Warren wasn't my old man in a bookstore after all, but having already gone there, I launched one last question. "Anything on ifrits?"

He rubbed his chin, whiskers crackling under his fingernails. "Not sure what that is. You may need an actual library, Bax, or use that internet."

He always called it "that internet" like it referred to some new crazy song the kids liked.

"I'll try that. Thanks." I smiled, masking my disappointment. So much for that idea.

Warren studied me, his breathing heavy. "Everything okay?"

"Just a long day." I threw him a wave over my shoulder, ignoring how his face fell. I didn't have time to sit through a missing finger story. Jason and Ashley were waiting at home.

"You're too young to be having a long day, my friend," he called as the door to Warren's Cosmos swung shut behind me. I waved goodbye again, not wanting to hurt his feelings, but I had to get home.

Ashley beat me there. She waited outside of my apartment building, sitting on the stoop, right where the old man had given me the ring. When she spotted me down the block, she sprang up and jogged toward me, her hands swinging with animation as she started talking. Surely, Ashley realized I couldn't hear her from that distance.

"Took you freakin' long enough to get here. We've been guarding the building so you couldn't slip by. Jason's checking upstairs to see if you somehow got here before us."

"Jason's upstairs?"

She nodded. "Be back down in a sec."

"So," she paused, "Jason suggested we use Janni to spy on my dad? I must say, I'm a little suspicious. Jason didn't say any more. I mean, you know I'd be on board calling Janni back for pretty much any reason, but why do we need details of Nick's case?"

"I guess—"

"'Bout time." Jason rammed through my building's front door. "What took you so long?"

"I stopped by Warren's Cosmos to ask if he knew anything about djinn." I nodded at Ashley.

She grinned with pride. "Your old man at the bookstore?"

"Yeah, but he couldn't help."

"Good try," Ashley began. "But my dad's meeting about Nick's case starts in thirty. I called the department secretary with some lame story about how I needed him, so she blabbed. But tell me why we need to find out information on the investigation?" Her attention shifted from me to Jason and back again. "I feel like, *once again*, you're not telling me something."

I sighed. "I had a dream last night where I watched everything happen. With Nick and the scout. Like, all the details. Plus, when I woke up, the jewel on Ifrit's box practically lit up our entire apartment."

Ashley took a minute to digest what I said. "Whoa. You think Ifrit killed Nick?"

I shrugged. "Not totally sure. But pretty sure."

"It may be a coincidence." Jason couldn't have said anything with less conviction.

"I have to ask." Ashley hesitated. "You didn't…"

"No! I didn't want him dead! I'm gonna pretend like you didn't ask me that."

Ashley held her hands up in surrender. "Sorry, but I had to ask. All right, so to recap, in order to determine if your dream was a spiritual peek into Ifrit's behaviors, you tell us exactly what happened. Then, we send Janni to spy on Dad. If the details of the case match your dream, then your ifrit had something to do with this. Right?"

The hairs on my neck stood up. "*My* ifrit? *You* were there, too."

"That's what I meant." She held up her hands again. "Don't be so sensitive. Let's get to it. Tell us every detail of the dream."

Chapter 12

Jason fanned the air in front of his face. "I'll never get used to that smell."

With Mom running errands, we summoned Janni in my bedroom. Too cold for the roof and too many people on the street. We didn't have much time.

"HOW CAN IT SERVE?" Janni crawled out from under my bed. He picked off a small dust bunny clinging to his fur. I needed to clean my room.

"Are we sure about this, guys? I mean, Janni isn't the most discrete spy." Janni could not be quiet, and we were about to send him into the middle of a police station. Talk about a risky plan.

"Don't forget"—Jason sat on my desk chair—"the first night we discovered Janni, he stole money from a bank without getting caught. If he can rob a bank, listening in on a police meeting should be a breeze."

"And my parents never realized he recorded them." Ashley leaned against my wall, arms folded.

We had to determine if my dream happened. Though the idea of my dream being a coincidence felt like a long shot—a crazy-long long shot.

"Janni, we need you to go to the police station. In Detective Bryant's office, there will be a meeting in, like"—I checked my phone—"five minutes. Do your spy-recording thing, like you did with Ashley's parents. We want to hear what they say about Nick Ruiz."

"IT CAN SPY, YES." Janni stroked his ears, straightening the fur. His large eyes sparkled under the sun coming in through my window.

"Do you hide in the air duct or something? I'm curious." Jason fiddled with the hem of his shirt. "You can't get caught."

"IT DOES THIS." Janni faded away. He didn't disappear entirely but became so translucent the light bent and bowed where he once stood. I could make out Janni's vague shape, but he blended into the gray wall behind him.

"You can turn invisible?" Ashley clapped her hands together. "Freakin' awesome!"

Janni reappeared, scowling at Ashley's hands. "GIRL IS SO LOUD."

I fought back a smile. We needed to stay on task. "Okay, Janni, go to that meeting and come back when it's done."

"IT WILL SERVE." Janni jumped.

Jason fanned the air in front of his face again. "How much time do you think we have until your mom gets back?"

"I'm thinking thirty minutes. There're only so many groceries two people need."

"Can I ask a question?" Ashley stared at the pile of laundry in the corner of my room. Clean or dirty? I couldn't remember.

"Yeah, I know. My room could use some attention. I've been a little busy."

She shook her head. "I'm just wondering…what happens next?"

"Next?"

Ashley hesitated, gathering her thoughts,

something I'd rarely seen her do before speaking. "On one hand, Janni comes back and gives us details that don't match your dream. Then we know it was a bizarre coincidence and something else triggered Ifrit's box. On the other hand, if the details match…then what? What do we do with that knowledge? Sending Janni to spy on Dad is the easy part. What comes next?"

Jason pushed his glasses higher on his nose as he shrugged. I let out a puff of air. The million-dollar question—what *if* Ifrit killed Nick? We didn't know if he'd kill again, or who his next target would be, or more importantly, how to stop him.

"I guess," I broke the silence, "if Ifrit did it, then we'd need to prevent him from doing it again."

"Easy to say." Jason rocked back on two legs of my desk chair. "But how do we do that?"

"Can we ask Janni about Ifrit?" Ashley asked. "There must be a connection between the two. They're both djinn. Janni showed us where to find Ifrit. We really haven't asked Janni much about Ifrit because he gets so scared at the mention of him."

"Not a bad idea. We should ask about the old man, too. I'm wondering what his part in all of this is. This whole roller coaster started when he gave me the ring."

Ashley pecked at her phone. "Well, they all have purple eyes. Maybe the old guy is another type of djinn?"

Jason and I watched Ashley typing, expecting her to miraculously stumble upon some answers.

Nick's murder could be an isolated event. Ifrit came out, killed once, then returned to his box, waiting for the next idiot to summon him—one and done.

Yeah, right. Things were never that easy. But we'd

find a way to stop him. No one else could die because of me. Guilt warmed my ears. They'd probably turned red.

"I swear, you guys, I never ever wished this. I never asked for it. I haven't seen Ifrit since we were all in the basement. Sure, I didn't like Nick, but I never wished that he…you believe me, don't you?"

I had to repeat it. I needed them to hear it again as much as I needed to say it again.

"We believe you, man." Jason gave me a half-smile.

"Yeah, me too." Ashley pulled up from her phone. "None of us knew what we were doing or what Ifrit would do. All Janni can do is turn invisible and jump. Shapeshifting and impersonation are another level."

Their words didn't erase the guilt eating at my insides, but they lessened it a little. I'd talked them into finding Ifrit. Especially Jason, who'd been hesitant from the start. My greed to find a more powerful djinn killed Nick.

I shook my head to focus. "Let's assume Ifrit is a shape-shifter, and my dream happened. Do you think he shifted into the waitress, too? It's awfully convenient how the waitress kept bringing liquor over to their table. I think Ifrit staged the drunk driving scenario."

Jason scratched the back of his head. "That'd mean he's not some crazy monster. He plots and plans. But here's what I don't get—how come Ifrit can leave the box whenever he wants? Janni can't. Ashley, didn't you say a djinn's inanimate object is like a prison? How can Ifrit come and go as he pleases?"

"That's what I read. They caused so much mischief that God imprisoned them in their vessel. Some version of that fact is pretty consistent across cultures."

"There's the problem." I smacked my palm on my mattress. "*Pretty consistent*. There're so many legends and stories about djinn, which one is the truth?"

"It's like trying to research God. How many different bibles are there?" Jason added.

"Here," Ashley read from her phone. "A website on djinn that I bookmarked says—"

Janni reappeared on the floor inside my bedroom door.

Ashley stopped reading. I stopped breathing. This was it—the moment. Part of me wanted to stop Janni from telling us anything, not ready to face the reality of what we'd have to deal with. But this was our responsibility. If Ifrit killed Nick, we'd fix it.

I knelt in front of Janni, my stomach a boulder in my gut. "Did you hear about the case?"

"YES. NICK RUIZ. CASE NUMBER 78-2017-67656."

Jason and Ashley waited for me to ask Janni to begin, but the words wouldn't form. My jaw had locked up.

Jason rested his hand on my shoulder, encouraging me.

"Tell us what you heard." I spat the words out.

Janni cleared his throat, preparing to give a speech. When he began speaking, he sounded like Mr. Bryant.

Mr. Bryant: Hit me, Bill. What have we got?

Bill: Well, sir, we don't have much. The whole situation is odd.

Mr. Bryant: Go on.

Bill: Parking lot security cameras confirmed a guy who resembles Armington arriving before Ruiz, then a little while later, talking on his cell in the parking lot before leaving. The footage is grainy. The visual ID isn't strong. The cameras also confirmed Ruiz arriving at the bar, going inside, then making a call on his cell right before he left.

Mr. Bryant: You order the phone records?

Another voice: Yes, sir. He called his girlfriend, Scarlet Lane. We interviewed her. She said he called to tell her he moved on to round two of the interview process. Told her he nailed the interview. That's the extent of their conversation.

Bill: Blood alcohol concentration on Ruiz's body came back at point zero seven. He rear-ended a van, then drove into oncoming traffic. No sign of anyone running him off the road, or an animal leaping in front of him, or anything. Not even skid marks on the pavement until the first collision.

Mr. Bryant: Wait, back to the girlfriend. Did she say he sounded intoxicated?

The other voice: No. She said Ruiz didn't mention drinking and didn't sound drunk.

Bill: But the BAC verified he had alcohol in his system.

Mr. Bryant: So he met someone. Likely Armington. Then this person bought him a drink. Assuming the bar didn't serve him directly.

Bill: Correct.

Mr. Bryant: Who paid for the drinks?

Bill: No credit card charges for Armington or Ruiz. They must've used cash.

Mr. Bryant: The bar's response?

Other voice: Of course, they said they don't serve minors. Aside from this, we don't have any reason to think they do. The only explanation is that Armington bought from the bar and served Ruiz himself. The waitress on duty swears she never saw Nick in her section.

Mr. Bryant: All right, fellas. Here's the biggie. Did we bring in Scott?"

Bill: We did. He denies it.

Mr. Bryant: Of course, he does.

Bill: But wait. Armington's alibi holds up. He was in Springfield—three hours away—presenting at a faculty meeting. So we have a room full of Missouri State professors who verify his presence. Plus, we have IT's record of him logging in and out of that conference room during the time Ruiz was at the Bar and Grill.

Mr. Bryant: What?

Bill: Before you ask, we circled back with Ms. Hamilton because we think we might have an impostor Scott Armington. She stated that she checked his ID when he asked for Ruiz, and when we showed her the real Armington's picture, she confirmed his identity.

Mr. Bryant: Someone with a fake ID, who fits Armington's description, arranged to meet Ruiz, got him intoxicated, then sent him on his way, where he mysteriously drove into oncoming traffic. Why? Any sign of sexual assault?

Other guy: None.

Mr. Bryant: We're missing something. Keep on it.

Other guy: You got it.

"THAT IS ALL." Janni shook his head, whipping his ears back and forth. He stared at me, waiting for his next instruction, but I couldn't speak.

"You dreamt Nick's phone call to Scarlet exactly as she described it to the officer." Ashley spoke carefully, watching for my reaction.

I bit my fingernail. The dream had happened. Ifrit murdered Nick Ruiz. I had confirmation but needed more. I needed certainty. "Janni, did Ifrit do this? Did Ifrit murder Nick Ruiz?"

Janni's ears fell back against his head. "IT DOES NOT KNOW."

My fists crashed down on my desk with a bang. "Come on! I'm sorry you're scared, but we have to know. Are we responsible for Nick's death? Did Ifrit kill Nick?" I already had my answer but needed Janni to say it.

Janni's big eyes narrowed, and his tiny hands balled into fists, matching mine. "I DO NOT KNOW WHAT IFRIT DOES WHEN I AM NOT THERE."

I groaned. "Fine." I plopped back onto my bed. "But why would Ifrit murder Nick when I didn't ask him to? Isn't that against the rules? When we first asked you about Ifrit, you said he would only do what I asked."

Janni scowled. "NO, IT SAID IFRIT ONLY DOES WHAT MASTER WANTS."

"But that isn't what I wanted!"

"YOU ARE CONNECTED TO IFRIT."

"How?"

"THE OLD MAN."

"With the purple eyes and the long nails?" Ashley cut in between us. "The one from Bax's stoop?"

Janni nodded.

I nudged Ashley aside. "So how does the old man fit into all of this? He gave me the ring, but that tied me to you. Are the three of you all connected?"

A bang vibrated my bedroom as the front door to

the apartment slammed the wall. "Hey, Bax! Little help with groceries, please?" Mom called. "What's that smell?"

Janni scrambled under the bed. "OH NO! TOO MANY PEOPLE MAKING LOUD NOISES!"

"Is something burning?" Mom's footsteps went to the kitchen to set down the groceries. "You okay?"

"Hold on!" I leaped from my bed, hissing at Jason and Ashley, both wearing looks of sheer panic, "What do we do?"

Mom's footsteps approached my closed bedroom door. In slow motion, the doorknob started to turn.

Jason saw it too, and with a gasp, he grabbed it, holding the door shut. "Get rid of Janni!" He pointed under the bed.

Mom rattled the doorknob. "Baxter? Open up."

I fell to the floor, looking under the bed. Janni hid in the darkness under the mattress, his hands covering his eyes. "Go away, Janni. We'll have to finish this later!"

"Wait, what about the odor?" Ashley asked, too late. From under the bed, the smell reignited as Janni jumped.

Not the best strategy for keeping him a secret. I should have told him to hide. He could turn invisible, for God's sake.

I dove across the room to open my window. The blinds banged as I dug under them for the window latch.

Ashley took my desk chair and crossed her legs a little too formally.

I threw open the window and dropped to the edge of my bed, grabbing my history book and opening it in my lap.

Jason released the doorknob, quickly stepping away so Mom would think the knob had stuck, not that he'd held it shut.

No way we could explain away the smell, and if the open window diluted the smell, how would explain an open window in October?

Mom threw open the door, nose in the air, sniffing. The doorknob smacked the wall. "What's that smell? Baxter? Oh, you have company. Why did no one answer when I called? Why did you have your door locked?"

Jason's gaze fell to the floor. Ashley's floated to the ceiling.

Mom stared straight at me. A muscle in her jaw twitched.

"I answered you. You must not have heard me."

Red blotches burst on Mom's cheeks, and her lips tightened. "Baxter Allen. Are you…smoking? Smoking pot?"

I coughed in surprise. "No!" I leaped to my feet.

I'd never done drugs. Never even smoked a cigarette. For a moment, I weighed the option of letting her think we were smoking. It'd give me a more believable story than "Sorry, Mom. You're smelling djinn."

The consequences for drug use in the Allen household, or how Mom would react to drug use, were a mystery. But it was too late now. I'd already denied it. Plus, I didn't have any butts or joints to back up my story.

"Jason?" Mom stepped toward him. Jason couldn't lie, and she wanted to take advantage of his honesty.

She was ruthless.

Jason shook his head and shoved his glasses so high on the bridge of his nose that they dug into his flesh. He held his breath, and Mom could see it.

"Answer me right now." She turned up the pressure, taking another intimidating step toward him.

Say something, Jason.

He couldn't stay totally quiet.

Jason glanced at me over Mom's shoulder, desperate for me to save him. His brown skin had never been paler.

"Oh no, Jason. Eyes on me." Mom showed no mercy. I had to do something.

Before I could intervene, Ashley abruptly got up to leave, catching Mom's attention. She thought she could escape?

"Wait a minute, young lady." Mom shifted her focus to Ashley. "Come back here."

Jason started breathing again.

Tears from somewhere formed in Ashley's eyes. "I have to go home!"

Come on, Ashley, Mom isn't that *scary.*

Mom closed in on Ashley. She recognized a new weak link. Tears meant a break in our chain.

"Ashley, were you doing drugs in here?" Mom rested a steel hand on Ashley's quivering shoulder.

"No!" Ashley broke into huge sobs. Jason stole a confused glance at me.

She was up to something.

"I tried to make my own perfume!" Ashley covered her face with her hands. "I stole some supplies from the Chemistry Lab. It smelled incredible this afternoon, and I thought I'd become a millionaire. But when I showed it to Bax and Jason, they started laughing because something happened over the last few hours, and now it freakin' stinks. I don't care about them, but if my dad found out I stole from school, he'd be so mad. Please don't tell him! Please, Ms. Allen! The boys are trying to protect me."

Ashley's story hung for a few seconds. Now, *I* had stopped breathing.

Mom raised an eyebrow, not easily fooled. "Then why is everyone acting nervous?"

I shrugged like a small child. "We've been so mean to Ashley in the past, we didn't want to get her in trouble." I kept my tone solemn and convincing. "Do you really think we'd do drugs?"

Wham!

I flipped it around on her in a sad, nondefensive way. I mentally patted myself on the back.

Mom scanned the room for evidence of our drug habit. "It does smell unusual in here. Then where's this bottle of perfume, Ms. Bryant?"

Uh oh.

When Ashley first met Janni, she said we needed an escape plan for his odor. How much detail did she weave into her plan?

Ashley reached into her backpack and produced a glass vial. The cork sealed in a murky brown liquid, and the label read "Black Fury." She handed it to Mom.

Mom removed the cork, took a whiff, and gagged. "Oh God, Ashley." She coughed.

Ashley wiped her eyes, which faintly glimmered with pride at her perfectly executed plan.

"It smelled amazing three hours ago! Please don't tell my dad. I didn't take much. I only made this vial."

Mom rolled the bottle in her hands, debating the story. Her gaze met each of ours, lingering uncomfortably. We held our ground. Even Jason kept his cool and nodded in agreement with Ashley's tale.

"Fine. I'll buy it." She handed the vial back to Ashley.

Fully committed, Ashley kept the tears streaming.

"No more stealing from school, Ashley." Compassion found its way back into Mom's voice.

"Can I go home?" Ashley sobbed. "Thank you, Ms. Allen. I'm so sorry."

"Go on." Mom dismissed her with a wave of her hand.

Ashley darted out of the room.

"I hope the two of you are being honest." Mom wagged a long finger at us. "If you're not, consider this your first and last warning."

"You got it, Mom."

We owed Ashley in a colossal way.

Mom folded her arms across her chest and sighed. "All right. Moving on. I bumped into Jason's mom at the grocery store. She invited us over for dinner. We're leaving in a few. Finish up your homework, guys."

"Cool." My heart rate began to even out. We'd avoided a drug bust. Or a djinn bust.

"And for the love of God, Baxter, close your window. It's October, and the heat's on," she added as she left.

Chapter 13

"More white?" Mrs. Franklin swirled the wine bottle in front of Mom. Exotic sculptures adorned every table of the Franklins' home. The various shades of browns and oranges throughout the house gave it a museum-like vibe.

"Thank you." Mom tipped her glass to Mrs. Franklin with a warm smile. She loved the Franklins. She admired their worldliness. Dr. and Mrs. Franklin both spoke French, the ultimate sign of sophistication for Mom. Not to mention, Dr. Franklin taught at Washington University, and Mrs. Franklin sat on every activist committee in existence.

Jason glanced over my shoulder, checking out his cell phone on the table across the room, next to mine. Both vibrated relentlessly. Jason's rumbled into mine, nearly pushing it onto the floor, but we both knew better than to check our phones during the enforcement of the No Phones During Dinner law. Another thing Mom admired.

"Can you fill me up, too, babe?" Dr. Franklin's smooth voice floated over the scratchy blues album playing beneath our conversation.

After filling Dr. Franklin's glass, Mrs. Franklin served herself. "So, Sara, there's a women's march next week if you're not working. Some ladies from the university are going."

"That'd be fun." Mom sipped her wine. "I'm so envious of everything you do for the community. Really."

Mrs. Franklin supported lots of causes. Equal pay for women, the education of girls in poor communities, and clean water in Africa, to name her current favorites. If Mom didn't work two jobs and had some actual free time, she'd totally join Mrs. Franklin's endless crusades.

"Stop it." Mrs. Franklin gave a modest wave of her hand. "We can't sit around and wait for change, can we?"

"I want to go!" Jason's sister lacked volume control, like Janni. It didn't matter the time or place, she shouted everything. "Pleeeeeeeease?"

"You can come." Mrs. Franklin pointed her fork at Michelle. "But if you want to hang with the older ladies, you need to act like one." She nodded to Michelle's napkin, still folded under her silverware.

"Sorry," Michelle sang, whipping her napkin out and shoving it on her lap.

"So, Bax." Dr. Franklin took a bite. "You feeling better? Jason told us about the assembly."

I choked on a mouthful of veggie-stuffed mushrooms.

Crap!

The shock of Dr. Franklin's question made the room spin. I'd avoided a note from Mrs. Bronson, only to have my best friend's dad out me during a dinner where I'd least expected it.

I swallowed, shooting a death stare at Jason.

"What?" Jason didn't understand why I shot darts at him with my eyes. Did I tell him I didn't want Mom to find out? Maybe not.

Mom took a very deliberate sip of her wine, watching Jason and me. "What happened at the assembly, Randal?" She watched me as she addressed Dr. Franklin.

Jason, seeing Mom's reaction and mine, mouthed a sincere, "Sorry."

Dr. Franklin also studied the exchange of glances. He didn't answer Mom's question, allowing me the opportunity to handle it. However, he did raise a stern eyebrow indicating if I didn't say something, he would.

I downed a mouthful of water, buying myself a few more seconds. "I had another VS episode last Friday."

"What?" Mom's fork clanked on her plate.

Unable to look at her directly, the corner of my eye caught her face. I cringed, rarely seeing that look. Hurt—true hurt. I'd kept something from her that Jason freely shared with his parents. She didn't understand Jason could share because it didn't happen to him. I'd be happy to share all of Jason's embarrassing moments with her.

"I'm sorry, Bax." Dr. Franklin wiped his mouth with a cloth napkin. "I didn't realize—"

"You didn't realize how on Earth a son wouldn't tell his mother about a health issue?" The background music overpowered Mom's weak tone. That killed me. Just yell at me.

For the first time in history, dinner with the Franklins became awkward. Michelle even kept her mouth shut, though she fiddled with her napkin furiously under the table as her five-year-old brain tried to figure out why the mood abruptly changed.

I needed to say something.

My focus stayed on my plate. "It's embarrassing, Mom. During an assembly, I couldn't answer a stupid question about football, so an episode snuck up on me."

"Did you talk to Mrs. Bronson? Why didn't she send me an email or anything?"

"I'm sure with all the Nick Ruiz stuff, she got distracted." I picked at the mangled stuffed mushroom on my plate.

"Well, you'd think she'd be able to multitask." Mom's soft tone sharpened. "I mean, nothing against the poor boy that…you should have told me, Baxter."

I scooted the green beans around with my finger as slow as possible. Michelle stared at my hand, mouth agape, amazed Mom didn't lecture me to use a fork. But neither she nor Mrs. Franklin said anything.

Mom sighed and straightened in her chair. "We don't need to discuss this now, but we'll continue it later. Believe me."

Ugh.

She needed time to think about her approach. I'd crushed her. Mom already harbored so much guilt about working too much. Now, she'd blame herself for being so out of touch with her son that she missed his horrible health episode. Which was the exact reason I didn't share it with her to begin with.

"Well," Dr. Franklin attempted to lighten the mood, "at least you're better."

Mrs. Franklin poured herself another glass of wine, having downed the prior one in the awkward silence, then cleared her throat. "So, Sara, about that march. It's in two weeks. Janet Parker is in—"

"And me!" Michelle shouted.

For once, Michelle's hollering worked to my

advantage and reset the dinner climate by breaking the tension. Mom shook off her disappointment and mentally regrouped, squaring her shoulders. She'd handle me later. Managing as much as Mom regularly did, she excelled at compartmentalizing issues, as Mrs. Bronson would say.

"That would be amazing, Jada." Mom smiled. "What's the date?"

Jason's fork tapped his plate. "Can we be dismissed, Dad?"

After a nod from Mom, Dr. Franklin said, "You bet."

He'd barely finished answering before Jason and I threw our chairs back from the table. We grabbed our phones and ducked into his room.

"We're not staying late, Bax. Don't go far," Mom called after us. "It's a school night."

"Got it!"

We slammed the door to Jason's room, finally able to talk about the *real* problem and not my stupid one.

"I'm assuming those million texts were from Ashley?" I started scrolling through them.

Jason paused, shoving his hands into his pockets. "Bax, man, I'm sorry. I didn't know you didn't tell your mom."

"It's fine." I really didn't want to continue that conversation. "I didn't tell you not to say anything. It's my fault."

"I figured you needed to tell your doctor or something."

"The doctor said I may never have another episode, or I might. There's nothing to treat."

"Yeah, I know—"

"Seriously, it's fine. I'll talk to Mom later. She'll get over it." I dropped my voice. "We should focus on the murderous djinn we unleashed. That's way more important than one of my stupid episodes that may or may not ever happen again."

"Do you think this whole djinn thing is causing your episodes to—"

"No. If Ifrit forced me to give a speech to a hundred people, then maybe we'd have an issue. Besides, if I didn't pass out in the creepy-ass basement where we let that monster out of his box, it ain't gonna happen now."

Jason smiled. "True."

"Can we change the subject? You know I hate talking about it."

"Sorry. Yeah." Jason turned his attention to his phone. He flipped through the texts with a finger. "Girl's been busy. Let's call her."

Jason's room wasn't much larger than mine, but he kept it neater, so it felt bigger. Clothes stacked and folded in his dresser, shoes neatly arranged on his closet floor, shelves lined with books in some kind of order. Unlike the lone soccer trophy on my shelf that the entire team received, Jason earned his numerous spelling bee and science ribbons.

He dialed Ashley and tapped the speaker icon.

"Oh my freakin' God! It's about time!" Her voice vibrated the phone. "Do you people have, like, five-course meals at the Franklins'?"

Jason cranked the volume down. "Yeah. That's how we roll in my house. Our personal chef flies in from—"

"Hey, Ashley," I interrupted, "we owe you. Thanks

for the save this afternoon with my mom." Ashley's perfume escape plan saved our asses, even if Mom still carried some lingering suspicions.

"Well, that's what friends do, right?" After she said it, she stammered, "I mean, or classmates or whatever. You're welcome."

Jason smiled and nodded in agreement.

I answered for both of us. "That *is* what friends do."

Ashley's tone softened. "Look, I know sometimes I can be a little—"

"We're glad you're on our side." I cut her off. She didn't need to apologize for being herself if that's what she was building up to.

After a short pause, Jason's phone crackled as Ashley's voice rose in volume. "Well, I told you guys we needed an escape plan. So I figured it'd be up to *me* to come up with one."

It wouldn't be Ashley if she just accepted the thank you. "But the perfume story only works once, so we'll need a new one for next time. Otherwise, Bax's Mom will throw us all into rehab."

I shook my head. "There won't be a next time. Once this Ifrit thing is over, we retire all djinn from our lives."

"Agreed." Jason eagerly nodded. "Speaking of which, you sent, like, a hundred texts. What'd you learn about Ifrit?"

"I read everything I could find and started writing down similar things mentioned in at least three different sources, like we talked about before. I worked under the assumption that if three sites said it, it'd have a higher probability of being true."

"Yup." Jason nodded.

"Here's what I found." She let out an exhale. "Ifrits are always depicted as evil or wicked. I found literally no mentions of a friendly ifrit. They tend to live in ruins or caves."

"Or buried under old buildings," Jason said.

"Right. They're associated with flames. Sometimes, they take on the shape of the deceased right before, or right after, they die."

"Like when he shape-shifted into Nick." My stomach turned. While I appreciated the information so far, everything Ashley said only worsened our situation. We were battling an actual demon. "How do we kill it?"

"Apparently, if you have a djinn who won't go back into his vessel, you need to recite an incantation, which is like a chant or a prayer. The incantation seals the djinn away and prevents it from coming out until it's summoned again."

I leaned in close to the phone. "Where do we find Ifrit's incantation?"

Ashley went silent for a moment. "The trail ends there. Each djinn has its own incantation. I found nothing on where to locate it, where to read it, if we need to drink a magic potion, burn sage, or do something like that while we read it."

"Burn sage? In case it farts?" Jason snickered.

"No, dumbass, people burn sage to get rid of ghosts in their homes."

"I'm a dumbass? Sorry I don't know the procedure for ridding a house of a poltergeist."

I ignored them. "We need to find the incantation—soon."

At least we had a direction, a first step in banishing Ifrit. Now, we just needed to find his incantation.

I paced in small circles in Jason's room. Unlike in my bedroom, I didn't have to worry about stepping on anything.

"What happens until we find this poem thing?" I stopped pacing to talk into the phone in Jason's palm. "Will Ifrit keep killing people until we banish it?"

"Not sure." Ashley typed on a keyboard in the background. "I mean, everything says djinn listen to their masters. So I can't figure out how Ifrit killed Nick without you ordering him to."

"Well, I didn't," I said for the hundredth time.

"I know, Mr. Defensive. You've said that, and we've said we believe you, but to answer your question, nothing I've read describes Ifrit as a stone-cold killer. More mischievous."

"Great!" I plopped onto Jason's bed. "Ifrit might kill people or simply decide to make my life a mess."

"Focus." The crease had returned to Jason's forehead, and he started squeezing a stress ball he picked up from his desk. "We need to figure out where Ifrit's incantation is. Should we check the cellar? Could be in that rubble."

"Good idea." I nodded.

"Tomorrow after school?" Ashley's voice cut out for a second. "It'd raise too much suspicion if we skipped school."

"Yeah, you're right. We're leaving here soon, and I've got to deal with something with Mom, anyway. It'll have to wait until tomorrow."

Jason looked up from his phone.

"It's fine," I whispered to him.

"It's a plan, then, boys. I'll see you at Bax's after school."

"Bax?" Mom called from the other room. "Let's hit it!"

"Later." Jason hung up.

"I'll see you tomorrow, dude." I fist-bumped Jason, preparing to face Mom.

****

After saying our goodbyes, we walked the stairs in silence. I swore I could hear Mom's mind grinding, trying to figure out how to approach me. Should she get mad and yell? Should she take the calm, understanding approach? Should she give me the silent treatment, letting me initiate the conversation?

She landed on the direct approach once we hit the street outside. "Why didn't you tell me about your episode?"

I sighed. "Because you'd make a big deal out of it."

"Your health *is* a big deal." Her voice remained calm.

Without breaking pace, Mom bent over and placed a dollar into a homeless woman's collection box. The homeless woman, wrapped in layers of mismatched, street-beaten clothes, mumbled, "God bless." We didn't have a ton of money, and Mom didn't grow up rich, but she always gave money to people in need.

I zipped my jacket to keep out the cold wind that barreled down the sidewalk. Over us, the moon lit up the night sky, on its way to a super blue blood moon. I'd have to remember to take a pic Friday night. I could use the extra credit.

"It's only the second time in, like, three years,

Mom. The doctor said each time could be the last."

"Everything going well at school?"

I knew she'd make this into a thing. "Yeah. Everything's fine. I got called on to answer a trivia question. I didn't know the answer while the entire school stared at me. So my VS acted up. Same old story."

She hesitated. "Everything good with us? At home?" She focused straight ahead. Her clenched fists shoved into her pockets bracing for the horrible thing I was about to drop on her.

"Of course, everything's fine." I hated when she did this. I had a medical condition that flared up when I felt anxious—end of the story. "This is why I didn't tell you. You always think you're somehow an inadequate mom. That moving apartments and schools caused this, that you work too much, that you don't make enough money, that Greg isn't around. I'm embarrassed it happened, but there's nothing more to it. There's no underlying cause. Other than speaking in front of people stresses me out."

Her shoulders dropped. "Any other episodes you haven't mentioned?"

"No. None since last year."

"We should set you up with someone besides Mrs. Bronson. A professional. Not that she isn't…you know what I mean."

I rolled my eyes. "Mom, for real. I'm fine. We already have the diagnosis, and it barely ever happens."

"I could take some time off—"

"Stop!" I cut her off. "I told you, this isn't about you. There's nothing you did to cause it and nothing you can do to prevent it. I'm thrilled with my life. I don't have some horrible childhood trauma causing this."

A twinge snagged me in the gut. If I was so satisfied with my life, why did I find the idea of a djinn—a powerful one—so irresistible? But Mom's parenting never figured into that. Money did. And Greg, to be honest with myself. The whole reason I accepted the ring from the old man in the first place was because of its connection to Greg and my curiosity about him.

Mom's hands came out of her pockets, and she slid her arm around my shoulders. "If you have stuff you want to talk about and aren't comfortable telling me, that's fine. In fact, it's more than fine. There are some things you can't tell a parent. You won't hurt my feelings."

"Got it. That's why I have Mrs. Bronson, right?"

"Right. Okay. I'll drop it but under one condition."

"What's that?"

"Even if you choose to tell Mrs. Bronson something you don't want to share with me, I still get to know about any episodes. Deal?"

"Deal."

Mom yanked me toward her as we turned on my street and gave me a massive bear hug. Usually, I'd pull away and make a crack about not wanting to be *that* guy hugging his mom in public.

But this time, I hugged her back, with a full-on, both-arms hug, because she needed it.

Maybe I did, too.

Chapter 14

Scarlet shuffled down the hallway of the modest, three-bedroom apartment. With two bathrooms and a separate dining room, it had more space than the place they'd lived in before her mom married Paul. Thanks to Paul's sales job and what he called its room for growth. Though Paul's career hadn't grown as long as she'd known him.

She brushed her hair behind her ear. Her heavy eyes stung with a mixture of exhaustion and crying. Everyone at school meant well, but the parade of sad head shakes and sympathetic texts kept the memory of Nick's death torturously vivid. She'd never forget him, of course, but she needed a break from the grueling grief.

A few drops from the cold water she'd splashed on her face trickled down her neck and settled into the neckline of her nightshirt. Nick loved the nightshirt. He loved when she wore anything green. He'd said it made her eyes sparkle.

As she collapsed onto the soft pink-flowered comforter, her phone vibrated.

Casey.

At eleven p.m.? She only called this late when she had a fight with Preston. They needed to break up. Enough with the constant drama. Scarlet tried to be a good friend, but at some point, a girl needed to decide—either the boyfriend stays or he goes.

But even someone as self-absorbed as Casey wouldn't be expecting a sympathetic ear tonight. Not at this hour and not so soon after.

"Hey." Scarlet answered to get it over with.

"How are you doing?" Casey asked.

"Fine, I guess." Scarlet relaxed. Normal Casey check-in.

"Just thinking about you, girl." Casey paused. "You're on my mind. I wish I could do or say something. I can't imagine what you must be going through."

"I know." How else could she respond? Lots of people said that exact thing to her over the past day, and she couldn't come up with a better response.

Scarlet fell back on her bed, relieved she wouldn't hear about Casey-Preston drama. "I miss him so much." Her voice cracked. Great, she finally stopped crying, just in time to start up again.

After a very brief pause, Casey said, "Don't get mad, but I have an idea."

Oh boy.

"About what?"

"I read this article," Casey started timidly, "and it suggested that maybe you should start dating again."

The phone almost slipped from her hand. She must've misheard. Casey could be self-centered but never blatantly insensitive. No, that was beyond insensitive. It was insane. Scarlet sat up. "Are you for real? It's been, like, literally one day. He died last night. Tell me you're joking."

"Hear me out. It's important to get out there again. According to what I read—"

"Stop, just stop. I'm not some spinster who's been in mourning for years. Jesus, Casey. What's wrong with you?"

"Girl, I'm trying to help. I saw Bax Allen today. I didn't remember him being that cute. You guys grew up together or something, didn't you?"

The phone shook in her trembling hand. "We didn't grow up together. Are you saying I should start dating Bax to get over Nick? Seriously?"

"Calm down. You guys used to live by each other, yeah?"

The blood drained from Scarlet's head. She unlocked her jaw to speak. "I can't believe we're having this conversation. I have to go." She hung up and threw her phone to the end of her bed.

What the hell?

Her phone started vibrating. Scarlet peered across the mounds of her comforter.

Casey.

"Are you kidding me?" She let the call go to voicemail.

Casey had to be drunk or stoned. The entire conversation didn't make sense. Scarlet buried her face in her hands. Her brain couldn't handle anything else. She needed to sleep.

Skipper scampered into her room and leaped onto the bed. He began licking her leg.

A reluctant smile snuck across her lips as she scooped her dog up in her arms, massaging her fingers through his fluffy white fur. Skipper always gave her love at the right time. He tilted his head back and licked under her chin as she wiped her eyes.

"What is wrong with her?" She replayed the

conversation in her mind. Was Casey in the middle of a nervous breakdown or something?

Like any loyal dog, Skipper whimpered in response and rubbed his wet nose on her forearm.

Scarlet debated sneaking a glass of wine from Mom's box o' wine in the fridge. She'd stolen a full plastic cup of Dinner Table White Blend every night this week. She should skip tonight.

Mom and Paul were out celebrating their anniversary at Mac's Corner Tavern, leaving her home alone. Just because their daughter's boyfriend died didn't mean they shouldn't get their drink on. Typical. Paul pretty much left Scarlet alone, but he truly loved her mom. And that seemed fine with Mom. Scarlet guessed it was okay with her, too.

She set down Skipper, who scrambled to the foot of the bed and got to work yanking the comforter with his teeth and paws, building his sleeping nest. Scarlet threw her robe to the floor, hit the light switch, and crawled under the covers, hoping to forget about the entire stupid day.

She'd just fallen asleep when a stench crept into her nose, pungent enough to drag her from sleep. It could be her mom smoking in the bathroom. No, that wouldn't have woken her. Besides, while she couldn't identify it, the odor didn't smell like tobacco. Then, it hit her. The smell reminded her of the time she burnt her hair on that cheap flat iron.

Shit! There's a fire in the house!

Scarlet bolted up in bed, snapping awake. Her head jerked toward the door, fully expecting flames lapping from underneath. Nothing—no smoke or orange glow under the crack.

Shadows quivered on the other side of her room.

Scarlet screamed. Scrambling up her bed, she pressed her back against the headboard. She flipped her lamp on, never taking her focus from the corner of her room.

A monster towered, straight out of a nightmare. The thing—half-man-half-goat-half-something-else—glared at her with glowing purple eyes atop a muzzle with smoke slinking from its nostrils. It cradled Skipper between its massive forearm and veiny bicep. The dog whimpered softly, afraid to make any noise.

Scarlet tried to jump off her bed and run but found herself stuck to the mattress, legs paralyzed. She screamed again.

The creature put one clawed finger over its wet, animal-like lips. "Quiet." Its growl spewed from deep in its chest.

She obeyed, swallowing hard and rubbing her eyes. It had to be a dream, but the creature seemed real. If it were a dream, would she be rational enough to question it?

"Scarlet Lane."

It knew her name.

"You will obey."

Her voice trembled. "What are you?"

"I am a servant." It stroked Skipper tenderly as a line of drool plummeted from its bottom lip to the dog's white coat. Skipper flinched under the burning saliva.

"I have tried to be reasonable, but you refuse."

"Huh?" Scarlet's gaze flicked to the door. "I've never seen you before."

The creature's purple eyes tracked hers. "You are home alone. No one will hear us."

Scarlet inventoried her room for weapons: her phone, a lamp, a book. Nothing useful. Besides, she probably didn't have enough strength to hit the massive thing hard enough to do any damage.

Maybe she could escape her bedroom and run for it. But, she'd need to be quick and leave Skipper. Surely the thing wouldn't hurt him.

After seeing Scarlet glance at the door for a second time, the creature's tail slithered from behind and wrapped around the leg of her desk. It slid the desk, light as paper, in front of her bedroom door, blocking it.

"What do you want with me?" she yelled, hoping someone in her building would hear her and call the police.

"You will love Baxter Allen."

She shook her head in disbelief. "Wait, what did you say?"

"You will love Baxter Allen."

The creature's mouth curled into a slight smile, then its voice morphed into a perfect imitation of Casey. "Girl, I'm trying to help. I saw Bax Allen today. I didn't remember him being that cute. You guys grew up together or something, didn't you?"

Scarlet's stomach dropped. That conversation was too insane even for a drunk Casey. "You?"

"I have given you a command."

Scarlet brushed her hair behind her ear, her mind racing. "A command? Bax is a nice guy, but I don't understand why—"

The creature lifted Skipper by the scruff of his neck. The dog's stubby legs kicked as he whimpered, dangling from the thing's clawed hand.

It chortled.

"Wait!" Scarlet reached out to Skipper.

"You will love Baxter Allen." It held Skipper at arm's length. The dog's legs thrashed, but he couldn't escape the creature's grip.

"Please, stop. I'll do—"

Before she could finish, the thing jerked its arm in one swift motion, snapping Skipper's neck with a deafening pop.

"No!" Scarlet screamed. She threw her hands over her face, unable to erase the image from her mind. It killed Skipper. Her puppy.

It waited for Scarlet to uncover her eyes before it let Skipper's lifeless body drop to the floor with a thud.

Scarlet sobbed, climbing across the bed on her hands and knees toward Skipper, no longer scared of the monster. But before she could get to him, the creature kicked the dog's body with one of its hoofed feet across the room. The dog smacked against the wall and dropped like a deflated soccer ball.

"Next, I will kill your stepfather, then your mother. One person will die each day you do not love Baxter Allen."

"How the hell am I supposed to just start loving someone?" She shouted at the thing through broken sobs. "That doesn't even make sense." She wiped her eyes. Skipper's body lay dead and lifeless.

The creature leaned down, its muzzle inches from Scarlet's face. Its rank breath poured over her like a rolling fog. She struggled to remain still, to suppress the sobs trying to explode their way out.

"You will figure it out, Scarlet Lane. And you will love him."

"Fine, I'll do it." She covered her face with her

hands. "Just leave!"

With her eyes closed, the warm stench of the beast's breath dissipated.

Scarlet opened her eyes.

She was alone.

Scarlet wiped the tears from her cheeks and gasped, out of breath. It was a dream. Maybe the past twenty-four hours had all been a dream: Casey hadn't called, a demon hadn't visited, Nick would be waiting for her morning text in a few hours, and Skipper would be patiently waiting by his food dish, his knobby tail wagging. Everything as boringly normal as last week.

She scanned her room, needing reassurance she'd awoken from a nightmare.

Her desk blocked her bedroom door. She didn't do that. The thing did. It wasn't a dream.

Her hands started trembling again as she searched her room, her gaze landing a few feet to the left of her desk.

There, on the beige carpet, Skipper—curled into a ball—huddled tightly in the corner, his entire body quivering.

"Skipper!" Scarlet leaped off the bed and ran to him, scooping her puppy into her arms. She held him tight against her, but he didn't lick her face like usual. Instead, he buried his cold nose into her armpit, shaking violently. A blistered, furless circle, the size of a quarter, marked his back from the monster's drool.

Scarlet's room was in shambles. The thing had visited her, but it didn't kill Skipper. Not this time. She'd been warned.

And next time, she knew the vision would be real.

****

I shot up in bed and grabbed my phone. 1:00 a.m.

"No, no, no." I rubbed my eyes as I slipped out from under the covers.

Tripping across my bedroom, still half asleep, I yanked open my closet door.

The jewel on Ifrit's box flooded my room with violet light.

Chapter 15

"You look like shit." My best friend always greeted me in the most uplifting way.

I dragged a hand through my curly hair, untangling it, knowing it wouldn't do much for my appearance. I'd spent the night wide awake. The images from Skipper's murder flashed like an old-fashioned slide show every time I closed my eyes. Scarlet's screaming echoed in my ears.

Ifrit ordered Scarlet to go out with me to save the lives of her family. Was that why he killed Nick? But now, she'd suspect I had something to do with the monster. Using my name openly connected me to Ifrit.

I'd snuck around the halls before morning bell to avoid her. I couldn't face her. Given everything she'd been through, hopefully, she'd stay home. Losing a boyfriend would wreck anyone.

Please take a sick day—for both of us.

"You look like shit, too." My weak-as-hell comeback. "We have a problem."

Jason shifted the books in his arms. "With supernatural beings? Yeah, I know."

"No, I mean another problem. I had another dream."

Jason froze. "Oh no. Who died? I haven't heard about any students."

"No students. No one died, but Scarlet—"

Jason glanced over my shoulder, then his head nodded. "Hi, Scarlet."

"Hi, Jason." The hairs on the back of my neck rose at the sound of her voice behind me. Her hand clamped on my shoulder like a vice grip. "Bax, do you have a minute?"

My stomach lurched. It always did when Scarlet talked to me, but this time, ricocheting bullets replaced the fluttering butterflies. I turned, overwhelmed with dread. Dreading how she'd look at me, what she'd be thinking of me.

Crying had swollen her bloodshot eyes. Like me, she probably hadn't slept since her visitor. When I blinked, Skipper's dead body emblazoned the back of my eyelids. Did her parents come home drunk and wonder why their beautiful daughter sat on her bed crying in a trashed room? Did they even notice?

Shame melted me into the floor. I ended up not spying on her or reading her journal, but I came dangerously close to it. Then, because of me, Ifrit murdered her boyfriend and threatened those she loved. Now, she had to pretend to like me. Ifrit's havoc continued to spread, all because of my greed.

"Hi." I took only slight, momentary breaks from staring at my shoes to glance at up her face. "What's up?"

The bell rang.

Thank God.

"We'll, um, catch up later, man." Jason gave my shoulder an awkward pat, then followed the rest of the students to class. He totally abandoned me, but he couldn't have done anything to help if he stayed.

"Yeah." I turned to Scarlet. "I need to head to

class, too." I started to pull away from her grip, wanting to avoid her at all costs. Wanting to avoid any conversation with her. But her hand didn't loosen.

"Just a second. Please, Bax." She guided us closer to the wall of lockers as the hallway slowly emptied.

She cleared her throat. "Casey told me dating again is the best way to heal grief." Her voice cracked. I forced myself to meet her gaze. Red eyes, quivering lips, a new slouch in her posture—she looked like a hostage held at gunpoint.

"Okay?"

Please don't say it. Please don't say it.

A few kids threw us curious glances as they made their way to class, but no one lingered. The hallway transformed into a ghost town.

She took a breath. "I'm not sure I'm ready, but if I did want to start dating again, I think I'd need someone I'm comfortable with. Someone I've known for a while. At a deeper level. Like you." Her entire body tensed. The words scalded her throat.

"Look, Scarlet," I stammered, "I don't think that's the right decision. You should be alone. I mean, we can talk or whatever, but dating isn't…you know."

Never in my wildest dreams had I imagined turning down Scarlet Lane.

Her face wrinkled with disgust. "Are you rejecting me? I'm coming to you as a friend. A friend who could be more." Her voice turned venomous. She hated me. She hated me so much.

"No, I think—"

"This is hard, Bax. You think it's easy to ask you out when my boyfriend just died?" Tears spilled from her eyes and cut down her cheeks, but she kept her face stoic. "I'm asking you for some, um, kindness, and you're treating me like we haven't known each other since kindergarten." She notched up her volume, even though, thankfully, the halls were empty.

I needed to end the conversation and buy myself some time to figure out how to handle her.

"Okay. Okay. Let's hang out this weekend or something."

She swallowed as if preparing to eat something vile, then slammed her face against mine, shoving her tongue into my mouth. Her hands rested on my cheeks, not as a gesture of endearment but to hold my lips against hers. Or to keep herself from being physically repelled off me.

The shock turned every muscle in me to stone. I was paralyzed. My chest tightened, and my lungs seared, needing oxygen.

And just as my mind caught up with reality, she released me. For a second, inches from my face, she paused. Our eyes met. Pain, wrapped around the most accusatory glare in the history of glares, punctured my soul. Hatred burned in her eyes. She suspected my involvement but had no way to accuse me of what happened in her bedroom without sounding like a lunatic.

She spun on her heels, anxious to be away from me. Any faster, and her departure would have been a sprint. "See you this weekend, babe!" she called over her shoulder. The phrase had never sounded so disturbing.

Down the hall, Malcolm watched us with his books clutched so tight their bindings were about to burst. His nostrils flared like a bull about to charge. He glared at me as Scarlet walked away, seemingly carefree. He couldn't see her face.

I backed against the lockers, even though Malcolm stood half a hallway away.

He mouthed a sentence under his breath, but even from my distance, I could hear his words as clear as if he stood towering over me. "You're a dead man."

I bolted to the bathroom, almost as fast as Scarlet had fled from me, afraid I'd throw up in the hallway. My mouth tingled. My cheeks stung where her hands had clutched the sides of my face, trapping me. My insides twisted with guilt and hurt.

After years of dreaming about her, *that* was my first kiss with Scarlet Lane.

****

It didn't take long for Malcolm to spread the word. No one said anything to my face, but I could feel the gossip radiating across campus faster than a gas fire. When I looked in someone's direction throughout morning classes, the whispering stopped, giggling turned to straight faces, and judgmental glances were exchanged.

I didn't have astronomy, so I could avoid Scarlet, but in history, Casey glared at me with absolute loathing, passing rapid-fire notes to Michelle, each with a nasty snarl in my direction.

At the lunch bell, I fled history, anxious to be away from Casey's evil stare. Though others awaited me in the hallway. I'd gone from invisible to laughing stock to asshole in under a week. I missed invisibility so much.

Jason waited at my locker, confirming the furious spread of rumors. "Is it true? She kissed you? Do I even need to ask? Yes, I do. What happened? I want details."

I kept my voice down as we walked to the cafeteria, not like anyone would hear us. A forcefield had formed around me, with other kids repelled at a safe distance, even in the crowded hall. Not a single person knocked into me, ran into me, or came within a few feet of me. An imaginary barrier imprisoned me.

Jason felt it too but tried to ignore it. "So?"

"Another dream. This time, Ifrit showed up in Scarlet's room. No shape-shifting. He appeared in his ugly, Big Bad form. He showed her how he'd kill her dog and threatened to kill her parents if she didn't go out with me."

"Holy shit! No more covert operations like with Nick. Just full-on threatened her into doing what he wanted. We have to find that incantation."

"Understatement of the year."

"At least no one in her life has died. Not yet."

I shook my head, the image of Scarlet's face before our kiss punched me in the gut again. "Yeah, but you should have seen her face. She knows I'm connected, but she can't tell anyone, or they'd think she's delusional."

"I'm sorry, man. You've always liked Scarlet. It must've been weird to have it go down like that."

"*Weird* is putting it mildly."

"So Ifrit is scouring your subconscious to find out what you want, but he's deciding how to make those wants real on his own."

I shook my head. "How on earth do I control my subconscious wants?"

In the cafeteria, we grabbed trays and walked to the lunch line. Not very hungry, I grabbed an apple I'd probably not eat and a carton of milk I'd probably not drink.

"Let's think about this." Jason grabbed an orange and a bag of potato chips. "If the pattern holds, then Ifrit only seems to do things when you're sleeping. That could be how he gets into your psyche."

"What about Nick? That happened around dinner time, and I dreamt about it later that night."

Jason scratched his head. "True, but there's some kind of correlation. Maybe he doesn't *do* stuff when you're sleeping, but sleep is when you see what he did because it opens your connection to him. Sleep may also be the time he digs around in your subconscious."

"If sleeping opens the connection, then—"

"We need to find the incantation before you sleep again and close the connection."

Easy—we just needed to find an ancient incantation hidden somewhere on the planet, and I couldn't sleep until we did. What could be so hard about that?

"What if it's not in the cellar?" My voice cracked. "And what about Scarlet? If I tell her about Ifrit, it really doesn't help our situation. I'm still to blame for it. What if she figures out Ifrit killed Nick?"

"One thing at a time." Jason kept his voice calm, neutralizing the hysteria in mine. "We'll clean up the damage after we banish Ifrit. Telling Scarlet now doesn't do any good."

We sat at our usual table as my name floated around us, buried in whispers. Eyes glanced at me until I met them, then they diverted to something else. The stinging judgement hovering in the air felt a million times more humiliating and demeaning than passing out at the assembly.

"What the freakin' hell is going on around here?" Ashley plunked her lunch down at our table. My apple rolled to the edge of my tray. "The entire school is gossiping about you and Scarlet. Does this have something to do with our friend from another dimension?"

I nodded. "Keep your voice down. Ifrit threatened to kill her parents if she didn't go out with me."

Ashley's mouth dropped open. "Wow. Didn't see that coming. I bet that's not how you envisioned getting your dream girl."

"Shut up." Every reminder of the kiss stung worse than the last.

"Didn't realize kissing Scarlet Lane was so horrible." Ashley's chuckle abruptly ended. "Sorry, bad joke."

"You didn't see her face." Out of the corner of my eye, Ashley and Jason exchanged glances. Jason gave her an it-was-that-bad nod.

"Well,"—Ashley took a drink of her milk—"we're searching for the incantation today after school, right?"

"It can't come soon enough." I picked up my apple, then put it back down, uneaten. "I'm gonna skip classes this afternoon. I can't focus on anything anyway. I need to find that incantation. I'm not waiting until after school."

Jason nodded. "I'm with you. This is important. Head out after lunch period?"

"Count me in, too," Ashley said, "I say we should—"

"Are you kidding me?" A voice pummeled me from behind. The familiarity ignited a chill that started at the back of my skull and slid between my shoulder blades.

Crap. Malcolm Reardon.

Jason mumbled an obscenity, keeping his focus on his tray.

I stiffened but stayed in my seat, praying Malcolm had hurled his question at some other unlucky soul. Based on Ashley's face across from me, though, my prayer was ignored.

"I wondered if my eyes were playing tricks on me, but the way you ran off when you saw me—like a scared little kid—I knew it was real." Malcolm's hands balled into tight fists, the veins on his forearms and biceps bulged. "You think Scarlet is gonna go out with you when Nick just…?" His voice dripped with rage. Not the pretend anger bullies used when they issued threats for your lunch money or your seat. He spoke with pure, sincere fury.

I swallowed hard. My throat had dried up. I needed to face him. I'd pissed all over the memory of his dead friend. He had every right to be angry.

Standing up from the plastic cafeteria chair, I turned around. "I told her—"

His iron fist slammed into my jaw.

Bolts of lightning shot across my entire body from the point of contact, and I stumbled backward into the table. Trying to catch myself, my palm landed on the edge of my tray, flipping it and catapulting my full carton of milk onto my back.

Students jumped to their feet for a better view.

"He hasn't even been gone a week, and you think you can put your little Flower hands on his girlfriend? Think again, fuck face." Rabid spittle flew from

Malcolm's mouth.

As my vision returned, the forms of Gerald and Brad took shape behind him. All three pounded their palms with their fists. I muttered a goodbye to the world of the living.

The crowd of onlookers grew as students gathered around.

Please draw the attention of a teacher.

Jason sprung from his chair and stood on my right. Ashley joined him on my left. If crippling terror hadn't consumed me, I'd have thanked them for their loyalty. But while I appreciated it, it wouldn't help. They meant well, but in a physical brawl, Jason and Ashley wouldn't exactly tip the scales in a fight against three football players. Not even sure if Malcolm would care about punching a girl.

"I don't want to date her or—" I struggled to say it "—or 'put my hands on her.' "

The crowd around us packed in close. Unlike in movies where the mob cheers for a memorable show, my classmates' faces mirrored Malcolm's to varying degrees. They all agreed with him. Their head nods confirmed it. They rendered their verdict. I disrespected Nick's legacy by taking advantage of his grieving girlfriend. They didn't surround us for bloody entertainment. They wanted to witness Malcolm administering painful justice.

My entire school hated me.

"It sure didn't look like you were pushing her away this morning." Malcolm's chest heaved under his stretched T-shirt.

"Seriously—" I begged, not sure how to explain. Not that it mattered. Before I could say anything,

Malcolm's fist launched into my gut. I doubled over.

"Back off!" Jason didn't sound remotely threatening. At least he tried.

"Here comes Mr. Buckwald," Ashley announced. "You'd better leave."

Gerald tapped Malcolm's shoulder. "She's right. He's on his way."

"We'll finish this later, Flower." Malcolm gave me a final murderous glare.

As the crowd registered what Ashley and Gerald said, they scattered before Mr. Buckwald could record names.

Malcolm leaned down, our noses an inch apart. He exhaled a burger-scented whirlwind across my chin. "Back off Scarlet, dipshit."

I nodded, not knowing how else to respond. How did I tell him I wanted to, but a djinn would kill her parents?

Mr. Buckwald grabbed Malcolm's shoulder from behind before he escaped. Malcolm stood a full head taller than the teacher and could have easily broken away but didn't. He wasn't that stupid.

"Something wrong here, gentlemen?"

"No, sir," Malcolm said with his back to Buckwald and me.

Mr. Buckwald raised one of his pencil-thin eyebrows.

"No, it's fine." I lowered my hands so they stopped clutching my stomach, even though the pain remained sharp. "We had a disagreement."

"Well, fighting is not how we settle a disagreement. Both of you to Mr. Clark. Right now."

Mr. Buckwald released Malcolm.

"On my way," Malcom muttered.

I rubbed my chin, stalling, wanting to give Malcolm a long head start. I needed as much space between us as possible.

"I guess we search after school, after all," Jason whispered.

"Plan on it."

If Mom found out I'd been in a fight, I'd never be able to meet up with Jason and Ashley to search for the incantation. Mrs. Bronson might have forgotten to email Mom about my episode, but Mr. Clark wouldn't forget to call her about a fight.

I was screwed.

Chapter 16

My fingertips grazed the doorknob before tepidly turning it. Unlocked. Mom left her shift early—not good. She needed to get back to work as soon as possible so we could find the incantation and stop my life from spiraling out of control.

Here goes.

Inside, Mom waited at our kitchen table, her laser scope glare fired from our kitchen, down the short hallway, and nailed me between the eyes. Still in her beige and brown front desk uniform, she held an ice-filled plastic bag wrapped in a towel. She shook her head as I opened the door. She never lost her eye lock on mine.

My backpack thudded to the floor outside of my bedroom like cannon fire in the dense silence. Forcing each foot forward, I shuffled toward the kitchen table, head hanging.

The chair creaked as I sat down. Mom let a few long seconds pass. Maybe she wanted me to say something first?

"They called me at work," she said finally. "I left midshift. I'm not getting paid while I'm here, by the way."

"I didn't do anything wrong!" My voice came out louder than I intended.

"Fighting, Baxter? Really?"

My head rolled back, and I answered to the ceiling. "I wouldn't call it a fight. *Malcolm* punched *me* twice. I never hit him. It was a public beating."

"Principal Clark said no detention, thank God, but still, fighting?" She slid the ice pack to me, leaving a trail of water on the table. I took it. The cold soothed my throbbing jaw.

Malcolm told Mr. Clark that Nick's death upset him, and he lashed out at me, unprovoked. Since Malcolm took responsibility and acted out of grief, Mr. Clark let us both off with a warning but said he'd notify our parents.

Malcolm didn't mention the kiss with Scarlet. Probably couldn't force the words out. He was a douchebag, but I couldn't blame him for hating me. Only an asshole would move in on Scarlet days after Nick died.

Mom leaned forward. With her fingertips under my chin, she turned my head right, then left. "You'll have a heck of a bruise. Why did this bully jump you?"

"He was friends with Nick Ruiz. So he freaked out when he saw me talking to Nick's girlfriend. Ex-girlfriend, I guess."

And if I didn't find that incantation, it wouldn't be the last time Malcolm freaked out. He would serve daily beatings for disrespecting Nick's memory. Malcolm wouldn't stop after Principal Clark's warning, he'd just be more thoughtful about hiding my torture.

Mom's demeanor softened. She rested her hand—still cold from holding the ice pack—on mine. "Are you sad about it? Nick's death?"

If Mom believed Nick's death traumatized me, she'd call into work and stay home. That couldn't happen. She had to go back.

"I didn't really know him. He hung out with the football players." I tried to sound casual without sounding soulless. "I mean, it's sad and all."

"I imagine losing a classmate is difficult." She stared at me for a few minutes, waiting to see if I started crying or something. When I didn't, she gave me a satisfied nod. "Okay."

Mission accomplished. Now, go back to work.

"No more fighting, Bax."

"You mean, no more getting sucker punched?"

She patted my hand.

"You heading back to the hotel?"

Keep it cool. Don't be overanxious.

"I told Mr. Albert I'd play it by ear."

"Mom, go. I'm fine."

She brushed a stray hair that had fallen loose from the restraint of her ponytail behind her ear and leaned back in the chair. "I feel like you should be grounded. You got in a fight."

"Malcolm admitted he started it! *And* he confirmed that I never even punched him back. Didn't Mr. Clark tell you that part?"

Mom's foot tapped on the linoleum, but with her work tennis shoes on, the tap resembled a muffled thudding. "He did."

"So what lesson am I learning by being grounded?"

She glanced at her phone. "Fair enough. No grounding, but no more fighting."

"Don't worry. That's not something I want to repeat."

"Don't get me wrong, no mom likes getting a call from the principal." She tilted her head, examining my jaw again. "But I also wanted to make sure you weren't hurt. Keep ice on it for a while, yeah?"

"A bruised jaw will totally round out my badass persona." I grinned.

"You're ridiculous." She got up from the table and grabbed her keys from the kitchen counter. "All right. I do need to go. I'll be home around ten."

"Sounds good." I reassured her with a wide smile.

I kept the ice against my jaw while Mom gathered her things together. It throbbed under the ice pack. I checked the time on my phone. Jason and Ashley should be home by now.

I texted them.

—*You guys coming over or what?*—

—*At Ashley's. Just got here.*—

Ashley chimed in.

—*Are you grounded?*—

—*No, Malcolm took the blame.*—

—*Good. He threw the punch.*—

—*Wait until Mom clears the hallway and come over. Time's wasting.*—

After the door clicked shut behind Mom, I sprang from the chair and tossed the ice pack into the sink. Always worried I'd lose it, I patted my pants pocket. Ring's there. I anxiously tugged on the hem of my T-shirt as I watched our front door.

Where were they?

Finally, the door swung open. About time. Ashley barreled in first.

She charged me, almost stumbling over her own feet, her mess of brown curls bouncing on her shoulders. "How's the jaw?" she asked, barely inside.

She skidded to a stop in front of me, leaned in

close, and examined me in a clinical sort of way. "It doesn't seem swollen or anything. At least, not yet. That's a plus."

"Hurts like hell."

Jason, unlike Ashley, sauntered in behind, moving with caution, afraid to approach me too quickly. He hovered at the edge of the kitchen, where the linoleum met the hardwood floor of the hallway.

"Hey," I said. What's up with him?

He took a deep breath. The crease in his forehead appeared. "Man, I wish I would've jumped on Malcolm or stepped in somehow. Done something. It all happened so fast. I'm sorry." Jason's gaze dropped to the floor.

This was typically Ashley's cue to make a snarky comment about how Jason couldn't beat up an ant, but she didn't. She just bit her bottom lip. They must've talked about this before they came over.

Jason seriously thought I expected him to get his ass beaten for me?

"It's all good, dude. There's no way the three of us could have taken down Malcolm, Gerald, and Brad."

"I know, it's just—"

"It's just nothing. For real. I do need you now, okay? So focus." I shoved him playfully in the shoulder.

"Yeah, okay. I'm focused." His shoulders relaxed.

I clapped my hands and spun back to Ashley, who leaned against the pantry door. The clap's vibration rang my throbbing jaw. "For the incantation, we should start where we found the box."

"In the cellar." Jason perked up. "Maybe we missed something in the brick pile."

"That's what I'm thinking. I'll ask Janni to fetch the keys once we're outside."

Jason and Ashley followed me down my building's stairwell. All three of us skipped over the broken stair and out the front door. Being last, Jason got stuck holding the door open for Mrs. Crawford, returning with a small bag of groceries.

When he could finally let the door swing shut without whacking Mrs. Crawford in the bottom, Jason leaped down the three cement stairs to meet us on the sidewalk. Barely waiting for him, Ashley and I tore off around our building to the cellar door.

The garbage truck must've completed its route because the dumpsters were empty, but they left tire tracks through some kind of liquid—too shiny to be water—from the dumpsters to the street. Fortunately, the lingering garbage odor would still mask Janni's arrival.

"Bring on the djinn," Ashley said.

"What if it isn't down there?" Jason's eyebrows crinkled tight above his eyes. "Do we have any other ideas?"

We needed this to work. If we didn't find the incantation in the cellar, I had no Plan B.

It will be there.

I rubbed the ring, setting the jewel aglow. As the icy chills finished cascading down my back, I shuddered, then said, "It will be there."

The hairs on my arms relaxed, and I clicked on my phone's flashlight to search the shadows of the alley. The sun hadn't set yet, but the alley stayed in a perpetual state of twilight or night. Daylight couldn't fully penetrate the space between the buildings.

Janni waddled out from behind a dumpster. He didn't mind that he walked through the sticky tire tracks. "HOW CAN IT SERVE?" His clasped hands hung over his stomach like a tiny waiter anticipating our order.

"I need you to get the landlord's keys for the basement again."

Janni's ears dropped. "WHY GOING THERE AGAIN?"

"Because we need to send Ifrit back to Neverland. He's wrecking my life. That's why."

"Hey, wait." Jason tapped my shoulder with the back of his hand. "Before we go through all that. Janni, if we recite his incantation, will it send Ifrit away forever?"

Jason always started with the obvious. Why not ask Janni about the incantation? This whole idea was just speculation from an internet search. "Nice thinking."

"YES. INCANTATIONS SEND DJINN AWAY. EVEN ME."

"Yeah, but you go away when we tell you. Like a good djinn." Ashley scratched him behind his ear.

"IT FOLLOWS THE RULES." Janni leaned into her hand with a moan.

"A good djinn, Ashley?" Jason rolled his eyes. "He's not a puppy."

Following Jason's lead, I kept with the direct approach. "Do you know where we can find Ifrit's incantation?"

Janni shook his head. "NO."

"Where's yours?" Jason asked. "That could give us a clue where to find Ifrit's."

Janni pointed to my pocket. "ON THE RING."

I pulled out the ring and rolled it in my palm. The dingy gold was smooth. "Where?" Even the jewel's setting had an unmarked finish. No etched words on the jewel itself, either.

"UNDERNEATH."

I flipped the ring over. On the inside of the band, beneath the jewel, were minuscule scratches. "Those?"

Ashley grabbed the ring from me.

"Hey!"

"Let me try something." She turned on her phone's camera, then zoomed in on the scratches. "They're tiny freakin' symbols. Look!"

I took the ring back, along with Ashley's phone. Sure enough, a series of symbols made up seven neatly ordered lines, invisible to anyone not looking.

"What language is that?" The miniature markings resembled pictures, like Chinese characters, but blockier.

"IT IS OLD. IT DOES NOT KNOW."

Ashley let out a *hmmm*. "Before we go down into the rat-infested basement, have we examined Ifrit's box for something similar?"

"No, and if it's this small—" I began.

"And it makes sense a djinn's vessel can summon him as well as banish him," Jason added.

I squeezed the ring in my fist. The incantation to set everything right could have been waiting in my room, nestled under some sweaters, the entire time.

"Let's go." I spit the words out as fast as I could. "Janni, jump to my room. We'll meet you there."

We charged back inside and up the stairs, taking several steps at a time. I tossed my keys on the kitchen table and left the front door open for Ashley, who'd fallen behind. Janni already waited on my bed, lounging against my pillow, feet straight out in front of him, like Mr. Cuddles.

I threw open my closet door and yanked the box down from my closet shelf, sending two sweaters tumbling to the floor.

"Do you see it?" Ashley panted in the doorway.

I rolled the box over in my hands, scanning for the incantation in the grooved, rough texture of the old wood. "Nothing on the outside."

"Be careful you don't accidentally rub the jewel," Ashley whispered. "We don't need Ifrit seeing what we're up to."

"Open the lid." Jason tapped my arm. "Check inside."

The old lid creaked on its rusted hinges. At first, nothing, then, we saw it. Obvious when you looked for it, carved on the underside of the lid, near the bottom corner. Not as small as the incantation on the ring, but not much more prominent. Like Janni's incantation, it consisted of seven lines.

Ashely held her phone up and compared it to the picture she'd snapped of Janni's incantation. "Same type of characters, but different incantation."

"They're the same language. Whatever that is." I held the box closer to my face as if that would suddenly enable me to understand it.

Jason plopped down on my bed. "Great. We found it. But how do you recite something you can't read? Is it a real language? What if it's like, djinn-talk?"

The possibility hadn't occurred to me. Maybe humans couldn't speak it at all.

"And you can't read this one either?" Ashley asked

Janni.

He shook his head. "IT HAS NEVER BANISHED ITSELF."

"Yeah, but you know who inscribed it, right?" Janni had to know something. Some clue to its translation.

"DJINN LIVED IN THIS WORLD, THEN BANISHED TO ANOTHER BY THE MAKER. THEN HUMANS FROM THOUSANDS OF YEARS AGO SUMMONED US BACK INTO THE WORLD OF MAN."

"Until those humans realized the problems djinn caused, so they created this incantation to send you all back. Right?" It lined up with Ashley's research. The history made sense, but it still didn't help me solve my Ifrit problem.

Janni scowled. "NOT ALL DJINN ARE PROBLEMS."

"No offense." I shut the box's lid.

"Let's think about this." Jason rubbed the crown of his head. "The writing is from an ancient civilization. Janni said one that existed thousands of years ago. How many thousands, Janni? Are we talking, like, Roman times or, like, first human times?"

Janni shrugged. "IT CANNOT TELL TIME."

Ashley took a picture of the box's incantation on her phone and handed the box back. "I'll try to find some matches on the symbols." She started typing on her phone.

I tossed the box to the bed. "If we find out it's Chinese or something, we'll still need a translator. How do we do that?"

"We'll figure it out." Jason's voice contained zero

confidence.

"We don't have time." I squeezed a pillow into my stomach. We'd hit another dead end, and Jason wanted to be positive. "Who else does Ifrit have on his list? I mean, the Scarlet thing is disturbing, but at least she's alive. I can keep taking punches from Malcolm, but what if someone else dies? What if I harbor some deep-down resentment for how Mom potty-trained me, or what if I'm mad at Mr. Clark for calling Mom? Will he bite it tonight?"

"Man, I don't know. But until we're officially out of options, let's not give up."

I belly-flopped onto my bed, the sudden bounce almost launching Janni right off it.

"I have an idea." Ashley clicked her fingernails on my desk. "What if we ask Ifrit to tell us what language it is or how to say it? Wouldn't he have to do what you ask? Maybe he can read the symbols."

"But if the incantation banishes him, why would he help us?" I had to yell with my face buried in my pillow. "Besides, Ifrit hasn't done anything I've asked before."

"Ashley's circling around something," Jason said. "We've focused on playing defense, what if we played some offense? You're right, he hasn't obeyed you, but you haven't commanded him. What if we summon Ifrit and order him to back off? Make him go to Antarctica and stay there until we call for him."

Offense instead of defense. I sat up. "Janni? Will that work?"

Janni picked at something in his arm hair. Hopefully, he wasn't dropping mystical fleas in my room. "IT DOES NOT KNOW."

"Well." I shrugged. "Should we try?"

Jason yanked the cord, and my blinds slammed down against the windowsill, shutting out the sunlight. "I'm not looking forward to seeing that thing again, but I think we give it a shot."

"We have to do something." I grabbed the box.

"I hate Ifrit," Ashley grumbled.

Janni stood on my bed. He wrung his hands together. "CAN IT GO? IT DOES NOT LIKE IFRIT."

"None of us do. But yeah, you can leave, Janni. No need to have you—"

Janni jumped before I could finish. I slid the ring into my pocket, wanting to keep it near me. "Didn't need to tell him twice, I guess."

I let out a long, uncomfortable sounding exhale. "Ready?"

Jason and Ashley nodded. Based on their faces, their stomachs were flipping over, too.

My pointer and middle finger ran over the purple jewel on Ifrit's box.

Heat swelled from deep in my core, warming my blood. Instantly, sweat dotted my forehead. My skin tingled, and the hair on my arms shot up, electrified. Then came the piercing needles behind my eyes. I squeezed them shut. Within seconds, the pain subsided.

The stench rolled into my room like smoke effects on a concert stage, saturating the air.

Ashley pinched her nose. "Gross."

The odor grew to an overpowering rankness. I blinked, and when my eyes opened, the lights had gone out, my room aglow in purple light from Ifrit's box.

"He's here." Jason's voice quivered.

Ifrit towered in the corner, his horns pressed

207

against the ceiling. He grumbled deep in his chest, and a thin stream of smoke slunk from his glistening nostrils. His purple eyes glowed, and he snapped his tail with a loud bullwhip crack.

We'd seen him before, but Ashley still choked on a short scream. Jason and I took a collective step backward. Every muscle in me tightened. Would I be able to command *him*?

Ifrit extended one of his massive, clawed hands, open palm up. "You summoned me?" His animalistic growl buried his words.

Ashley clutched the back of my shirt, tightening the neckline against my throat.

I swallowed. "You need to stop…stop doing things to people in my life."

His mouth curled into something resembling a smile. "I give you what you want."

"No, you don't." I forced my voice louder, more assertive. I summoned my courage. "I never wished Nick murdered or for you to force Scarlet to like me."

Ifrit bent at the waist, his head sliding forward to meet me. His hot breath scalded my face, but I stood my ground. I was his master and needed to act like it.

"Really?" He sniffed me like a dog. "You did not want Scarlet to be yours?"

"No! I mean, yes, but not like that. I never wished for that."

He retracted, sitting back on his haunches. "The most powerful wishes are not said with words."

"Bullshit." My fear swirled into anger, fueling my bravery. I wouldn't let him hurt anyone else. Sure, he could crush me without flexing a muscle, but I summoned him. He had to do what I commanded.

That's the rule.

"The most powerful wishes aren't said with words?" I repeated. "How do I control that? You're supposed to be my djinn."

Ifrit's head cocked, and he rose, his pointed tail whipped out from behind him, snapping across my room.

CRACK.

It shattered my lamp.

I jumped, bumping into Ashley. We both stumbled backward. We'd made a mistake summoning him.

"You think you do not wish these things, but you do."

"I don't!" I stepped toward him and squared my shoulders, my hands in tight fists, readying for a physical battle I'd lose. I had to show him who was in charge if I wanted this to end. "I never wanted Nick to die!"

"But how else could Scarlet be yours?"

"You threatened her! That's not *being mine*."

"I know what you want, Baxter Allen. When you summoned me, you let me into your mind. We are connected."

"You're a monster." My voice cracked. I didn't want any of this. My mind didn't think those things. He's a liar.

Ifrit took a step forward with one of his thick goat legs. "Then *we* are a monster."

Tears of anger, fear, and sadness blurred my vision. What had I unleashed on the world? If what he said were true, then I made him a monster. He acted on my impulses—my unspoken wishes and wants. I was to blame for Nick, for Scarlet, and for whatever else he would rip from of the depths of my mind and choose to act upon.

We are a monster.

I swiped my wet eyes with my forearm and squared my shoulders again. "Go to some deserted island. I don't care where. Stay there until I summon you. Do nothing else in my name. Nothing! I command it! Do you understand?"

He emitted a deep, mocking cackle. "Goodbye, Baxter Allen."

Ifrit vanished.

The lights in my room flickered back on. The jewel on his box faded to dark.

Wiping my cheeks before Ashley or Jason saw, I turned around. Ashley's eyes were as wide as Jason's.

"Did it work?" Jason whispered.

"I-I don't know."

"I guess we wait and see." Ashley's hands trembled. When she saw I noticed, she shoved them into her pockets, self-conscious. Not that she had anything to be self-conscious about.

"In the meantime," I inhaled a shaky breath, "we need to translate that incantation. And until then…"

"Until then?" Jason searched the room, as if expecting Ifrit to return at any moment.

I swallowed. "You heard him. We're connected. We are a monster."

"Bax, that doesn't—" Jason began.

I held up my hand. "We're connected. Like you said earlier, sleeping seems to open that connection. It gives him access to my subconscious or something."

"So?"

"So until we translate the incantation," I paused,

"I'm not sleeping."

"At all?" Jason shook his head. "How will that work?"

"Not sure, but I'm not risking it."

Chapter 17

Hundreds of tiny needles danced over my skin. My heart pounded faster than machine-gun fire in *Archer Annihilation*. It could have been the lack of sleep or the excessive coffee—most likely, a combination of both. My eyes burned from staring at the computer screen throughout the night, but I pushed through, desperate to find any information on the incantation. Every time my eyelids started drooping, I rolled to the floor, powered through some sit-ups and push-ups, and then snuck to the kitchen for more coffee, careful not to wake up Mom.

I sifted through endless sites on djinn, djinn incantations, ancient alphabets, and historical civilizations. Academic websites tended to be the most boring—but most reliable—sources, and they all agreed djinn lore started somewhere in Asia or the Middle East. Archeologists found mentions of djinn on Arabic, Chinese, and Sumerian artifacts. So, I narrowed my research to those three languages, comparing their characters to Ifrit's incantation.

As soon as the computer loaded a picture of the Sumerian alphabet, a caffeine-free rush jolted me awake. The symbols resembled both Janni's and Ifrit's incantations. After I read Sumerian was one of the oldest recorded languages, it made perfect sense. But that also created a huge obstacle—how in the hell would I find someone who can translate the language of a long-lost civilization?

I'd already peed my brains out but needed to stop for coffee on the way to school if I intended to keep the no-sleep thing going. I grabbed my backpack on my way to the front door, wanting to leave before Mom noticed my bloodshot eyes.

I yanked open the door. "Bye, Mom—"

Mr. Bryant stood in our doorway with his fist raised, about to knock.

"Morning, Baxter." He smiled pleasantly as he lowered his hand.

"Oh, hey." Mr. Bryant never just stopped by to say hi. Especially first thing in the morning.

"Can I snag you for a sec? Is your mom home?"

Snag me for a sec?

Being a detective, Mr. Bryant never wore a uniform, so I couldn't tell if he was on duty. I didn't see Ashley in the hallway with him.

My insides turned to ice.

Ashley! She used to annoy the crap out of me, but I never—on any subconscious level—wanted something terrible to happen to her. We'd become friends. No way I harbored any bad feelings toward her, no matter how deep.

That couldn't be it. If something had happened to her, Mr. Bryant wouldn't calmly ask to snag me for a sec. He'd be upset, angry, worried, or all of those things.

Maybe she confessed about Nick. How would that have sounded? *So, Dad, we unleashed a djinn that impersonated a college scout and killed the high school football star.*

"What's going on?" I kept the panic from my voice. Mr. Bryant was a detective. He'd notice it. That's his job.

He patted my shoulder and shot me his pleasant smile again. "I have a few questions about Nick Ruiz. Police business. Since it's official, I need your mom here while you and I talk. It'll be quick. I know you're on your way to school."

Shit!

"Questions for me? About Nick? Right now?"

Innocent people didn't fire off rapid questions. I had to keep it together. I took a deep breath, then stepped aside, holding the door open. "Sorry. I stayed up late working on a project, plus, I probably drank too much coffee. Mom, Mr. Bryant's here!"

"Hey, Tom." Mom came out of her bedroom holding a makeup compact and brush, in the middle of getting ready for work. "Come on in. Have a seat."

She led us into the kitchen. Mr. Bryant took a chair at the table with a relieved grunt, not appearing to profile me like a suspect. Unless he was so discrete, I couldn't tell.

"I think winter's finally coming," he said.

"Gonna be a cold one, I hear. Coffee?" Mom set her makeup on the kitchen counter and pulled out a coffee mug.

"Half a cup. Thanks, Sara. I'm sorry for the surprise visit. I promise I'll only be a few minutes."

"No problem." Mom poured his coffee, then made one for herself. "Thanks for making coffee, Bax. What can we do for you, Tom?"

"Well, I'm investigating Nick Ruiz's death." Mr. Bryant's brown eyes matched Ashley's, but he had a rounder face, with a jawline edged by a thin beard.

"Horrible story." Mom sat down, warming her hands on the Best Mom Ever coffee cup I bought her for Mother's Day years ago. "So young and so much potential, from what I've read. Could have really gone places."

I twitched as Mom sung Nick's praises. She'd never even met him. She fell in love with him by reading his obituary. No one saw the cocky asshole I did.

Mr. Bryant sipped his steaming coffee. "I contacted his parents, his friends, his girlfriend, Scarlet Lane, etcetera, and something's not right."

"Scarlet Lane?" Mom raised an eyebrow and tilted her head. "The same girl who used to live across the hall?"

Mr. Bryant nodded. "Her family lived in our place before we moved in, yes."

Mom watched me suspiciously. I'd told her Malcolm punched me for talking to Nick's girlfriend. I might have failed to mention her name. Who knew Mom would've remembered Scarlet's name? Did it even matter?

"Yeah. They were dating," I mumbled.

Mr. Bryant noticed our exchange. "What am I missing?"

"Well, Tom," Mom began, her eyebrow still high on her forehead, "You probably know this, but Bax got into a fight with another student who claimed he put the moves on Scarlet."

I shifted in my seat, as uncomfortable about this entire conversation as I was with Mom's use of the phrase *put the moves on Scarlet,* but I kept my mouth shut.

"Malcolm Reardon, yes. Mr. Clark told me." Mr. Bryant rotated his coffee mug in his hands. "Which is why I'm here. You see, Mr. and Mrs. Lane said Scarlet has been acting strange the past day or two."

Mom shook her head. "I can only imagine what that girl must be going through."

Mr. Bryant rubbed his chin. "Malcolm told Mr. Clark he lashed out at you for talking with Scarlet. That right, Bax?"

"Yeah."

He glanced at Mom, then said to me, "The Truman High Rumor Mill is saying you and Scarlet are a thing."

My face grew warm.

A thing?

"That true?" Mom tip-tapped her fingernails on the kitchen table. "Interesting."

Now she and Detective Bryant went full-on interrogation mode. Awesome.

"We're not *a thing.*" I picked at a loose thread in the chair's cushion. I hated my classmates. Gossip had us practically married after one kiss.

"Several students said they heard that you kissed in the hallway."

My face almost caught fire. I could deny the kiss. Malcolm was the only witness, but Scarlet would corroborate Malcolm's story. She had plenty of motivation to convince everyone of our *thing.* Besides, a kiss wouldn't connect me to Nick's death. It'd make me a jerk, not a murderer.

"Well, she kissed me. Out of grief or something." My words spilled out fast and short.

"Please understand, Baxter," Mr. Bryant softened

his voice as he scratched his beard. "I need to follow every path and paint a full picture of Nick if I'm gonna figure out what really happened. Something about the drunk driving story doesn't add up. But if you were with Scarlet while she dated Nick, that would add a whole new dynamic—"

"Tom," Mom interrupted, "are you implying Baxter might have killed Nick in a jealous rage? He's just a boy, for Christ's sake."

I tensed, holding my breath. A crash of something barreling into empty trash cans outside made me jump.

"No, no, no. Not at all, Sara. Of course not. Like I said, something doesn't add up. I'm curious if Nick found out about Baxter and Scarlet and fell into a self-destructive phase."

"Well, I'm not dating her." I couldn't stay silent. "And never have."

And thanks to Ifrit, I never will. He crushed that fantasy into smithereens.

"So the Truman High Rumor Mill story isn't true?" Mr. Bryant tapped his pointer finger, keeping a slow, steady beat to a song in his head.

"No, it's not." I stared at his stupid finger. "Look, she is acting strange, so her parents are right. And yes, she kissed me in the hallway, but I asked her to stop because she seemed like she was in a bad place. Emotionally, I mean. But we aren't dating. That kiss happened once. Once."

Mr. Bryant glanced at Mom. "Will Scarlet tell me the same story?"

My stomach fell to the floor. No, she'll tell him we're dating. She'll tell him she's in love with me. She'll do her best to convince him of that to save her parents and dog from murder.

"I can't speak for her. Scarlet's upset and not acting normal. That kiss came from nowhere. That's the truth. We've never gone to a movie together, eaten dinner together, or sat together at lunch. That kiss was the extent of any romantic relationship between us. If she does answer differently—and I'm not sure why she would—ask her to give you examples of our relationship. She'll have none."

The image of Scarlet's face flashed in my mind. Her lips inches from mine, immediately after our kiss. Her emerald eyes scorched with hatred, unable to comprehend how I'd sent a monster to threaten her family. The words she spat at me were still loud in my ears, *See you this weekend, babe!* as she fled from me before she started crying again.

"Anything else I should know, Bax?" Mr. Bryant stared, likely doing some cop trick to test my honesty.

"There's nothing to tell." My voice cracked with guilt. I'd never hurt someone like I hurt Scarlet. The feeling ate at my insides like a wolverine clawing to get out of my stomach. I fought back the urge to vomit.

"Last week, Scarlet Lane barely spoke to me. She's always been nice, but Scarlet dates guys like Nick. Not guys like me. Why do you think news of the kiss spread so quickly across the Truman High Rumor Mill, as you call it? Scarlet kissing someone right after Nick's passing is crazy. Scarlet kissing *me* is absolute insanity. Everyone at school knows it."

The words stung as they rolled over my tongue. I said it. Happy, Mr. Bryant? I'm a loser.

After a few seconds of silence, Mr. Bryant pushed back from the table. "Fair enough. I won't belabor it. If

Scarlet's behavior continues, will you call me, Bax?" He slid a business card to Mom. "Her parents are worried."

I nodded, keeping my attention fixed on the table.

"I appreciate your time. Both of you. I don't want to make you late for school, Bax. Sara, I'm sorry for barging in." He took one last drink of his coffee, then set the mug down.

"No need to apologize. I hope you find out the truth about Nick." Mom escorted Mr. Bryant to the door.

I kicked my chair back, grabbed my backpack, and stomped to the door, hoping to slip out behind Mr. Bryant and avoid a follow-up interrogation by Mom. I couldn't deal with that.

Mom slammed the door behind Mr. Bryant before I could escape. She leaned against it.

"Hold on, Baxter. Why didn't you tell me that Scarlet—"

"Please don't, Mom." I spoke to the closed door, unable to look at her. "Yes, the girl I've crushed on forever finally started paying attention to me. Yes, she kissed me. Yes, it was because she's grieving the guy who she really loved. Yes, it hurt like hell to tell her to go away, but I did because it was the right thing to do. And no, I don't want to relive every high school humiliation with you. So please don't ask why I didn't tell you."

I yanked the door open from under her hand and slipped into the hallway, not looking back in order to hide the tears pooled in my tired, bloodshot eyes.

****

The morning rumble of Truman High hummed in

my ears: distant talking, banging lockers, books hitting the floor. The hypnotic drone soothing me to sleep while my heart raced from the onslaught of caffeine. I tossed the paper coffee cup into the trash and smacked myself in the cheek.

Jason wasn't waiting at my locker, so I couldn't share the new information I'd learned. Oddly, Ashley wasn't around either. If she'd known her dad stopped by to question me, she'd be badgering me about what happened.

I grabbed the beat-up algebra book from my locker. How would I keep myself awake in algebra? As I shut my locker, a voice floated over my shoulder. "Hey, Bax."

Her voice caused me to shiver with dread. I turned around, holding my textbook tight against my chest, a barrier to separate us.

The enchanting sparkle in Scarlet's eyes became venomous flames. God, she hated me. She hated whatever I'd done, even though she couldn't articulate what *it* was. She knew a connection existed between the creature and me. No one else benefited from her going out with me.

I played dumb. "Look, Scarlet, I'm not sure what's going on, but I'm not comfortable seeing you. I mean, I like you, but—"

Pink blotches erupted on her porcelain cheeks. Her nostrils flared. "Well, I'm falling in love with you, so this thing is happening. Like I said, because I love you."

The phrase tore at my insides. I kept playing dumb. It's the only option. "You don't love me. I don't know what is up with you, but—"

"You don't? Really?" Her jaw muscles quivered under her clenched teeth. Her raised voice caused students to look over, ready for the Daily Baxter Allen Spectacle.

"No, I don't! I don't know." I wanted to tell her the truth, but that wouldn't fix anything. It'd only confirm I had something to do with Nick's death. She'd never overlook or forgive that.

"Well, I've always liked you," her lips barely parted, "so I'm glad we can be together now. I'll see you at lunch."

"You have to stop this!" My brain—running on coffee fumes—scrambled for some combination of words to explain we needed to keep a distance. To make sure she understood that she's setting us both up as suspects in Nick's death if she continued down this path. That said, if she did leave me alone, I couldn't protect her parents from Ifrit.

"The cops visited me today." I lowered my voice. "They think you're acting strange."

Her eyes narrowed. "They came to visit *you*? So they think what?"

"I-I don't know. That it's suspicious how you keep telling people we're together right after Nick's death."

A sinister glimmer of pleasure twinkled in her bright eyes, making the hairs on my forearms tingle. She folded her arms across her chest. "Really? I guess it *is* pretty awful to be dating someone else so soon. Do you agree?"

"Yes! That's why you need to stop."

"Well, I can't...can't...deny my love." She winced. The words burned her throat.

"'Deny my love?' You don't even talk like that.

Scar—"

She spun, stomping away. I didn't need to see her face to know she'd started to cry.

I spun around and slammed my forehead into the cold metal of my locker, making the mistake of closing my eyes for more than a blink. They instantly grew heavy, begging me to let them rest. My legs became liquid. My algebra book slipped from my hands to the floor. The hallway commotion around me melted into peaceful quiet.

Wake up!

I stood up straight again, shaking my hands out, then bent over and picked up my textbook. The commotion returned, hammering my ears again. I took a few deep breaths.

"Hey, man, you tired?" Jason nudged me, almost knocking me over. "I'd swear you just fell asleep standing up."

The most glorious two seconds of my life.

"You're a mess." He only half-smiled.

"I think I figured out the language of the incantation." If I didn't spit out what I had to say soon, I'd pass out on my feet again. "It's Sumerian."

"Wow."

"Yeah, wow. Now, I need someone who can translate a dead language. One that people stopped using a couple thousand years ago."

Jason didn't hesitate. "Dad might be able to recommend someone at the university."

Dropping one hand on each of Jason's shoulders, I leaned into him, letting a smile spread across my face like an insane person. "Shit. Of course! Can you ask him? Like, right away?"

"Yeah."

"Can you do it soon? I can't stay up like this forever. I'm dead on my feet."

Jason dropped his voice. "Ifrit doesn't do stuff every single time you sleep, right? You should get some rest."

"I can't risk it. Ashley's dad stopped by my place this morning to question me about Scarlet's weird behavior. This thing keeps snowballing."

"Really? What did you tell him?"

"That she's grieving, and I'm trying to give her space." I shook my head, wanting to erase the painful conversation that happened seconds before Jason found me dosing off. "When can you ask your dad about translating Sumerian?"

"I'll call him after Algebra. He's teaching right now."

Malcolm and Gerald rounded the corner. They were shoving each other and yelling loudly, but noticed me as soon as they entered the hallway.

Malcolm gave Gerald a hard shove away from him. His laugh faded, laser-focused on me.

Too many kids still filled the hallway for him to come at me directly. At least, not the day after our conversation with Mr. Clark.

I hoped.

Wrong.

Malcolm didn't care. His stride quickened, parting the river of students as he set a direct course for me, his mouth curled into a snarl.

I didn't wait for the bell. I jumped in front of Jason into Mr. Beatty's classroom. I'd never been so thankful to see Mr. Beatty at his desk reviewing papers.

"Early, Mr. Allen? Come on in."

The bell rang, but I barely heard it with my heart beating in my ears. I collapsed into my seat, safe from Malcolm—for now.

Jason would call his dad right after Algebra, and with any luck, I'd skip out after lunch to meet with someone who read Sumerian. Then I'd banish Ifrit, get some sleep, and try to reassemble my life tomorrow. That's the plan.

My entire body melted into the uncomfortable desk chair as Mr. Beatty welcomed everyone and said something about a quiz.

Within seconds, I drifted off to sleep.

Chapter 18

Tom stared at his computer screen; his eyes watered from the harsh glare. He never understood how people worked on computers all day long, staring for endless hours at a monitor. One of his oldest friends made big money as a programmer. Not for him.

With the file of Nick Ruiz open on his computer, Tom scribbled more notes about the case on the yellow pad next to his keyboard. A big fat question mark followed each note. The case was "unfortunately closed," in Chief Walton's opinion. Tom couldn't argue it. While strange, it appeared someone impersonating a football scout invited Ruiz to a bar, got him liquored up, perhaps to kidnap him, rape him, or something else unseemly, but then left him at the bar unharmed. Maybe the pervert saw someone he recognized, and that frightened him off. Then Ruiz had no choice but to drive home and ended up going right off the road. Still, something didn't feel right.

Tom glanced at the clock. *11:00 a.m.* He'd been sitting at his desk all morning. His doctor lectured him every visit about how he needed to be more active. When he joined the force, he never expected to spend so much time in an office. Sure, a desk job lowered his risk of being shot, but it wouldn't save him from a heart attack.

Ashley tried getting him to wear a watch to count

his steps. Yeah, right, like he'd wear a bracelet to work. The guys would laugh him right out of the station.

Scooting his chair back, he stretched his arms to the ceiling. His back popped in response. Time to get active.

Tom opened his office door. The conversations, paper rustling, and phones ringing in the bullpen flurried around him. Across the way, a small group of officers and staff sang Happy Birthday to Monica, the new receptionist. He'd introduce himself later.

"Hey, Tom."

"Hey, Bart." Tom waved.

Crossing the bullpen, Tom opened the door to the stairwell. He promised Jennifer and Ashley he'd walk flights of the Police HQ stairs. Get his blood moving. It helped him refocus, too. However, his stair workout didn't seem to be shrinking his gut, which expanded each year. Getting older sucked.

Tom took a breath and started up the stairs, mindful of keeping his breathing steady and deep. He hit the first landing, turned, continued up to the next landing, turned, and then up to the second floor. As he began his walk up to the third floor, a woman in a delicate pea-green dress rounded the corner. She had wispy brown hair speckled with premature gray and breasts way younger than the rest of her.

"Hello, Claire." Tom nodded.

"Well, hi, Tom." Claire's southern accent gave her an endearing charm. She had to be ten years older than him but didn't look or act like it. She was the chief's assistant but always brought Tom a coffee when he needed a switch from the dishwater coffee in the breakroom.

"Tom, this whole stair idea is incredible. Really helps keep the midday drolls away. Genius."

He smiled. "Can't take all the credit. Heard about it from Roger."

"Roger Pinkerton?" Claire covered her smile with a modest hand. "He doesn't look like he walks many stairs."

Tom chuckled but didn't say anything.

"We should walk together sometime." Claire lightly grazed the back of her neck with her manicured fingertips as she winked.

Tom's cheeks grew warm. Claire had a naturally flirty way, but she just winked at him. Unless he misread her. It could be her contact lens bothering her. She did have *that* kind of personality. He joked it away. "Claire, we'll have the entire floor whispering by the second landing if we walk together."

She giggled again. "Is that a bad thing?"

Tom's heart skipped. He didn't recognize Claire's forwardness. What should he say? Should he call it out? Politely remind her he's a happily married man of eighteen years? What if she didn't mean anything by it, and saying something embarrassed her, hurting their friendship? Jesus, was he back in high school or what?

Claire's soft fingers brushed his forearm, sending a clear message. "How about instead of bringing you coffee, next time we go out for coffee? Or lunch?"

Alarms sounded in Tom's mind. A blaring DEFCON One alarm. Claire—an actual woman—just asked him out. That hadn't happened since his bachelor party, and strippers didn't really count.

He eased his arm away from her. "I'm very sorry, Claire. I have a wife and daughter."

J. L. Sullivan

Taking a step back, she rested a hand high on her chest. "Oh my, but you don't wear a wedding band."

Tom glanced at his hand. He'd forgotten. "I'm embarrassed to say, my ring has gone and shrunk on me. In other words, my finger got fat. We're saving up to put in an extension."

"Well, aren't I a fool?" She diverted her eyes to the scuffed gray-green wall.

"No, no, no, Claire! Perfectly innocent mistake. How were you to know? Really, it's not a big deal, not at all. In fact, I am quite flattered. You are way out of my league." He grinned awkwardly.

She took a deep breath, held it, then blew it out. "Well, I'd appreciate you not reporting me to HR."

Tom laughed, more out of discomfort than her joke. His big laugh carried up the stairwell. "I wouldn't dream of it. Besides, you didn't do anything wrong."

"Well, you finish your stairs and have a good afternoon, Tom." She continued down, passing by him. Her perfume lingered behind.

As she disappeared around the corner, his heart sank. He loved Jennifer and would never cheat on her, but he hoped he hadn't damaged Claire's and his friendship.

With a sigh, he started up the stairs again for a couple more flights.

Third floor.

Fourth floor.

He started to pant, pausing to catch his breath. Damn, he'd gotten out of shape. That may be enough for today.

"Tom?" Claire called from below, her voice echoing in the stairwell. "You still up there?"

228

He took in a few quick breaths, not wanting to appear winded when she arrived. "Up here."

She rounded the corner to the fourth-floor landing to meet him.

"There're no hard feelings, right?" She struggled to catch her breath, too.

He smiled. "Of course not, Claire. None at all."

"I am glad to hear that." As she said the words, her lips thinned, and her eyebrows met over her nose. "But I wish you would have accepted my offer. Now I have to do it the hard way."

"Claire? What do you mean, the hard way?" She'd never so much as scowled at another living thing. Was she angry?

With the strength of ten men, Claire grabbed Tom's forearms and flung him around her, launching him down the stairs like a doll.

He hit the steps, which jabbed his belly, then the momentum rolled him, shoulders over legs, down the flight. Pain exploded in his mouth as he bit down on his tongue, biting through it. The inside of his head rattled.

When his body crashed to a stop on the landing, he tried to steady his spinning head and crawl to his knees. He'd lost his mind for sure. Claire couldn't have just done that.

A gust of wind shot by him like a passenger train. Claire appeared, straddling him with a wide stance, a pink-heeled shoe on each side of him.

"Claire?" His eyes were playing tricks on him. "What's—"

She stepped to one side and grabbed his left leg. Like a golf club, with two hands, she swung him, sending him hurtling down the stairs again.

He rolled this time, shoulder over shoulder. His chest popped, sending searing pain through his torso. His failed attempt to stop himself with his hands caused his arm to snap at the elbow. Pain shot through him like he'd touched a live wire.

She waited at the next landing. Her pea-green sundress rode high on her thighs as she squatted like a quarterback ready to hike.

Claire yanked him by the hair, launching him face-first down the next flight. His chin smacked against one concrete stair, then the next, then the next. The hard edges punched him over and over as they dragged down his chest and gut. By the third punch into his groin, the pain became numb.

He skidded to a stop at the landing. The blood dripping into his eyes made it difficult to see. His head spun. Up and down seemed like the same direction.

He reached out blindly, needing something to ground him. Needing a reference point. His fingers grazed the beveled wood of a door frame.

A door!

He couldn't seem to control his right arm, so with his left, he clawed up the door, searching for the damn doorknob. He tried to yell for help, but his lungs lost the ability to expand. He could only take short, shallow puffs.

"Now, Tom." Claire's southern accent became sinister.

Panicked, Tom wiped the blood from his eyes with his working hand as it shook fiercely. He'd talk and reason with Claire. But as he opened his mouth, his tongue, swollen and cut, scraped against his broken teeth.

Claire leaned down, her dress falling forward, any remaining ladylike modesty gone. The sweet perfume floating around her changed, smelling more like burnt hair. "A lady doesn't take no for an answer," she whispered into his ear.

When she stood back up, her green eyes faded into a dull purple.

Blood ran into Tom's eyes, blinding him. As he raised his hand to clear his sight, his body rose into the air. Two dainty hands lifted him, one under his shoulders and one under his ass.

"Claire, wait," Tom tried to say, but instead, just gurgled blood.

After an effortless heave, Tom sailed through the air.

He floated weightlessly for a split second, the wind rushing by him, all sound drowned out. Almost peaceful. Then he slammed on the stairs, face first, the inertia continuing his descent head over feet, rolling and sliding down the final flight of steps. His body didn't stop until the ground floor when he crashed into the door leading to the police station.

Everything went black.

****

I woke with a loud gasp, unable to breathe. A rocket launched along my spine, stiffening my back. My knees slammed against the underside of my desk with a bang.

No, no, no, no.

My commotion alerted Mr. Beatty, along with the rest of the class. He pointed his dry erase marker at me. "Should I bother to ask you to repeat what I shared with your fellow students, Mr. Allen?"

My hands trembled, barely hearing my teacher.

Desks, Mr. Beatty, and an algebra book wet with drool, but no Police Station stairwell. I was in Algebra class.

"I'm sorry. I—"

"You can report to Nurse Masson." Mr. Beatty shook his head in a dramatic gesture of disappointment. "I'm going to attribute this to your illness, not disrespect toward your classmates or me."

Jason, from the front of the classroom, had turned around in his chair like everyone else. "Did it happen?" he mouthed.

I nodded. Vomit swirled in my gut, then erupted up my throat. I swallowed it down before it escaped.

Mr. Bryant.

"Can you stand, Baxter?" Mr. Beatty took a few steps down the aisle.

I pushed up from my desk. One hand remained on the desktop, with my legs wobbling under me.

"Mr. Johnson, please help Baxter to Nurse Masson's office."

"W-Who me?" Andy Johnson acted as if Beatty just asked him to perform a ballet in front of the class.

"I can walk." I let go of my desk. "I'll go see Nurse Masson."

At least it would get me out of class, and give my brain a chance to catch up.

Chapter 19

"Nurse Masson said you're all good." Mrs. Bronson crossed her legs, hands folded and resting on the notepad in her lap. We faced each other in the black vinyl chairs near the window. She never liked having sessions sitting on opposite sides of her desk. The framed picture of her chocolate lab on the table between us stared at me with sad eyes. His name was Rider or Diver—I couldn't remember.

"Like I said, I stayed up too late and fell asleep. It wasn't an episode." I checked out the clock on her desk, thinking only about Ifrit/Claire throwing Mr. Bryant down flight after flight of stairs. I flinched, his snapping bones and desperate gasps to avoid choking on his own blood still rang in my ears.

Please let me out of here.

Every lost minute meant more time where I didn't contact a Sumerian translator and increased my odds of falling asleep again, unleashing Ifrit on an unsuspecting person in my life.

Mrs. Bronson did her patient pause thing, giving me time to change my answer. For a moment, I'd forgotten what I said.

"My episodes happen when I'm under pressure and embarrassed, right? Not when I'm sitting through Beatty's algebra class."

"Baxter." Mrs. Bronson scribbled on her pad,

noticeable bags hung under her eyes. "Staying up too late doesn't help vasovagal syncope. In fact, it can make it worse. Not getting enough sleep stresses the body. Stress is your trigger, not just anxiousness."

Wrong. If stress were the trigger, I'd have spent this entire week passed out.

"I had a project to do." I stuck to my story.

"What project?"

Crap.

The homework excuse worked on Mom and Jason's parents, not on a woman with access to my academic schedule.

She glanced at my foot, rapidly tapping on the floor. I stopped.

"Look, I stayed up late playing video games. Is that a crime?"

"I'd hoped we'd meet after your episode at the assembly." She flipped through her notebook. "I don't think meeting every three weeks is enough. I'll be honest, Baxter, I'm concerned about you."

"Why?" I glanced at the clock again.

"Well, Nick's death is weighing on everyone. That happened right after your episode, followed by your fight in the cafeteria, and now you're falling asleep in class. Why shouldn't I be worried?"

Nick's death weighed on me, but not because I mourned the loss of the first professional football player to come out of Truman High. And why did everyone keep calling Malcolm's sucker punch *a fight?*

"They're all unrelated. Coincidental."

"Tell me more."

Ugh.

Thirty minutes before the final bell. I had to

convince her I wasn't in a downward spiral to end the session.

"First, the assembly episode happened because I couldn't answer a trivia question while the entire school stared at me. Second, I knew *of* Nick but didn't really know him. I feel bad for his family and friends, but I'm not one of them. Third, Malcolm attacked me in the cafeteria because that's how he grieves. I never hit him, so that doesn't qualify as a fight. And fourth, I stayed up too late playing video games. Irresponsible, yeah, but hardly a sign of a mental breakdown. They're all unrelated."

She waited to see if I wanted to add a fifth. When I didn't, she nodded, scribbling on her pad. We weren't done. I had to give her something to get out of here. Something we could explore together in a future session.

"Maybe a classmate's death did make an impact, now that I think about it." I slowed my words, pretending to just come to a realization. "I mean, the idea someone my age could suddenly die is kinda…freaky."

Guilt might have been the more appropriate way to describe how I felt.

"Really?" She straightened in the subtlest way. "Tell me more." Her favorite phrase.

"Nick acted like an asshole. He and his friends called me Flower because of the assembly, in case you hadn't heard. Despite that, I didn't want him to die." Saying it out loud to someone other than Jason or Ashley liberated me, part of a weight lifted.

"You didn't have anything to do with Nick's situation. You understand that, don't you?" She set her pen down to focus on me.

"Yeah."

"Baxter, losing a classmate is tough, but your opinion of Nick—positive or negative—didn't cause his death."

If she only knew how dangerously close she circled to the truth. I needed to end this conversation.

"I know." I struggled to restrain myself from rechecking the clock. Mrs. Bronson's calm, rhythmic way of speaking, the sun rays from the window warming my shoulders, and the drone of the ventilation system pumping in air made my eyelids grow heavy. My nap in Algebra didn't help. In fact, after the adrenaline from the nightmare faded, exhaustion began slithering back. I had to figure out a way to sleep without dreaming. I couldn't keep this up.

"Baxter?" Mrs. Bronson waved her hand. "You still with me?"

"Huh? Sorry, I'm exhausted."

"I can see. Why don't you go home before the bell rings? Get some sleep tonight. I'll write you a sick pass."

Awake again, I jumped out of my seat. I'd planned on begging for a pass. "Thanks."

"Wait, wait, wait." She rose to meet me. "I'm going to schedule a time to follow up, but what I want you to do before then is write down your feelings about Nick's death."

"Homework?"

She rested her fists on her hips. "I won't read it. Sometimes writing helps. Bring it to our next session for discussion. You're tired now, but I'd like us to explore how Nick's death has impacted you. Sound like a plan?"

I nodded. "Sure." Whatever. I had to get home.

After she nodded, I took measured steps to her office door. The instant her door clicked shut behind me, I sprinted down the hallway. Without breaking stride, I checked my phone. No messages from Jason. Weird.

I stopped running and texted him.

—Call me after final bell.—

Then, I took a detour, jogging down the east hallway to grab my backpack from my locker. I skidded to a stop in front of it.

Vandalism decorated the beat-up metal door. Someone had drawn a flower—a daisy, more specifically—in black marker on it. Below it, they'd scribbled *DICK* with an arrow pointing to the flower. Under that, someone had started writing *ASSHO* without finishing.

A public branding forever emblazoned on my high school home base. Awesome. I shook my head. Nope, not this time. It wouldn't set me off.

I ignored it, yanking out my backpack. I had more important things to deal with and was way too tired for some graffiti to bother me.

Slamming the locker shut, I raced home.

****

Six o'clock and still no calls or texts from Ashley or Jason. I'd texted them twice, but no response.

Jason saw me wake up in Algebra. By now, he probably heard about Mr. Bryant and put the pieces together. Which made it even weirder he wasn't texting me back. Plus, Jason needed to find us a Sumerian translator at his dad's school—soon.

I scoured the web, figuring a beat-up detective in a police station would make news but found nothing. I even searched Mr. Bryant's name reluctantly, relieved when I didn't find any mention of his death.

My tired eyes burned from staring at my laptop screen. I shifted gears and typed "dreamless sleep" into my browser. Since Ifrit connected to my subconscious through dreams, I needed to shut them down. Skipping sleep altogether couldn't continue.

A couple of medical websites warned how sleeping pills interrupted REM sleep, which was when people dreamed. REM was also when the brain reset for the next day. So without REM sleep, a person's mood and memory could be negatively impacted—thus the warnings. I'd have to deal with that later. If sleeping pills meant no REM sleep, and no REM sleep meant no dreams, then I'd found my temporary solution. Bingo.

I searched *over-the-counter sleeping pills.*

Moxidryl.

I searched *How much Moxidryl should I take to fall asleep?*

It was frighteningly easy to figure out how to knock myself out. The internet made taking drugs super easy.

Out of the corner of my eye, my phone lit up, catching my attention. I grabbed it. Just an email notification advertising *Archer Annihilation* T-shirts.

"Come on, man."

I redialed Jason.

This time, the third ring stopped midtone.

"Jason! Where have you been? Did you ask your dad? Wait, first, how's Mr. Bryant? Ashley's not returning my texts. Is he okay?"

"Hey." Jason mumbled a one-word, monotone reply.

My stomach wretched. "Oh no, is he…"

"In the hospital." Jason stopped me from finishing. "Critical condition, but he'll make it. Lots, and I mean lots, of broken bones. No one can figure out what happened. They think he tripped down the stairs, but he somehow hit a landing, then kept falling to the next landing. Down four flights. Almost like someone repeatedly pushed him."

"Or something," I mumbled.

Silence hung between us. Silence never hung between us. We were best friends.

Jason didn't ask about my dream, and I didn't offer. Details didn't matter at this point.

"How's Ashley?"

"Not great."

"Does she know about my dream?"

Jason paused. "Yeah, she knew her dad stopped by your place this morning, and she heard you fell asleep in Algebra. She concluded that Ifrit didn't appreciate the interrogation." Jason chose each word with care, something he never did around me.

"I've been trying to get ahold of her to apologize."

"Don't, Bax."

"Why?" I squeezed the edge of my comforter in a fist. I knew why.

Jason sighed. "She, um, she asked me to tell you not to call or text her."

"She knows I would never—"

"She does. She doesn't think you did it intentionally. Obviously."

Whatever. I had to contact her. At least text her

again. I couldn't stay silent like a criminal or like we weren't friends.

"And, Bax." Jason cleared his throat. "I think we should take a step away from each other, too. Some space."

The phone almost slipped out of my hand. A step away from each other? My throat closed tight. I couldn't breathe. I needed Jason and Ashley. What if the incantation didn't work? What then? They were the only people in the world who could help me banish Ifrit.

"W-what? You don't blame me, do you?" Every muscle in my body tensed, dreading his answer. They'd been with me since the beginning. They knew how Ifrit worked. That I couldn't control him.

"No," Jason said meekly.

"You do!" I leaped from my bed.

Jason paused a bit too long. "Man, we don't blame you. That's the truth. We're scared. Scared of accidentally pissing you off, causing Ifrit to come after us. Honestly, I'm terrified telling you we need some distance is like asking Ifrit to throw me down four flights of stairs—or worse."

His words stung. I couldn't think of a response. Of course, I scared them. I couldn't control Ifrit. We kept saying the djinn were *ours*, but Janni and Ifrit had always been mine. And as long as Ifrit roamed the world, he endangered everyone in my life.

"Bax, we started this with you, and we really wanted to help end it. We owe you that much, but we're not sure what else to do. You're safe from Ifrit. He won't touch you. We're not."

"I might have found a way to stop dreaming." If I

didn't dream, Ashley and Jason could feel safer. "Sleeping pills. They should keep Ifrit out of my subconscious."

"That's great news." Jason's words fell flat.

More silence.

I scrambled to think of something to say. Something to keep Jason on the phone. What could I say to reassure him when I couldn't control Ifrit?

"I didn't forget about asking my dad," Jason said. "I'll email you the name of a professor who can translate Sumerian."

I'd forgotten. The incantation had temporarily disappeared from my mind. "Oh, yeah. Thanks."

"Well, I'd better go."

"Wait!" I sounded desperate but didn't care. "We'll be friends again when this is over. Right?"

"We'll *still* be friends. I mean, if you don't hate me for bailing on you."

"I will." I forced an awkward sound that resembled a chuckle. "But I understand why. I hate it, but I understand."

Jason sniffed. Crying? "Well, I'd better—"

"I have an idea!" Nope, not letting him hang up. "What if I summon Ifrit? I'll command him to leave you and Ashley alone. Plus Ashley's parents, and yours, and Mom. I'll come up with a list and block him. I'll try that."

"Our offensive maneuver didn't work the last time we tried. He basically laughed at us. Remember?"

"Jason, please." I wanted to convince him not to hang up and leave me alone in this battle, but any association with me had become life-threatening. I couldn't guarantee their safety. That should be my priority.

"Okay. Later."

He hung up with a click that hit my ears like a sonic boom, leaving a void of crushing loneliness.

I inhaled, held it, then exhaled, clearing my mind of any negative feelings toward Jason or Ashley, no matter how deep down. I understood why they tapped out, but that didn't make the conversation burn any less.

I'd told Ashley we were friends after the perfume incident, and I meant it. Now, because of me, her dad was in critical condition for doing his job. No matter what she told Jason, I couldn't just leave her alone. Not when I caused Ifrit to go after her dad. Especially when she literally lived across the hall from me.

I marched out of our apartment and down the hall to Ashley's, my footfalls heavy on the wood floorboards, pounding with determination. My stomach, however, twisted with nerves. What if her mom answered? What would I say? Her mom wouldn't know I caused the accident. She wouldn't ask about it.

I knocked on her front door.

I'd apologize and see if I could do anything to help. Not sure what, but I'd offer.

Not a peep from inside.

I knocked again.

Jason's words rang in my ears. *I think we should take a step away from each other, too. Some space.*

I waited before knocking again, listening for any signs they were home.

My knuckles barely made contact with her door on my final knock. Someone would have answered if they were home. They were probably at the hospital.

Running a hand through my hair, I slid to the floor,

my back against her cold front door. I banged my head against it. I'd be taking a step away from her after all.

No, one more try.

I pulled my phone from my pocket and dialed. Three rings, then to voicemail.

"Hey, Ashley, it's me." I didn't have a plan, but after a deep breath, I just started talking. "I am so sorry for all of this. I'm sorry about your dad. Jason said you don't want to talk to me. I understand, but…the other day at the park when we saw Scarlet. You told me how after my episode in fifth grade, you didn't say anything, and now realize, looking back, you should have said something. That I didn't have any friends and was probably lonely."

I swallowed the frog in my throat. "Well, we're friends now. I can't just step away. So, please know I'm sorry and am working really hard to fix our situation. I understand why you're mad, or sad, or both. Whenever you are ready to call me back, I'll be here. Even if you just want to yell at me or curse me out. Whatever you want. Okay? Okay. Bye."

The quiet of the hallway beat in my ears. I slipped the phone into my pocket and slid up the door to my feet, heading back to my apartment.

Jason and Ashley had to distance themselves. Ifrit left them no choice. Maybe that was his intent. Drive me into isolation from the world.

He wouldn't win. I didn't care what Jason said. I'd give it one last shot with Ifrit. Command him to leave everyone alone. I had to try.

Back in my bedroom, I rolled my blinds closed, then grabbed Ifrit's box from under my stack of sweaters. Last time, Ifrit mocked us when we told him to go to a deserted island until summoned, so I had to be more specific to protect the people I loved. It couldn't make things any worse.

I dragged my thumb over the hideous jewel, the heat instantly rising within me. Sweat beaded my forehead. My arm hair stood at attention. As my blood burned and the invisible needles stung the back of my eyes, the distinct, repulsive odor rolled in.

I spun around, searching my room.

Charcoal-colored smoke crawled along the floor around Ifrit, lapping up my carpet. He rubbed his clawed hands together, flexing the veiny muscles of his forearms.

"Hello, Baxter Allen." Ifrit snarled.

The sight of him still sent shivers down my back, but I focused on my friends' safety, not my fear. I refused to cower.

"I forbid you to do anything to anyone else without my permission." I pointed at him, commanding him like a dog. "That includes Jason Franklin, Ashley Bryant, either of their families, my mom, any teachers at school, or other kids at Truman High. Nothing. Do you hear me? You don't hurt any human. No more!"

A grumble of a laugh vibrated from his mouth between the saliva drippings. He leaned forward, his snout inches from my face, his breath like the heat from an oven. I held my ground, even with the heat searing my skin.

"I grant wishes. I grant wants."

"No, I command you to stop granting my wishes or wants!"

Ifrit rose to full height, his curled horns pressing into the ceiling, imprinting dents. "You don't command me. We are one."

Ifrit's tail whipped around and, with a sharp crack, sliced me across the cheek.

My hand flew to my face. I quickly dropped it back to my side. He wouldn't see my pain. I clenched my fists, willing the sting away, ignoring the blood trickling down my chin. I wouldn't give him the satisfaction. "I'm not you. Not at all."

His pointed tongue traced his razor teeth. "Ah, but you are."

Tears of desperate rage blurred my vision. I refused to let them escape by blinking. "Go away!"

He vanished.

I dove onto my bed and shoved my face deep into my pillow. I yelled, then yelled again. I didn't scream words. I just screamed. Tears soaked my pillow, diluting the blood from my cheek that stained it. He would never go away.

I slammed my fists on my mattress, pounding, the vibrations running through the bed springs and ricocheting back. He'd be with me forever—a constant threat to anyone in my life.

Minutes passed, and as the adrenaline from my tantrum faded, exhaustion crept over me. It soaked into every pore of my skin.

Focus, Bax. Get yourself together.

Crying like a baby wouldn't solve anything.

Jason promised to send the name of someone who could translate Sumerian, but it was too late for that to happen tonight anyway. And if tomorrow would be my final showdown with Ifrit, I needed some rest.

I scribbled a note to Mom that my stomach ached, and I grabbed the Moxidryl from the bathroom. Then, downing the pills with some water, I collapsed into bed.

Almost instantly, the coma-like sleep shut my entire body down.

Chapter 20

I peeled my dry eyes open after my drug-induced sleep, wiping the crusty gunk out of them. My mouth tasted like I'd chugged a bucket of sand overnight. I'd crashed hard with no recollection of new nightmares. Maybe it worked.

It only took a few seconds awake, though, before vivid details about Mr. Bryant reminded me why I'd taken the sleeping pills to begin with. The horrible conversation with Jason followed.

"They'll be safer this way. That's what's important." I buried the feelings of betrayal down deep, hidden from Ifrit. I didn't have time to dwell on disappointment. Time to translate an incantation.

In the mirror over my dresser, my finger gingerly skimmed the cut on my cheek, two inches long and crusted over with dried blood. I might be in just as much physical danger as those in my life.

Mom banged dishes around in the kitchen. Local news blared from the TV. I couldn't make out the words, but newscasters spoke with a familiar cadence.

I grabbed my phone.

Please have a text from Jason.
Please have a text from Jason.

An email notification flashed on my phone's screen—from Jason!

I tapped it.

Hey—Dr. Bashir at Wash U can translate Sumerian. He studies Ancient Languages. Dad asked him to help us with a school project. I figured you'd want to go in person. His office hours are nine a.m. to eleven a.m. today. Below is his address. Good luck. We finished Archer Annihilation, and that involved taking down an entire kingdom. Ifrit will be a piece of cake.

I smiled, the *Archer Annihilation* joke igniting hope that life could return to how it used to be. Back when my biggest worry was missing curfew to play a video game.

I absorbed every detail of his email, rereading it. One step closer, I couldn't waste time. I'd skip first period to visit Dr. Bashir during his office hours. Mrs. Conway loved me, and I had a B plus. Having never missed one of her classes, she'd let me off with a warning and may not even report it.

"Bax, come have breakfast," Mom called from the kitchen. "I gotta leave soon."

"In a minute." I printed out the pic of Ifrit's incantation, folded it, then shoved it into my pocket. I couldn't lug Ifrit's box with me and risk raising suspicion. I doubted many high schoolers owned an ancient Sumerian artifact.

"Bax, I want to see you before I leave."

"Coming!"

I detoured to the bathroom, wet some toilet paper, wiped as much of the dried blood off my cheek as I could, then splashed water on my face. Not perfect, but it'd have to do.

Mom ate her cereal, dabbing her mouth with a napkin when I walked in. She had turned the TV off, sitting in silence, reading on her phone. Usually, we passed by each other on mornings with work and school, frantically getting ready.

"Hey." I poured myself a bowl of cereal. No dirty dishes in the sink, and the scent of lemons freshened the air. She'd already cleaned the kitchen. How long ago did she wake up?

"What was going on in there?" She sipped her coffee, holding her mug with both hands. "You sounded very busy for first thing in the morning."

Something was up with her.

"Finishing up a history project." I didn't even think about it. The lie just rolled smoothly out of my mouth.

"Ah." She squinted. "The swelling on your jaw seems to be going down."

I touched the bump. I'd forgotten about it. "Doesn't hurt anymore."

She cocked her head. "You cut yourself?"

"Yeah, shaving." I shrugged, playing it cool. I shoved a spoonful into my mouth, pretending to only half pay attention. Pretending not to notice she wanted to talk about something.

"You need to take care of that handsome face." She worked her cereal with her spoon. She never played with her food, especially with such concerted effort.

I didn't have time for a long conversation. Bashir's office hours started at nine.

"Bax—"

Here it comes.

"—Mrs. Bronson called."

A glob of milk-soaked cereal solidified in my throat.

Shit.

I had escaped The Call for too long. Mrs. Bronson

couldn't have waited one more day? Just until this nightmare ended? One day?

"She's worried about you. So am I. She told me about algebra class."

She paused. Waiting for my reaction.

I gave her an overly dramatic, confused look, as if she'd started speaking in some other language—maybe Sumerian.

"I stayed up late playing video games. I told her that." I never lied to Mom more than in the past few weeks. I shoveled that into the Guilt Bucket with everything else. "It really wasn't VS like she thinks. Which is why I didn't tell you. That's why I went to bed so early yesterday. I was exhausted."

She chose her words carefully, swirling her remaining coffee in the mug. "You realize, hon, staying up late playing video games isn't exactly student of the year behavior."

Lying to her formed a rock in my gut. I couldn't keep worrying and disappointing her. "I've never done it before. It was a one-time thing. I'm a kid. I'm allowed to mess up sometimes."

She nodded. "Okay." She took a final sip of her coffee but kept watching me.

I needed one more day—less than that. In an hour or two, I'd read the translated incantation, and life would return to normal.

Mom squared her shoulders. "Here's the deal, Bax. The VS, the fighting, whatever is up with you and Scarlet, falling asleep in class, even that cut on your cheek—which is not a shaving accident, by the way— all started around the time I smelled that odor in your room. I noticed yesterday you broke your lamp. Are you on drugs? You won't be in trouble. I want to help you, but you need to be honest with me."

My lamp? I'd forgotten Ifrit's tail smashed it.

Mom's hand clutched her spoon, about to bend it in half.

I hated myself for doing this to her.

"No, Mom. I'm not on drugs."

She stared at me—her way of waiting for my confession.

"I'll take a drug test if you don't believe me."

"Not fair, Bax. You have to admit, you've had a very sudden change in your behavior."

"I knocked over the lamp in my sleep, and the cut originally came from Malcolm's punch, but I scraped it shaving, making it bigger. That's why it doesn't look like a razor nick."

Lying seemed to be a skill I'd mastered.

She closed her eyes. "I got a referral from Mrs. Bronson for a doctor. A psychologist."

"Something we can't afford."

"We'll make it work. Don't worry about the money. You've had three VS episodes now since last year."

"Two! Algebra wasn't VS, just a need for sleep. I know the difference."

She released her spoon from her death grip and sighed. She patted my hand. "All right, fine. The point is, you're the most important person to me, Baxter. I think seeing a psychologist may help."

Denying it wouldn't work. If Mom wanted me to see a psychologist, I'd do it. Besides, if the incantation banished Ifrit, this would all be behind me.

"Okay, I'll see whoever Mrs. Bronson referred.

And I promise I'm not on drugs."

Every muscle in Mom seemed to relax, a weight lifted off her. "I believe you." She stood up, smoothing out her hotel uniform shirt. "I'll be home early. It's Friday. Movie night?"

I smiled. The mention of movie night—an event so distant, like Jason's joke about *Archer Annihilation*—unleashed a warm, fuzzy rush over me.

"My turn to pick." I grinned.

"Don't remind me." She ran some water over her bowl and coffee mug in the sink, then wiped her hands on her jeans.

"I'm gonna finish up a few things on that project before school. I'll lock up." I gave her the widest smile I could muster.

"Sounds good. See you tonight, hon."

I couldn't remember when I'd become so phony. The rock in my gut grew bigger. I had to translate the incantation fast.

****

I searched the poster-sized directory for the building address in Jason's email. An endless maze of tan brick buildings between meticulously maintained green space filled the campus. Paths cut between each building going in every direction. I'd never find Dr. Bashir.

Not an encouraging start to my first visit to a college campus. Mrs. Bronson started challenging me to think about where I'd be in three years. I had no idea where I'd go to college, if I went at all. If I didn't solve my djinn problem, though, God help the admissions board who rejected my application.

Not funny, Bax.

"Where is the Histories Building?" I finally asked a guy with a ponytail strolling by.

He wore baggy corduroy pants and a button-down shirt, half-open, even in the chilly October morning. He held one hand up to block the sun from his eyes and pointed with his other. "Probably that building over there, by the statue."

"Awesome. Thanks."

I jogged past a fifteen-foot-tall statue of a bald guy with glasses, holding a thick book. He pointed to the sky, lecturing the clouds.

Behind him, a four-story building with black numbers over an ornate stone archway matched the address in Jason's email. I'd found the place.

Inside, students lounged on green and dark red couches, legs up, shoes off. Some studied, but most socialized. I expected academic discussions, but from the sound bites floating around me, college student conversations mostly centered around drinking and who's hot—girls, boys, and in some cases, teachers. College seemed a lot like high school with older kids and fancier buildings.

At the top of some marble stairs, I rounded a corner and found Dr. Bashir's office. Through the open door, a man concentrated on his computer screen while pounding on his keyboard. He had light brown skin with shiny black hair and a gray goatee.

"Hello?" I knocked, sticking my head inside. "Dr. Bashir?"

He dragged his attention from the monitor, seeing me over the top of wire-rimmed glasses. "Yes?"

"I'm Baxter Allen."

He blankly stared for a moment. "Ah yes, Dr.

Franklin's son's friend. Come in. Have a seat." He stood, his demeanor softened, and he signaled to the chair across his desk. The scent of cinnamon floated up from a glass jar plugged into the wall.

"What can I do for you, Baxter?"

I slid the picture of Ifrit's incantation toward him. "We're doing a project for class. On ancient languages. Can you help us translate this? I think it's Sumerian."

Dr. Bashir lifted the paper and examined it through the bottom half of his glasses. He skimmed the page as his bushy eyebrows crinkled and unwrinkled several times.

I shoved my hands under my thighs. He studied too intensely. Reading shouldn't take this long. I hoped I didn't have the wrong language.

"Tell me about your project." He didn't take his eyes from the paper.

Why did he need to know that? "Um—"

"I ask so I can understand the context for these words."

Crap.

I worried the box would raise suspicion, not that the incantation itself would be incriminating. What if the incantation said "Kill all humans?"

I couldn't leave. No plan B. So I played dumb.

"What do you mean?"

"This is Sumerian Cuneiform. You're right. It's ancient. Where did you get it?" He still absorbed the words on the page.

"The internet." I spouted off the story I'd concocted on the bus ride to campus. "Our assignment is to compare different languages and describe how the characters vary. Find patterns in them. For example, how do Korean and Mandarin characters differ? But Jason and I wanted to also see if we could translate them. We're thinking of comparing Sumerian to Arabic."

Dr. Bashir's chair creaked as he leaned back. "Jason's always going the extra mile, that one."

"Yeah, awesome partner. We found some software to translate Arabic, but Sumerian has been harder to translate." I loosened my grip on the arm of the chair.

"No surprise. Few people can read it anymore. You found this online, you said?"

"Yeah." I scrambled. While I'd come up with a fake project, I didn't spend much time on the details. "It's a zoomed-in pic from a relic at a museum."

"Makes sense." He nodded, and his mouth curled into a reassuring smile.

I held my breath. Read something from it. Anything.

"Everything is on the internet nowadays." He smoothed his goatee. "Sumerian Cuneiform is a dead language that died back in the first century. One of the first forms of writing. Then in the nineteenth century, linguists and historians started researching it."

I glanced at the clock. "Can you read it?"

"No, I can identify it's Sumerian, but that's about it. There're only a few people in the world who can truly interpret Sumerian Cuneiform."

My lungs deflated. He had to translate it. How in the hell would I find one of those *few people?*

"Well, can I email them or something?" I struggled to keep my voice from breaking with desperation.

Dr. Bashir must've heard the quiver in my words because he gently patted the desk with his palm. "I can

255

see why you and Jason are friends. Both so determined."

If you only knew.

"You're in luck." Dr. Bashir picked up the phone and dialed, grinning at me as he waited for someone to answer. "Amed? It's Omar."

Pause.

"Excellent. You?"

Pause.

"Good, good. Listen, I won't take much of your time. I have a young man here who is trying to translate Sumerian Cuneiform for a school project. Could I send it to you?"

Pause.

"Yes, I have your email. If it's not too much trouble. There's no rush."

No rush? There was a massive, gigantic, enormous rush! Lives literally depended on it.

"Excellent. I'll send it right over. Thank you, my friend."

Dr. Bashir hung up. He spun on his chair and scanned the picture on his desk printer. "Amed is one of the smartest people I know, but is very busy. We're lucky he can help. He said if it isn't too complicated, he'll email us right back. Do you have time to wait?"

"Absolutely." I slumped into the chair, relieved. "Thank you very much. Thank you, thank you."

"I am curious, though." Dr. Bashir rubbed his goatee again. "On what website did you find this? You said it came from a museum? I'm no expert, just some of the random words I could read seemed…interesting for a museum display."

I shrugged, scrambling to craft more details for my

fake story, something I'd learned online. "It came from an exhibit with a bunch of like, prayers and stuff. In Chicago. No, New York. I can't remember. We searched all over for something that looked cool and found it."

"Cool it is. I ask because, as I said, the context of the words I recognize intrigues me." His phone rang. "Hang on, please."

As he talked to the caller, I fixated on his computer screen. I fought the urge to reach over and keep hitting refresh to see the new email notification as soon as it popped up.

Dr. Bashir's conversation droned on.

Nothing from Amed.

Blah, blah, blah.

No new email.

Blah, blah, blah.

Bing.

An email from amedrs@brecken.edu.

I straightened in my chair. Amed was his name, and "edu" would be another university.

Dr. Bashir rambled on and on with the caller, staring mindlessly out the window. This wasn't a cocktail party.

Look at your monitor!

I cleared my throat. Twice. Then coughed.

Dr. Bashir glanced at his screen. He shot me a smile and pointed to his monitor, like I'd stopped staring at the unopened email since it arrived. He clicked a few times, and his printer hummed to life.

"Hold on for a second, Chris." He pressed the mute button, skimmed the page, then handed me the printout. "It is interesting indeed. Here you go. Keep me posted on your project. I'd love to read your paper."

"Sure!" I ripped it out of his hands.

I read as I walked, nearly tripping down the marble stairs.

Omar,

It is, in fact, Sumerian Cuneiform. Loosely translated, I'd say this is an old prayer, or perhaps part of a longer poem. Ask your friend where he got it. I've never seen anything like it.

Here's what I'm thinking it says based on my first pass:

Neither slumber nor sleep will be overtaken by It. Dreams belongeth unto the soul who dreamt.

May It never intercedeth with the desires of Man, on his behalf or with Will.

Here forward, It is commanded to return to Otherworld, from whence it came.

Never again to know that which is in front of Man, nor behind him.

May It encompass nothing of knowledge and Will.

Spending the rest of time in darkness, forever away from Man.

"Whoa." It sounded legit.

Out of habit, I whipped out my phone and started to text Jason. I stopped myself, remembering his request.

Didn't matter. It'll all be over soon, and everything will go back to normal. On the short bus ride and jog back home, I fantasized about getting my simple, pathetic life back. The one I'd written off as so horrible. The one with an invisible social status, movie nights with Mom, no girlfriend, and a tiny apartment. It never sounded sweeter.

I yanked the wooden box from my closet. Anxious with excitement, I clasped it with both hands, afraid I'd drop it.

"It's over, Asshole," I said to the unsummoned djinn. "I'm taking back my life."

Setting the box on my bed, I unfolded the translated incantation. I paused. Were there rules? Did I summon Ifrit first, then read it? Did I need to burn candles or something? Ashley said burning sage banished spirits. If only ancient artifacts came with instructions. What if I only had one chance? I couldn't blow it.

Stop it!

I had to try the incantation before Ifrit hurt anyone else. Time's up. I'd try reading it without summoning him. That way, if it failed, I wouldn't have him staring me down.

I crossed my legs on my bed, incantation in my lap, my hands on each side of the old wooden box.

Here goes.

"Neither slumber nor sleep will be overtaken by It. Dreams belongeth unto the soul who dreamt. May it never intercedeth with the desires of Man, on his behalf or with Will."

The jewel glowed, and my bedroom lights dimmed. In my chest, the heat rose, scorching my blood and raising the hairs on my arms. The pain behind my eyes warned me of his arrival.

"Here forward, It is commanded to return to Otherworld, from whence it came. Never again to know that which is in front of Man, nor behind him. May It encompass nothing of knowledge and will. Spending the rest of time in darkness, forever away from Man."

My bedroom lights went dark, but the jewel glowed brilliantly, blinding me. Silence hung in the air for a moment.

Then came Ifrit's growl.

I jumped off the bed, leaving the box, and spun around.

The purple jewel cast sharp shadows of furniture on my bedroom walls while a hazy twilight cloaked the corners of my room. I rubbed my eyes, hurrying them to adjust to the purple lighting.

Ifrit only needed that brief second to emerge from the darkness.

His chest heaved, and his fur-covered shoulders and arms glistened with wetness. His thick brow wrinkled over his narrow violet eyes, and he crouched in a battle-ready stance, arms out, ready to defend himself. He appeared surprised and confused, ripped from wherever he came, instead of appearing by his own will or a call from the purple jewel.

"You are a fool." He dragged one of his clawed hands down my wall, leaving gouges in the plaster.

"Go away! I banish you forever back to your box!"

His head darted around my room, expecting something. His movement seemed panicked. When he didn't see whatever he'd expected to see, his shoulders relaxed.

I'd missed a piece of the puzzle.

A deep throaty laugh erupted from him. "I am not so easy to banish, Baxter Allen."

No, this couldn't be happening. The incantation had to work. This was the only solution. Now, Ifrit knew I'd translated it. What piece of the equation had I missed?

"Go away!" I sounded like a baby but didn't care.

"We have so many desires yet to fulfill." His muzzle morphed into a sinister smile.

"Keep it up, and there won't be anyone left in my life for you to torture. You don't want that, do you?" I picked up the box, the purple jewel glowing brightly. I wound up and hurled it at the wall as hard as I could.

The glowing jewel spiraled with the box as it sailed through the air causing the shadows to quiver and rearrange themselves on the walls. But despite the rotted wood, the box smacked the wall, then bounced to the floor. Not a single splinter loosened.

"If my vessel were so easily destroyed, Baxter Allen, do you think I'd have survived the passage of millennia?"

"Go away!" I repeated, unable to think of anything else to shout. I had nothing else to say and nothing else to threaten him with. The incantation had failed. My friends were gone. Ifrit terrified Janni. No one remained in the battle but me.

Wait.

"The old man! He'll defeat you. I'll find him and send you back to hell."

Ifrit chortled as a thin flame flickered out of his mouth. "The old man?"

With the speed of a single blink, the old man stood where Ifrit had. He hunched over, watching me from the top of his purple eyes. His long fingernails curled out of the ends of his sleeves. His coat, the reddish-brown of my building's brick.

"What?" I took a disbelieving step forward. "You?"

His dead stare met mine. He spoke slowly, like that

first night. The act of speaking absorbed all of his energy. "It took hundreds of years to collect enough energy to create this illusion outside of my vessel. Even then, I needed the approaching lunar anomaly to energize my projection with strength enough to actually hold the ring."

Lunar anomaly. The familiar phrase from Mr. Buchanan's class: the super blue blood moon.

The old man smiled, his skin cracking to the point of shattering. "The air is electric with anticipation. That air gifted me with enough extra charge to present the ring to an unsuspecting human. After that, I did very little. Once a human discovers Janni and tastes what djinn can do, it is only a short while before greed fuels the urge to find a stronger djinn."

He played me from the beginning. I took a step back, falling to a seat on my bed. He'd planned this all along. He wanted me to discover Janni and grow greedy for more. Greedy enough to summon him into this world.

"Do not feel bad." He raised one long, twisted fingernail to scold me. "Greed has fueled man throughout his existence. No matter how wealthy, man always wants more. Bigger. Better."

He gave me the ring, but it couldn't have been random. He'd mentioned Greg's name. "But you knew my dad's name. How did you know that?"

The old man smiled again, his entire face wrinkled mosaic. "I never mentioned your father until you touched the ring and established the binding connection between us."

I dropped my head into my hands. "No, no, no."

There was never a connection to Greg. Ifrit

manipulated me from the start. He'd read my mind. This all started because I took that dumb ring.

When I looked up again, Ifrit had shifted back into his monster form. "We are joined for all time, you and me."

I squeezed my eyes shut and screamed, "Get out!"

When I opened my eyes, he'd vanished. The lights came back on, and the jewel faded to dark.

I gasped for breath. The old man never existed. He'd only been a ploy to tempt a greedy idiot like me. To seduce me with a harmless janni, then tease me with the idea of a stronger one. And I fell for it. Now, my greed tied us together for the rest of my life.

And on top of that, the incantation didn't work.

Left with no choice, I grabbed my phone and texted Jason and Ashley.

—*I am sorry for everything, but I need your help. Please.*—

I stared at my phone for several minutes.

No response.

I'd confront them at school.

Chapter 21

The incantation had failed. Failed. I'd missed a piece of the formula. When Ifrit appeared in my room, he looked around frantically, almost scared, expecting something else to be there, but what?

Jason and Ashley would help me figure it out. They had to. I'd beg them. They wanted to distance themselves from me, and I agreed at first, but would that really erase them from Ifrit's radar? Even if they weren't near me, they'd always be on my mind, which made them targets. Hell, anyone that crossed my thoughts became a potential target. I never hung out with Nick, but simply existing in my world put him within Ifrit's grasp.

A car honked, snapping me to attention. "Watch out!" its driver yelled out the window. I'd crossed the street without paying attention. Just my luck, I'd survive Ifrit, but not the walk to school.

I stopped. The odds of not surviving the walk to school just skyrocketed.

Ahead, as if hanging out on a leisurely summer day—and not a school day—Malcolm, Brent, and Gerald shoved each other, harassed passing cars, and drank out of a silver flask. Brent shouted about a woman's tight ass as she strolled by them. She flipped him off. His buddies laughed as he grabbed the flask from Gerald, took a swig, then swallowed with a grimace.

Great, just what I needed. I didn't have time to deal with them. I had to meet up with Jason. Malcolm hated me sober, hatred that was probably a million times more dangerous drunk on a weekday morning.

Before they saw me, I hung a right down Pine, a detour I often took on the way to school, but usually, only when I could afford the time. Midway down the block, I ducked into Warren's Cosmos. The silver bell at the top of the glass door greeted me.

I'd stall for a few minutes until Malcolm and his gang moved on. If they didn't, I'd jog the long way to school. Either way, I'd still be there before third period to catch Jason.

"Morning, Bax." Warren nodded.

"Hey." I glanced over my shoulder and out the window, checking for Malcolm. How long could someone sit on a street corner heckling people before it got boring? I groaned. Malcolm's threshold for entertainment seemed pretty low.

Warren watched me, tapping his fingers on the counter.

Oh, right.

"Anyone come in asking about *Shade Slayer, #276?*"

"No, Bax. Sorry."

I moseyed up a random aisle, flipping through some comic books. Just being at Warren's calmed me. I inhaled the familiar mustiness. I traced the brightly colored paper and laminated covers stacked in wooden crates and crammed on the tables. A new cardboard cutout of a life-sized hero I didn't recognize stood guard.

I checked my phone. No return texts from Jason or Ashley.

I grabbed a random comic book and handed it to Warren. I didn't even care enough to read the title. Warren started punching the keys on his antique register. It chimed, the drawer slid out, and he counted my change. As he gave me the money, he stalled with his hand hovering over mine, a reminder to ask about his missing fingers.

He had his I've-got-a-good-one-for-ya glimmer in his eye, but I couldn't bring myself to ask—too distracted. Besides, if Malcolm hadn't moved on by now, I'd have to take the long route.

Realizing he wouldn't have the opportunity to share his story, Warren's shoulders dropped as his hand lowered. He lived for those stories.

It was official. I alienated absolutely everyone in my life.

Warren nodded at my cheek. "What happened?"

I touched the scrape from Ifrit's tail. Wouldn't he love to know? I paused before taking my comic book off the counter. Maybe it was my turn to tell the story.

I glanced back toward the door to make sure the street outside remained Malcolm-free. "Well, I found an ancient box with an oversized purple jewel on the lid. I rubbed it, which summoned an evil djinn called Ifrit. He's huge, with a ram-like head and legs, a long, pointed tail, and a fire deep in his throat. He's been haunting me ever since. I tried sending him to a faraway place, but he wouldn't listen. That's how I got this." I pointed to the cut.

"Then, I found an incantation to banish him. I read that, but it didn't work. It shouldn't have failed. It's supposed to send him back. I'm missing part of the banishing ritual, and I don't know what it is. Any ideas?"

Warren raised one of his bushy eyebrows and folded his arms. His stool creaked as he leaned back against the wall, and his leathery skin pulled into a proud smile. "Very interesting. You asked about djinn the other day."

"Same one. If I don't get rid of him, he'll be with me forever."

Warren's gaze floated to the ceiling, then drifted back down, pondering. Most people would have laughed me out of the room. But like the endless stories explaining how he lost his fingers, in Warren's Cosmos, the reality of a story didn't matter.

"You're certain the incantation should do it?" He rubbed his chin, his whiskers sounding like sandpaper on his rough fingers. "You have that on good authority?"

I nodded. "Positive."

"Well, I'm no expert on beings from the astral plane—" his words came out slow and with care, "—but from stories I've read, when you summon demons into this world or send them back, usually, it requires some kind of cosmic power. Don't it?"

"What do you mean?"

"Well, think about it, Bax. In most fantasy or horror stories, words aren't enough. You need something celestial as a power source. Magicians use enchanted staffs or talismans to summon demons. Even classic monsters used power sources. Dr. Frankenstein brought his monster to life with lightning. Heck, werewolves only shape-shift during a full moon.

There's always an energy that fuels summoning spells or activities. Maybe that'll send your demon back."

Warren's words rolled over each other in my mind. *Werewolves only shape-shift during a full moon.*

"Like a blood moon?" My heart began to thud.

Holy crap. Warren may be on to something. Slow down. Think it through.

Warren tapped his stubbed fingers on the counter. "Blood moon. Isn't there a blood moon tonight?"

"Technically, a super blue blood moon." I took a step back from the counter.

The missing piece. The power source.

I shoved the change into my pocket. "They're rare. They only happen every one hundred and fifty years."

"Sounds like a celestial power source if I ever heard of one." Warren rubbed his chin again. "And there are lots of stories about blood moons making strange things happen."

My heart thundered in my chest. "Mr. Buchannan told us how ancient people believed blood moons unlocked mystical powers."

"You should try reading your incantation tonight."

Read the incantation during the super blue blood moon.

Of course!

Ifrit said he shape-shifted into the old man after hundreds of years but could only hold the physical ring because of the energy from the approaching super blue blood moon. So if the *upcoming* lunar event enabled his illusion to hold the ring, then the *actual* lunar event might charge the incantation enough to send him back.

"Are you writing a story or something? About demons?"

I wished.

"Actually, yeah."

Thanks for the idea, Warren.

"Gonna try and write my own comic book."

Warren patted his palm on the counter. "Well, I think you're on to something. You've got an intriguing premise."

"Thanks for helping me fix a plot hole." I grabbed the comic I bought and dropped it into my backpack. "And I want to hear how you lost your fingers, just not now. I'll be back tomorrow. Cool?"

"You bet. They aren't growing back before then. At least, I don't think." He winked.

I had to get to school and talk it through with Jason. The logic of Warren's idea made sense. All monsters needed a power source. No one ever just read an old poem and banished a demon. Even during exorcisms, priests used holy water, crucifixes, and crap like that to send the devil back to hell. And Ifrit was definitely my devil.

I jogged, able to make up some time. Late morning, pedestrians and cars were sparse. I glanced at my phone, no texts. I'd be there by the end of the third period, and hopefully, I could convince Jason and Ashley to help vet Warren's theory. If the moon theory worked, I only had one shot. If I missed another piece of the puzzle tonight, I'd be stuck with Ifrit for the next one hundred and fifty years.

"Well, look who's playing hooky today?"

The voice glued my shoes to the sidewalk, midjog, and I almost fell forward.

Malcolm.

I'd been so lost in my thoughts, I jogged right into

them.

Before I could will my feet to start moving again, Malcolm, Brent, and Gerald surrounded me like a pack of wolves circling their prey.

Keeping my head down, I tried to push through an opening between Brent and Gerald, acting like I hadn't seen or heard them. Malcolm grabbed my shirt between my shoulder blades and yanked me backward. I skidded to the concrete on my ass.

"Where ya headed, Flower?" Malcolm's voice slurred, his bloodshot eyes half-open.

I climbed to my feet, struggling to keep my breathing even to appear calm. I'd never been in a fight. Malcolm's recent sucker punch was the closest I'd come. I made confident eye contact with each one of them. Not sure it did any good.

My heart pounded. Would they lay into me all at once, or would I fight one at a time? Were there rules for this kind of thing, like an "honor among thieves" type of agreement?

And where the hell was Ifrit? Surely my fear of Malcolm swarmed around somewhere in my subconscious. No, too easy. Instead, Ifrit chose to torture Ashley's dad for doing his job.

Act casual, Bax. Don't let them sense your fear.

I batted the dirt from my jeans. "I'm headed to school. You?"

"You're late." The breeze blew from behind Brent, washing me in a wave of stale pot. They'd been partying all night.

"I have to go." I turned to leave again, searching for a way through the bully barrier. With a couple of side steps, Gerald blocked my only exit from the center of the circle.

Trapped.

"We want to talk." Malcolm sniffed a hunk of snot back and gulped it down. "You're already late for school. You can spare a few."

"Look," I fought back a stammer, "I really have to go. I've got—"

"Bullshit, Flower!" Spittle flew from Malcolm's lips, his eyes crazed. "You don't have to go nowhere. You're scared we're gonna kick your ass for trying to bang Scarlet. And you should be."

Malcolm's glare pelted my skin like icy shards. He'd always been a bully who I avoided, but the way he glowered at me now freaked the hell out of me.

He dropped the flask into his pants pocket, his breathing labored and heavy, like a rabid dog.

"I'm not trying to bang her." I needed to buy some time, but no pedestrians—or escape—were in sight. They tightened their circle, putting me within arm's reach of all three of them.

"I'm not sure what you did, Flower." Malcolm's nostrils flared. "But don't you see how she looks at you? She's scared of you. It's fucking weird. You threaten her?"

I shook my head, taking a step back. Gerald pressed the palm of his hand between my shoulder blades, keeping me from backing up any farther.

"What is it?" Malcolm tilted his head. "Did you threaten her? Is that how you get chicks? Threaten them? You a rapist, Flower?"

"No." Even though Gerald's palm dug into my back, I leaned against it as Malcolm moved closer. I struggled to inhale. My throat had closed. My entire chest became a stone block.

"You have naked pics of her you're threatening to leak?"

"No. I told her I don't want to date her."

Malcolm stood so close, I stared into his T-shirt. His pot and vodka breath pounded down on the top of my head. Gerald's hand still pressed into my back.

"Well, I'll make it easy for you. You aren't going to date her anymore."

"Fine." I braced for impact and squeezed my eyes shut.

And it came.

He shoved me in the chest, pressing Gerald's palm into my back once before he dropped it, allowing Malcolm to freely shove me again.

"I said no more!" His spit rained on my hair.

"Fine. I agree. I won't."

Gerald's arms looped under my armpits and over my shoulders, pinning my arms back. I squirmed, about to become a murder victim in the middle of the street.

Brent stepped to the side for a better view of the beating. This time, Mr. Buckwald wouldn't save me.

"I can't hear you!" Malcolm drove his fist into my stomach, forcing the air out of me.

"I said—"

His fist rammed me higher, cracking the bottom of my rib cage. A searing bolt of pain shot through me.

"I can't hear you!" he shouted again, smacking me openhanded across the face.

"I said I won't—"

He slammed his forehead against mine. Orange explosions blistered my vision. My legs turned to mush, but Gerald propped me up.

"You're a fuckin' coward, dating Nick's girl." He panted. "Drop him."

Gerald released my arms, and I stumbled forward, doubled over, coughing. Before I could stand up straight again, Malcolm's fist swiped up from underneath me, hitting my jaw and throwing me backward. I crashed onto my back. My head smacked the sidewalk.

The city around me rumbled with life, even though the street around me was dead. No one on their way to work who'd stop and ask, "What's going on here?" No cop walking the curb issuing parking tickets and no shop owners taking out the trash. No witnesses.

It didn't matter. I deserved it. Intentional or not, Nick died because of me. Ashley's dad may die because of me, and the girl of my dreams hated me. I deserved a beating.

Malcolm's shoe drilled me in the side. I curled into a protective fetal position. His shoe repeatedly hammered at my shin and forearms. My hands tried to protect my face.

Bam.

Bam.

Bam.

A pause. Malcolm panted, catching his breath.

"That's enough, man." Brent's voice?

A zipper unzipped. Then came the warm stink of urine showering my head.

Brent's caution to Malcolm disappeared beneath his laughter. All three started pissing on me. I held my breath, not wanting to inhale piss. I kept my lips pressed together, even though my lungs screamed for oxygen.

"Stand up, goddammit." Malcolm zipped up his fly. Gerald and Brent followed suit. "Now!"

I couldn't stand. My shins and arms throbbed. Blood trickled down my chin. Maybe from my nose, maybe from my lip. My head wobbled loosely on my shoulders. The inside of my chest burned.

"Stand up, Flower. I'm not saying it again," Malcolm snarled.

I rolled over and dragged myself to a hunched over standing position. The rocks embedded in my skin stung, and the slimy wetness of blood and urine dripped off my chin, some making its way between my lips. I couldn't stop it.

I somehow remained standing on my mushy legs and faced him, ready to take what he doled out but hoping he'd keep me alive through the super blue blood moon so I could make things right.

"You're tough, Flower." Malcolm wound up, his force concentrated into a blow to the side of my head.

I fell backward but don't remember hitting the ground.

Chapter 22

Ben threw his keys to the table, dotted with nicks, and kicked off his steel-toed shoes. He unbuttoned his blue uniform shirt and, in the mirror, caught a glimpse of the oil stain on his T-shirt. After a quick lick of his thumb, he scrubbed the stain, but it had already seeped into the cloth.

He popped open a beer. It hissed as he collapsed into the recliner. He reached back, grabbed a comic book, and flipped on the baseball game. Nothing better than comic books and baseball. One of the few ways he could relax.

Five to three, his team lost. He hurled the comic book at the TV. Five hundred bucks down the drain, plus the bookie's fee. So much for relaxing.

He chugged his beer. A belch exploded from his mouth, but the sound of the train clamoring by outside swallowed it. The walls of his studio apartment vibrated, rattling the dishes in the kitchenette behind him.

Ben cranked up the TV volume until the train passed. He'd grown so used to it, adjusting the volume had become an involuntary reflex. Working the hours he worked, he'd developed the ability to tune the world out so he could sleep during the day. He'd become a master at tuning out what he didn't want to hear.

His phone buzzed.

Cursing at another disturbance, he heaved himself out of the recliner and searched for his phone. It lit up a stack of comic books on his two-person kitchen table.

He squinted at the screen—a local number. A residence, not a telemarketer. He vaguely recognized the name.

"Yeah?"

"Greg Allen?" The voice chirped like a canary.

Ben tallied his debt. No collectors should be contacting him yet. He'd paid off most of it. At least, the overdue part. He glanced at the phone's screen again. The woman's name seemed so damn familiar.

"Ben Allen. Greg's my middle name. Who's this?"

"Right, sorry. I remember you as Ben, but I saw a note you go by Greg now."

"Nope. Ben."

"Well, Ben, I'm Sherry. Sherry Miller. From North Central? We graduated together."

That's it. Dark hair, blue eyes, and massive tits, she was one of the smart, too happy, always energetic girls. One of those girls with extremely vanilla opinions because she never wanted to piss anyone off. She claimed to like everyone, even though she only hung out with a select few. Every subject in school was her "fave," and she mastered every extracurricular activity. Why the hell was *she* calling?

"What do you need, Sherry?"

"Can you believe it's been twenty-five years? What *have* you been up to?"

Had he knocked her up? No. She wouldn't give him a passing smile in high school, too far below her standards.

"Not much. You?"

"Well, guess what? I'm organizing our reunion! I'm trying to get everyone on a mailing list. I'm not thinking anything crazy and overplanned. Dinner and drinks at a hotel or something after the holidays. Mid-January, here in Chicago. Destination reunions are the new thing, but I'm like, 'Um, no, who'd do that?' Spend *that* much moolah on a reunion? No thanks." Twenty-five years may have passed, but that didn't slow her speech. Annoying as hell.

"Uh, I'm not sure." He hated high school as much as he hated the peppy girls with big tits who never gave him a passing smile.

"It'll be fun! We'll catch up. The whole gang is coming. Mark Thompson, Keenan Jones, Brad Baker…" She droned on with names Ben didn't give two shits about.

Then, as he started to hang up, a name caught his attention. "Oh, and I'm calling Sara next. Looks like her area code is in St. Louis. You two aren't together anymore? Too bad."

She'd found Sara? "Um, no, sadly. She's down in St. Louis."

"Do you get down there often?"

"Yeah, sure. My son lives with her." He forced a casual chuckle as he picked up a plate, crusted with dried food, and tossed it onto the stack of dirty dishes in the sink so he could get to the paper and pen underneath it.

He hear that right?

"Sara and Bax are down in St. Louis. You got it." He sat on the wobbly kitchen chair, ready to write down any information Sherry let slip.

"Oh my gosh, it is so great you two still get along.

For your son, especially. Buck, is it? Most broken marriages end ugly, you know." Sherry's voice dripped with phony sentimentality.

"Bax is his name, and not us. We just grew apart." He needed details. "Now, what contact info do you have, Sherry? They recently moved. Which is why I'm asking. I can confirm it for you. I bet you have their old address."

"Oh my gosh!" Papers rustled on her end. Had this woman aged? She talked like she never left high school. "You're a lifesaver. I haven't called her yet, but the address we have is on Euclid Avenue. Is that the new one?"

The corner of his mouth curled into a smile. He jotted the location down. "Yep, Euclid Avenue in St. Louis. You know, I need to call her to talk about Thanksgiving schedules and stuff. Why don't you let me tell her about the reunion? Save you the effort."

No need to risk Sherry tipping off Sara.

"That'd be amazing. Super helpful."

"Consider her called." He stared at the street name on the coffee-stained pad of paper in his hand. Asking Sherry to confirm the address may sound suspicious. City and street were all he needed. He could figure out the rest.

"Great," Sherry said, "So we'll be—"

"Sherry, hon, I gotta run. You just send me the info. Sara and I will be there."

"Awesome!"

He hung up.

Yeah, awesome.

Ben pounded the rest of his beer, invigorated for the first time in years. He tossed the can to the trash but missed. It landed on the floor, clanging among the other empty beer cans.

His exhaustion from the day disappeared. He'd all but given up. Now, all these years later, he'd found her. All the years of searching and the bitch who stole his son fell right into his lap. Just like that. Thanks to Sherry Fucking Miller.

He opened the refrigerator. A couple of sandwiches wrapped in deli paper, condiments, a few apples, and a shelf of beer. He cracked open another beer and shuffled into his bedroom.

In the top drawer of his dresser, he shoved the socks aside and unburied the handgun. He double-checked it—not loaded—then tossed it to the bed. Under his wadded-up boxers, he unburied a plastic bag—one of three bags filled with hundred-dollar bills. He threw it to the bed next to the gun.

He probably wouldn't have to use the gun, but he wanted it, just in case. To show her he meant business. Sara would freak the hell out when she opened her front door to see him standing there. He clenched his fists, imagining the lies she'd fed his son over the past thirteen years.

Ben dug into his pants and pulled out his wallet, thick with everything but cash. He flipped through old receipts and found a picture of Sara Allen. God, she was hot. Young, too. They both were. Their marriage wasn't perfect, but she didn't need to leave him. She sure as hell didn't need to take Bax. She packed him up like one of her stupid dresses, not giving him a say in it, then they vanished.

She'd humiliated him. His beautiful wife and son, gone from his life. He told people they'd split mutually, and people in Ben's life were smart enough not to ask any questions about it.

But that's history. Now, he'd pay her a visit. Teach Baxter a valuable lesson—you can't run away from problems. You need to face them.

And he'd teach Sara you can't take a boy from his dad.

Ben admired himself in the mirror with a grimacing smile, exposing his chipped front tooth. Then he laughed a deep belly laugh. He hadn't felt so full of life in—God, he couldn't even remember.

He'd be taking a trip to St. Louis.

****

My eyes opened, blinded by the pristine white ceiling. Blood pumped in my brain like a drumbeat as I rolled my head to the side of the paper pillowcase.

I wasn't dead. That's encouraging.

A pale blue curtain surrounded the area around my bed. As my ears became conscious, hospital noises sprung to life on the other side of the curtain: medical speak, beeping equipment, and the clanging of devices.

Malcolm jumped me. Drunk or high or both, he and his buddies ambushed me on my way to find Jason and Ashley. My jaw still throbbed from the impact of their fists, my stomach still tight under their pummeling shoes, my dry chin still felt wet from their piss.

Next to me, Mom flipped through a magazine on a gray plastic chair, legs crossed. She didn't notice I'd woken up. Celebrity gossip completely absorbed her.

Mom.

The dream smacked me upside my thudding head. Greg—I mean Ben—in his dive apartment, complete with a stack of comic books. Ben getting the call about his reunion and using it to figure out where we lived. Ben acting like we fled from him, not the other way around.

Mom never told me many details, but she led me to believe *he* left *us*. She also told me Greg was his first name, not his middle name. No wonder I couldn't find any record of him. Her cryptic insinuations implied they'd drifted apart until one day, thirteen years ago, they mutually ended it. He collected comic books and worked as an electrician. That was the extent of my knowledge about him. If Mom lied about his name, what else had she lied about?

I never pressed her for information. Why would I? Lots of parents divorced, and despite Mom's incessant worrying about my well-being, I never missed Greg-Ben. Like I always reminded her, I was curious about him, but it ended there. You can't miss someone you don't remember. She always took my curiosity as a knock on her parenting, so I never pushed her for information.

Ifrit, however, thought differently. In his twisted way of granting my wants and wishes, he found Ben and gave him a map right to us.

No purple eyes in the dream, but Sherry Miller existed only as a voice on Ben's phone. She had to have been Ifrit. The call was too convenient. Now, Ben traveled to St. Louis with a gun and a mission to teach Mom a lesson.

"Mom?" My dry voice scratched.

Startled, she dropped the magazine to the floor and leaped to her feet. "Baxter!" She rushed to my bedside. "You're awake." Her face glowed with relief.

"You thought I wouldn't wake up?" I swallowed,

trying to wet my throat.

"Don't be silly." She stroked my hair gently, like a child's.

I pulled my head away, too distracted for soothing. "How'd I get to the hospital?"

"Mr. Bevin found you on the sidewalk. You still had your backpack and phone, so I'm not sure why anyone would do this to you for no reason."

I didn't have time to go into it. Not without a hundred follow-up questions from her. "Mr. Bevin?"

"Warren Bevin. From the comic book store you visit. He called the ambulance."

I shifted a little in bed, which sent electric bolts of pain from my chest to every extremity. I squeezed my eyes shut, waiting for the pain to pass. Then, I lifted the sheet and glanced down at myself. A purple and blue bruise three inches round blistered the lower left half of my rib cage.

I dropped the sheet. "How bad is it?"

"You fractured a rib and needed a few stitches in your head, but other than that, you're fine. Do you know what happened? The police want to talk with you."

Images of Ashley's dad rolling down four flights of stairs flashed in my mind with the mention of the word *police*. Mom must not know about Mr. Bryant, or she would have said something. "I got jumped. I didn't recognize them. Maybe a gang initiation or something."

Mom tilted her head. She didn't believe me.

Come on, Mom. Just let it go.

Her watch read 5:00 p.m. If the dream happened in real time, Chicago was only a five-hour drive away. "How long have I been here?"

"The hospital called me late morning, I guess. Then we waited a few hours. You woke up a few times, briefly. Probably don't remember. Then when you were actually seen by a..."

Ben could arrive any minute. The dreams weren't always in real time, but they were usually close. He could be trolling our street right now, waiting for us to show up.

I clutched the sheet. I had to confirm Greg was the guy from the dream. I had to confirm who could be on their way to St. Louis right now. "Mom, what happened between you and Greg?"

She took a step back as if an invisible hand smacked her.

"Greg? What made you think of him at a time like this?"

I didn't back down like usual. Our lives depended on it. "You've never told me anything about him, and I've always respected that, but I have to know."

She stiffened like she usually did, and her face tightened. "You're getting older now, I guess. So why don't you focus on healing? Once we get home, I promise to answer all of your questions."

"No, Mom, now. It's important."

She laced her fingers between mine. Cinnamon and lavender wafted off her. She must've been working at the candle store. "There's nothing to say. Some marriages don't last. It happens. I don't think it's right to talk badly about him. He is your father."

"Badly? You don't talk about him at all."

Her focus drifted to the foot of my bed. She couldn't look at me. I usually dropped it at this point. Not this time. She left me no choice. "Where does he live?"

"I-I don't know."

"What if I found him online? Could I invite him over?"

She swallowed. My words hurt her, but I kept going, shoving the knife deeper. "Is Greg actually his middle name, and Ben's his first?"

Her face grew pale, and her hand flew to her mouth. "Wait, what? Jesus, Baxter, did you contact him? Did he do this to you?" She examined the stitches over my ear as if just seeing them for the first time. "He did this to you, didn't he? Didn't he? Why wouldn't you—"

And there's my answer. The Ben in my dream, the one in Chicago on his way here, was very real. She expected him to beat the shit out of me during our reunion.

I always assumed her reluctance to talk about him came from pain at their separation. Not fear of a dangerous loser.

"No, Mom. He didn't do this. A bunch of kids jumped me. I haven't contacted him."

Her head fell back, and she spoke to the ceiling after taking a shallow breath. "But you found him?"

"I found Ben Allen in Chicago online and took a guess. Mom, tell me why I shouldn't email him. What else have you told me about him that isn't true?" I confirmed the man in my dream was my dad, all I really needed, but I wanted the story.

She rubbed her eyes. Several times, her mouth opened, no words came out, then she closed it. Finally, she assembled a few sentences. "Oh, Baxter. We married young. He drank too much. Sometimes he'd do things he'd regret."

"Like hit you? Just say it."

She squared her shoulders, preparing to answer. She gave me only a single word. "Sometimes."

"Did he hit me?"

She shook her head. "No, but I couldn't be sure he never would. One time, you spilled your milk, and he freaked out like he did. I thought he might."

"Hit me?"

She flinched every time I said it. "Yes, but he didn't. I decided to leave before that happened. I didn't want to wait for him to do it. The next day, while he was working, I packed up, took you, and we drove here."

Even though she'd started to cry, she didn't take her attention from me or back away from my bedside.

"He never found you?" I battled back tears of my own. I hated seeing her relive something so painful. I hated that the man I'd built up in my mind turned out to be a monster. I hated myself for summoning a stupid djinn into the world who hurt everyone I loved.

She sniffed but kept her head up. "No, hon, he never found us. Bad-mouthing him wouldn't have done any good. You always treasured that dumb comic book so much. You loved the idea of him. Why would I take that from you?"

"Is the other stuff true? The little I know? Electrician? Comic books?"

She nodded. "I only changed his name, in case you searched for him. Which turns out, didn't matter."

I grabbed her hand and squeezed. My stomach collapsed as I watched the tears drip off her chin. I had forced this conversation, so it happened. I'd made her cry. Now I had the answers I needed. Time to pull it together and focus. Time to fix what I started. After all these years in hiding, Ifrit delivered us to Ben wrapped in a bow—no time to waste.

"Any other questions?" Mom wiped her eyes and chuckled through a sob. "I'm on a roll."

I shook my head even though tons of questions swirled in my mind, but they could wait.

Mom took a deep inhale, then exhaled. "Well, I'll go tell the doctor you're awake so he can check you out and hopefully discharge us."

"Sounds good." I wiped my own eyes and gave her a comforting smile.

Mom yanked open the curtain to step out and then shut it behind her. Briefly, before the curtain closed, across the room and through the window, the sun began to set. I had to throw Ben off our trail and banish Ifrit before the end of the super blue blood moon.

I have to hurt you one last time, Mom.

I crawled out of bed as my fractured rib zapped me. White lights exploded in my vision before fresh tears flooded my eyes. I held still, waiting for the pain to subside. I couldn't bend over, and deep breaths hurt.

Ifrit and I were ready to battle, for sure.

I had pants on, so without bending over, I slipped into my shoes. No shirt or jacket anywhere in the curtained-in room.

Did Mom have them? Were they still with the nurses?

I couldn't wait. Mom would be back soon.

"Now what?" I scanned the area around my bed. "This will have to do." I snagged the hospital gown hanging in the corner, moving with care to avoid another shot of agony from my rib cage. I tucked the blue gown into my pants and tied it in the front, knowing there'd be no way I'd be able to reach back and tie it behind me without passing out from the pain.

Picking up my phone, I turned the camera on myself—hospital gown tied crookedly and on backward, a section of hair shaved over my right ear, the skin beneath it lined with stitches, a bruise under my left eye, and bottom lip swollen. A smile spread across my ridiculous, battered face. What a mess—and the night just started.

I poked my head out from between the blue curtains. The hospital bustled like a TV ER. Men and women in scrubs and white coats hurried from patient to chart to the computers behind each bed. Some wore sad, sympathetic faces, some wore happy, smiling ones.

No Mom.

I straightened my spine, taking long, confident strides across the floor, ignoring how I must've appeared to other patients and the medical staff. Fortunately, the sick patients and busy staff had other things to worry about than a kid walking around the ER—ample cover for me.

The skinny lady at the check-in desk talked on her headset while she typed, so I strolled by her, straight for the exit. She didn't seem to notice me. After all, a hospital's not a prison.

As the wide ER glass doors swished shut behind me, I let my shoulders drop.

Escape complete.

The autumn air sensed the confidence of my small win and whipped through the thin hospital gown, icing my torso.

Should have stolen a jacket.

The sun hadn't completely set, but the enlarged, pumpkin-colored full moon had already begun its ascent.

Mom would freak out when she returned with the doctor and found me gone. After a safe head start, I'd text her so she wouldn't worry. Not that a text would prevent her from worrying.

"Give me a night to figure this out, Mom. I promise everything will go back to normal tomorrow—it has to."

Chapter 23

As I sprinted to catch the bus, my head throbbed under the stitches. The pounding of my feet on the sidewalk caused my rib cage to scream. Onboard, the bus driver kept her suspicious eye on me through the long rearview mirror, but the other passengers barely seemed to notice my bruises, stitches, and hospital gown.

Mr. Buchanan would have been proud—I'd never watched the night sky more in my life. Through the scratched bus window, the moon illuminated bright pink as the sun's light disappeared, and with each minute, the pink settled deeper into a reddish-orange hue. According to the National Weather Service website, the super blue blood moon would peak at 10:38 p.m. I still had time to prepare.

Based on the state of his apartment in my dream, I guessed Ben didn't have a reliable car for the road trip, which meant he'd likely buy a train ticket to St. Louis. According to the schedule, the last train left Chicago at 1:00 p.m., arriving here at 8:00 p.m., but it looked like it sold out two days ago. So I hopefully had until tomorrow to deal with him.

A text notification popped up on top of the train website.

Mom again.

I'd stalled long enough, time to reply.

—I have to take care of something. Everything is all right. I'm safe. Be home later.—

She immediately texted back.

—Baxter!!!! I'm worried. Come home. The doctor didn't even release you. He wanted to examine your ribs again. What is going on???? Is this about Ben???—

—No. Not about Ben. I'm fine.—

Although, it was about Ben. Oh yeah, and an evil djinn.

The bus squealed to a stop, and I got off, walking the last few blocks home at a fast pace. I needed to beat Mom home. Without me at the hospital, nothing kept her there, so I had to get in and out of our apartment as quick as possible.

Near our building, I scanned the street. The loitering pedestrians didn't resemble Ben, and only empty parked cars lined the curbs. Ben wouldn't know what I looked like, which gave me an advantage.

I leaped two steps at a time up the stairwell, skipping the broken one. I tossed my keys to the small table by our front door—where they slid off to the floor. Then, I hurried to collect my supplies, working without lights and keeping an attentive ear for any indication of Mom's return.

My heart pounded as I grabbed a notebook, pen, and Janni's ring. I used a broom to scoop Ifrit's box down from my closet shelf since lifting my arms sent jolts of pain through my midsection. After shoving everything into my backpack, I threw in a bag of chips and some water bottles. This could be a long night.

I checked up and down the hallway for Mom, then flew back down the stairs. No sign of her outside, either. Finally, some luck.

In the alley, I paused to catch my breath. Panting tore at my rib cage, so I tried short, shallow breaths to avoid passing out. As my breathing evened and my lungs absorbed the stench of garbage around me, a strange invigoration energized me.

My plan had begun.

"Let's do this."

I texted Jason.

—*Hey, I'm*—

The abandoned sentence stared at me. Jason asked for distance, and I never made it to school to beg him and Ashley for help, thanks to Malcolm. I scrolled to the text I sent them this morning. Still no reply. My text hung out there like a high five no one would slap.

My short-lived adrenaline rush dissipated as loneliness settled onto my shoulders. I missed my friends a lot, but I'd have to finish this on my own. Given everything I put them through—Ashley in particular—I owed it to them to respect their ask.

I'd fix this. I didn't have time to sulk.

I swept my phone's flashlight across the pavement. Finding a space clear of rotting garbage or puddles of liquefied food, I sat down, trying not to think about rats or roaches scurrying onto me. I scribbled the instructions for Janni on a piece of paper, read it, corrected it to make it as easy to understand as possible, then reread it.

Could Janni read? I bit the end of my pen. Janni's ability to follow my instructions would make or break my plan.

He could read. He had to.

I dug the ring out of my pocket, stood up, and

rubbed the purple jewel with the pad of my thumb.

The alley around me glowed purple. Familiar chills tingled my skin, starting on the top of my head and flash-freezing the stitches above my ear before they scampered down the rest of me. After they settled, I sniffed. Garbage masked Janni's odor, which swirled just underneath.

The black silhouettes of motionless dumpsters, cans, and bags hung close against the brick walls. I searched the shadows, figuring a white monkey-creature would be easy to spot, even in the dark alley, but the darkness was still.

My stomach dropped. I summoned Janni too many times. I must've hit a limit.

Panicked, I started to rub the ring's jewel again, still aglow from the first summoning.

"HOW CAN IT SERVE?"

I whirled around, almost tripping over my own feet. "Jesus! Don't you ever come straight at people?"

He started to respond, but then closed his mouth. His ears sunk back against his head. Janni's purple eyes rose to the sky, the dark orange moon vividly reflected in them. "IT DOES NOT LIKE NIGHTS LIKE THESE."

The super blue blood moon meant something to him. Something that made him nervous. I suppressed an excited smile. "Why? Tell me why."

"THE MOON CHANGES THE AIR." His furry brow wrinkled in the middle. "YOU ARE HURT."

"I'm fine." I tightened the hospital gown, suddenly self-conscious.

"IFRIT HURT YOU." Janni's shoulders dropped with a tiny sigh. "IT WARNED YOU."

"I know, I know. Believe me, I'm very aware of my mistake, but right now, I need your help."

"HOW CAN IT—"

"Serve, yeah, got it. First, go get the cellar keys from the landlord like you did before."

"OKAY." Janni jumped.

Here we go.

The breeze chilled my shaved head and blew through the thin hospital gown as I waited. Above, the moon's deep orange glow intensified, coloring the night sky a few shades brighter. The super blue blood moon arrived. No time for a backup plan. This one had to work.

Janni waddled out from behind a garbage bag, the jingling key ring at his side. Its weight made him lean to the right. He hoisted it up and handed it over.

"Thanks. Now, here's the hard part. Can you find a guy named Ben Allen?"

"WHO?"

"My dad." The words felt foreign in my mouth. "I need you to fix something Ifrit did."

Janni fell back on his haunches, pondering. He scratched his chin with one of his monkey hands in a bizarrely human-looking act. "IF IFRIT FOUND HIM, THEN IT CAN TRY. USUALLY, IT NEEDS MORE DIRECTION. EARTH IS A BIG PLACE. IFRIT IS MUCH STRONGER."

"He lives in Chicago, if that helps."

Janni rested his hand on his head, his big eyes checking on the moon again. "CHICAGO."

"Can you do it?" I swallowed the rising panic. Of all the things that could have gone wrong with my plan, finding Ben should have been the easy part. Since I'd met Janni, he'd never needed overly specific instructions on where to go or what to do.

"IT CAN FOLLOW IFRIT TRAIL TO BEN ALLEN. BUT IF IFRIT FINDS ME, JANNI WILL BE IN TROUBLE. LOTS OF TROUBLE."

"I really need you to do this, Janni. Mom and I are in danger. I'll handle Ifrit."

Janni lifted his finger like they did in movies to see which way the wind blew. "IT CAN FEEL THE TRAIL. IT SHOULD WORK."

I smiled. "Awesome. Here's what you need to do." I handed him the instructions. "Can you read that? I wrote everything down. You must follow each step."

He read the page. "THERE ARE MANY WORDS."

"You can read, right?"

Please, please, please.

"IT CAN DO THIS."

I let out a tense breath. Step one complete. "Just follow it step by step."

He rolled up the paper in his pink hands. "IT WILL TAKE AND HELP YOU, BAXTER ALLEN."

"Come find me when it's done." I patted him on the head. "Thank you."

Janni's animal snout twitched like a puppy getting his belly rubbed. "WELCOME. MOON MAKES ALL DJINN STRONGER, SO IT WILL BE EASY."

He jumped.

"Wait, what?"

I stared at the empty space, my mouth hanging open.

The moon makes all djinn stronger?

Could the energy from the super blue blood moon

help Janni find Ben while also helping Ifrit resist banishment? What if the moon empowered Ifrit and I couldn't get rid of him? No, that couldn't happen. It couldn't.

My phone vibrated. Probably Mom. Sheepishly, I checked, dreading her text.

A breath caught in my throat. The phone almost slipped out of my hand. Jason!

—I heard you were in the hospital. You okay?—

The excitement made it hard to type. I kept having to backspace and start over.

—Yeah. Jumped by Malcolm. Bruises. Some stitches.—

—That sucks.—

—I deserve it.—

—No, you don't. You try the incantation?—

—Failed.—

—!!!!!!—

—New plan. Reading it during the super blue blood moon. Hoping incantation needs power from space.—

—Good thinking!!! Moon power works on werewolves.—

I smiled. Jason and I always thought alike. That's why we were best friends.

—Need help?—

—I appreciate it, but you should stay out of it. Be safe.—

—We're already deep in it.—

—We?—

—Look up.—

At the mouth of the alley, the streetlights elongated the shadows of Ashley and Jason, stretching them toward me like superheroes showing up in time for the final epic battle.

My laugh echoed off the brick walls of the alley.

They came!

I charged them, practically tackling them to the ground. One arm around each, I mashed us into a tight group hug. They squeezed me back. Ashley giggled.

I ignored the searing pain in my chest for as long as I could before I eased them away.

Jason adjusted his glasses, squished crooked on his nose. "Not a hugger? You started it."

I untied one of the hospital gown ties to show them the bruise. "Fractured rib. Don't take it personally."

"Gift from Malcolm?"

"How'd you guess?"

"Well, it goes with the stitches." Ashley eyed the shaved part of my head. "And given your outfit, I'm guessing you made a quick escape from the hospital?"

"Yeah." Seeing Ashley triggered flashes of Ifrit torturing Mr. Bryant. I cringed. "I can't tell you how sorry I am." I spoke to her shoes, unable to look her in the eye.

"I got your message. Thanks for saying those things. It's not your fault, Bax. I know that. I'm not gonna lie, though. I was freakin' angry."

Freakin'.

Ashley's annoying traits seemed way less annoying. "I would have been angry, too. How is he?"

"I'll fill you in later. Bottom line—he'll be fine. Said he knew who did it but won't say who. Dad said they provided a verified alibi, so he didn't want to drag them through the mud until he could prove it. If he even could. And, he said if it *was* that person, it didn't make any sense at all. Not sure what all that means. I think he's still half out of it."

"I can fill you in, if you want to know?"

Ashley shook her head. "Doesn't matter right now. Tell me later. Moon time is ticking. Let's do this thing. I'm sure you have a plan that needs my editing."

The grin practically took over my entire face. I wanted to hug them both again but wasn't ready to brave the pain so soon after it finally resided. "I have to ask, what changed your minds? Why'd you come back? Not that I'm complaining."

Jason shrugged. "We figured abandoning you put us in just as much danger as helping you end it."

"Plus, we heard you were in the hospital and guessed you could use some help." Ashley bit her bottom lip. "And, if I'm honest, finding out Dad would survive got me back on board."

"I get it."

The incantation would work. I'd never been so sure. We'd send Ifrit straight back to oblivion.

"Oh," Jason lowered his voice, even though no one was around to hear us, "and your mom came by my house looking for you. Ashley said she checked there, too. She's pretty worried."

"Wait." I shook my head. "She went by Ashley's tonight? I just left my place, like, minutes ago."

Ashley nodded. "You probably barely missed her."

"Too close. But if I'm considered AWOL, how'd you know to check here?"

"Really?" Ashley folded her arms. Ms. Know-It-All had returned. I missed her. "Reading the incantation where you summoned Ifrit seemed like a logical step. The moon thing's a good call, too, by the way. How'd you think of that?"

"Old man in a bookstore." I laughed.

"See?" Ashley's loud voice rang in the alley, louder than Janni's. "Those old guys in bookstores always know things!"

"Okay, okay." Jason grabbed my shoulder with one hand and Ashley's with his other. "What have we missed since you translated the incantation? Talk quickly."

I filled them in, grateful to have my friends back and not have to go into the banishment—or cellar—alone. I told them about Dr. Bashir translating the incantation, the failed attempt at reading it, Malcolm jumping me, and finally, the dream about Greg turning out to be Ben.

"Your mom has been in hiding this whole time?" Jason leaned against the brick wall. "That's crazy. You think Greg—I mean Ben—is really coming?"

"Not if Janni comes through. But right now, I can't do anything else about that."

"Well, let's hope your plan works." Jason pushed off the wall.

"The clock's ticking." Ashley tapped the invisible watch on her wrist.

"Right. So," Jason recapped, "we go into the cellar, near where we found Ifrit's box and read the incantation at 10:38. How long will the eclipse go on?"

"It's called totality." Ashley jumped in, reading off her phone. "The super blue blood moon will be in totality for one hour, sixteen minutes, and four seconds. We have time."

I nodded. "But I'd rather finish sooner than later. In case it backfires and we need to try again or something."

"Do we have a backup plan, boys?"

"We don't need one," Jason and I said together.

Jason dropped his backpack and took out a large flashlight. "I grabbed this from home."

"Great. I got the box."

Ashley scrunched her face. "Rats, here we come."

Chapter 24

The heavy cellar door slammed shut above us, kicking up a small cloud of dust while sending a tremor rumbling over my shoulders. I ran my phone's flashlight across the floor, scattering a cluster of shiny black bugs. Ashley must've seen them, too, because her clutch on the back of my hospital gown tightened.

"I have a fractured rib. Go easy back there."

"Sorry." Her grip loosened.

We crept between the rotting shelves, tripping over each other every few steps. Jason turned his flashlight on lantern mode, brightly lighting our immediate area. At the same time, the beams from Ashley's phone and mine swept our surroundings, chasing every shadowy movement our eyes tricked us into thinking we saw. I'd never walked so slowly or so keenly aware of every subtle sound or flicker in the darkness, even though we were the first to walk in the cellar in decades.

A mangy brown rat scampered across our path, and Ashley let out a bizarre squeak as she suppressed a scream.

"Did you just try to talk to that rat in his native language?" Jason chuckled, relaxing some of the anxiousness hanging over us.

"Whatever." The smile sounded in her voice.

"Up there." I shined my light ahead.

Jason stepped up next to me with his brighter

flashlight. "You sure this is the right corner?"

"Definitely." The cement chunks and broken brick remained piled on the floor, right where we'd found Ifrit's box. I should have left that stupid thing buried. If only I'd listened to Janni's warning.

No time for that.

"And look." I swung the beam of my flashlight over to the only shelf in the cellar that didn't form a straight row with its neighbors and the only one with a splintered leg. "There's where he appeared and shoved the shelf aside."

Jason lit up the area where the foundation met the brick of the building. "And there's the hole where erosion must've pushed the box out. Do you think someone, like, dropped Ifrit's box in the wet cement when the building was under construction? I mean, the building's over a hundred years old."

"Given the shit storm Ifrit causes," Ashley shook her head, "would it surprise you if someone snuck in here during construction and buried it? Kind of a good idea if your goal is to keep the box out of people's hands. I'm sure whoever hid it never guessed time would unearth it."

My fingers traced the cold cement around the opening. "Ifrit said it took him hundreds of years to form the illusion of the old man. So he hasn't been out of his box since way before the building existed. I wonder if he could have created the illusion if his box was still buried."

Neither Ashley nor Jason commented. The quiet of the cellar swelled in my ears. Unintentionally or not, we were stalling, delaying our confrontation. I checked my phone—*10:30 p.m.*

Almost time.

"Okay, guys. We have an hour and sixteen minutes." I hid my trembling hands in my pockets before they could notice.

"Plenty of time to read a freakin' poem, right?"

"Thank you for coming back." I nodded at each of them. "It means a lot."

Jason grunted. "Stop acting like this is your death march, man. It's gonna work."

Ashley handed me the incantation and then shined her light on the paper while Jason illuminated the brick pile. Jason held up his phone, showing us the time.

We stared at his screen. The minutes crawled by.

10:33 p.m.

10:36 p.m.

10:37 p.m.

I held the incantation in front of me. I couldn't hide my shaky hands in my pockets anymore. Jason and Ashley pretended not to notice.

My eyes burned from staring at the phone screen.

Blink, Bax.

10:38 p.m.

Here we go.

I inhaled, slowly exhaled, then began. "Neither slumber nor sleep will be overtaken by It. Dreams belongeth unto the soul who dreamt."

The old cement floor vibrated. Concrete pebbles jumped in place. The heat simmered in my core.

It was working!

"May It never intercedeth with the desires of Man, on his behalf or with Will. Here forward, It is commanded to return to Otherworld, from whence it came."

The shelves bounced on the concrete, dust and debris rolled from them and rained onto the floor. Inside the hole where the cement met the brick, where we imagined the box came from, a swirl of thick blackness began to spin. Beads of sweat, which quickly chilled in the basement, broke out on my forehead.

The size of a softball, the dark matter in the opening spun like a black hole in space. It drew the air into it. Slowly at first, but as it turned faster, the cellar air breezed past our heads, sucked into it.

We found the missing piece. Either the moon, the location, or maybe both. At this point, I didn't care. We were gonna banish Ifrit forever.

The jewel on Ifrit's box exploded with bright purple, lighting up the entire cellar.

"Holy crap." Jason clutched his flashlight. "Keep going. Finish it, Bax."

The short incantation went on for millions of lines. My hair tingled. The energy around us pulsated like a living organism.

I concentrated on the paper in my hands. "Never again to know that which is in front of Man, nor behind him. May It encompass nothing of knowledge and will."

The black hole grew, spinning faster and absorbing the concrete wall until it was as tall as me. The air whipped past us into the vortex. Decades of dust pelted the backs of our heads, bounced over us, then flew into the void. My flimsy hospital gown flapped. Next to me, Ashley's hair slapped the fresh stitches in my head.

I shouted the last line, yelling over the swirling tornado. "Spending the rest of time in darkness, forever away from Man."

A deafening roar rose in the cellar, shaking the walls and ceiling. Shelves scooted on the old concrete, inching toward the human-sized black hole. I leaned back against the vortex's pull, not wanting to lose my footing and end up whisked into whatever lay beyond.

Ashley's hands tightened around Ifrit's box. Jason squeezed his flashlight.

Then, he appeared.

A few short yards from the vortex, Ifrit materialized, rising to life. His muscled legs flexed as he planted his hooves firmly, struggling to resist the draw of the vortex.

I pointed to Ifrit. "Look! It's pulling him in. When I'd summoned him with the incantation before, he didn't see the vortex. That's how he knew I'd failed."

Ifrit's tail, usually slithering behind him, stretched out toward the black hole. One of his hands grasped a nearby shelf. The wood splintered under his grip.

"You have discovered the way." Ifrit's growl sliced through the vortex's swirling wind.

My backpack slid along the concrete. I threw it over my shoulder. "Go away. You're banished!"

"I gave you everything you wanted. Even your father." His eyes glowed a bright violet, and the flickering flame in the back of his throat lit up like an inferno.

"I don't want any of it!"

"You are a fool. If I had asked if you wanted Scarlet Lane, would you have said no? If I had asked if you wanted to meet your father, would you have said no?"

I covered my ears, not wanting to hear him. If he had asked me, I would have absolutely said yes. I would have never asked about consequences—never.

"Do not feel bad. I have served hundreds of masters. All as stupid as you." A chortle erupted from him.

I tossed my backpack to Jason, picked up a piece of brick from the ground, and threw it. It bounced off Ifrit's chest like a pebble.

Almost there. Just get in the damn vortex!

A rat, clawing at the floor, slid past us, then caught air and shot into the vortex.

Ashley grabbed my forearm. "Why isn't he going in? What should we do?"

The swirling black hole vibrated, answering Ashley. Thousands of voices screaming over each other poured from it—tortured souls screeching in pain. The sound punctured the wind. We covered our ears.

Slime-glistened black tentacles crept from the opening of the vortex. Like octopi legs with no body, they slinked with infinite length across the concrete toward Ifrit. As if frozen in place, Ifrit allowed the tentacles to slither up his legs and secure themselves around his ankles and calves.

Ifrit roared, shaking the cellar, making me flinch, but the tentacles kept hold, unintimidated. With a loud crack, the shelf Ifrit clutched snapped under his claw.

Even though his hooves remained planted, Ifrit began sliding toward the vortex as the tentacles dragged him, leaving concrete ruts in their wake. Having lost the shelf, Ifrit leaned back, clawing the wall behind him. He couldn't resist the pull.

"It's working!" Jason yelled in my ear.

"Humans always want what they don't have. Then they blame others for the consequences." He growled at us.

The tentacles dragged Ifrit, leaving deep claw gouges in the wall. As the vortex drew nearer, the tentacles slithered up Ifrit's legs, around his torso and chest, lacing around him like a cocoon. Only his head remained exposed.

He roared.

With a final yank, Ifrit's feet left the ground, and he flew into the void, whisked away by the tentacles. Together, they disappeared into the blackness.

We stared at the swirling black, waiting for it to shrink and close.

"Is it over?" Ashley yelled over the drone of the whipping wind.

Something moved inside.

An unmistakable black claw launched from the blackness. It punctured the floor like a grappling hook.

"No! Go the fuck away!" I leaped toward the vortex, but Jason grabbed my shirt.

I broke free. This was our only chance to banish Ifrit. Now or never.

I grabbed a cement chunk and threw it at the claw with all my strength. I missed. The rock bounced once on the floor, then into the black hole.

Following my lead, Jason started throwing whatever he could find. So did Ashley. Jason made the first direct hit, but Ifrit's hand didn't even twitch.

Picking up another rock, I stepped closer and threw it. This time, I hit Ifrit's hand. He roared, though it sounded muted from inside the vortex. I took another step closer and made contact again. This time, his hand twitched, his grip loosened.

"Hit him with everything," I yelled over the

swirling wind, commanding an army.

Another chunk flew at the hand from behind me. It missed.

With another basement-shaking roar, Ifrit's pointed tail whipped out from the void, lashed across the cellar floor, and wrapped securely around my ankle.

Oh no—

The tail yanked, throwing me flat on my back. My head cracked against the cement. Starbursts exploded in my vision.

I scrambled, but the tail began dragging me toward the vortex. I clawed at the ground, trying to stop myself. Without footing, I slid forward, feet first. My back scraped across the concrete like sandpaper.

Jason and Ashley grabbed at my shoulders but couldn't secure a grip on the loose hospital gown that had come untied as I slid forward. Looking down the length of me, beyond my feet, the vortex grew bigger and bigger, closer and closer.

My flailing arms searched for my friends' hands. My fractured rib sent surges of pain shooting through me as my outstretched arm waved over my head, my breathing frantic.

I grazed fingertips but couldn't connect.

Ashley screamed. Jason shouted my name, hysterical.

The vortex drew nearer.

Jason finally grabbed my hand. I squeezed, desperate to secure our hold on each other.

"Don't let go!" His pull on my arm sent fire bolts across my midsection. Tears rained from my eyes. I didn't let go. I couldn't let go.

But Jason's grip came too late and too insecure.

With a mighty yank, Ifrit's tail thrashed, and my hand slipped from Jason's.

Over the rumble of the winds and my friends yelling my name, the dark hole flew at me.

The chaos of the cellar dropped into silence.

Frigid blackness enveloped me.

Chapter 25

Infinite, bottomless blackness.

Like outer space, my arms and legs swung with
ease. I was swimming, but without the resistance of
water. The lack of something tangible to hold, along
with the sensation of floating, made my stomach
queasy.

My arms were still through the sleeves of the
hospital gown, but the rest of it floated behind me like a
cape underwater. Ashley and Jason's desperate attempt
to save me from Ifrit pulled the cloth ties apart,
allowing the dense cold to wrap itself around me,
stinging the shallow cuts on my back. I tied the hospital
gown shut, tucking it back into my pants, but my
muscles still shivered.

Behind me, the tunnel of light I'd fallen through
glowed brightly—a lone star in a starless galaxy. As the
only point of reference, I couldn't determine how far
away the beacon was. A mile? Hundreds of miles?

I pumped my arms and legs, attempting to swim
back to the gateway, but the frictionless space just
rolled around my limbs. There was nothing to propel
me forward.

Ifrit dragged me here, then vanished. Why? To
float lifelessly until starvation killed me? Or boredom?

There had to be a way out, back to the gateway.

The blackness quivered ahead.

Like a spaceship materializing from a speck on the horizon of space, something floated steadily toward me. It glided silently on a straight trajectory, headed for the gateway. Could I be that lucky? I'd just grab onto the object and ride it to the tunnel. Then, when close enough, I'd jump off, propelling myself through the gateway and back into my world.

Stay calm. Focus.
Wait for it.
Wait for it.
Wait for it.

The object drew closer, taking shape from the blackness. A woman, Egyptian maybe, floated on her back. Her delicate silk robes rippled elegantly around her like a spirit. Her rigid, flat body lay on nothing. She had light caramel skin, and her ebony hair melted into the vortex around us. She rested peacefully. On her stomach, a jeweled oil lamp glimmered. A lamp that, before recent events, I would have associated with genies.

She floated closer. My heart thundered in my ears. She'd be my ride out.

Here we go.

I reached for her.

The smile melted off my face. My fingers fell inches short of making contact.

"No!" My voice cracked with panic. "Come on, come on."

I pumped my legs and arms in every direction, but my flapping limbs didn't move my body any closer. The narrow gap—mere inches—remained between us. I spun in place, swinging my arms and wiggling my fingers, trying to get all possible length from my body. I just needed the hem of her rippling dress or a few strands of her floating hair.

The woman glided by, oblivious to my crazed flailing. Frantically, I kept reaching with both arms, determined to stretch, determined to catch my ride out of the vortex. I refused to let a couple of stupid inches beat me.

She continued past me, a one-woman funeral procession, taking my opportunity to escape with her.

"Wake up! Don't leave me here!"

She floated on, peacefully at rest, my ride to the gateway vanishing. In all the infinite space around me, I'd missed my escape by a finger length.

The beautiful woman shrunk to a speck in the blackness, then disappeared entirely. Gone.

Ifrit set me up. He showed me the way out, knowing it'd be just out of reach. The odds of the woman passing by so close were too improbable. Ifrit orchestrated that. He enjoyed watching my torment from somewhere in the depths of this place.

"You did that, didn't you? Why did you bring me here?" The endless nothing of the vortex absorbed my words. "Why?"

His familiar grumble floated through the blackness as smoothly as the Egyptian lady paraded by me. His subtle chuckle slinked beneath his animal growl.

Ifrit rode the empty space toward me on an invisible chariot. The fire in his throat burned, and smoke curled from his snout, trailing behind him like an old-time train. His tail wavered left to right like a shark's.

He eased to a stop in front of me.

"Why did you bring me here?"

The corners of his muzzle turned up into a sinister smile. "You wished to banish me, so now you will know the fate you so casually bestowed."

"Casually? Are you kidding me? Let me out of here!" The emptiness nullified the impact of my shout.

"You are no longer my master. You are a mortal visitor. Nothing more."

"Visitor? You mean prisoner. Am I in the box? Your box?"

"The box is only a doorway." Ifrit glided closer, able to manipulate the nothingness while I floated lifelessly, entirely at his mercy.

"Please let me go. Please."

"Let you go? I waited entire human lifetimes to be free of this place. Lifetimes. Now I am back because of you. For that, you shall suffer."

I swallowed the vomit rising in the back of my throat. Ifrit intended to punish me. He'd never release me. I'd spend the rest of my life in the vortex, limply floating, subject to whatever he wanted to do to me. Until I died in this place.

His arm lashed out, striking like a cobra. He locked his hand around my neck. His clawed fingertips pierced my skin.

Surprise created a gasp in my throat that couldn't escape.

He squeezed.

I grabbed his wrist with both hands, trying to push him off, but his stone arm didn't budge. I punched his thick wrist. His grip didn't loosen. He wouldn't torture me after all. He'd just kill me, short and sweet.

My head warmed with trapped blood, unable to drain back to the rest of me. My vision narrowed. My neck muscles strained.

No way. Not without a fight.

I kicked as hard as I could into Ifrit's stomach. He didn't flinch.

My sight became blurred with exploding orange spots. Thanks to my episodes, I knew the feeling. Darkness swelled inside. The spots grew together into a solid curtain, then the orange faded to black. My head became fuzzy, and my throat collapsed.

I passed out.

****

Gasping, the sudden inhale of frigid air charged my fractured rib, stinging me with a jolt and thrusting me back to consciousness. With only blackness in front of me, I looked over my shoulder. The gateway home still glowed, but hope felt as distant as the gateway itself.

I massaged my neck. Spending the rest of my life with Ifrit strangling me over and over while I hung in space like a lifeless doll sent shudders over me. Ifrit's meddling in my real life didn't compare to this nightmare. There had to be a way back home.

The stillness vibrated.

I squinted into the darkness to my left.

A shape glided by, faster than the Egyptian woman. It traveled away from the gateway and well out of my reach. If closer, I might have grabbed it. The idea of moving somewhere—anywhere—seemed like a good idea. Doing *something* seemed like a good enough plan.

No, bad idea. The tunnel of light was my only way home. Aimlessly flying farther into the vortex would be like giving up. I wasn't there. Not yet.

Besides, as the shape came into focus, I

reconsidered spending my days in oblivion with it. A cloud of smoke surrounded this djinn, which resembled a huge man's bodiless head propelled forward like a turtle-paced comet. With pointed ears, pencil-thin eyebrows, and two small fangs poking out from beneath his upper lip, the face appeared to be in a meditative sleep, like the Egyptian woman.

As the spirit leisurely cruised by, a clawed hand sprang up from behind the head. Ifrit climbed over the top of the djinn, shoving it aside. The head continued its new redirected trajectory, still asleep.

My muscles tensed. I raised my fists, bracing for another murder attempt as the nothing carried Ifrit toward me.

"What do you want with me?" I shouted. "Why did you drag me here? Just to kill me?"

Ifrit cocked his head. "But I have not killed you."

"Was that what you wanted to do?"

He slid closer and folded his arms across his broad chest, almost appearing humanlike. "Since time began, no mortal has entered this dimension, only djinn."

"Why bring *me* here, then?"

"So you'd see where I exist when you stole my freedom."

Did he expect me to feel sorry for him? Not after what he'd done. No way. Not after he'd killed, manipulated, and tortured people in my life.

"Fine, I see it. It sucks. Can I go now?"

Ifrit's pointed tongue lashed out over his lips. "Sucks?"

"Sorry, did I offend you by saying your kingdom sucks? You seem to be the guy in charge around here. That makes this your kingdom, right?"

He growled. "Then behold my subjects." Ifrit waved his hand at the djinn head disappearing into the nothing. "I am no more than a caretaker of nothing. Djinn sleep until summoned into your world. Blissful until ripped out of this dimension and thrown into yours. If this is my kingdom, then I rule over a vast emptiness littered with spirit corpses."

"They just float around until summoned?"

A cloud of gray smoke puffed out of his nostrils. "They are unaware of time. Until brought to life."

What a horrible way to exist. Floating unconscious in blackness, waiting to be summoned. Djinn only lived the brief moments humans called them to life. They depended entirely on strangers. Strangers who wanted something from them. Strangers who used them to create a different life for themselves—a more remarkable one.

My cheeks grew warm with guilt, even in the coldness of the vortex. People never used djinn for the greater good. If a genuinely selfless human had discovered a djinn, the world would be free of disease, war, and poverty. But those things existed. That meant humans have always used djinn to selfishly serve themselves.

I was no better. Disappointment settled on me like a ton of steel. Like the hundreds of selfish humans before me with an opportunity to make a positive change, I didn't.

"So if the other djinn sleep in this place, why don't you?"

"I cannot. As caretaker of this dimension, I am aware of every second of every millennium in this darkness, with nothing."

Ifrit lived through the endless loop of summoning and banishing. He experienced it alone, over and over, for thousands of years. No wonder he hated people.

His purple eyes flickered, and a strange sympathy tugged at me. "I'm-I'm sorry, but I don't belong here."

"You do now. You will live here forever, or as long as your mortal body allows."

His words sprouted goosebumps on my arms. "What?" My eyes widened, my temporary sympathy devoured by fear.

"No way." My voice quivered. "Send me home."

"Aren't you curious how a mortal can survive in this dimension? You will be the first."

"No, not curious at all. Couldn't give two craps." Frenzy hurried my words. Did he keep me here to punish me, out of loneliness, or did he want to play scientist?

He didn't know the answer. He'd never done this before. I had the honor of being the first.

Lucky me.

By the time the crack of Ifrit's tail rang in my ears, it had already snapped across my cheek. My eyes closed as my head flung to the side.

When I opened them, a white ceiling blinded me as I lay flat on my back, on something solid.

I jerked my head to the side of the paper pillowcase. A pale blue curtain surrounded the area around my bed. As my ears became conscious, hospital noises sprung to life on the other side of the curtain: medical speak, beeping equipment, and the clanging of devices.

Next to me, Mom flipped through a magazine on a gray plastic chair, legs crossed. She didn't notice I'd woken up. Celebrity gossip absorbed her.

My thumb and fingertips rolled the stiff sheets between them, testing their realness. I inhaled, ignoring the pain of my rib cage expanding, taking in the sanitized, chilled air of the hospital.

This was all familiar. Had I gone back in time? Did Jason and Ashley find a way to bring me back?

The skin of my newly shaved head was smooth, except for the stitches. I lifted the sheet. The purple and blue bruise three inches round blistered the lower left half of my rib cage.

I was in the hospital, so the beating happened. I reviewed what else took place up until this point in time. Malcolm wouldn't have jumped me if Ifrit hadn't threatened Scarlet, which could have only occurred if Ifrit murdered Nick.

So I still needed to get to the cellar before the end of the super blue blood moon. This second chance could be my last chance.

My head throbbed. How did Jason and Ashley turn back time? With Janni?

"Mom?"

Startled, she dropped the magazine to the floor and leaped to her feet. "Baxter!" She rushed to my bedside. "You're awake." Her face glowed with relief.

She rested her hand on my head, stroking my hair. "You fractured a rib and needed a few stitches, but other than that, you're fine. Your father will be elated. You worried us for a while there."

"Wait, my...father?" I shook my head.

The light blue curtain clanged as its rings slid along the bar, and Ben stepped inside. He pulled the curtain closed behind him.

"Hey, buddy." The opposite of the Ben in my dream, this guy wore a yellow golf shirt and dress slacks, clean-shaven, with his hair stylishly swept to the side. His eyes sparkled, and his broad smile beamed with pride. "So glad you're okay."

I choked, propping myself up on my elbows, ignoring the pain in my chest. "What the hell?"

"Hey now, watch the language, buddy." Ben grinned.

Buddy?

My friends hadn't brought me back in time, they created an alternate dimension or alternate timeline. The thought made the hairs on the back of my neck stand at attention.

Mom gave Ben a warm smile, lacing her fingers between his.

I swallowed, my throat gritty.

"You okay, buddy? You're safe. No one will attack you here."

Stop calling me buddy.

I rubbed my eyes. As I lowered my hand, a fresh smear of blood stained my palm. I traced the cut on my cheek. My fingertips came back red.

Ifrit's tail sliced my cheek twice. Once in my bedroom, and then in the vortex. The cut on my cheek didn't come from Malcolm beating the crap out of me but from Ifrit's tail. Right before I showed up in the hospital with this cleaned-up version of Ben.

"You're not real." I rubbed my eyes again, trying to end the weird dream.

"Hon, you're—" Mom started.

"You're not real!" I yelled at the ceiling.

I didn't want some fake life with Ben in it. I

wanted my old life back, before the ring and before the box. I wanted movie night with Mom, *Archer Annihilation* with Jason, and dinner with his parents. I wanted to fantasize about Scarlet, knowing she'd never date me. I wanted my perfectly imperfect life back.

I wished I could go back in time and never accept that stupid ring. That's the alternate reality I wanted.

"Not real!"

I blinked.

Black nothing replaced the sterile whiteness.

Ifrit hovered in front of me. His eyes glowed brightly. I floated limply before him.

"See what I can do for you?" Ifrit growled. "I can still give you what you want, or I can give you eternal nightmares. We can try both. We have plenty of time."

"I don't want some fake reality. I don't want anything from you. I want what's out there." I pointed to the gateway. "That's what I want."

"How about life as a superhero, with the strength of twenty men? A rock star with beautiful women pining over you?"

"Stop it!" The darkness chilled the tears in my eyes. I swiped them dry. "I'm not your entertainment to help you pass the time."

"You are an ingrate." Ifrit slithered closer. Heat radiated off him, sizzling the coldness of the vortex.

I should bargain with him—make a deal with the devil that was worth his while.

"Look, the tunnel is still open. Send me back. If you do, I'll summon you on the outside again. I promise. You can keep messing with my life."

The purple in Ifrit's eyes faded. He glanced at the gateway.

Come on, accept it. Just accept it.

"The gateway has not closed." He snarled, just realizing it. "This place wants to vomit you back to your world."

I took in a short breath. Then why wouldn't it spit me out?

"I wonder, though, once the eclipse ends, if the gateway will close." Ifrit mused to himself, thoughtfully trying to figure out the riddle.

I spun in place. The tunnel of light shrank. Hadn't it? No, my mind played tricks on me. "I promise, I'll summon you again from the outside. I promise."

Ifrit's head darted from the tunnel back to me. "Too miserable? After only a few minutes? How will you feel after trillions of minutes?"

He turned to leave. I bored him.

"Wait!" I couldn't let him go. I couldn't let him leave me alone.

"Yes, Baxter Allen?"

What else could I say? I needed to keep him talking. If I kept him talking, maybe he'd reveal a way out.

Ben.

"I have a question." I hurried to formulate it.

Ifrit cocked his head.

"You grant what you think I want. Like how you tortured Ashley's dad to protect me because I'm your connection to out there." I pointed to the gateway. "But why did you show Ben where we lived? You saw what I saw. He'll hurt us."

Ifrit's eyes flickered purple. "Ben has no intention of harming you."

"He packed a gun in his suitcase! He wanted to

teach Mom a lesson."

"But he would not harm you." A hesitant, almost confused tone laced Ifrit's response. "He has a desire to know you and you a desire to know him."

"He'll kill my mom!"

"She is not my concern." Ifrit turned to leave again.

"If you want to be out of here so badly," I shouted after him, "why do you do such horrible things to people who summon you? If you did *normal* wish granting, we'd be best friends."

He turned his thick neck, pondering a response. He answered over his shoulder. "But this is how I am."

"You're not. You're lonely. You want to be around people, or other creatures, or whatever."

"You do not know what it means to be djinn."

"I don't, but if you—"

"*Silence!*" Ifrit roared into the blackness, his back still toward me, his tail rippling behind him. "Someone summons."

"They're summoning you?" Jason and Ashley came through! They're pulling him back out. They'd better have a plan, though.

"Man summons another."

"Another djinn?" My shoulders dropped—not Jason and Ashley.

Ifrit vanished.

"Wait! You can't leave me here," I shouted to no one.

Once again, I floated alone in the emptiness.

Chapter 26

My only escape twinkled mockingly behind me, far away, likely to disappear with the end of the super blue blood moon. I tried demanding, reasoning, begging, even bartering, but Ifrit responded to none of it. He couldn't decide what to do with me other than keeping me imprisoned, which seemed fine with him.

Would I grow old in the vortex? Would I get hungry at some point? Could I sleep? If I floated in space for long enough, my muscles would deteriorate. Not to mention I'd go insane with nothing but empty blackness all around me twenty-four seven. People can't spend years without human contact. That's how prisoners of war got all messed up in the head. So if I managed to escape one day, I'd have PTSD or something. *If* I escaped.

As my bleak future stabbed me over and over in the brain, my heart rate increased. My knees—even though they held no weight—melted. Cloudiness crept into the edges of my peripheral vision.

Oh no.

An episode brewed inside me. I wasn't even speaking in front of people.

Are you kidding?

My ears pounded as blood tried to fuel my brain through shrunken arteries. My vision narrowed.

I couldn't. I refused to have an episode. If the

gateway only stayed open for the rest of the super blue blood moon, I couldn't waste time on a stupid anxiety attack. If I passed out, I'd miss my only chance at escape.

Think.

Mrs. Bronson gave me tips to avoid a full-blown episode.

First, clear my mind. Worrying about an eternity in the vortex wouldn't help. If that's my fate, I'd have plenty of time to stress out about it. No time now. Stay rational.

Second, close my eyes. Focus.

Third, slow my breathing. Long, deep breaths while counting to four. As my chest expanded, pain seared my fractured rib, but I didn't stop, the discomfort a needed distraction from my swirling thoughts.

Inhale. One, two, three, four.
Hold. One, two, three, four.
Exhale. One, two, three, four.
Repeat.
Repeat.

I forced everything from my mind, concentrating on the rhythm of my breathing. No thoughts of the vortex. No thoughts of Ifrit or Janni. No thoughts of Scarlet or Nick or Mr. Bryant or Ben. Just the steady beat of the cold air entering and leaving my lungs. I floated high among clouds, above the Earth, far from the nothingness.

The pounding in my ears eased to a steady thud. My throat opened. The muscles in my legs became solid. The cloudiness in my peripheral vision evaporated.

Episode averted. I beat it.

I smiled in the vast emptiness, aware again of my surroundings. Mrs. Bronson would have been proud. First time I ever kicked an episode's ass.

And with my final, cleansing breath, my clear mind smacked me with a single word.

Incantation.

What would happen if I read the incantation in the vortex? It may summon Ifrit, or maybe it would cause a reverse disruption, sending me back into my world. Since the gateway remained open, the super blue blood moon would still power the words. Ifrit said the vortex remained open because it wanted me out. Maybe it just needed some help.

With nothing to lose, I dug into my pocket for the incantation. My fingers brushed against the ring. Mortals hung in the vortex like rag dolls, but Ifrit rode the emptiness like a superhero above the clouds. Could Janni do the same?

I pulled the ring out of my pocket, gripping it tightly, terrified to drop it into the nothing. I swiped my finger over the purple jewel and waited—and waited.

Then, it happened.

Chills trickled over me, icier than the dense air. I shuddered. The ring glowed, lighting up the darkness with a purple hue. I laughed out loud. Janni would get me to the gateway and back to my dimension.

Within seconds, Janni glided through the darkness, his floppy ears trailing him like a cape. My tiny, hairy superhero.

"YOU ARE HERE?" Janni took in our surroundings, searching the blackness.

"Janni!" He flinched as I yelled his name. "I can't

tell you how happy I am to see you."

"WHY IS BAXTER ALLEN HERE? IT HAS NEVER SEEN A HUMAN HERE." He scratched his head, still looking around. "JANNI HAS NEVER BEEN AWAKE HERE, EITHER—"

"I need your help, and we don't have much time." I spoke so quickly, the words fumbled around in my mouth.

"IT FOUND BEN AND—"

"Not now," I interrupted. "You need to haul me to the gateway over there before totality ends. I don't know how much longer we have."

The light from the gateway sparkled in Janni's glassy eyes. "JANNI IS NOT THAT STRONG."

I grabbed Janni's tiny hand, colder than the vortex air. "There's no gravity in here. I won't be heavy. You have to try."

Janni puffed up his pink cheeks, tightened his grip on my hand, and started floating toward the gateway. As my arm extended, pain shot through my chest. I squinted, trying to ignore it, fighting the instinct to yank my arm back and return it comfortably against my torso.

Like Ifrit, Janni rode the nothing like a gentle wave, dragging me behind. The gateway grew closer.

"Can you go any faster?"

His right arm outstretched in front of him, looking even more like a superhero, while his left hung at his side, my hand wrapped tightly around it.

A roar erupted, unleashing a shockwave that rippled through the vortex. The nothingness quivered.

"No!" Ifrit's yell filled the vastness.

Without letting go, I looked back. Ifrit sped toward

us, the space between us shrinking rapidly.

"He's coming!"

Janni glanced back, his eyes glowing purple. "OH NO!"

"Hurry! Don't worry about him. Just keep going."

Tears streaked my cheeks from the searing pain in my chest, but I didn't let go of Janni's tiny hand. I couldn't.

The gateway's light grew brighter in front of us.

Behind us or below us—direction in the nothingness didn't exist—Ifrit closed the gap.

"Stop, djinn, I command you." Ifrit's voice quaked the emptiness. "You will spend eternity in agony."

Janni whimpered but continued flying.

"Faster, Janni!" I shouted prompts to cover Ifrit's threats and keep Janni focused. "You have to keep going. Don't look back."

I couldn't do anything from inside the vortex, but after we escaped, I'd protect Janni. I'd keep him summoned and by my side all the time, safely out of Ifrit's clutches.

The light grew bigger. Almost there.

Ifrit's tail whipped behind him like a beached eel. His massive arms reached out, snapping at my feet. His constant growl vibrated the space around us.

"I command you to stop, djinn!"

Janni dove into the gateway, pulling me with him.

The light blinded me. The cold concrete shocked my bare arms. I didn't wait for my eyes to adjust. I clawed myself out of the vortex and onto the frigid cement floor. My chest screamed in pain, but the happiness at seeing the musty, rat-infested cellar smothered it.

"Baxter!" Jason and Ashley shouted at the same time. They scrambled toward me.

I dug my fingertips into the floor, pulling with every muscle. Jason and Ashley each took a wrist and yanked. An orange explosion of pain exploded across my vision. The intensity consumed me, tearing through my midsection like a machine gun.

Don't pass out. Stay conscious.

And as they heaved, Ifrit grabbed my ankle.

"He's got my foot!"

"Try harder," Jason screamed at Ashley.

"I am!"

As they yanked me forward, Ifrit pulled me back, my torso ready to rip in half at any moment.

With my free foot, I stomped backward, kicking Ifrit's hand. Over and over, I pounded the sole of my tennis shoe on him, trying to loosen his hold. The excruciating pain in my chest sent wave after wave through me. Tears drenched my cheeks, but I kept pounding.

Janni's hands wrapped around my forearm, helping Jason and Ashley.

Finally, summoning the remainder of my strength, I launched my foot down on Ifrit's hand. His grip relaxed. I stomped again. This time, my leg broke free, and I launched into Jason and Ashley, who tumbled backward to the ground, the three of us in a pile. Janni had rolled safely to the side, avoiding getting squashed under us.

The black hole continued to swirl, its suction whipping dust and debris into a windstorm in the cellar. My ears rang, shocked from the dead silence of the djinn dimension.

I panted. Everything ached as I rolled over.

Why hadn't the vortex closed?

I lifted my head, looking down the length of my body to the black hole. One of Ifrit's hands clung to the cement as he attempted to climb back out.

"No fucking way."

Feeding off the jolts of pain, I crawled to a stand. Bolts of electricity shot through me. I grabbed a broken brick. I'd cut his hand off if it came to it. No way he'd crawl his way back here.

The windy drag of the vortex and the burning in my rib cage made me dizzy. The room swayed back and forth. After a few wobbly steps, it stopped.

Concentrate.

Before I took another step, the slimy tentacles slithered out from the vortex. They slunk around Ifrit's hands, uncurling his fingers. With a final, deafening roar, the tentacles dragged Ifrit back into the nothing.

The instant his hand disappeared, the black hole shrank. The tornado winds slowed to sporadic gusts, then to a heavy breeze. Finally, the vortex vanished.

Silence crashed down on us. My skin vibrated from the vortex's windstorm even though the cellar air settled back into its dead stillness. Clouds of dust, floating in the light from our flashlights, hovered before settling to the ground.

Jason, Ashley, and I panted, trying to catch our breaths. My entire chest throbbed. With each gasp, electric pain radiated from my fractured rib to the rest of me. I lay flat on my back, staring at the shadowy rafters above me. A steady parade of tears flowed from the corners of my eyes into my ears. The mildew odor in the old cellar never smelled sweeter.

Despite my pain, I laughed, overcome with exhaustion.

I rolled my head to the side. Ashley lay on her back next to me, her fear of spiders and rats forgotten. After what she'd seen, what could a rodent do?

"Is it over?" She struggled to catch her breath.

"I think so. The vortex must've been waiting for me to leave or for totality to end, whichever came first. Janni, tell me it's over."

With his back against the leg of one of the old shelves, Janni's tiny chest rapidly pumped. "IFRIT IS GONE."

"The best sentence in the history of sentences." Jason wiped the sweat from his upper lip on his shirt sleeve. He stood, then helped Ashley up.

"Some help, please?" I extended my hand, holding my breath as they pulled me up.

Once standing, I didn't let go of their hands. "Thank you, guys. If you weren't here, I'd have spent the rest of my life in the djinn dimension, which…well, I'm glad I'm back."

"I want to hear about that place so freakin' bad, but I'll give you some time before I badger you with questions."

"Janni." I turned to him. "What can I do to make sure Ifrit doesn't punish you for helping me?"

Janni shook his head, his ears swinging. "IFRIT CANNOT HURT DJINN WHEN THEY SLUMBER."

"So you'll be okay?"

He shrugged. "AS LONG AS WE ARE NOT ON EARTH TOGETHER."

"That's excellent." I rubbed the top of his head, and he made a purr-like noise.

"DOES BAXTER ALLEN WANT TO HEAR ABOUT BEN?"

I'd almost forgotten. We weren't in the clear yet. I needed some good news.

"Yeah, tell me what happened. How'd it go?"

"JANNI WILL SHOW YOU."

"How?"

He pointed to the ground in front of him. "KNEEL."

"Kneel?" Jason asked. "What are you doing, Janni?"

Without needing an explanation, I knelt on both knees.

Janni leaned to the side to speak to Jason over my shoulder. "IT WILL SHOW BAXTER ALLEN, BUT IT CANNOT REACH." He raised his arms, and I bent down further so he could rest one of his cold hands on each side of my head.

He closed his eyes, but the purple glowed under his eyelids.

Chapter 27

The entire apartment trembled with the passing train. Ben's hair still dripped from his shower as he packed. In his boxers and stained T-shirt, he read his ticket for the hundredth time. He'd leave for St. Louis early tomorrow. The excitement of seeing Sara's face when he showed up gave him the chills. Sleeping wouldn't be easy tonight. This fantasy had been thirteen years in the making.

A single drop of water slid off his nose and hit the paper ticket. He swiped the water with his thumb before it absorbed into the paper. He didn't want to ruin his ticket. Ben placed it on top of the clothes crammed into his battered suitcase. More clothes than he needed, but they covered the gun and bags of cash underneath them.

His phone vibrated.

At ten thirty?

The caller ID read "Missy O'Leary."

He didn't know the name, but he couldn't afford any hiccups with his trip. "Yeah?"

"Mr. Allen?"

"Who's this?"

"It's Missy O'Leary from North Central High!" Her voice oozed with enthusiasm.

Jesus Christ.

How did all the bitches from high school get his number?

"I already got a call from Sherry."

"I know. I have a note here. That's why I'm following up."

Ben scratched his armpit as he sat on the edge of his bed. He caught a whiff of his fingers. He'd forgotten deodorant. "What do you need?"

"My note says you told Sherry you were still in touch with Sara. Your ex-wife?"

Shit.

"I am. We're real close. I mean, not married anymore, but with a son. You know how it goes." Ben took a swig of his beer.

"I'm happy to hear that. I went ahead and tried contacting her."

Ben almost crushed the phone in his hand. He told Sherry he'd call Sara and let her know about the stupid reunion. The bitch better not have tipped her off. "And?"

"Well, the contact info from Sherry said St. Louis. I called that number, but a man answered who said no one named Sara lived there. And he said he's lived there for fifteen years."

An invisible fist rammed Ben in the gut. He glanced at the ticket lying on the pile of clothes in his suitcase. Served him right for relying on a grown-up cheerleader for information. Although, if they weren't idiots, they wouldn't have volunteered someone's personal information to a guy they hadn't seen in twenty-five years.

"Anyway," she went on, "we did find a Sara Allen in Detroit. This Sara has a son who's fifteen."

Bingo.

"St. Louis? I don't think Sherry mentioned St.

Louis when we talked earlier. Sara lives in Detroit. With our son, Bax. Is his name Bax?"

Missy laughed. "The directory doesn't list his name, but if I gave you Sara's address, could you verify it? I don't want to keep calling random people. Sherry said you knew where she lived."

Could he be any luckier? Could they be any stupider? Twice?

A giddy smile spread across Ben's face. "Of course."

"You're a lifesaver." Missy shuffled some papers. "We found a Sara Allen at 7001 Delmar Street, Detroit, MI 68932."

Ben scribbled the address as fast as he could.

"That's the right contact info, Missy, but you know what? I already called Sara and told her about the reunion. We're both planning on being there. Just waiting for the details. No need for you to waste time on a phone call."

"Oh, really? You're the best."

Ben needed to get off the phone to change his train ticket but also needed to reassure Missy. Make sure no one suspected anything until he could get to Detroit.

"I bet when Sherry called the other day, I misheard St. Louis instead of Detroit. Listen, Missy, Sara is lucky to have people like you making sure she's included in the reunion." Ben rolled his eyes, barely able to choke out the words.

Missy giggled. "Well, you're sweet, but really—"

"Gotta run." He hung up.

Ben punched the address into his phone. He found the listed phone number.

Blocking his cell, he dialed. He couldn't take any

more chances. He needed to double-check this time.

After three rings, a young man answered. A teenager. "Hello?"

Baxter.

Ben hung up.

Found you.

God bless the morons who worked on his high school reunion planning committee. Saved him a trip to St. Louis. Who knows how long he'd have wandered around that city looking for Sara and Bax?

From his laptop, he logged on to exchange his ticket. Hopefully, there weren't any penalties. As the site loaded, a knock thudded in the other room.

His head jerked toward the front door.

No one ever visited him—ever. And his neighborhood wasn't a prime target for salespeople. No discretionary income in this building.

Knock, knock, knock.

He pulled on his jeans and scanned the suitcase—no sign of the gun or cash under his clothes.

Knock, knock, knock.

He shuffled to the door, examining the rest of the apartment for questionable evidence. Nothing out of the ordinary. The studio apartment needed someone to do the dishes and scrub the bathroom, but nothing illegal.

As his hand touched the doorknob, the knock came again. This time followed by, "Open up. Police."

Ben froze, immobilized.

Police?

Some of his betting wasn't on the up-and-up, but hardly anything requiring a visit from the cops. And the robberies happened ten years ago. The only possibility could be they somehow found out he'd been selling copper piping he stole from work.

He sold it to a metal distributor who paid cash, no questions asked. They didn't even know his name. If his boss suspected him, wouldn't he have confronted him before reporting it to the cops?

Knock, knock, knock.

"Mr. Allen, we have a few questions for you," the cop in the hallway called.

Ben squared his shoulders. Innocent men acted with confidence since they had nothing to hide.

He opened the door. Two cops—a short, fat one and a tall, handsome one. Perfect casting for a buddy movie.

"Yeah?"

While the short one talked, the handsome one peered over Ben's shoulder into his apartment. "I'm Officer Hart, and this is Officer Braxton. Are you Benjamin Gregory Allen?"

"I am."

"Are you here alone, sir?"

"Huh? Yeah, of course. Why?"

Hart nodded. "We received a call about a domestic disturbance from one of your neighbors."

Neighbors? He'd lived in the building for seven years and couldn't tell you the first name of anyone on the floor. With the hours he worked, he never even passed anyone in the hall.

"It's just me here, Officer."

"You mind if we look around?"

Ben paused. Why not? He'd tucked his gun and the money in his suitcase. If they intended to save a woman from distress, they wouldn't rifle through this stuff.

"That's fine." He stepped aside.

The two officers entered. Braxton's nose twitched, though he tempered his reaction to the smell in the apartment. Asshole.

Less than a few steps in, Hart signaled to Ben's kitchen. "Can you tell me what that is?"

"What—" the words disappeared. On the small table outside the narrow kitchenette, Ben's gun and a stack of cash had been neatly and visibly arranged, as if he'd just finished counting it.

"What the hell?" In his bedroom, his clothes had been scattered across the floor like someone had rummaged frantically through his suitcase to dig out the cash and the gun. He'd only been at the door for a minute. Had he lost his mind?

"Not a good practice to have your firearm laying out, sir." Hart leaned over the table, careful not to touch anything. "You have the paperwork for that handy?"

He didn't have any shoes on but could make a run for it. They didn't have a warrant, but he'd still need to explain an unregistered gun and pile of cash.

Braxton must've seen the surprise—or guilt—on his face. "That *is* a registered firearm, isn't it?" The cop's hand crept ever so slightly to his holstered gun.

"Of course, it is." Horrible lie, with no chance they'd believe him. How would he produce the papers?

"Can I ask why you have so much cash lying around?"

How the hell did that stuff get out of his suitcase? He checked on it right before he answered the door. The room shrunk around him and beads of sweat collected on his brow.

Stay calm.

"I don't trust banks." Ben forced a short, awkward

chuckle that sounded like a cough. "I keep it in a mattress, old-school-like."

"You mind coming to the station and answering some questions, Mr. Allen?" Hart widened his stance on his stubby legs. Ben would be able to outrun him, but probably not Braxton.

If they had anything, they'd arrest him, but if he refused to go with them, it screamed guilt. Stall for more time.

"Is there a problem, Officer?"

"Not if you can show me the paperwork for your piece."

Ben looked from Hart to Braxton. Trapped.

Sensing the rising tension, both cops now rested their hands on their holstered guns.

"Come with us, Mr. Allen." Hart kept his voice steady.

Ben held his hands up to calm the cops. He'd go answer questions. They didn't give him much of a choice.

Over Hart's shoulder, near the kitchen table, something moved. Ben didn't see anything specific, but the yellow flowers in the wallpaper wavered. The light bent in an odd direction in a small, one-foot-tall area close to the floor.

Ben rubbed his eyes, but then it was gone.

Chapter 28

Janni lowered his hands from the sides of my head, and I grunted as I pushed myself up to a stand. Everything hurt.

"What happened?" Jason's eyes were wide under his glasses. "Is he coming?"

Janni's vision replayed in my mind. "Before you guys got here, I gave Janni instructions to throw Ben off our trail. Janni did his impersonation trick to make Ben think we lived in Detroit. Then, he answered some random person's phone and impersonated me to confirm it. Just for good measure, Janni called the cops and led them to Ben's pile of cash and his gun. I remembered the bags of money from the first dream, so I took a gamble he'd been involved with something illegal. Sounds like he steals copper piping from his job and sells it. He mentioned some robberies, too."

"Can you get arrested for stealing copper?" Ashley brushed the dust off her shirt sleeves.

I shrugged. "Who knows. I figured, at a minimum, it'd put him on the cops' radar. With any luck, they'll lock him up. If he gets off with probation, at least that'll keep him in Illinois."

I'd spent so much of my life wondering about Ben, I'd become blinded by the man I'd created in my mind and almost led the monster right to us. If landing Ben in jail saved Mom and me, so be it. Ben wasn't who I'd imagined.

Jason chose his words carefully. "What if Ben doesn't go to prison, and instead, goes to Detroit, finds out it's not you, and then decides to try St. Louis after all?"

"Then I'll have to deal with it. At least I bought us some time."

"You could send Janni to check on him in a few days," Ashley winked at Janni as if doing him a favor, "to see what happened with the police."

I patted Janni's head. "No offense, but I'm not sure I want to summon any djinn back to Earth any time soon."

"IT NEEDS A BREAK."

Ashley threw her hands up. "Fine, but we always wondered how we could use Janni for something other than fetching things and spying. We finally found it— manipulating criminal deadbeat dads. But if you want to check on Ben the old-fashioned way—police records online—I guess we can do it that way, too."

Unlike on the swings, Ashley calling him a deadbeat didn't bother me this time.

"CAN IT LEAVE NOW? IT HATES CELLARS."

"We all hate cellars." I took Janni's tiny hand. "Thank you for everything."

Janni nodded. "IT WILL NEVER BE FAR, BAXTER ALLEN."

Janni's hand slipped out of mine as he jumped back into the Djinn-verse. His furry body to float lifelessly through the deep blackness, at peace with everything.

"Hey, check out your hair." Ashley snapped a pic on her phone.

She handed it to me. Flecks of gray speckled my

dark hair. Still more brown than gray, but noticeable.

"Well," I chuckled, "I don't think people will notice my hair with the stitches, the swollen lip, my shallow breathing, the cuts on my face, and the backward hospital gown."

"You're a mess." Jason threw his backpack over one shoulder and mine over his other.

Ashley grabbed Jason's flashlight. "Let's get out of here before the rats start coming out of their holes again."

I followed my friends out of the cellar. "And let's never come back here again."

****

The front door swung open. Mom sat at the kitchen table, clutching her glass of wine, filled to the brim. She rose when she saw me but didn't speak. Her eyes—red from crying—were currently dry. Mom never wore much makeup, but her makeup from earlier left dark shadows under her eyes.

I let my backpack slide off my shoulder and fall to the floor with a thud before beginning the hundred-mile walk to the kitchen. Every sore muscle in my body screamed out with each step.

Mom's gaze never released its lock with mine. Time to take my beating.

"Sit." She pointed to the table.

I obeyed.

She took a loud gulp of her wine, letting the silence linger as she sat back down. "I'm not sure where to start, Baxter."

"Then let me." I'd take the lead. "First, I'm sorry."

"There'd better be a second and third coming quickly because 'sorry' won't cut it."

"I—"

"I know you're upset about Ben." Mom had no patience or tolerance for me to lead the conversation. She'd been stewing over what she wanted to say all night. "I shouldn't have dropped that on you in the hospital. That's on me. But that didn't give you the right to disappear. I was so worried. I called the Franklins, I stopped by the Bryants. I didn't know what to do. You cannot send me a cryptic text and get a pass to do what you want. I'm your mother. Not your roommate." Her hands formed clenched fists.

I'd really hurt her—again. But this would be the last time.

"I'm sorry. I was upset." This contained some truth. "Why weren't you honest with me about Ben?"

"Oh, Baxter, what good would it have done for you to know your father is…like he is?"

"It would have stopped me from imagining a guy somewhere who abandoned us for no reason at all." I stared at the red wine, the kitchen light's reflection wavering on its surface. I couldn't look her in the eye. "Plus, it'd have saved me a ton of money from all those comic books I bought."

She cracked a reluctant smile. "Where did you go tonight?"

Argh. Stop making me lie.

"To the park for some air."

She pointed to the hospital gown. "In that, with your shaved head? I'm surprised they didn't arrest you."

"Nah, I blended in with the other crazies."

"Not funny. You could have been hurt." She shook her head. "For a second time today."

"I really am sorry."

"Now." She sighed. "I'm gonna ground you."

"I know."

"No *Archer Annihilation* for a month."

"A month?" I quickly added, "Okay."

"By the way, when I stopped by the Bryants looking for you, Mrs. Bryant was on her way to the hospital. Mr. Bryant suffered a horrible accident at the station. Fell down the stairs. Nancy said he'll be okay, but it sounds like they weren't sure for a while."

I'd have to see Mr. Bryant at some point. He'd never find out about my involvement, but I'd always know what I did. I'd almost killed him.

"Speaking of injuries, how're you doing?" She took the ice pack out of the freezer and slid it toward me. "We're sure getting a lot of use out of this lately."

"My chest hurts pretty bad. I may take one of those pain pills. Did you bring them home?" The idea of sleeping soundly and dreaming normal dreams never sounded so incredible.

She took a bottle out of her pocket and rolled them across the table. They stopped when they hit the ice pack. "You need to take it with food. Why don't I throw a frozen pizza in the oven?"

"Sounds awesome." I pressed the ice pack on my rib cage over the hospital gown. "Maybe I can put on a real shirt, and we watch a movie?"

"*That* sounds awesome." Mom's face lit up. I missed that look.

I stood, but before going to my room, I stopped. "Mom?"

She was already on her way to the freezer. "Yeah?"

"One last thing, and then I'll drop it."

Even with her back to me, I saw her stiffen.

"I'm very thankful for you and our life. It isn't perfect. Sometimes I think about how it could be better, but I'm never ever gonna forget how great it is. Never again." My throat constricted on the last few words. I swallowed hard. "My life isn't horrible because you work too much, or Ben isn't around. You're an incredible mom and have built an amazing life for us. So stop questioning if I feel differently about it. That's that. End of conversation."

Mom smiled. She wiped the corner of her eye with her shirt sleeve. "Thanks, hon. You're pretty incredible, too."

With superhuman mom speed, she zoomed across the kitchen and wrapped her arms around me. Bolts of pain shot through my chest, but I clenched my jaw and hugged her back—tight.

When she let me go, she swiped more tears from her face. "Go change."

As I headed for my room, she called through a smile, "I'll start looking for the cutest romantic comedy ever made."

****

The morning chill deterred most people from the park. I checked my phone. I'd arrived early with a twisted knot for a stomach. I'd almost left several times while I waited but didn't. I forced myself to do the right thing.

Right on time, Scarlet walked through the park's rusted iron gateway, underneath the iron eagle perched on top. She studied the ground as she walked, avoiding any eye contact with me until absolutely necessary. I'd emailed her last night, asking if we could meet. The email was a total of one sentence long. She never replied.

Hours passed as she crossed the small park, head down the entire time. A gust of wind flew across the grass, but she didn't adjust her red hair whipping her in the face. She forcefully shoved her hands into the pockets of her jacket, zipped all the way up.

When she finally stopped in front of me, she dragged her eyes up to connect with mine, the act of which seemed to cause her pain. They flickered for an instant to my shaved head and stitches, but she didn't ask. She brushed her hair behind her ear.

I took a deep breath, hoping the words beat the vomit out of my mouth.

"It's over."

Her emerald eyes narrowed. She remained silent. Did she hear me? Had the words left my mouth or were they still swirling in my head?

I cleared my throat and tried again. "I am sorry, Scarlet. I can't imagine what you've been through. No, I can imagine it. And I can't explain everything. Not that you'd believe me, even if I did."

I waited for her to say, "Try me," but she didn't. Instead, her bottom lip quivered subtly, and her jaw tightened.

"I promise it's over." Another wave of cold air whipped by us, freezing my stitches. "Over between us and…and everything else."

She knew I had something to do with the demon in her bedroom even though she couldn't prove it. She connected me with Nick's death. She just couldn't explain the connection.

Her green eyes glistened, but she didn't wipe them

dry. "Do you promise? You cannot lie, Bax."

I nodded. "I promise. Again, I'm so sorry."

We stood as still as the algae-covered statues in the waterless fountain behind us. For a moment, I envisioned her giving me the smile I loved, throwing her arms around me, and telling me we could still be friends.

Instead, with lightning speed and thunderous power, her hand flew from out of nowhere and smacked me across the face.

My jaw, still swollen from Malcolm's beating, sent a jolt of pain across my cheek and down my neck.

I contained any reaction and turned to face her again, waiting for her to administer another. I deserved it, and she earned the right to deliver it.

But she only slapped me once.

"I'll tell Malcolm to back off, for what that's worth."

My shoulders dropped. "Thank you."

Her empty gaze pierced mine. "I'm not doing that for you. I need to put this behind me."

Then, without saying anything else, she spun on her heels and left. The fallen leaves crunched under her footfalls.

We'd never be friends. I'd be lucky if she even looked at me again. There'd be no more accidental run-ins during assemblies or Jason making fun of me drooling over her.

And I'd have to be okay with that. Just like I'd have to be comfortable with the name Flower until Malcolm's anger faded. He'd always be angry, just like Scarlet would never speak to me again, but hopefully, over time, Malcolm and Scarlet's hatred would lessen to a general dislike. I'd have to be okay with that, too.

I meandered out of the park, making sure to give Scarlet a long head start. The leaves rustled around me. The bitter cold relieved my throbbing jaw while at the same time stung my stitches.

My greed caused so many people pain, and in Nick's case, death. I couldn't change that. Hell, I'd almost used Janni to read Scarlet's journal—but didn't. One of the few decent decisions I'd made lately.

Just one more thing to do before everything was finally over.

****

The silver bell dinged against the glass as I shoved the door open with the cardboard box in my arms. The mustiness engulfed me. Its warm familiarity blanketed me in a comforting calm I desperately needed. I squinted, giving my eyes a moment to adjust from the sunlight to the indoor light.

"Bax!" The sound of Warren's husky voice brought a smile to my face. "I've been wondering how you were doing."

"I'm good," I called.

Warren let me take my time going up the aisle to the counter, even though he sounded anxious to talk with me. I absorbed the stacks, rows, and boxes of superheroes, supervillains, monsters, and demons all around me one last time—at least for a while. No more comic books for me. No more connection to Ben and what he did, what he meant to do, and the years I'd wasted chasing a father figure I'd fictionalized in my mind. It stung too deep.

Finally arriving, I heaved my box up onto Warren's counter. "Thank you for the other day."

"Calling the ambulance? 'Course. I heard a commotion and saw the end of what happened. Did you know them?" Warren's navy T-shirt—too tight for his barrel-like midsection—had a small golden logo with two overlapping letters, *P* and *H*, the symbol for a new female superhero named Purple Hawk.

"Kind of, but not really."

Warren glanced at the stitches in the side of my head. "I'm glad you're okay."

"Just banged up a little." I lifted the flap of the box. "These are for you."

"For me?" He dug into the comics I'd bought from Warren's Cosmos over the years, organized in neat stacks. Most were in pristine condition since I'd only read them once. The number of crime fighters in the box would terrify the evilest of evildoers, but comic books had no place in my life anymore.

"Well, let's see…" Warren's big fingers pounded the old cash register.

Chang. Chang. Chang.

"No, Warren. I'm not looking to sell them. You can have them."

He stopped typing. His caterpillar eyebrow crunched in the middle. "Why?"

"You've done so much for me. It's the least I can do."

The stool squealed as Warren leaned back. "Like calling the ambulance? That's just being a good human."

"Not that. Well, not just that." My stomach fluttered. I didn't think it'd be this hard when I packed up the comics at home. Warren's Cosmos had been a significant part of my life for so long.

Warren pulled *Shade Slayer, #276* from the box. The most worn comic book in the collection, by far. He flipped through the pages, the bright colors faded with time. "Even this one?"

The sight of it made me cringe. "Especially that one." I'd memorized every word of it by ten years old. I'd read it over and over since then, but maybe I hadn't really seen it in years.

He eyed me but didn't ask me to elaborate. "Well, I'm gonna keep this box in the back for a few weeks. If you change your mind, you let me know."

"I won't. I'm taking a break from comics. Probably permanent."

He nodded. "So I see. Before you totally give them up, did you ever finish yours?" He pointed to the cut on my cheek, the mildest of my injuries at this point. "The one you were writing about djinn?"

The mention of the word djinn made me shudder. One more thing to do at Warren's Cosmos before I left. It was a long shot, but it worked before.

"I do want to finish that before I quit comic books entirely. And it's almost done. Your super blue blood moon idea was perfect, by the way."

"Glad to help." He smiled with pride.

"I have one final story detail I can't figure out. Maybe you have another good suggestion in you?"

Warren chuckled. "I might have just one more in me."

I smiled, resolving to come back and visit Warren, even if I didn't buy any more comics. Maybe I'd occasionally buy one and give it away or something.

"How would my hero get rid of the magical box he used to summon and banish the djinn? It's pretty much indestructible, so he can't throw it in the trash where someone else might find it."

Warren's fingertips—what remained of them—crunched on his chin's stubble. "Again, I'm no expert, you understand, but magic items are generally crafted by an element. Magic swords are forged by enchanted fire. Sorcerer's staves are carved from ancient wood. Usually, one of the four elements—earth, fire, water, or air—is used to create a magic item. So, it'd stand to reason that one of the four elements can be used to destroy the item or make it dormant. Your hero could melt it, throw it in the ocean—"

"Bury it?"

"I believe you said yours was a wooden box? With a jewel? Both wood and jewels come from the earth"—Warren raised one of his caterpillar eyebrows—"in your story."

"You were right about the moon."

The box and ring came from under my building, dormant in the foundation. Even though returning to the cellar gave me the shivers, reburying them there seemed safer than in a park where a heavy rain might expose one of them and start the whole thing over for some unsuspecting person. Ifrit said it took him hundreds of years to build up his strength to project the old man's image. So the box needs to be safely hidden for at least that long.

I refused to summon any more djinn, so getting into the basement without Janni's help would be a challenge. Maybe I'd make up a school project on architecture. I'd enlist Jason and Ashley. The three of us would figure it out. It'd have to be the three of us since nothing would get me back into that cellar alone.

"I hope to read your story sometime." Warren ripped me out of my thoughts.

"You bet." I needed to get going. Every minute the box sat in my closet buried under my sweaters, I risked Ifrit's return. But I couldn't leave Warren's Cosmos with a simple goodbye.

"I have one last question for you." A smile crept across my face. "What happened to your fingers?"

Warren laughed a deep, robust laugh I'd never heard before. He jiggled everywhere. "Well, Bax, that's an interesting story, and there are no magical items involved."

"Good!"

Warren launched immediately into it, always ready with his next tale. "A friend of mine—Jedediah—owned and operated one of the largest logging operations in North America. You know what logging is?"

I nodded. "Of course."

"Just checkin'. You're a city boy. Anyway, Jedediah called me about twenty years ago in need of some help. So off to Alaska I went…"

I couldn't stop smiling even if I tried, which I didn't. Warren would probably never tell me the truth about how he lost his fingers. If he did, chances are, it'd be boring and not some elaborate story about noodlin' or logging in Alaska. Real-life stories were sometimes dull, which was fine by me.

I meant what I told Mom. My life was pretty great. I didn't need a Something Big to make it remarkable. Superpowers came with weaknesses like kryptonite. Inheriting an island nation came with the headache of running a government. We lived in a decent apartment.

I had two best friends, up one from a month ago. And I wanted to believe my episode of VS in the vortex—the one I beat down—would be my last.

No one would ever make my life into a movie, but that didn't mean it sucked. What I did with my life would be all mine, and it'd be remarkable.

A word about the author...

J. L. Sullivan writes young adult stories inspired by gritty urban environments and the tales that percolate within abandoned buildings and desolate alleys. He lives in St. Louis with his wife, two daughters, and a dog named Princess Penelope Picklesworth.

Visit the author at: http://www.jlsullivan.net

Thank you for purchasing
this publication of The Wild Rose Press, Inc.

For questions or more information
contact us at
info@thewildrosepress.com.

The Wild Rose Press, Inc.
www.thewildrosepress.com

CPSIA information can be obtained
at www.ICGtesting.com
Printed in the USA
BVHW050921130522
636961BV00012B/209